SWORD ART ONIINE

001

W9-BUN-476

SWORD ARt OnIinE
PROGRESSIVE

REKI KAWAHARA
ILLUSTRATION BY abec
DESIGN BY bee-pee

"...We're all going to die anyway."

"A little bit overkill, if you ask me."

◆ **Asuna**

A player trapped inside *Sword Art Online*. Without a care for her life, she throws herself into battle against monsters.

◆ **Kirito**

A swordsman aiming to beat the top floor of Aincrad. He adventures as a solo player, working only to strengthen himself.

"You met your quota of upgrading materials for your Wind Fleuret during our hunt, right?"

"All right. I'll take your weapon and materials."

Nezha

A blacksmith who runs his business in the east plaza of Urbus, the main city of the second floor.

"Ugruoooaaah!!"

Illfang the Kobold Lord

The boss of the first floor of Aincrad, lurking deep within the twentieth level of the labyrinth.

"Vrrrooooooo!!"

Baran the General Taurus
The boss of the second floor of Aincrad, lurking deep within the twentieth level of the labyrinth.

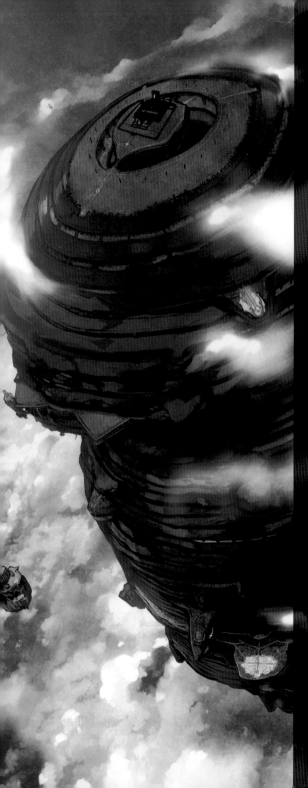

FLOATING CASTLE AINCRAD
Floor Data
■ FIRST FLOOR

Aincrad is broadly conical in sha
so the lowest floor is the largest.
circular floor is about six miles ac
with a surface of o r thirty qu
miles. Because of it size, there
large variety of terra in to be fou
At the southern tip of the landm
is the Town of Beginnings, a city o
half a mile across, surrounded b
semicircular wall. Outside of the
are rippling plains illed with bo
and wolves, as well as insect mons
such as worms, beetles and wa
Across the field to the northeast
deep forest, while ne northeast ho
swampy lowland dotted with lal
Beyond these regions lie mounta
valleys, and ruins, each full of powe
monsters.

Aside from the Town of Beginnings,
floor is dotted with a number of ot
settlements of various sizes, the m
prosperous of which is Tolbana, a va
town closest to the floor's labyrinth
the northern end of the floor is a so
tower three hundred yards across
a hundred yards tall—the first-fl
labyrinth.

The boss of the first floor is Illfang
Kobold Lord, who wields a cur
blade. Illfang is always accompan
by three Ruin Kobold entinels cla
metal armor and armed with halber

■ SECOND FLOOR

A savanna realm covered in plains
boulders, the seco d floor is roug
the same size as the first floor. Me
loom over the plains, dotted with sr
caves through which undergrou
rivers run. The second floor is divi
into a wide-open northe f
a narrow southern half. est
fields are home to dangerous
oxen, while the wastelands bey
that are prowled by even more dea
creatures.

The main city of the second flo
which contains the teleport gate t
allows travel to other floors, is Urb
a settlement carved directly do
into a three-hundred-yard-wide m
top, with only the outer perime
left standing. Just two miles to
southeast of Urbus is a small villa
called Marome.

The boss of the second fl
(according to the beta test) is Ba
the General Taurus. Baran uses
golden two-handed battle hammer.
is accompanied by Nato the Colo
Taurus. Tauruses are a dangerous r
in particular, due to their paraly
causing sword skill, Numbing Impac

SWORD ARt ONliNE PROGRESSIVE

VOLUME 1

Reki Kawahara

abec

bee-pee

NEW YORK

SWORD ART ONLINE PROGRESSIVE Volume 1
REKI KAWAHARA

Translation by Stephen Paul

SWORD ART ONLINE PROGRESSIVE
© REKI KAWAHARA 2012
All rights reserved.
Edited by ASCII MEDIA WORKS
First published in Japan in 2012 by KADOKAWA CORPORATION, Tokyo.
English translation rights arranged with KADOKAWA CORPORATION, Tokyo, through Tuttle-Mori Agency, Inc., Tokyo.

English translation © 2015 by Yen Press, LLC

Yen On
1290 Avenue of the Americas
New York, NY 10104
www.yenpress.com

Yen On is an imprint of Yen Press, LLC.
The Yen On name and logo are trademarks of Yen Press, LLC.

First Yen On Edition: March 2015

ISBN: 978-0-316-259361

10 9

LSC-C

Printed in the United States of America

SWORD ART ONLINE
PROGRESSIVE

ARIA ON A STARLESS NIGHT

FIRST FLOOR OF AINCRAD, NOVEMBER 2022

1

JUST ONCE, I SAW AN ACTUAL SHOOTING STAR.

It wasn't on a camping trip under the stars, but from my bedroom window. This wouldn't be such a rare thing to those who live in places with clear skies or that are properly dark at night, but my home of fourteen years, Kawagoe in Saitama Prefecture, was neither of those things. Even on a clear night, you could only see the brightest of stars with the naked eye.

But one midwinter night, I just so happened to glance out of the window and caught a glimpse of a momentary brilliance falling vertically through a starless night sky pale with the light of the city. I was in fourth or fifth grade at the time, and in my innocent youth, I decided to make a wish...only to squander it on the most pointless thing imaginable: "I wish the next monster would drop a rare item." I was in the middle of grinding for a level-up in my favorite MMORPG at the time.

I saw another shooting star of the same color and speed three (or perhaps four) years later.

But this was not with the naked eye, and it did not flash against the gray night sky. It happened within the murky depths of a labyrinth created by the NerveGear—the world's first full-sensory immersive VR interface.

The way the fencer fought brought the word "possessed" to mind.

He darted out of the way of the level-6 Ruin Kobold Trooper's crude axe so tightly, I felt a chill run down my back. After three successful evasions, the kobold's balance was entirely lost, and he unleashed a full-power sword skill into the helpless beast.

He used Linear, a simple thrust that was the first attack anyone learned in the Rapier category. It was a very ordinary attack, a twisting thrust straight forward from a centered position, but his speed was astonishing. It was clearly not just the game's motion-assistance system at work, but rather the product of his own athletic skill.

I'd seen party members and enemy monsters use the same skill countless times during the beta test, but all I could catch this time was the visual effect of the sword's trajectory, and not a glimpse of the blade itself. The sudden flash of pure light in the midst of the dim dungeon brought the memory of that shooting star to my mind.

After three repetitions of the same pattern of dodging the kobold's combo and responding with Linear, the fencer had dispatched the armed creature—one of the toughest in the dungeon—without taking a scratch. But it was not a lazy, easy battle. Once the final thrust had ripped through the kobold's chest and sent it bursting into empty polygonal shards, he stumbled back and thudded against the wall, as though the creature's disintegration had pushed him backward. The man slid down the wall until he sat on the floor, breathing heavily.

He hadn't noticed me standing at a tunnel intersection about fifteen yards away.

My normal activity at this point would be to silently slink away and find my own prey to hunt. Ever since I'd made the decision one month ago to work as a self-interested solo player, I had never gone out of my way to approach another person. The only exception would be if I saw someone battling and in mortal danger, but the fencer had never dipped below full health. At the very least, he didn't seem to need anyone barging in and offering to help.

But still…

I hesitated for five seconds, then made up my mind and strode forward in the direction of the sitting player.

He was skinny and undersized, wearing a light bronze breastplate over a deep red leather tunic, tight-fitting leather pants, and knee-high boots. His face was hidden beneath the hooded cape that hung from head to waist. Everything aside from the cape was proper light armor for a nimble fencer, but it was also similar to my swordsman's wear. My beloved Anneal Blade, a reward for a high-level quest, was so heavy that I needed to cut down on bulky equipment to keep my moves sharp—I didn't wear anything heavier than a dark gray leather coat and a small breastplate.

The fencer flinched when he heard my footsteps but didn't move farther. He would have seen the green color of my cursor to reassure him that I was no monster. His head stayed hung between his upturned knees, a clear sign that he wanted me to keep walking past, but I stopped a few feet away.

"A little bit overkill, if you ask me."

The slender shoulders under the thick cape shrugged again. The hood shifted back just an inch or two, and I saw two sharp eyes glaring out at me. All I could see were two light brown irises; the contours of his face were still shadowed.

After several seconds of a glare just as piercing as those rapier thrusts, he tilted his head slightly to the side. It seemed to suggest that he didn't understand what I meant.

Inwardly, I heaved a sigh of resignation. There was one massive itch in the back of my mind that kept me from continuing on my solitary way.

The fencer's Linear was chillingly perfect. Not only were the pre- and post-motions extremely brief, the attack itself was faster than I could see. I'd never been in the presence of such a terrifying and beautiful sword skill before.

At first, I assumed he must have been another former beta tester. That speed had to have come from plenty of experience gained before this world had plunged into its current deadly state.

But when I saw that Linear a second time, I began to question my assumption. In comparison to the excellence of his attack, the fencer's battle flow was downright perilous. Yes, the defensive strategy of dodging enemy strikes with a minimum of movement led to quicker counterstrikes than blocking or parrying, as well as saving wear and tear on equipment. But the consequences of failure far outweighed those positives. In a worst-case scenario, a successful hit by the enemy might be treated as a counterattack that included a brief stun effect. For a solo fighter, getting stunned was a kiss of death.

It didn't add up—brilliant swordplay combined with downright reckless strategy. I wanted to know why, so I approached and wondered out loud if it might be overkill.

But he didn't even understand that extremely common online term. The fencer sitting on the floor here could not be a beta tester. He might not have even been an MMO player before coming to this game.

I took a quick breath and launched into an explanation.

"*Overkill* is a term used when you do way too much damage for the amount of health the monster has left. After your second Linear, that kobold was nearly dead. It only had two or three pixels left on its HP bar. You could have finished it off easily with a light attack, rather than going for a full sword skill."

How many days had it been since I'd said so many words at once? How many weeks? For being a poor Japanese student, my explanation was as elegant as an essay, but the fencer showed no response for a full ten seconds. Finally, a soft voice muttered from the depths of the hood.

"Is there a problem with doing too much damage?"

Finally, at long last, I realized that the squatting fencer was the rarest of encounters in this entire world, to say nothing of deep in a dungeon—not a male player, but a woman.

The world's first VRMMORPG, *Sword Art Online*, had opened its virtual doors nearly a month before.

In your average MMO, players would be hitting the initial level cap and the entire game world would have been thoroughly explored from end to end. But here in *SAO*, even the best players in the game were barely around level 10—and no one knew what the cap was. Barely a few percent of the game's setting, the floating castle Aincrad, had been mapped out.

SAO was not quite a game anymore. It was more of a prison. Logging out was impossible, and the death of the player's avatar resulted in the death of the player's body, period. Under those stark circumstances, few people dared risk the danger of a dungeon's monsters and traps.

On top of that, the game master forced every player's avatar into their real-life gender, which meant there was a massive shortage of females in the game. I'd assumed that most of them were still camped out in the safe haven of the Town of Beginnings. I'd only spotted women two or three times in this massive dungeon— the first-floor labyrinth—and they were all in the midst of large adventuring parties.

Thus it never occurred to me that this solitary fencer at the edge of the unexplored territory deep in the dungeon might actually be a woman.

I briefly considered mumbling an apology and leaving in haste. I wasn't on a crusade against the men who always made it a point to talk to any female player they saw without hesitation, but I most definitely did not want to be identified as one of them.

If she'd responded with a "mind your own beeswax" or "I can do what I want," I'd have no choice but to agree and move along. But the fencer's response seemed to be an honest question, so I stopped and tried to come up with a proper explanation.

"Well...there's no penalty in the game for overkilling—it's just inefficient. Sword skills take a lot of concentration, so the more you use them, the more exhausted you get. I mean, you've still got to get back home, right? You should try to conserve more energy."

"...Get back home?" the voice from the hood questioned again. It was a ragged monotone, seemingly exhausted, but I thought it was beautiful. I didn't say that out loud, of course. Instead, I tried to elaborate.

"Yeah. It's going to take a good hour to get out of the labyrinth from this spot, and even the closest town is another thirty minutes from there, right? You'll make more mistakes when you're tired. You look like a solo player to me; those mistakes can easily turn fatal."

As I spoke, I wondered to myself why I was lecturing her so earnestly. It wasn't because she was a girl, I thought. I'd started this conversation before realizing her gender.

If the roles were reversed and someone was haughtily lecturing me about what I should do, I'd certainly tell them to go to Hell. Once I realized how contradictory my actions were to my personality, the fencer finally reacted.

"In that case, there's no problem. I'm not going home."

"Huh? You're not...going back to town? But what about refilling on potions, repairing equipment, getting sleep...?" I asked, incredulous. She shrugged briefly.

"Don't need potions if I don't take damage, and I bought five of the same sword. If I need sleep, I just get it at the nearby safe area," she said hoarsely. I had no response.

The safe area was a small room located inside the dungeon that was never in danger of spawning any monsters. It was easily distinguished by its colored torches in each corner of the room. They were useful as a foothold when hunting or mapping out a dungeon, but they weren't meant for more than an hour-long nap. The rooms had no beds, only hard stone floors, and the open doorway didn't keep out the incessant sounds of monstrous footsteps and growling in the corridor outside. Even the stoutest of adventurers couldn't get honest sleep under such conditions.

But if I was to take her statement at face value, she was using that cramped stone chamber as a replacement for a proper inn room in order to camp out permanently inside the dungeon. Could that possibly be right?

"Um...how many hours have you been in here?" I asked, afraid to know the answer.

She exhaled slowly. "Three days...maybe four. Are you done? The next monster's going to spawn soon, so I need to get moving."

She put a fragile, gloved hand against the dungeon wall and unsteadily climbed to her feet. With the rapier dangling from her hand as heavily as a two-handed sword, she turned her back to me.

As she walked forward, I saw ragged tears in the cape that spoke to its poor condition. In fact, it was a miracle that after four days of camping out in a dungeon, the flimsy cloth was intact at all. Perhaps her statement about not taking any damage wasn't an idle boast...

Even I didn't expect the words that tumbled out of my mouth at her receding back.

"If you keep fighting like this, you're gonna die."

She stopped still and let her right shoulder rest against the wall before turning around. The eyes I'd thought were hazel under that hood now seemed to flash a pale, piercing red.

"...We're all going to die anyway."

Her hoarse, cracking voice seemed to deepen the chill of the dungeon air.

"Two thousand people died in a single month. And we haven't even finished the first floor. There's no way to beat this game. The only difference is when and where you die, sooner...or later..."

The longest and most emotional statement she'd uttered so far passed her lips and hung in the air.

I instinctively took a step forward, then watched as she quietly crashed to the floor, as though hit by an invisible paralysis.

2

THE MOMENT SHE HIT THE FLOOR, THE ONLY
thought that passed through her brain was the mundane question "I wonder what happens when you pass out in a virtual
world?"

Falling unconscious was a momentary shutdown of the brain,
caused by the stoppage of blood flow. Blood might stop flowing
for a variety of reasons—heart or blood vessel malfunctions,
anemia, low blood pressure, hyperventilation—but under a VR
full dive, the physical body was already utterly stationary in a
bed or reclining chair. On top of that, everyone stuck in this
particular game of death had presumably been transferred to
a nearby medical facility, where they'd be undergoing regular
monitoring and the administering of necessary drugs and fluids.
It was hard to imagine someone passing out from purely physical reasons.

These thoughts ran through her fading consciousness and
eventually coalesced into a simple statement: *I just don't care
anymore.*

Nothing mattered. She was going to die here. If she passed out
in the middle of a labyrinth guarded by deadly monsters, there
was no way she'd emerge safely. There was another player nearby,
but he wouldn't risk his own life just to save a stranger.

Besides, how would he save her? The weight that a player could carry in this virtual world was strictly controlled by the game system. Deep in a dangerous dungeon like this, any player would be heavily laden with potions and emergency supplies, not to mention all of the loot they'd procured along the way. It was impossible to imagine anyone carrying another human being on top of all that.

Then she realized something.

For fleeting thoughts escaping her brain just before she fell unconscious, they were certainly lasting quite a while. Plus, it was only hard stone beneath her body, so why did she feel something so soft and gentle pressing against her back? She felt warm, somehow. There was even a light breeze tickling her cheek.

With a start, her eyes snapped open.

She wasn't in a dank dungeon surrounded by clammy stone walls. It was a clearing in the midst of a forest, surrounded by ancient trees engraved with golden moss and thorny bushes bearing small flowers. She'd passed out—no, been sleeping—on a bed of grass as soft as carpet in the middle of the round clearing, measuring roughly eight yards across.

But...how? She'd lost consciousness deep in that dungeon, so how could she have traveled all the way to this outdoor area?

The answer was ninety degrees to her right.

There was a gray shadow huddled at the foot of an especially large tree at the edge of the open space. He cradled a large sword with both hands and had his head resting on the scabbard. His face was hidden beneath longish black bangs, but based on the equipment and profile, it had to be the player who'd been talking to her moments before she passed out.

He must have found some way to carry her out of the dungeon and to this forest. She scanned the line of trees, until on her left she finally spotted a massive tower stretching upward to the roof, a few hundred feet away—the labyrinth of the first floor of Aincrad.

She turned back to her right. Perhaps sensing her movement,

the man's shoulders twitched beneath the gray leather coat, and his head rose slightly. Even in the midst of the midday forest sun, his eyes were as black as a starless night.

The instant she crossed gazes with those pitch-black eyes, a tiny firework went off deep in the back of her mind.

"You shouldn't…have bothered," growled Asuna Yuuki past gritted teeth.

From the moment she'd been trapped in this world, Asuna had asked herself the same questions hundreds of times, if not thousands.

Why did she decide to play with that brand-new gaming console, when it wasn't even hers? Why did she put the helmet on her head, sink into the high-backed mesh chair, and utter the start-up command?

Asuna hadn't bought the NerveGear, VR interface-of-dreams-turned-cursed-tool-of-death, or the game card for *Sword Art Online*, vast prison of souls—that had been her much-older brother, Kouichirou. But even he'd never been one for video games, much less MMORPGs. As the son of the representative director of RCT, one of the biggest electronics manufacturers in the country, he underwent every kind of education necessary to be their father's successor, and everything that didn't fall under that duty was eliminated from his life. Why he became interested in NerveGear—why he chose *SAO*—was still a mystery to her.

But ironically, Kouichirou never got a chance to play the first video game he'd ever bought. On the very day that *SAO* launched, he was sent on a business trip overseas. At the dinner table the night before, he'd tried to laugh off the frustration, but she could sense that he really was disappointed.

Asuna's life hadn't been quite as strict as Kouichirou's, but she too had little experience with games aside from free downloads on her phone, even up to her current age in ninth grade. She was aware of the presence of online games, but the entrance exams for high school were fast approaching, and she had no reason or motive to seek them out—supposedly.

So even she had no explanation why, on the afternoon of November 6, 2022, she'd slipped into her brother's vacant room, put the already prepared NerveGear on her head, and spoken the "link start" command.

The only thing she *could* say was that everything had changed that day. Everything had ended.

Asuna locked herself inside an inn room in the Town of Beginnings, waiting for the ordeal to be over, but when not a single message had made its way through from the real world in two weeks, she gave up hoping for rescue from the outside. And with over a thousand players already dead and the first dungeon of the game still unbeaten, she understood that defeating the game from the inside was equally impossible.

The only choice left was in how to die.

She had the option of waiting for months, possibly years, within the safety of the city. But no one could guarantee that the rule that monsters couldn't invade towns would never be broken.

Asuna preferred to leave the city rather than curl up into a ball in the dark, living in fear of the future. She'd use all of her instincts to fight, learn, and grow. If she ultimately ran out of steam and perished, at least she didn't spend her remaining days regretting the decisions of the past and mourning her lost future.

Run, thrust, and vanish. Like a meteor burning up through the atmosphere.

Such was Asuna's mindset as she left the inn and headed out into the wilderness, totally ignorant of a single MMORPG term. She picked out a weapon, learned a single skill, and found her way deep into the labyrinth that no one else had successfully conquered.

Finally, at four in the morning on Friday, December 2, the accumulation of so many battles caused her to black out with exhaustion, and her quest should have ended. The name Asuna carved into the Monument of Life beneath Blackiron Palace would be struck through, and everything would come to a close.

It would have. It should have.

"You shouldn't have," Asuna repeated. The slumping, black-haired swordsman dropped his eyes dark as night down to the ground. He seemed to be slightly older than she, but the surprising naiveté of his gesture surprised her.

A few seconds later, her original suspicion returned as a cynical smile crossed his lips. "I didn't save you," he said quietly. It was the voice of a boy, but something in it disguised his actual age.

"...Why didn't you leave me back there, then?"

"I only wanted to save your map data. If you spent four days at the front line, you must have mapped out a good chunk of unexplored land. It would be a waste to let that disappear."

She sucked in a breath at the logic and efficiency of his explanation. She was expecting the same answer that most people she'd met had given her, some claptrap about the importance of life, or the need for everyone to band together. She'd been prepared to cut through all of that nonsense—verbally, of course—but the practicality of his answer left her speechless.

"...Fine. Take it," she muttered, opening her window. She'd finally gotten used to the menu system, tabbing over to access her map info and copying it to a scroll of parchment. Another button command materialized the scroll as an in-game object, and she tossed it at the man's feet. "Now you've got what you wanted. So long."

She put a hand in the grass to get to her feet, but her legs wouldn't stay steady. The clock in her window showed that she'd been out almost a full seven hours, but her exhaustion hadn't entirely worn off yet. She still had three more rapiers, though. She'd told herself before she left that she'd stay inside the tower until the last one's durability level was below halfway.

There were still a few suspicions lurking in the back of her mind. How had the swordsman in the gray coat managed to bring her out of the dungeon to this forest clearing? And why did he take her all the way outside, rather than just to the nearby safe zone within the tower?

They weren't worth turning back to ask him about, however. So Asuna turned to her left, in the direction of the black, looming labyrinth, and started to march off.

"Hang on, fencer."

"..."

She ignored him and kept walking, but what he said next made her stop in her tracks.

"You're doing all of this for the purpose of beating the game, right? Not just to die in a dungeon. So why don't you come to the meeting?"

"...Meeting?" she wondered aloud. The swordsman's explanation reached her ears on the gentle forest breeze.

"There's going to be a meeting tonight at the town of Tolbana near the tower. They're going to plan out how to beat the boss of the first-floor labyrinth."

3

AINCRAD WAS BROADLY CONICAL IN SHAPE, SO THE lowest floor was therefore the largest. The circular floor was about six miles across with a surface of over thirty square miles. In comparison, the city of Kawagoe in Saitama Prefecture, home to over three hundred thousand, was a little over thirty-eight square miles.

Because of its size, there was actually a considerable variety of terrain to be found. At the southern tip of the landmass was the Town of Beginnings, a city over half a mile across, surrounded by a semicircular wall. Outside of the city were rippling plains filled with boars and wolves, as well as insect monsters such as worms, beetles, and wasps.

Across the field to the northwest was a deep forest, while the northeast held swampy lowlands dotted with lakes. Beyond these regions lay mountains, valleys, and ruins, each full of appropriate assortments of monsters. At the northern end of the floor was a squat tower three hundred yards across and a hundred yards tall—the first-floor labyrinth.

Aside from the Town of Beginnings, the floor was dotted with a number of other settlements of various sizes, the largest of which—though only two hundred yards from one end to the other—was Tolbana, a valley town closest to the floor's labyrinth.

The first visit by a player to this tranquil town lined with massive windmills was three weeks after the official launch of *Sword Art Online*.

By that time, over eighteen hundred players had perished.

The mysterious fencer and I left the forest—not together, but at an awkward distance—and passed through the northern gate of Tolbana.

A purple message in my field of vision stating SAFE HAVEN indicated that we were within town limits. Instantly, I felt the exhaustion of the long day settle onto my shoulders. A sigh escaped my lips.

If I felt this bad after only leaving the town that morning, the fencer behind me must have felt much worse. I turned back to check on her, but her knee-high boots did not falter. A few hours of sleep couldn't have erased the fatigue of three days of straight combat, so she must have been putting on a brave front. It seemed like returning to town ought to be cause for relaxing both mind and body (and in this virtual setting, they were the same thing), but she didn't appear to be in the mood for suggestions.

Instead, I kept things short and sweet. "The meeting's at the town square, four in the afternoon."

"…"

The face within the hood nodded slightly, but she kept walking right past me.

A slight breeze running through the valley town rippled her cape as she passed. I briefly opened my mouth but found nothing to say. I'd spent the last month vigorously avoiding all human contact as a solo player; I had no right to expect anyone to welcome me with open arms. The only concern I'd had was in saving my own life.

"Strange girl, yah?" a voice muttered from behind me. I tore my gaze away from the fencer and turned around. "Seems to be on death's door, but never dies. Clearly a newbie, but her moves are sharp as steel. Who can she be?"

The voice, a high-pitched wheedle that rose into an odd nasal whine at the end of each sentence, belonged to a slippery little player an entire head shorter than me. Like me, she wore only cloth and leather armor. The weapons on her waist were a small claw and some throwing needles. It didn't seem like the kind of stuff that would get her out to this dangerous zone, but this person's greatest weapon did not have a blade.

"You know that fencer?" I asked her automatically, then grimaced, anticipating her answer. Sure enough, the little woman held up a hand, all five fingers extended.

"I make it cheap. Five hundred col?"

The smiling face had one very distinct feature. She'd used a cosmetic item to draw three lines on either cheek in the style of animal whiskers. Combined with her short mousy-brown curls, the overall effect was unmistakably rodent-like.

I'd asked her why she chose that appearance before, but her only response was "You don't ask a girl the reason she puts on make-up, do ya? I'll tell you for one hundred thousand col." So the answer was still a mystery.

I silently swore to myself that one day, I'd actually cash in a rare item and pay the exorbitant fee, just to force an answer out of her.

"I don't feel comfortable trafficking in a girl's private information," I muttered sternly.

"Nee-hee! Good mindset to have," she said smarmily. Argo the Rat, the first information trader in Aincrad, chittered with laughter.

Watch out. Five minutes of chatting with the Rat, and she'll have worked a hundred col outta you, someone had warned me once. But according to Argo, she'd never once sold a piece of information whose verification was unclear. She always paid a source for info she considered worth something, and only turned it into a product to sell once she'd made sure the story was solid. It seemed clear to me that a single piece of poor intel sold for cash would ruin her reputation, so while it wasn't exactly the same as farming ingredients in dungeons and selling them to NPCs, as a business, it had its own set of perils.

Although I knew my skepticism was sexist, I couldn't help but wondering why a female player would choose to dabble in such dangerous work. But I knew that if I asked, she'd quote me another price of one hundred thousand col, so I cleared my throat and asked a different question.

"Well? Is it the usual proxy negotiation today, rather than your main business?"

Now it was Argo's turn to scowl. She looked back and forth, then prodded my back with a finger, guiding me to a nearby alleyway. With the boss meeting a full two hours away, there were few players milling about the town, but it seemed to be important that she not be overheard—probably something to do with her reputation as a guardian of secrets.

Argo came to a stop in the narrow alley and rested her back on the wall of the house (inhabited by an NPC, of course) before nodding.

"Yeah, that's right. They'll go up to twenty-nine thousand eight hundred col."

"Twenty-nine, huh?" I grimaced and shrugged. "Sorry...my answer's the same, no matter the number. Not gonna sell."

"That's what I told the client, but what can ya do?"

Argo's main business was selling information, but she used her excellent agility stat to moonlight as a messenger. Normally she simply passed along brief verbal or written messages, but for the past week, she'd been a pipeline to me from someone very insistent, if not downright pushy.

He (or she) wanted to buy my Anneal Blade +6 (3S3D).

The weapon-strengthening system in *SAO* was relatively simple for a modern MMORPG. There were five parameters: Sharpness, Quickness, Accuracy, Heaviness, and Durability. For a price, an NPC or player blacksmith could attempt to raise a particular stat for you. The process required specific crafting materials depending on the stat, and there was always a probability that it would fail. This was similar to the way it worked in other games.

Each time a parameter was successfully raised, the weapon name gained a +1, or +2, and so on, but the actual statistic being affected wasn't clear until you tapped on the item properties directly. Since it would be a pain to say "plus one to accuracy and plus two to heaviness" each time when trading with other players, it was common to abbreviate the information instead. Therefore, a +4 weapon with 1 to accuracy, 2 to heaviness, and 1 to durability would be labeled "1A2H1D."

My Anneal Blade +6 (3S3D) increased sharpness and durability by three points each. It took quite a lot of persistence and good fortune to improve it that much on the first floor. Few players bothered to work on the Blacksmithing skill—which had no bearing on your odds of survival—and despite the dwarfish appearance of the NPC blacksmiths, their actual skill was sorely disappointing.

Even the base weapon was the reward of an extremely tough quest, so the sword's current values had to be about the maximum a player could expect to find on the first floor. But it was still starter equipment. I might pump it up a few more times, but I'd find a better sword on the third or fourth floor, and the process would begin all over again.

For that reason, I had a hard time fathoming the motive of Argo's client to pay the massive sum of 29,800 col for such a weapon. In a face-to-face negotiation, I could simply ask the buyer, but without a name to track down, there was no way to find out about them.

"And how much are they paying you to keep quiet? A thousand?" I asked. Argo nodded.

"Yeah, I'd say so. Feel like upping the ante?"

"Hmm...one k, huh? Hmmmm."

This "hush money" was a fee that Mystery Bidder X was paying Argo to keep their identity hidden. If I offered to pay 1,100 col, Argo would pass that along via instant message, until they came back with 1,200 col. Then I'd be asked to pony up 1,300, and so on. If I ended up winning the bidding war, I'd learn who wanted to buy my sword, but I'd end up losing a significant amount of cash. That would clearly be an idiotic outcome.

"Great...So you're an information broker who makes money even when you *don't* sell? Gotta admire your dedication to your business," I grumbled. Argo's whiskered face broke into a grin and she hissed with laughter.

"That's the best part about it, see? The moment I sell a piece of intel, I've got a brand-new product to sell: So-and-so just bought such-and-such information. It's twice the profit!"

In real life, an attorney would never reveal the name of her client, but given the Rat's motto of "all information has a price," she didn't seem to honor that taboo. Anyone who wanted to make a deal with her needed to know beforehand that their own information could be sold, but when her product was so excellent, who could complain about the price?

"If any female players want my personal information, let me know so I can buy theirs first," I said wearily. Argo cackled again, then put on a serious expression.

"Okay, I'll tell the client you refused again. I'll even throw in my opinion that they won't get through to ya. So long, Kii-boy."

The Rat turned and waved, then darted back out of the alley as nimbly as her namesake. After a momentary glimpse of her brown curls vanishing into the crowd, I felt sure she'd never get herself killed.

I'd learned several things over the first month of *SAO*, the game of death.

What separated a player's likelihood of life or death? There were an infinite number of variables—stock of potions, knowing when to leave a dungeon, and so on—but somewhere at the center of those swirling factors was the presence of a person's core, something they could believe in unconditionally. You might call it one's greatest weapon, a tool necessary for survival.

For Argo, that was information. She knew everything crucial:

where the dangerous monsters were and the most efficient places to hunt. That knowledge gave her confidence and a cool head, which raised her chances of survival.

What was my core? It had to be the sword on my back. More precisely, it was the feeling I got when my blade and I became one. I'd only managed to reach that mental zone a few times, but it was the desire to control that power at will, to be the unquestioned ruler of that realm, that drove me to stay alive. The reason I'd put points into sharpness and durability rather than quickness or accuracy was simple: the former were pure numerical increases, but the latter adjusted the system itself. They changed the sensation of swinging the sword.

But in that case...

What about the fencer on the frontier of the labyrinth? What was her core? I'd transported her outside of the dungeon (using means I could never tell her), but if I hadn't been there, would she really have died? I could easily imagine her unconsciously getting to her feet as the next kobold approached, using her shooting-star Linear to dispatch the beast.

What drove her to undergo such a ferocious string of battles? What had kept her alive up to this point? She must have some source of strength I could only imagine.

"Maybe I should have paid Argo the Five hundred col," I muttered, then shook my head and looked upward.

The white-painted windmills that were the defining symbol of Tolbana had just a tinge of orange to them. It was a bit past three o'clock—time to grab a bite to eat before the undoubtedly long and tedious boss raid meeting.

When the meeting started at four, things would get ugly.

Today, for the first time, one hidden fissure between *SAO* players would come into clarity: the unbridgeable gap between new players and beta testers...

There was only one piece of information that Argo the Rat refused to sell to others, and that was whether a person had been a beta tester or not. She wasn't alone in that philosophy. All the former testers, who could recognize one another by name or voice, if not by face, intentionally avoided reaching out to each other. The previous encounter was no different. Both Argo and I knew the other was a beta tester, but we went light-years out of our way to never discuss it.

The reason was simple: Being publicly outed as a beta tester could be fatal.

Not because of monsters in a dungeon. Because if you wandered alone in the game map, you could be executed by a lynch mob of new players. They believed that the deaths of two thousand players within a month could be laid at the feet of the beta testers.

And I couldn't totally deny that charge.

4

FOR HER FIRST MEAL IN THREE OR POSSIBLY EVEN four days, Asuna chose a heel of the cheapest black bread the NPCs in town sold, as well as the free water available at the many fountains around the place.

She'd never particularly enjoyed eating in real life, but the total emptiness of eating in this world was hard to describe. No matter how gorgeous the feast might appear, not a single grain of sugar or salt reached her real body. It seemed to her that they should have eliminated the concept of hunger and fullness altogether, but the virtual body craved food three times a day, and the pangs did not disappear unless virtual food was eaten.

She'd learned how to shut out the feeling of hunger through sheer willpower while lurking in the dungeon, but there was no hiding the need once back in town. As an act of protest, she always chose the cheapest possible option, but it made her angry, in a way, that even the rough black bread eaten a scrap at a time actually tasted pretty good.

Asuna was sitting on a simple wooden bench next to the fountain square at the center of Tolbana, chewing away with her hood pulled low. For only costing a single col, the bread was fairly large. Just as she'd finished half of it—

"Pretty good, isn't it?" came a voice from her right. Her fingers stopped in the act of ripping another piece free, and she threw a sharp glare in that direction.

It was the man she'd just left behind at the town entrance a few minutes ago, the black-haired swordsman in the gray coat. The meddlesome stranger who'd somehow transported her unconscious body outside of the dungeon, keeping her journey going when it should have ended.

Her cheeks suddenly grew hot at the thought. After all of her bold statements about dying, not only was she alive, but he'd seen her chowing down on a meal. Her entire being was wracked with shame, and she froze with the crescent of bread in her hands, uncertain of how to respond.

The man eventually coughed politely and asked, "May I sit next to you?"

Normally, she would silently stand up and leave without a second glance, but in this unfamiliar situation, she was at a loss. Taking Asuna's lack of response as silent permission, he sat down on the far right corner of the bench and rummaged in his pocket, giving her as much space as possible. When his hand reappeared, it was holding a round, black object—a one-col roll of black bread.

For an instant, Asuna forgot her shame and confusion and looked up at him in simple astonishment.

If he was good enough to have reached that deep a spot in the labyrinth, and have such excellent equipment, this swordsman must have enough money to afford a full-course meal at a nice restaurant. Was he just a cheapskate? Or...

"Do you *really* think that tastes good?" she asked, before she could stop herself. His eyebrows took on an expression of hurt dignity, and he nodded vigorously.

"Of course. I've eaten one every day since I got to this town. Of course, I throw in a little wrinkle."

"Wrinkle...?"

She tilted her head in confusion beneath the hood. Rather than explain out loud, the swordsman reached into his other pocket and produced a small porcelain jar. He set it down on the bench between them and said, "Use this on your bread."

For a moment, she wasn't sure what he meant by "use it on the bread," then realized that it was a common video game phrase. Use the key on the door, use the bottle on the spring, and so on. She reluctantly reached out and touched the lid of the jar with a fingertip. She selected "use" on the pop-up menu that appeared, and her finger started glowing purple, the signal for "target selection mode." By touching the black bread in her left hand, the objects would interact.

With a brief jingle, the bread was suddenly white, coated—no, covered—with a thick substance that appeared to be—

"…Cream? Where did you get this?"

"It was the reward for the 'Revenge of the Cows' quest in the last town. It takes a long time to beat, so I don't think many people have bothered to finish it," he said seriously, using the jar on his bread with a practiced motion. It must have been the last of the container, because the jar flashed, tinkled and disappeared. He opened his mouth wide and took a large bite of his cream-slathered bread. His chewing was so vigorous she could practically hear the sound effects, and Asuna realized that for the first time in ages, her stomach pangs were not an unpleasant pain, but the healthy sign of honest hunger.

She took a hesitant bite of the creamy bread in her hand. Suddenly, the rough, dry bread she'd been eating had turned into a heavy, rustic cake. The cream was sweet and smooth, with a refreshing tartness like yogurt. Asuna took a few more rapturous bites, her cheeks packed full with a numbing sense of contentment.

The next thing she knew, there was not a single crumb left of the item in her hands. She looked over with a start to see that she'd finished her food just two seconds before the swordsman. Overcome with shame again, she wanted to get up and run off but couldn't bring herself to be so rude to the man who'd just treated her to a tasty meal.

Breathing heavily, attempting to get her mind in order, Asuna finally managed to squeak out a polite response.

"........Thanks for the food."

"You're welcome."

Done with his meal, the swordsman clapped his fingerless-gloved hands together and continued. "If you want to do that cow quest I mentioned, there's a trick to it. If you're efficient, you can beat it in just two hours."

"..."

She couldn't deny the temptation. With that yogurt cream, her cheap black bread turned into a proper feast. It was only an artificial satisfaction created by the game's flavor modeling system, but she wanted it again—every day, if possible.

But...

Asuna looked down and quietly shook her head. "I'll pass. I didn't come to this town in order to eat good food."

"I see. Why, then?"

While the swordsman's voice wasn't particularly melodious, there was a boyish inflection to it that was not displeasing to her ears in the least. It was perhaps this feature that led her to speak what was on her mind, something she hadn't done with anyone else in this world.

"So that...I can be myself. If I was going to just hide back in the first city and waste away, I'd rather be myself until the very last moment. Even if it means dying at the hands of a monster...I don't want to let this game beat me. I won't let it happen."

The fifteen years of Asuna Yuuki's life had been a long series of battles. It started with the entrance exams to kindergarten and followed with an endless succession of tests big and small. She'd beaten them all. Losing in a single instance would mean that her life was no longer of any worth, and she'd successfully shouldered that pressure since the very start.

But after fifteen years of winning, this test, *Sword Art Online*, would likely be the end of her. It was too mysterious to her, a culture steeped in foreign and unfamiliar rules, and it was not the kind of battle that could be won alone.

The only means of victory was reaching the very top of the giant floating castle, a full hundred floors above, and beating the final enemy. But a month after the start of the game, one-fifth of the players were already gone, and most of them were experienced in the ways of these things. The forces left behind were too weak, and the path ahead was so very, very long…

As though the faucet holding her innermost feelings had been opened the tiniest bit, the words trickled drop by drop out of her mouth. The confession came in fragments, pieces of logic that didn't add up to full sentences, but the black-haired swordsman sat and listened in silence. When Asuna's voice had died away in the evening breeze, he finally spoke.

"…I'm sorry."

A few seconds later, Asuna skeptically wondered why he would say that.

She'd only met him today. He had no reason to apologize to her. She peered to her right and saw that he was hunched over on the bench, his elbows on his knees. His lips shifted, and more faint words reached her ears.

"I'm sorry… This current situation—the reason you feel so pressured—is my…"

But she couldn't make out the rest. The especially large windmill in the center of town started ringing its wind-powered clock bell.

It was four o'clock, the time of the meeting. She looked up and saw that a large number of players had gathered across the fountain square.

"Let's go. You invited me to this meeting, after all," Asuna said, getting to her feet. He nodded and slowly rose. What was he going to say? It ultimately didn't matter, because she was never going to speak with him again, but the thought dug into her side like a tiny thorn.

I want to know. I don't want to know. Even Asuna didn't know which desire was stronger.

5

FORTY-FOUR.

That was the number of players who gathered at the fountain in Tolbana.

I had to admit, it was well below my expectations—my hopes. An official party in *SAO* could be up to six players, and a throng of eight of those, forty-eight people in total, was a full-size raid party. My experience in the beta test had taught me that the best way to tackle a floor boss without any casualties was two raid parties trading off, but this wasn't even enough for one.

I sucked in a deep breath for a sigh, but held it in when a voice came from behind me.

"There are...so many..."

It was the fencer in the hooded cape. I turned and shot back, "Many...? You call this many?"

"Yes. I mean, they're all here for the first attempt at this floor's boss monster, right? Knowing that they could all die in the process..."

"...I see."

I nodded and gazed around at the small groups of fighters huddled throughout the square.

There were five or six players I knew by name, and another fifteen or so were familiar faces I'd come across along the frontier. The remaining twenty-something were all new to me. Naturally, the gender balance was extremely uneven. As far as I could tell, the fencer was the only woman in the group, but with her hood pulled so low, it wasn't quite apparent, and I was certain that anyone else observing would assume it was all men. Across the square, Argo the Rat was perched upon a high wall, but she would not take part in the battle.

The fencer was right—they were all going to face the first floor boss, an enemy no one had seen before, at least in the official Aincrad. Of all the battles one could tackle on the first floor, this would carry the highest risk of death. That meant that every player here was prepared for the possibility of death, in order to serve as a stepping-stone for those who came after them. However...

"I'm...not so sure," I muttered. She turned to me, her eyes flashing doubtfully within the hood. I chose my words carefully.

"I don't think it applies to everyone, but I think a fair number of them aren't doing it out of self-sacrifice, but because they just don't want to be left in the dust. If anything, I'd be one of the latter, myself."

"Left in the dust? Behind what?"

"Behind the frontier. The thought of dying is frightening, but so is the idea that the boss is being defeated without you."

The cloth hood dipped slightly. I figured that being a total beginner at MMOs, she wouldn't understand what I was saying. But I was wrong.

"Is that the same kind of motivation...like when you don't want to fall below the top ten of the class, or you want to stay above the seventieth percentile, or whatever?"

"..."

Now it was my turn to lose my voice. Eventually, I agreed. "Yeah...um...I think so..."

The shapely lips visible through the hood crinkled into a tiny smile, and I heard a few quiet snorts of breath. Was she...laughing? The wielder of that ultra-precise Linear, who told me to mind my own business when I brought her out of the dungeon?

I was almost about to rudely stare directly under the hood, but I was saved from that faux pas by the sound of loud clapping and a shout that echoed across the square.

"All right, people! It's five minutes past already, so let's get started! Gather 'round, folks—you there, three steps closer!"

The speaker was a swordsman clad in glimmering metal armor. He leapt nimbly up onto the lip of the fountain at the center of the square from a standing position. A single jump of that height wearing heavy armor made it clear that he had excellent strength and agility.

Some within the crowd of forty-odd began to stir when he turned to survey the group. It made sense—the man standing on the lip of the fountain was so brilliantly handsome that you had to wonder why he would bother playing a VRMMO in the first place. On top of that, the wavy locks framing his face were dyed a brilliant blue. Hair dye wasn't sold at NPC vendors on the first floor, so he must have gotten it as a rare drop from a monster.

If he'd gone to all this trouble just to look good in front of the crowd, I assumed he must be disappointed, given that there was only one woman in the group (and it wasn't clear she was one, given the hood), but the man flashed a dashing smile that suggested he would never stoop to thinking such a thing.

"Thank you all for heeding my call today! I'm sure some of you know me already, but just in case, my name's Diavel and I like to think of myself as playing a knight!"

Those closest to the fountain started jeering and whistling, and someone cried, "I bet you wanted to say you're playing a 'hero'!"

There were no official character classes in *Sword Art Online*. Every player had a number of skill slots, and they were free to choose which skills to equip and advance. As an example, players who focused on crafting or trading skills might be referred to as blacksmiths, tailors, or cooks...but I'd never heard of anyone called a knight or hero.

Then again, if someone wanted to be known by that title, that was their prerogative. Diavel had bronze armor on his chest, shoulders, arms, and shins, as well as a longsword on his waist and a kite shield on his back. Added up, they certainly made a proper knight's outfit.

Watching his proud display from the back row, I quickly consulted my memory. The equipment and hair were different, so it was hard to tell, but I could have sworn I'd seen that face a few times before in towns around the first floor. What about before, in the *other* Aincrad? I didn't recognize the name...

"Now, you're all top players in the game, active around the front line of our progress, and I hardly need remind you of why we're here," Diavel's speech continued. I stopped trying to remember and focused on his words. The blue-haired knight raised a hand and gestured to the massive tower—the labyrinth of the first floor—outside the town limits.

"Today, our party discovered the staircase that leads to the top floor of that tower. Which means that either tomorrow or the day after, we'll finally reach...the first-floor boss chamber!"

The crowd stirred. I was surprised as well. The first-floor labyrinth was a twenty-level tower, and I (and the fencer) had been just around the start of the nineteenth level today. I had no idea that others had mapped so much of that floor already.

"One month. It took an entire month...but we still have to be an example. We have to beat the boss, reach the second floor, and show everyone back in the Town of Beginnings that someday we *can* beat this game of death. That's the duty of all the top-level players here! Isn't that right?"

Another cheer rose. Now it wasn't just Diavel's friends but others in the crowd who applauded. What he said was noble and without fault. In fact, anyone seeking fault in it had to be crazy. I decided the knight who stood up and took on the role of uniting the scattered players at the frontier deserved some applause from me, when—

"Hang on just a sec, Sir Knight," the voice said calmly.

The cheers stopped and the people at the front stepped aside. Standing in the middle of the open space was a short but solid man. All I could see from my position was a large sword and spiky brown hair that conjured the image of a cactus.

The cactus took a step forward and growled in a rasp totally unlike Diavel's smooth voice, "Gotta get this offa my chest before we can play pretend-friends."

Diavel didn't bat an eye at this sudden interruption. He beckoned to the squat man with a confident smile. "What's on your mind, friend? I'm open to opinions. If you're going to offer yours, however, I'd ask you to introduce yourself first."

"...Hmph."

The cactus-headed man snorted, took a few steps forward until he was right in front of the fountain, then turned to the crowd. "The name's Kibaou."

The spiky-haired swordsman with the fierce name glared out at the gathering with small but piercing eyes. As they swept sideways, I had the fleeting impression that they stopped on my face for a moment. But I'd never heard his name and didn't remember meeting him before. After his lengthy survey of the gathering, Kibaou growled again.

"There gotta be five or ten folks in this midst what owe an apology first."

"Apology? To whom?"

Diavel the knight, still standing on the edge of the fountain behind him, grandly gestured with both hands. Kibaou spat angrily, not bothering to turn around. "Hah! Ain't it obvious? To the two thousand people who already died. Two thousand people died because *they* hogged everythin' to themselves! Ain't that right?!"

The murmuring crowd of forty or so suddenly went dead silent. They finally understood what Kibaou was trying to say. I did, too.

The only sound through the heavy silence was the distant strains of the NPC musicians playing the evening BGM. No one

said a word. Everyone seemed to understand that if he spoke up, he would be branded one of *them*. It was certainly that fear which gripped my mind at the moment.

"Mr. Kibaou, when you refer to 'them,' I assume you mean… the former beta testers?" asked Diavel, arms crossed, a look of grave severity on his face.

"Obviously," Kibaou said to the knight behind him with a glance, the thick scale mail sewed to a leather frame jangling as he turned. "The day this goddamn game started, all them beta testers up an' ran straight outta the first town. They abandoned nine thousand folks who didn't know right from left. They monopolized all the best huntin' spots and profitable quests so's they could level up, and didn't spare a backward glance for no one. I know there must be more'n one or two standin' here right now, thinkin' they can get in on the boss action without anyone knowin'. If they don't get down on hands and knees ta apologize, and donate their stockpile of col an' items for the cause o' fightin' this boss, I ain't gonna put my life in their hands, is what I'm sayin'!"

Just as the "kiba" in his name—the word for fangs—suggested, he ended with a snarl of bared teeth. Unsurprisingly, no one spoke up. As a former beta tester myself, I clenched my teeth, held my breath, and didn't make a sound.

It wasn't as though I didn't want to shout back at him, to ask him if he thought no beta testers had died yet. A week earlier, I bought a piece of intel from Argo—technically, I had her look into something for me. I wanted a total of dead beta testers.

The *SAO* closed beta, which ran during summer vacation, only had a thousand open slots. Every member also got exclusive first rights to buy the official package edition when it was released. Based on the number of people logged in at the end of the beta, I estimated that not every person was going to keep playing when the game was released. It would probably be seven or eight hundred—that was my guess as to the total number of beta testers present at the start of the game of death.

Finding out *who* was a beta tester was the tricky part. If there was a β mark next to the player's color cursor, that would clear up the matter at once, but (fortunately) that was not the case. And physical appearance was not a factor either, as the GM Akihiko Kayaba had ensured that every player was now modeled after their own real-life appearance. The only hint to go on was player name, but many of them could have changed names between the beta and the full release. The reason Argo and I recognized each other as beta testers had to do with the circumstances of our first meeting, but that's a story for another time.

At any rate, Argo's investigation should have been incredibly hard. Yet she came back to me with a number after just three days.

In her estimation, the total number of beta testers who were now dead was about three hundred. If that figure was correct, it meant that of the two thousand dead, seventeen hundred were new players. Put into percentages, that meant the death rate of new players was 18 percent—but the death rate of beta testers was closer to 40.

Knowledge and experience did not always translate to safety. At times, they could be one's downfall. I myself nearly died on the very first quest I followed after the game of death began. There were external factors as well. The terrain, items, and monsters were virtually the same in the finished game as in the beta, but just the slightest little difference could pop up, as small and deadly as a poison needle...

"May I speak?"

A rich baritone voice echoed throughout the evening square. I looked up with a start to see a silhouette proceeding from the left end of the gathering.

He was large, easily over six feet tall. The avatar's size was supposed to have no effect on stats, but he made the two-handed battle axe strapped to his back look light. His face was just as menacing as the weapon. His scalp was completely bald and chocolate brown, but the chiseled features on his face fit that bold look quite well. He didn't even look Japanese—for all I knew, maybe he *was* of a different race.

As the burly man reached the edge of the fountain, he turned and bowed to the crowd of forty before turning his attention to the woefully outsized Kibaou.

"My name's Agil. If I have this right, Kibaou, you're claiming that many newbies died because the former beta testers didn't help them, and therefore they ought to apologize and pay reparations? Is that correct?"

"Y...yeah."

Kibaou was momentarily taken aback, but he recovered and stood straight, glaring back at the axe warrior Agil with his glinting eyes. "If they didn't abandon the rest of us, that's two thousand wouldn't be dead right now! And that ain't just two thousand random folks, that's the best of the best from other MMOs that we lost! If those beta assholes had the decency ta share their loot and knowledge, we'd have ten times as many folks here...In fact, we'd be on the second or third floor by now!"

Three hundred of the people you're mourning are those "assholes," *jerk!* I wanted to yell, but I held back the impulse. I didn't have any proof backing that number, and in more self-centered terms, I just didn't want to be singled out. This much was clear: Outing myself as a former tester could not possibly help my situation.

The four or five hundred testers left were hiding among the players new to the game. In terms of level and equipment, they likely weren't any different from the other top players. But if I stood up and revealed my background, not only would it fail to smooth over tensions between the two groups, it would probably just end with a witch hunt. The worst possible outcome was in-fighting between new players and testers among the elite players on the frontier. We had to avoid that outcome at all costs. Whether in the fields or the dungeons, the "outdoor" areas of *SAO* were free rein for attacking other players.

"So you claim, Kibaou. While I can't argue with the loot, we've certainly had the information out there," Agil spoke in his rich baritone while I hung my head pathetically. He reached into the pouch on the waist of the leather armor stretched over his rippling muscles and produced a simple book made of bound sheets of parchment. On the cover was a simple rat icon with round ears and three whiskers on either side.

"You got one of these guidebooks too, didn't you? They were handing them out for free at the item shops in Horunka and Medai."

"F-for free?" I murmured. As the icon on the cover suggested, it was a guide to the area that Argo the Rat sold to other players. It contained detailed maps and lists of monsters, their item drops, and even quest information. The large splash text on the lower half of the cover that said "Don't worry, this is Argo's guidebook" wasn't just a cheeky bit of fluff. Admittedly, I'd bought the entire set myself to keep my memory fresh—but from what I recalled, they went for the hefty price of five hundred col a book…

"I got one, too," the hitherto silent fencer whispered. When I asked if it had been for free, she nodded. "It was stocked at the item store on consignment, but the price was listed as zero col, so everyone took one. It was really helpful."

"But…what the hell…?"

The Rat—a scheming dealer who would sell her own status numbers for the right price—giving away information for free? It was unthinkable! I shot a glance back to the stone wall where she'd been sitting minutes ago, but there was no one there. I made a mental note to ask her the reason the next time I saw her, then reconsidered when I heard her voice inside my head saying, "That'll cost ya a thousand, dig?"

"Yeah, I got one. What of it?" Kibaou snarled, bringing me back to the present scene. Agil put the strategy guide back in his pouch and crossed his arms.

"Every time I reached a new town or village, there was always one of these books at the item shop. Same for you, right? Didn't it strike you as too quick for the information to have been compiled already?"

"What's the point if it's too quick?"

"I mean that the only people who could have offered this information and map data to the informer are the former beta testers."

The crowd stirred. Kibaou's mouth shut, and Diavel the knight nodded in agreement. Agil looked at the group again and spoke in his loud baritone. "Listen, the information was out there. And yet people still died. I'm thinking it's *because* they were veteran MMO players. They assumed that *SAO* worked on the same principles and standards as other titles, and failed to pull back when they needed to. But now's not the time to be holding anyone responsible for this. It seems to me that this meeting is going to determine whether we meet the same fate or not."

Agil the axe warrior's tone was bold but reasonable, and his argument was so sound that Kibaou had no immediate retort. If anyone other than Agil had argued the same thing, Kibaou would likely have accused him of being a beta tester himself, but in this case, he could only stare daggers at the large man.

Behind the two silent debaters, standing on the edge of the fountain with his long flowing hair almost purple in the light of the setting sun, Diavel nodded magnanimously.

"Your point is well taken, Kibaou. I myself nearly died on several occasions due to my ignorance of the wilderness. But as Agil says, isn't this the time to look forward? If we're going to beat the floor boss, we'll even need the former testers…no, *especially* need the former testers. If we exclude them and get wiped out, then what was the point of it all?"

It was a sweeping speech more than worthy of a noble knight. Many in the crowd nodded in agreement. As the mood seemed to tilt toward forgiveness for the testers, I sighed with relief and not a small amount of shame. Diavel continued.

"I'm sure you all have your own thoughts on the matter, but for now, I would like your help in clearing the first floor. If you simply can't bear the thought of fighting alongside beta testers, then we'll miss you, but I won't force you to participate. Teamwork is the most important part of any raid."

His gaze slowly swept across the crowd until it fixed on Kibaou. The cactus-headed swordsman met the gaze for several long moments, then he snorted loudly and growled, "Fine...I'll play along for now. But once the boss fight's over, we're gonna settle this once and for all."

He turned, scale mail rattling, and walked back to the front row of the crowd. Agil spread his hands, signaling he had nothing else to say, and returned to his spot.

In the end, this scene was the highlight of the meeting. There was only so much detailed planning to be done for a battle when we'd only just reached the floor the creature was on. How does anyone plan a boss fight when no one's even seen it yet?

Well, that wasn't quite true. I knew that the first-floor boss was an enormous kobold, that he swung a huge talwar, and that he was accompanied by a retinue of about twelve heavily armored kobolds.

If I revealed that I was a former beta tester and offered my knowledge of the boss, our odds of success might rise. But if I did that, people would ask why I hadn't spoken up before, and it might inflame the undercurrent of anger against the testers again.

Plus, my knowledge was only of the previous incarnation of Aincrad, and there was always the possibility that the release version of *SAO* had a redesigned or rebalanced boss. If we formulated a plan based on the beta information and charged into the room only to find it had a different appearance and pattern of attack, the ensuing confusion would be the downfall of the raid. Ultimately, until someone opened the door to the boss chamber and got him to pop into the world, we couldn't begin to plan.

This was the excuse I told myself to hold my silence.

At the end of the meeting, Diavel led an optimistic cheer and got the rest of the gathering to shout in approval. I raised a fist in solidarity, but the fencer beside me did not even pull a hand out of her cape, much less join in the cheer. She turned around to leave even before the call of "Dismissed!" rang out. Before she went, she spoke in a whisper that only I could hear.

"Whatever you were about to say before the meeting... Tell me, if we both survive the battle."

As she headed into a dim alley, I silently answered.

Yes, I'll tell you. I'll tell you how I left everything else behind for the sake of keeping myself alive.

6

THERE WAS NO DISCUSSION OF ANY STRATEGIC MERIT at the meeting, but it had apparently served the valuable purpose of bolstering morale, as the twentieth level of the labyrinth was mapped with unprecedented speed. On Saturday, December 30, the day after the meeting, the first party (again, Diavel's band of six) discovered the double doors of the boss chamber. I knew when it happened because I was solo adventuring nearby and heard the cheers.

Boldly enough, they opened the door to catch a glimpse of the resident within. At the fountain-side meeting in Tolbana that evening, the blue-haired knight proudly announced his findings.

The boss was an enormous kobold that towered over six feet tall. His name was Illfang the Kobold Lord, and his weapon fell into the Curved Blade category. He was attended by three Ruin Kobold Sentinels with metal armor and halberds.

This much was the same as the beta. From what I recalled, the sentinels respawned with each of the four stages of the boss's HP bar, making a total of twelve over the course of the battle, but as usual, I didn't have the guts to say this out loud. It would become clear as they tried a few test skirmishes, I told myself. As it turned out, I needn't have worried, because something cleared it all up in the midst of the meeting.

Coincidentally, the NPC shop stall in the corner of the fountain square began selling a very familiar item. Three sheets of parchment bound together, more of a pamphlet than a book. It was *Argo's First-Floor Boss Guidebook*. Price: zero col.

The meeting was temporarily adjourned so that everyone could "purchase" a copy from the NPC and pore over the contents.

As usual, the amount of information was impressive. The first three pages were stuffed with all manner of details: the just-revealed boss's name, estimated HP, the reach and speed of its talwar, damage, even sword skills. The fourth page covered the accompanying Kobold Sentinels, including a note that they spawned four times, making a total of twelve.

On the rear cover of the book was a message in a red font that had not been present on any of Argo's other guides. It read: *This information is from the* SAO *beta test. Details may not match the current version of the game.*

When I saw this, I looked up, searching for Argo around the square. But I saw no sign of the Rat or her plain leather armor today. I looked back down and murmured, "She's really going out on a limb…"

This red warning was going to topple Argo's usual stance of "this is just information I bought from some former beta tester, identity unknown." Anyone who read this warning would suspect that the Rat herself was a former tester. There was no proof, of course, but with the widening gap in sentiment between the new players and beta testers, she was clearly putting herself at risk of being the first hunted down.

On the other hand, it was clear that this guidebook would remove the need for tiresome and dangerous scouting missions. Once all forty-plus players had finished reading, they looked once again to the blue-haired knight standing on the lip of the fountain, as though putting their decision in the hands of a leader.

Diavel's head stayed down for many long seconds, deep in thought, before he finally straightened up to address the crowd.

"Let us be grateful for this information, my friends!"

The crowd murmured. This was clearly a call for peace with the beta testers rather than antagonism. I thought Kibaou might leap up to protest, but the brown cactus hair near the front the gathering stayed firmly in place.

"Regardless of its source, this guide is going to save us two or three days of scouting out the boss. I'm actually quite grateful for this. It's the reconnaissance missions that carry the greatest risk of fatalities, after all."

Heads of various colors nodded throughout the square.

"If these figures are correct, the boss's numerical stats aren't too dangerous. If *SAO* was a normal MMO, we could probably take it out with an average level three—no, five levels below the enemy's. So if we work on our tactics and come equipped with plenty of pots for healing, it should be possible to win without any deaths. No, let me rephrase that: We're not going to have any deaths, period. On my pride as a knight, I swear this to you!"

Someone in the crowd raised a cheer, and a round of applause followed. Even as a twisted solo, I had to admit that Diavel had a gift for leadership. The guild function didn't unlock until the third floor, but he would certainly have his own on the day we reached that far.

But my breath caught in my throat at his next words.

"All right, now I think it's time to actually start planning out the battle! After all, we can't start taking roles until we've formed a proper raid party. First off, form into parties with your friends and others around you!"

.... *What?*

He sounded like a PE teacher at an elementary school. I did some quick calculations. A full party in *SAO* was six members, and there were forty-four present, so...that made seven parties with two left over. Should we shoot for average, and have four parties of six and four parties of five? But that was unlikely to happen on its own if our leader didn't make the order...

All of my high-speed thinking went to waste. In less than a minute from Diavel's suggestion, there were seven full parties of six members each. Obviously he already had his own party of six, but I didn't expect lone wolves like Kibaou and Agil to find their own groupings so fast. I began to wonder if I was seriously the only person who didn't receive some kind of invitation.

But I wasn't.

After a quick scan of the crowd, I spotted a familiar hooded cape standing slightly apart from the rest, and slipped over to her side.

"So you got left out too, eh?" I asked, only to be greeted with a stare like molten steel. She muttered an angry response.

"...I'm not a castoff. I just didn't want to butt in, because it seemed like everyone else already had their own friends."

I wisely decided not to point out that she had perfectly defined a castoff, and put on a serious face instead. "Why don't you team up with me, then? A raid goes up to eight parties, so it's the only way we can participate."

Basing my suggestion on the properties of the game system was a success, as she looked briefly hesitant, then snorted and said, "I might consider it, if you send me the invite."

Since retorting "It was my idea first, so *you* should send the invite" was the kind of childishness that I'd grown out of since being trapped in here last month, I nodded obediently and tapped the fencer's cursor, sending a party invite. She accepted flippantly, and a second, smaller HP gauge appeared on the left side of my field of vision.

I stared at the list of letters below the bar.

Asuna. That was the name of the strange fencer with the preternaturally swift Linear.

Diavel the knight's leadership was not limited to his speech-making. He examined each of the seven full parties that had been formed, and with a minimum of switching members, had tweaked them into distinct groups with their own purpose in the battle. There were two heavily armored tank squads, three groups of attackers with high offensive power, and two support teams armed with longer-range weapons.

The two tank squads would switch off pulling aggro from the Kobold Lord—absorbing his attacks and attention. Two of the attack teams would focus on the boss, while the third was in charge of holding off his followers. The support teams, equipped with long, shafted weapons, would employ delaying and interrupting skills as much as possible to prevent the enemies from attacking.

I thought it was a good arrangement—simple and less likely to fall apart. The knight returned my esteem by examining the leftover party (the fencer and I, of course) for a few long moments before offering some pleasant advice.

"Can you folks back up team E to make sure none of the roaming kobolds gets through?"

Translated, it felt like he was asking if we could hang out near the back and not get in anyone's way. I could sense the fencer named Asuna preparing to make a very unfriendly gesture, so I held a hand in front of her and smiled.

"Got it. That's an important role. You can count on us."

"Thanks a lot." The knight flashed his pearly whites and returned to the fountain.

An angry voice hissed in my ear. "How is that important? We're not going to get a single hit on the boss before it dies."

"W-well, what else can we do? There's only two of us. We can't even switch in and last long enough for pot rotation."

"Switch...? Pot...?"

At her mistrustful murmuring, I stopped to consider. She had left the Town of Beginnings as an absolute newbie with no prior experience, and made it this far on her own, using nothing more than a bundle of five baseline rapiers bought from an NPC and the sword skill Linear.

"I'll explain everything later. It'll take too long to go over right here." I figured there was a more than likely chance she'd shoot back that she didn't need to know anyway, but to my surprise, she was silent for several moments before nodding meekly.

* * *

The second meeting of the boss strategy committee ended with quick greetings from the leaders of teams A through G and an official distribution plan for the cash and items the boss would drop. The large axe warrior Agil was the leader of tank team B, while the antagonistic Kibaou led attack team E. The E-team was the group assigned to stop the roving kobolds, so as the leftovers, it was our job to assist Kibaou. I didn't really want anything to do with him, but he didn't actually know that I was a former tester—for now. In the end, Argo the Rat never showed up to the meeting. I wasn't going to blame her, of course. Her guidebook was more than enough help.

The col dropped by the boss would be automatically split evenly between all forty-four members of the raid, and the items were on a simple finders-keepers basis. Contemporary MMOs had transitioned to a system in which players could elect to claim an item and roll dice to see who would win it, but *SAO* chose the more primitive method. The items would automatically drop into a player's storage, and no one would be any the wiser. In other words, if the group decided that all items from the boss should be distributed by dice rolls, all players would have to voluntarily give up those items to the lottery first. As I knew from personal experience in the beta, this was a sore test of one's willpower. Several times, I'd experienced the nasty breakup of a party when no one stepped forward with loot after a big fight, meaning that *someone* must be lying about their gains.

It was likely Diavel's intention to prevent this unsavory outcome by enacting the finders-keepers rule. Our considerate knight in shining armor.

At five thirty, like the day before, we closed with a cheer and the gathering broke apart into small groups to find pubs and restaurants to visit. I rolled my shoulders, which seemed unnaturally stiff, wondering if it was just an illusion or some kind of actual physical tension that was bleeding through to this virtual world.

"So...where will you be giving me this explanation?"

I wondered what she was talking about for a moment, then spun around in nervous surprise. "Oh...I-I can talk anywhere you like. How about a pub around here?"

"...No. I don't want anyone seeing."

I was briefly stung by her implication but recovered my pride by choosing to interpret her meaning as "seen with a man" rather than just "seen with me."

"Okay, how about an NPC's house? But still, someone could wander in...We could get a room at an inn so we could lock the door, but that's obviously out."

"Of course it is."

This time, I suffered piercing damage from that retort, which was as sharp as the end of her rapier. I could manage a conversation with a female player because this was a virtual world, but just a month before, I had been a terribly awkward and antisocial middle-schooler who could barely talk to his own sister. Wasn't I supposed to be sticking to my guns as a solo player? Why was I in this situation in the first place? Obviously I wouldn't be any use in a boss battle without joining a group, but the other seven groups were all men, so I'd have felt much less awkward if I'd just worked my way in with them instead...

As my mind ran in ever more self-pitying circles, the fencer sighed and continued, "Besides, the inn rooms in this place barely live up to the name. They're like tiny boxes with a bed and table, and they expect you to pay fifty col a night? I don't care about food, but the sleep you need is real, so they could at least give us better accommodations."

"H...huh? You think so?" I asked, surprised. "You know there are better places available if you search them out, right? They just cost a little more."

"How hard do you have to search? There are only three inns in town, and they're all the same."

I finally understood. "Oh...I see. You only checked the places with the big INN signs, right?"

"Well…isn't that self-explanatory? An inn's an inn."

"Yeah, but that only refers to the cheapest possible places to spend the night here on the ground floor. The inns aren't the only place to pay col for a room."

Her lips suddenly pursed.

"W-well…why didn't you say that earlier?" she shot back. I knew I had the upper hand now, so I proudly described my favorite spot in town.

"I stay on the second floor of a farm in town for eighty a night, but it comes with all the milk you want, has a comfy, spacious bed and a nice view, not to mention the bath…"

At that last phrase, she struck. With the speed of the Linear I'd seen deep in the dungeon, her hand leapt out and grabbed the collar of my gray coat, almost hard enough to set off the game's anti-crime code. Her voice was steely and menacing.

"…What did you just say?"

7

AS SHE'D MENTIONED EARLIER, IT WAS ASUNA'S BELIEF that out of all the actions possible in this virtual world, the only real one was sleep.

Everything else was a sham. Walking, running, talking, eating, and fighting. All of these things were simple digital codes sent to and from the *Sword Art Online* server. Nothing the in-game avatar did caused a single twitch of a finger on the real-life body, reclining in bed. The only exception occurred when the avatar lay down for the night, and the real brain engaged in what must be sleep. So, above anything else, she wanted to make sure she got a good night's sleep at the inns in town. It proved to be harder than it seemed.

The constant stress and rhythm of battle in the wilderness and dungeons left no time for reflection, but when she returned to town and lay down in bed, she fell into an endless replay of her actions from a month before. Why had she indulged such a strange whim that day? Why wasn't she satisfied just by touching the NerveGear? Why did she put the formidable headgear on and say "link start"?

Whenever she fell into a light sleep reflecting on that particular regret, she had nightmares. It was a crucial time for her—the winter of her third and final year of middle school—and because of this stupid game, Asuna's classmates were no doubt laughing at her failure. Her relatives were pitying her for falling off the career path that had years left to play out. But worst of all, her parents, staring down at her comatose body in some hospital room, their faces hidden...

She'd twitch and wake up with a jolt, then check the clock in the lower left corner of her vision to find that at best, she'd only been asleep for three hours. After that, no amount of lying in bed with her eyes closed would bring sleep back. In a way, if she'd just been able to get a good night's sleep, Asuna wouldn't have driven herself to punishing dungeon crawls for three or four days at a time.

So as the col piled up in her purse, Asuna wished more and more for a nice room and bed to spend it on. The inns in this world were cramped and dim, and whatever material the beds were made from, they were noisy and tough. She didn't need Italian-made high-resistance polyurethane foam...but maybe simple latex would at least lengthen her rest from three hours to four. And beyond that, a bathtub, or at least a shower, would be nice. As far as bathing went, her real-life body was almost certainly being regularly cleaned at the hospital, but this was an issue of comfort. She was ready to die alone in a dungeon if that's what it came to, but if she could just have the chance, just once, to stretch out her legs and soak in a nice, hot bath...

This fervent wish shot to the forefront of her mind at the black-haired swordsman's words.

"......What did you just say?" Asuna repeated, not realizing she'd grabbed him by the collar. Unless she'd just suffered some hallucination, she could have sworn he'd just said...

"A-all the milk you can drink...?"

"After that."

"C-comfy, spacious bed and a nice view...?"

"After that."

"W-with a bath...?"

So she hadn't misheard. Asuna let go of his coat and continued, flustered.

"You said this room was eighty col a night?"

"I...I did."

"How many extra rooms does this inn have? Where is it? I'll take a room, just show me the way."

Finally he seemed to understand the situation. He coughed and solemnly stated, "Um, well, I told you I was renting out the second floor, right?"

"...You did."

"What I meant was, I'm renting out the *entire* second floor. There are no open rooms. And they didn't have any to rent on the first floor."

"Wha...?" She had to hold her feet firm to keep from slumping to her knees. "Then...the room's all..."

He seemed to understand what she was trying to ask, and responded regretfully, his eyes wandering. "Well, I've gotten a good week's worth of enjoyment out of the place, so I'd love to switch with you...but I actually bought the maximum length of stay in advance—ten days. And the transaction can't be canceled."

"Wha...?" Again, she nearly flopped over but held her ground. Asuna was terribly conflicted. He'd just told her there were places to stay aside from the inns, and some were much nicer. Therefore, if she just searched around Tolbana, perhaps there would be another spot with a bath. On the other hand, there were currently several dozen players around town for the purpose of beating the floor boss. Most likely, any nicer room would already be taken, which was no doubt the reason he'd reserved his for such a lengthy stay.

Should she try checking at the last town before this? But the fields around there were full of dangerous beasts after sundown, and they were meeting at the fountain at ten the next morning. She wasn't all that jazzed about this group effort to fight the boss, but now that she was participating—however marginally—she was not going to show up late or skip it entirely.

That left only one option.

For several seconds, Asuna's body and soul were a battleground of conflicting desires. She would never in a million years consider this option in the real world. But everything here was only digital data, not real, including her own avatar. And this was no longer a total stranger. They'd shared bread with cream, they were taking on the same role in the boss battle, and, hang on, hadn't he just said he was going to explain something to her earlier? That explanation would serve as a good excuse...right? Of course.

The swordsman was still studiously looking everywhere but at Asuna when she lowered her head and said in a voice barely loud enough to reach his ears, "...Let me use your bath."

The farm at which the swordsman was staying was at the edge of a small field to the east of Tolbana. The building was much larger than she expected; the combined size of the stable and the house itself might even be as large as Asuna's house in real life.

A pristine stream ran through a corner of the plot of land, pushing a small waterwheel with pleasant creaks. The two-story house was occupied on the first floor by an NPC farming family. When Asuna stepped through the front door, the farmer's wife flashed her a beaming smile. She couldn't help but notice the grandmother snoozing in a rocking chair next the fire had a golden *!* over her head—the sign of a quest—but decided to let it pass for now.

The swordsman led her up a set of heavy stairs to a short hallway with a single door at the end. He touched the knob and it opened automatically with the clicking sound effect of a lock unlatching. If Asuna had touched it, nothing would have happened. Even lockpicking skills had no effect on the door to a room rented by a player.

"Um...well, come on in."

He pushed the door open and gestured her in awkwardly.

"...Thanks," she said quietly and took a step inside—then screamed. "What the—? It's so big! And...and this is only thirty col more expensive than the place I'm renting? It's so cheap..."

"Being able to find spots like this is a special skill—it's just not on your character sheet. Of course, in my case..."

He stopped mid-sentence. She looked at him curiously, but he merely shook his head. Asuna gave the room another once-over and sighed.

The room they were standing in now had to be at least three hundred square feet. If the door on the east wall led to the bedroom, it must be about the same size. On the west wall was another door with a placard reading BATHROOM over it. The oddly decorative script seemed to have a sorcerous suction to it, drawing Asuna closer. While the design of the place was rustic, it was very comfortable and homey. The swordsman removed his sword and boots and sank into the cushy sofa.

After a luxurious stretch, he looked up as though just remembering Asuna was there, and coughed awkwardly.

"Um, well, as you can see, the bathroom is that way, so...b-be my guest."

"Ah...th-thanks."

It felt a bit rude to visit someone's room and plunge right into the bath, but it was far too late to observe restraint now. She accepted his offer and was heading for the door when his voice drifted over her shoulder.

"Oh, just so you're aware, bathing isn't quite the same as in real life. The NerveGear doesn't handle liquid sensations all that well...so just don't expect too much."

"As long as there's plenty of hot water, I'm not asking for anything more," she said in all honesty, and opened the bathroom door. She slid inside and pulled the knob shut behind her.

Except for maybe a lock, she thought. Alas, when she turned around to check, her wish was unfulfilled. There were no buttons or latches around the door. She tried tapping the door just in case, but as she wasn't the current owner of the room, Asuna could not call up a menu.

On the other hand, at this point the presence or absence of a lock was largely irrelevant. She was already in the bathroom of a boy she'd met just yesterday, about to use his tub. The black-haired swordsman—whose name she still didn't know—was hard to gauge in terms of personality and age, but he was not the kind of person to barge into a bathroom without warning...she thought. And if he did try it, they were within the safe limits of town, which meant the anti-crime code was in effect.

Asuna tore her gaze away from the door and looked to the south.

"...Wow..." she murmured.

Even the bathroom was large. The northern half was the changing area, complete with a thick, soft carpet and shelves of untreated wood on the walls. The southern half was polished stone tile, most of which was covered by a large white bathtub in the shape of a boat.

High on the brick wall was a faucet in the shape of a monstrous face, and clear liquid was shooting out of it with terrific force. The hot water and its thick white steam filled the bathtub up to the very lip and cascaded onto the tile floor, where it ran down into a drain in the corner.

Common sense said there was no way the medieval European manors this building was modeled after contained such deluxe hot-water plumbing. Asuna was not going to fault the design inaccuracies of this virtual world, however. Weak-kneed, she opened her menu window and hit the equipment removal button on the mannequin that took up the right half of the screen.

All the things she'd been wearing for days and weeks—the hooded cape, the bronze armor that covered her chest, the long gloves and boots, and the rapier at her waist—disappeared instantly, and her long chestnut hair fell across her back. All that remained were a woolen three-quarter-sleeve tunic and tight leather pants. The equipment button now read REMOVE ALL CLOTHES, so she pressed it again. The top and bottom disappeared, leaving only two pieces of simple underwear.

Asuna gave the door another quick glance, then pressed the button one last time, which now read REMOVE ALL UNDERWEAR. With just three button presses, her virtual avatar was completely unequipped, and she felt a chill on her virtual skin. The floating castle with the odd name of Aincrad did seem to follow the concept of seasons, and the room was quite chilly, in keeping with the early December date.

She quickly crossed the room and straddled the ceramic tub. When her left foot sank into the water, the sensory signals hit her brain like a wall. She stuck her head into the flow of water from the faucet, resisting the urge to slide entirely under the surface just yet. Only when the warmth covered her entire body and took the chill of the air off did she slip down into the hot water on her back with a splash.

"…Aaaaahh…"

There was no holding in that sigh of contentment.

As the black-haired swordsman had warned her, it wasn't a perfect representation of a bath. Most of the details were just slightly off—the connection between skin and water, the pressure on the body, the glimmering reflection of light on the underside of the face.

But as with eating, there was enough preset "bathing sensation" programmed into the system for her to be able to close her eyes, stretch her limbs, and relax. It was a bath. And not just any bath, but a deluxe one nearly six feet long and full to the brim.

She sank up to her lips, eyes closed, letting every muscle relax, and thought, *I can die happy now. I have no regrets left.*

Ever since she had left the Town of Beginnings two weeks earlier, Asuna's thoughts had followed one stark philosophy: As long as this deadly game was effectively impossible to beat,

all ten thousand players would eventually die. In a world where everything was false, dying sooner or later made no difference, in which case she'd rather keep moving forward as fast as she could, until she could no longer go on.

At the strategy meetings the last two days, Asuna had observed the scene with cold disinterest. Who was a former beta tester (whatever that was), how the loot would be distributed—these things didn't matter. Tomorrow morning, they would attempt the greatest challenge of the first floor of Aincrad, which had already claimed two thousand victims. A mere forty-something people would never overcome such a hurdle on the first try. There was a very high possibility that they would all die, if they didn't retreat in ignoble defeat first.

The reason Asuna was so willing to go out of her normal comfort zone for this bath was because she just wanted one more before she died. Now that her wish had been fulfilled, she was completely prepared to disappear from this world forever at tomorrow's boss battle...

That black bread with cream on top.

What I wouldn't give for one more of those before I die...

Asuna was disturbed by the desire that suddenly rose within her. She opened her eyes and sat up slightly.

That flavor wasn't bad. But it was an absolute fake. It was a polygonal model attached to some simple variables that dictated its taste. But then, the same could be said of this bath. What looked like hot water was simply an in-game boundary with transparency and refraction numbers calculated to look real. The warmth that enveloped her body was just a string of numbers being sent to her brain by the NerveGear.

But...*but*.

Even back in the real world, the world in which she'd lived her entire life up to a month before, had she ever wanted to eat something as badly as she did now? Had she ever wanted to take a bath as badly as she did before this very moment?

The full-course menus of organic food that she'd dutifully but mechanically eaten as her parents commanded, or the virtual roll of bread her body craved so much it made her drool: Which was the "real" thing?

Sensing that she was considering something very, very important, Asuna held her breath.

8

WHO KNEW THAT JUST KEEPING MY GLANCE FROM drifting toward the bathroom door required such a difficult saving throw against temptation?

I was lying deep in the sofa, training all of my concentration on the copy of *Argo's First-Floor Boss Guidebook* I'd received earlier that day. But no matter how many times my eyes passed over the simple, easy-to-read font, none of the contents stuck in my mind.

Well, it's still better than it would be in real life.

Let's say this was my house in Kawagoe, Saitama, and my mother and sister were away, and a female classmate of mine came in to take a bath for some reason. What would I do? The answer was obvious. I'd silently sneak out of the front door, hop onto my beloved mountain bike, and take off down Prefectural Route 51 toward Arakawa.

Instead, fortunately, I was upstairs in a large farmhouse on the outskirts of Tolbana on the first floor of the floating castle Aincrad, and I was not a geeky teenage MMO fanatic but Kirito the swordsman. As long as my body was this virtual avatar, nothing would happen to me, even after Asuna the fencer exited from the bathroom. Of course, there was always the possibility that this was a clever trap, and that while I was taking my bath, she'd empty the chest in this main room and disappear, but the most she'd find in there were some low-level ingredients from wimpy monsters. In fact, there was no need to take my turn after her. She'd emerge and I'd say, "Good luck tomorrow," and send her on her way. The end.

I shook my head rapidly and was setting the guidebook down on the coffee table when I heard something.

There was a rhythmic sound at the door—to the hallway, not the bathroom—*tap, tap-tap-tap*. Someone was knocking, but it was not the farmer's wife. That particular rhythm was the signature of someone else.

I leapt up with a start and nervously turned around to stare in the direction of the thick oak door and the person standing on the other side—Argo the Rat.

Out the south-facing window into the front yard, onto the donkey tied up outside the stable, then down the path through the forest and to the labyrinth, the thought occurred to me, however briefly. But riding mounts in *SAO* was an extremely difficult task. They would behave better as the Riding skill increased, but I didn't have the slot space to waste on a hobby skill like that.

Instead, I hopped off the sofa and went to check on the bathroom. Lady Asuna would be in the midst of her luxurious bath right now. If Argo caught even a hint of this fact, there would be a new piece of information in her book of secrets: *Kirito is the kind of man who entices a girl into his bedroom on their first meeting.* I couldn't possibly serve as a model for solo players if news like that got out.

But fortunately, all doors in this world were totally soundproof, with certain exceptions. As far as I knew, there were only three things that could travel through a door: shouts, knocks, and battle SFX. Normal conversations and the sounds of the bath would not leak through, even with an ear to the door.

So I could let someone into the room, and they would have no idea that anyone was bathing in the tub. And if the fencer happened to open the door while Argo was here—well, there was always that donkey.

The above thoughts flashed through my brain as quick as combat reactions, and I approached the hallway door, steeled myself, and opened it. Once I confirmed who it was, I gave her my prepared line. "Strange for you to come visit my room directly."

Argo the Rat's whisker-drawn face looked suspicious for a moment, then she shrugged.

"I guess. The client says I have to get an answer out of you before the end of the day."

She strode comfortably across the room and thumped down into the exact spot on the sofa I'd just been using. I closed the door and turned to the tray in the corner to pour two glasses of fresh milk from the large pitcher there, very carefully keeping myself from glancing at the bathroom door as I returned to the sofa and set the milk on the table. Argo raised an eyebrow and smirked.

"Seems almost too considerate for you, Kii-boy. Slipped a little sleeping powder in there, didja?"

"You know that stuff doesn't work on players. Even if it did, we're inside town limits."

Argo paused a moment to reflect, then admitted I had a point. She raised the glass and downed the entire thing in one swallow.

"That was good. Pretty high taste settings for being all-you-can-drink. Think you could bottle it up and sell it?"

"Unfortunately, it's only valid for five minutes after leaving the building. Even worse, it doesn't just disappear, it turns absolutely disgusting..."

"Ooh, I didn't know that. Nothing scarier than free food."

I kept praying that she'd get to the damn point, but there was no telling what would happen if she sensed my impatience. With a straight face, I picked up the guidebook I'd left on the table and smacked it.

"Speaking of free stuff, what about this? Now, I'm a happy customer of your work, but I was buying these books for five hundred col each. Then at yesterday's meeting, Agil the axe-warrior says you're giving them out for free?" I said sourly. She hissed with laughter.

"It was thanks to you and the other front-runners purchasing the first batch that I was able to make a second printing to distribute for free. But don't worry, all the first printings have an authentic Argo signature inside."

"...I see. Well, that's a great reason to keep buying."

This free distribution must have been Argo's way of taking responsibility for her beta tester background. I wanted to open up and ask her about it directly, but even between us, there was an unspoken taboo about discussing the beta. Plus, as a former tester who'd never lifted a finger to help the player population, I didn't have the right to ask.

Argo swung her brown curls and cut through the heavy silence. "Welp, do you mind if I cut to the chase?"

Please, please, please, I silently screamed, nodding politely.

"As you can probably guess from the fact that I mentioned a client, this regards the potential buyer of your sword. If you accept today, the offer will be thirty-nine thousand, eight hundred col."

"...Th..."

Thirty-nine?! I nearly screamed, but held it in. After a deep breath and several seconds, I finally spoke.

"...I don't mean to disrespect you...but are you sure this isn't a scam of some kind? Forty thousand is more than this weapon is worth. The basic Anneal Blade costs about fifteen thousand col, right? With another twenty thousand, you can buy all the materials to augment it up to plus six without any trouble. It might take a little time, but with just thirty-five thousand col, you could get the same weapon as mine."

"I said the exact same thing three times, just to be sure!"

Argo spread her hands, a rare expression of disbelief on her face. I crossed my arms and leaned back into the sofa, all thought of the situation in the bathroom forgotten now that this new topic demanded my attention. The idea of losing money from this situation burned me up inside, but I felt worse letting my curiosity go unanswered. It took an act of will to make a counter-offer to Aincrad's first information dealer.

"Argo...I'll pay one thousand five hundred col for the name of your client. Check with the other side to see if they'll add to that."

"...All right," Argo nodded, opening her window and shooting off an instant message with fingers flying.

When the response arrived a minute later, she twitched an eyebrow and shrugged broadly.

"It says they don't mind telling you."

"..."

I was now thoroughly baffled, but I opened my window and extracted 1,500 col anyway, stacking the six coins on the table in front of Argo.

She grabbed them and flipped them one-by-one into storage with her thumb, nodding to signal the completion of the deal.

"Actually, Kii-boy, you already know his face and name. He caused quite a scene at the strategy meeting yesterday."

"...You mean...Kibaou?" I whispered. She nodded.

Kibaou. The man who burned with a righteous fury toward former beta testers. He was the one paying forty k for my sword?

I did recall that the weapon hanging across his back was a one-handed sword, just like mine. But yesterday was the first time we'd been face-to-face. And it was over a week ago that Argo had brought the first offer from this particular client to me.

The information that I'd paid 1,500 col for left me even more confused than before. I crossed my legs on the cushion to think over this development. Just to be certain, Argo asked me, "I take it there'll be no deal on the sword again?"

"Nope..."

I was not going to part ways with my favorite sword for any sum of money. I nodded my assertion and sensed the Rat getting to her feet.

"Welp, I better be off, then. Make good use of that guide, hear?"

"Yeah…"

"Oh, and before I go, I'm gonna borrow your other room. Gotta change into my night equipment."

"Yeah…"

As I scanned my memory, I did recall that when Kibaou had stood in front of the crowd and glared at everyone, his eyes stopped on me for a moment. Did that mean he wasn't suspecting me of being a beta tester, but that he was scoping out my sword? Or could it be both…?

Hang on a second. What did Argo just say?

I looked up, 80 percent of my mind still concentrating on the topic of Kibaou. Out of the corner of my eye, I saw Argo turning the doorknob. Not the main door to the upstairs hallway or the bedroom door on the east wall—the one beneath the plate proclaiming BATHROOM.

And as I watched, stunned, the Rat disappeared into the bathroom.

Three seconds later—

"Whoa—?!"

"…*Eeyaaaaaaa!!*"

A tremendous scream shook the building. The next thing I saw was a player that was not Argo burst out of the door.

No memory remains of what happened next.

9

10:00 AM, SUNDAY, DECEMBER 4.

The game had launched at one o'clock PM on Sunday, November 6, so in three hours, it would be exactly four weeks since it all began.

When I first noticed the lack of the log-out button, I assumed it was simply a system error, and at worst, it would be a matter of minutes before order was restored and I could leave. But before long, Akihiko Kayaba, in the guise of a faceless GM, assigned us to the task of clearing all one hundred floors of Aincrad. At the time, I foresaw an imprisonment lasting a hundred days. In essence, I expected that we'd average about a floor a day.

Now it had been four entire weeks—and we hadn't even finished the first floor yet.

I could only laugh at how optimistic I'd been, and depending on the outcome of today's boss battle, it could become brutally clear that time wasn't the real issue with our escape. The forty-four players in the fountain square of Tolbana were the best of the best in the game at the present time. If this squad fell entirely or even lost half of its members, the news would spread throughout the floor, and a prevailing view would form: *SAO* was unbeatable. No one could say how long it would take for a second raid party to be formed—there might never be another attempt at the boss. Even grinding for levels wasn't an option, as the effective experience gain from the monsters on the first floor had long passed its peak.

Everything rode on whether or not the stats of Illfang the Kobold Lord, boss monster of the first floor, had been altered since the beta. If the king of the kobolds was only as tough as I remembered him being, it shouldn't be impossible to get through the fight without any fatalities, even with our limited levels and equipment. It just depended on whether or not everyone could remain calm and perform their duties knowing their lives were on the line...

My brain overheating with all the mental calculations, I looked to the player at my side, took a short breath, and let it out with an awkward smile.

Asuna the fencer's side profile, half-hidden by her deep hood, seemed no different from the time I'd first seen her in the labyrinth, two mornings before. It was both as fleeting and fragile as a shooting star, and as sharp as steel. Compared to her calm manner, I was a nervous wreck.

I continued staring until she suddenly turned and shot me a cold glare.

"...What are you looking at?" she whispered, voice quiet but full of menace. I shook my head rapidly. She'd warned me this morning that if I so much as recalled the reason why she was furious, she'd force-feed me an entire barrel of sour milk. Whatever happened, it was a blank blur in my mind.

"N-nothing," I tried to say nonchalantly. She flicked me another glare as sharp as the tip of her rapier and turned away. I began to wonder if this foul mood might affect today's battle. True, no one else was relying upon us for help—we were practically extras—but still.

"Hey," came a decidedly unfriendly voice from behind. I spun around.

A man with short brown hair fashioned into spikes stood before me. I flinched backward. Of all the people I expected might talk to me today, Kibaou was the last.

I stood there, dumbfounded. He glared up at me and growled, "Now listen up and listen good—y'all stay in the back today. Don't forget your role: You're our party's support, nuttin' more."

"..."

I was already quiet by nature, but no one could have come up with a better response. This was the man who'd tried to buy my weapon for forty thousand col yesterday and hired an agent to ensure his identity stayed hidden, both of which failed spectacularly. Typically, a person under those embarrassing and awkward circumstances would rather stay at least fifty feet away from me.

But Kibaou's attitude seemed to suggest that I *ought* to be feeling intimidated. He sneered at me arrogantly one more time and spat, "Be a good lil' boy and pick off the spare kobold scraps we let drop from the table."

And with a glob of spittle on the ground for a final flourish, Kibaou turned on his heel and strode back to his party, team E. I was still staring in dull amazement when a voice beside me snapped me back to my wits.

"What's up with him?"

It was Asuna, the other half of "y'all." Her stare was about 30 percent scarier than the one that had just been fixed on me.

"D-dunno...I guess he thinks solo players shouldn't get full of themselves," I murmured without thinking, then tacked on a silent addendum.

Or perhaps that beta testers shouldn't get full of themselves.

If that hunch was correct, Kibaou almost certainly suspected that I was a former beta tester myself. But on what evidence? Even Argo the Rat would never use the identity of beta testers as a business product. And I'd never spoken a word of my beta history to anyone.

I watched Kibaou's retreating back with the same sense of unease I'd felt yesterday.

"...Huh...?"

And without realizing it, I let out a grunt of understanding.

Yesterday, he had tried to buy my Anneal Blade +6 for the massive price of forty thousand col. That was an undeniable fact. He clearly meant to use it in today's boss fight. Putting aside whether he could handle the extra weight of the points I'd put into durability, his motive seemed obvious enough to me: He wanted to show off a powerful weapon at a crucial moment to add to his influence and leadership qualities.

But if that were the case, he ought to have used that forty thousand col on a different set of weapons or armor when the deal fell through. Today was the big day.

But Kibaou's scale mail and the one-handed sword on his back were the same as what he'd worn at the planning meeting. It wasn't a bad weapon, but he had the time and more than enough money to arrange something better. In fact, at my advice, Asuna had upgraded her weapon from the store-bought Iron Rapier to a rare drop weapon, a Wind Fleuret +4. What was the point of keeping forty thousand col in storage when you were about to undertake a battle that could easily be fatal?

I had no more time to follow that line of thinking. Diavel the blue-haired knight was standing in his familiar spot on the lip of the fountain, exercising his clear, loud voice.

"Okay, everyone—first, thanks! We've got all forty-four members from all eight parties present!"

A cheer ripped through the square, followed by a spray of applause. I begrudgingly abandoned my musing and clapped along with the others.

With a hearty smile for the crowd, the knight raised a fist and shouted, "To be honest, I was prepared to call off the entire operation if anyone had failed to show up! But...it seems that even entertaining that possibility was an insult to the rest of you! I can't tell you how happy I am. We've got the best damn raid party you could possibly want...except for a few more bodies to round us up to a nice even number!"

Some laughed, some whistled, some thrust their fists just like him.

There was no doubting Diavel's leadership. But inwardly, I wondered if he was getting the crowd a little *too* revved up. Just as too much tension could lead to poisonous fear, too much optimism caused sloppiness. It was easy to laugh off a few mistakes in the beta, but failure here would lead to death. Being on the uptight side was preferable in this case.

I scanned the crowd around me and saw the axe-warrior Agil and team B, arms crossed, their faces hard. They could be counted on in a pinch. Kibaou had his back turned to me, so I couldn't read his expression.

After everyone had gotten out their jeers, Diavel raised his hands in the air for a final cheer.

"Listen up, everyone...I just have one thing left to say!" He reached down and drew his silver longsword, brandishing it high. "Let's win this thing!!"

I couldn't help but feel that the roar of excitement that ensued bore more than a little resemblance to the screams of ten thousand I'd heard at the center of the Town of Beginnings four weeks earlier.

10

THE PROCESSION FROM TOLBANA TO THE LABYRINTH tower prickled at Asuna's memory. After a few minutes of mulling it over, she finally realized what she was remembering.

The school field trip from this January. They'd traveled to Queensland in Australia. Her classmates were thrown into a tizzy by the shift from midwinter Tokyo to blazing midsummer on the Gold Coast. They were rapturously excited, no matter where they went.

There was nothing—not a single thing—that linked the two experiences, but she felt the atmosphere emanating from the forty-odd players marching through the tree-lined path was very similar to her schoolmates'. Endless chattering, frequent bursts of laughter; the only thing that seemed different was the presence of monsters that could burst out of the trees at any moment. But with these confident warriors, they'd be able to dice up any foes in seconds.

Asuna and the swordsman at her side were at the rear of the procession. She turned to him and started up a conversation, choosing to overlook the atrocity that had occurred the night before.

"Hey, before you came here, did you play other...MMO games? Is that what you call them?"

"Um...yeah, I suppose." He bobbed his head, still a bit intimidated.

"Does traveling around in other games feel like this? You know...like a hike..."

"Ha-ha. I wish," he laughed, then shrugged. "Unfortunately, it's not like this at all in other titles. See, if you're not in a full dive, you have to use a keyboard or a mouse or a controller to move around. You barely have any time to type anything in the chat window."

"Oh...I see..."

"Of course, there are also games with voice chat support, but I never played any of those."

"Ahh."

Asuna tried to imagine a mob of game characters running silently on a flatscreen monitor.

"I wonder...what the real thing would feel like."

"Eh? Real thing?" He turned a skeptical glance on her. She tried to describe the image in her head.

"I mean...if there really was a fantasy world like this one... and a bunch of fighters and magicians teamed up on an adventure to defeat a terrible monster. What would they talk about on the road as they traveled? Or would they just march in silence? That's what I mean."

"......"

The swordsman fell silent for a few awkward moments, and when Asuna finally looked at him, she became aware that the question she'd posed was actually quite childish. She turned away and tried to mumble a brief "never mind," but he spoke first.

"The road to death or glory, huh," he murmured. "If the people made a living of doing that, I bet it would be no different from going out to a restaurant for dinner. If you have something to say, you say it. If not, you don't. At some point, I bet these boss raids will be just as ordinary. Assuming we can do enough of them to make them that way."

"Heh...ha-ha."

She couldn't help but giggle at the silliness of that statement, then apologized quickly to cover it up.

"Sorry, didn't mean to laugh. But…that's really weird. This place is the polar opposite of ordinary. How can you make anything here become normal?"

"Ha-ha…Good point," he chuckled quietly. "But today makes it four whole weeks in here. Even if we do beat this boss, there are ninety-nine more floors ahead. I was expecting this to take two, maybe three years. If it lasts that long, even the extraordinary will become ordinary."

Once, the enormity of those words would have thrown Asuna into shock and despair. But now the only thing that blew through her heart was the dry wind of resignation.

"You're very strong. I don't think I can do that—survive in here for years and years…That's much more frightening to me than dying in today's battle."

The swordsman gave her a brief glance, thrust his hands into the pockets of his gray coat, and murmured, "Y'know, there'll be even nicer baths on the higher floors, if we can get there."

"…R-really?" she asked without thinking, then gasped. She fought down her rising embarrassment and gave him a quiet warning. "So…you remembered. In that case, I'll be feeding you an entire barrel of sour milk."

"Which means you'll have to survive this battle first," he shot back, grinning.

11

AT ELEVEN O'CLOCK AM, WE REACHED THE LABYRINTH.
At twelve thirty, we were on the top floor.

I was secretly relieved that we at least hadn't lost anyone so far. After all, the majority of our group's members were no doubt experiencing their very first raid at near-full capacity. And in this world, every "first" experience was fraught with the possibility of accidents.

I did get the chills on three separate occasions. Teams F and G, who were equipped with long weapons like spears and halberds, were ambushed along their flanks by kobolds in narrow corridors. During close battle in *SAO*, accidentally grazing another player with a swing caused no damage (and hence no crime), but it acted as a blocking obstacle that canceled out any low-level sword skills. It happened more often to spears, given their long reach, making surprise attacks by close-range enemies quite dangerous.

Diavel made excellent use of his leadership qualities in the face of this predicament. He boldly commanded the other members aside from a single team leader to stand down, used a heavy sword skill to knock the monsters off-balance, then switched out for close-range fighters. It was the kind of strategy that only someone familiar with leading a party could employ so quickly and assuredly.

In that sense, perhaps it was presumptuous for a solo player to be concerned about "too much excitement" before we'd left. Diavel had his own philosophy on how to lead, and as a member of this raid who'd come this far, it was now my duty to put my full trust in him.

Finally, the massive doors were visible ahead. I stood up on tiptoes to see over the rest of the group.

The gray stone surface was adorned with reliefs of terrible humanoids with the heads of beasts. In most MMOs, the kobold was nothing more than a typical starting monster, but in *SAO* they were fearsome demihumans. They brandished swords and axes, which meant they could use sword skills of their own. Because skills were far faster, stronger and more accurate than simple swinging attacks, even a low-level skill could deal astonishing damage if it landed a critical hit on a defenseless target. The fact that Asuna had made it to the top level of the labyrinth using nothing more than the simple Linear attack proved just how powerful sword skills could be in the right hands.

"Listen up for a sec," I murmured to Asuna, leaning close. "The Ruin Kobold Sentinels we're supposed to fight are only like bodyguards for the actual boss, but they're plenty tough. Like I explained yesterday, their heads and chests are armored, so just hurling Linear at them over and over isn't going to work."

The fencer's glare shot back at me from under her hood. "I know that. I have to hit them straight in the throat."

"That's right. I'll use my sword skills to knock back their pole-axes, and then you switch in and finish them off."

She nodded and turned to the giant doors. I stared at her profile for a few more seconds.

The only difference is when and where you die, sooner or later, she'd claimed on our first encounter. I couldn't let her prove that statement. Asuna's Linear suggested an incredible talent, and she had no idea. Not all shooting stars burned up in the atmosphere. Some of them withstood the fires and made their way to earth.

If she survived today's battle, I was certain that she would be known all throughout Aincrad as the fastest and most beautiful swordsman in the game. Countless players crushed by fear and desperation could look to her guiding light. I was certain of it. That role was something I could never fulfill myself, with my beta testing past.

I swallowed my determination and faced forward. Diavel had just arranged the seven other parties into perfect formation.

Even our charismatic leader couldn't simply lead a lighthearted cheer now. Humanoid monsters would detect the shouts and come running.

Instead, Diavel raised his longsword and gave a hearty nod. Forty-three others brandished their weapons and signaled back.

His blue hair waving, the knight put his other hand on the center of the door.

"Let's go!" he shouted, and pushed hard.

Was it always this vast?

My first thought upon setting foot in the first-floor boss chamber after four months was skepticism.

It was a rectangular room that stretched away from us. It had to be roughly sixty feet from side to side, and closer to three hundred from the far wall to the door. Given that the rest of the floor had been mapped out, the empty space remaining on the map was a good indication of the size of the room, but it seemed much larger in person than it did on the page.

That distance was actually rather troublesome.

The giant doors on Aincrad's boss chambers did not close during a battle. If all seemed lost, there was always the option of running back to the door to avoid total defeat. However, turning your back to the opponent left a player defenseless against long-distance sword skills that could cause movement delay, if not a total stun effect. Therefore, it was better to retreat backward while still facing the boss. In a vast room like this, that distance might seem endless. Retreat would be easier in the higher-floor boss battles, after players had earned the teleport crystals that allowed instantaneous escape. On the other hand, they were extremely expensive, so using them would be a very costly retreat, indeed.

As I pondered the various scenarios for withdrawal, a crude torch on the right wall of the dark chamber audibly burst into life. One after another, torches lit themselves down the walls.

With each successive source of light, the gamma level in the room increased. Cracked paving stones and walls. Countless skulls of various sizes. An ugly but massive throne at the far end of the chamber, and a silhouette seated upon it...

Diavel brought down his sword in its direction. At that signal, forty-four warriors raised a valiant roar and raced through the chamber.

First down the chamber was a hammer-wielding fighter with a large heater shield like a metal plate, the leader of team A. Just behind them and to the left were Agil the axe warrior and his team B. On the right were team C, made of Diavel and his five party mates, and team D, led by a man with a very tall greatsword. Behind that line were Kibaou's team E and the two polearm teams, F and G.

And last of all, two forgotten stragglers.

Just as the leader at the head of team A reached sixty feet from the throne, the previously immobile figure leapt up ferociously. It did a flip in midair and landed with an earth-shaking crash, then opened a wolflike jaw and roared.

"Grruaaah!!"

The appearance of Illfang the Kobold Lord, king of the beastmen, was exactly as I remembered it. His burly body was covered in grayish hair and easily over six feet tall. His reddish-gold eyes glinted menacingly, thirsty for blood. In his right hand was an axe fashioned from bone, and in his left, a buckler of skins and leather. Hanging off the back of his waist was a massive talwar that had to be nearly five feet long.

The kobold lord raised his bone axe and swung it down upon the leader of team A with all of his strength. The thick heater shield took the brunt head-on, and a bright flash and fierce shudder filled the room.

As though that sound was a signal, three heavily armed monsters leapt down from holes high on the side walls. These were the Ruin Kobold Sentinels that accompanied their leader. Kibaou's team E and their backup team G descended on the three to draw their attention. Asuna and I shared a look and dashed over to the nearest kobold.

And so it was that at 12:40 on December 4, the first boss monster in Aincrad was finally challenged.

Illfang's HP gauge had four bars. He fought with his axe and shield through the third bar, but at the final stage, he would throw them aside and produce his giant talwar. The change in his attacking patterns was the biggest challenge in his fight, but this transition was detailed fully in Argo's guide. At yesterday's meeting, we'd spent plenty of time studying the change in his sword skills once switching to the talwar, and how to counteract them.

As I dealt with the sentinels that slipped away from teams E and G, I kept an eye on the state of the front line. It seemed like the strategy would hold strong. The switches and pot rotation of the tanks and attackers were working smoothly, and the average HP readouts of all the individual parties listed on the left side of my vision showed a solid 80 percent across the board.

Please, please let this hold up, I prayed with all my being— something I never did as a solo player.

12

AT THE POINT THAT HE'D TRANSPORTED HER OUT OF the labyrinth tower (through unknown means), Asuna had a feeling that the black-haired swordsman was talented. But upon properly witnessing him in battle for the first time, she realized just how inadequate that description was.

He was *strong.*

In fact, there was something within his fighting that couldn't simply be summed up by strength. Something that transcended power or speed, something that suggested the next dimension.

Asuna had no experience with online games or full-dive systems, so she didn't know how to put this idea into words. If she had to describe it, he was "optimized." There was no wasted movement in anything he did. His skills were precise and his strikes were heavy. With a quick swipe, he knocked the kobold warrior's frightening halberd high up into the air, shouted a "switch" command, and floated backward. When Asuna leapt in to take his place, the kobold was still in the process of recovering its balance, leaving her enough time to unleash a Linear thrust into its weak throat. It was all very simple.

She thought back to what he'd said on their very first meeting: "Your attacks are overkill; they're inefficient." To which she'd asked what was wrong with being thorough. At this point, she understood that there was *plenty* wrong with that. Eliminating waste created better poise, and poise widened her viewpoint. These Kobold Sentinels were supposedly much tougher than the Kobold Troopers she'd been fighting back then, but she could clearly see the creatures' every swipe and kick.

After her Linear struck its critical weak point, the kobold only had a sliver of life left. The old Asuna would have evaded the enemy's attack by a hair, then unleashed another Linear, but that would have been overkill. As soon as the pause after her sword skill had worn off, she jabbed the same spot with minimal effort. That was enough to reduce the enemy's HP to zero. It burst into blue shards and disappeared.

"GJ," came the swordsman's voice from behind her. She didn't know what that was short for, so she offered him a neutral "You too."

At this point, the boss kobold's first HP bar had just emptied. Diavel cried, "On to the second," and more Kobold Sentinels poured out of the holes in the walls.

Briefly forgetting that they were supposed to be sheer backup, Asuna joined her partner in dashing after the nearest kobold. The sword in her hand was brand-new to her, but it already felt familiar and precise in the palm of her hand. It was as though everything in the sword, from its leather handle to its sharp, glimmering point, was an extension of her own arm.

If this is what constitutes a true battle in this world, then what I was doing before today was something similar, but very different. There must be something more. This swordsman is far, far ahead of me down that path. This is a virtual, illusionary world, and everything I do here is false . . . but . . . this feeling, at least, is truth: that I want to see what he sees.

The swordsman knocked the sentinel's axe high overhead. The next moment, Asuna shouted the command to switch on her own, and leapt in with her new favorite blade.

13

THE BATTLE OF THE KOBOLD LORD AND HIS COHORTS against forty-four players was going far smoother than I ever expected.

Diavel's team C took down the first HP bar, team D was responsible for the second, and now teams F and G were the main attack force halfway through the third bar. The worst that had happened so far was the tanks in teams A and B going down to the yellow zone on their HP. No one had fallen into the red danger zone yet. Team E and the two extras had made such easy work of the kobold's helpers that team G, the other backup group, was able to switch over to the main boss.

What stood out to me most was the effort of Asuna the fencer. Her Linear skill had already impressed me on our first meeting, and with a better weapon, it was even sharper, piercing the throats of the Kobold Sentinels with ease and precision. The amount of time it took from initial motion to damage infliction had to be half of the ordinary time when allowing the automatic system assistance to take over. I'd been studying and practicing ways to intentionally boost my sword skills since the beta, and even I wasn't sure if I could match that speed.

And this was from a total newbie who only knew one skill. A shiver ran down my back at the thought of her limitless potential if she added more knowledge and refined her instincts.

If possible, I wanted to see that transformation happen with my own eyes—but I quickly stashed that idea away. When I'd taken the path of a self-interested solo player one month ago, I'd lost any right to connect with others. My very first friend in this world, Klein, was probably still busy leveling up around the Town of Beginnings, trying to keep all of his party members alive...

Unrelated to my own bitter reminiscence, Asuna was just finishing off her second victim. Ruin Kobold Sentinels were rare monsters that did not spawn anywhere else, so even if they weren't as lucrative as the boss itself, they still dropped plenty of experience, col, and items. The money was set to automatically divide between all the raid members, but the experience belonged only to Asuna and me for our direct effort in defeating the creature, and the looted items were her bonus for inflicting the killing blow.

For that reason, if Kibaou was being perfectly honest, he wanted team E to do all of the killing itself. But the two of us, the supposed "leftovers," were dispatching our targets much faster than their full party of six. Surely he couldn't complain about that.

But just as the thought passed through my mind, Kibaou's gravelly rasp issued from behind me.

"Yer plan backfired, eh? Serves ya right."

"...What?"

I turned around, confused. Only two of the three sentinels that spawned in the third stage of the battle were left, and they were nearly dead. We had enough time for a brief conversation before more of them showed up. The cactus-headed swordsman squinted hard at me and raised his voice.

"Drop the lame act. I already know exactly why y'all slipped yer way into this boss fight."

"'Why'? You mean...to defeat the boss? What other reason could there be?"

"Oh, so you're gonna deny it? You know what you're after!"

We clearly weren't seeing eye to eye about the substance of

the conversation. I clenched my teeth in frustration and anger. Kibaou finally came out and said what was on his mind.

"You think I don't know? I've heard all about yer style... *how you've always used dirty tricks ta steal the LA on all the bosses!*"

"Wha...?"

LA. Last Attack.

In a way, he was right. I'd made a solid practice of trying to leave the smallest amount of health possible and then unleashing my most powerful sword skill in order to gain the largest LA bonus possible. But that had nothing to do with our current circumstances—it was only during the *Sword Art Online* closed beta that had ended long ago.

Kibaou knew that I was not only a beta tester, but the way I'd played. But...hang on. He'd just said he had "heard about" my style. Which meant it must have come from someone else. But who would have...?

A second burst of understanding shot through my brain.

Kibaou had been attempting to buy my Anneal Blade +6 for a preposterous price through Argo the Rat. Yesterday, he'd finally upped his offer past the market rate to forty thousand col. However, when I refused his offer, he did not spend that money elsewhere.

No. He *couldn't* spend that money. It wasn't his.

Kibaou was just another proxy, like Argo after him. That's how he was able to talk to me the next day as though nothing had happened. The true buyer was someone else, and that was the source of the forty thousand col. By placing another person between them and Argo, no amount of money I paid back up the line could buy the true purchaser's name.

This conspirator had given Kibaou beta information, manipulating him and inciting his hatred of former testers. Which meant that this mystery buyer's intention was not to gain the Anneal Blade +6 for improved attack points. Perhaps that was a side benefit, but the real point was something else. They wanted to drive down my attack power, to prevent me from making use of my skill at earning LA bonuses...

"Kibaou...Whoever told you that story, how did they gain that information about the beta test?"

"Ain't it obvious? They put up a grip of cash to buy the info from the Rat. All so's they could sniff out the hyenas among the raid party."

That was a lie. Argo might sell her own status numbers for the right price, but she would never sell beta test information.

I ground my teeth in fury but was momentarily distracted by a shout of triumph from up ahead. The boss's lengthy, four-stage HP bar was finally on its last step. I couldn't help but watch. After they'd eliminated the third bar, polearm teams F and G retreated, leaving the fully recovered team C to charge in and clash with the boss. Diavel the blue-haired knight, party leader and commander of the raid, sparkled dazzlingly in the darkness of the grimy dungeon.

"*Ugruooooaaah!!*"

Illfang the Kobold Lord roared, his loudest and fiercest yet. The final trio of Ruin Kobold Sentinels appeared from the holes in the walls.

"Go ahead, take one o' them lil' kobolds. Get your LA in," Kibaou snarled, his voice dripping with scorn, and ran back to his team E partners.

I hadn't recovered from the shock and confusion of our conversation, but I had no choice but to turn back to find Asuna.

"What were you talking about?" she asked quietly, but I had no time to do anything but shake my head.

"Nothing...Let's just take down those enemies."

"...Okay."

We turned our blades on the closest approaching sentinel.

The next instant, I sensed *something*, and looked back to the main battle as briefly as I could.

The Kobold Lord had just thrown aside his bone axe and leather buckler. He roared once again and reached back behind his waist, gripped a handle wrapped in crude rags, and pulled out the long, malevolent talwar.

I'd seen this transition in attack patterns many times during the beta. From this point until he died, Illfang would use only Curved Sword skills. He made a terrifying sight in his berserk rage, but was actually easier to deal with than before, if you just knew how. His attacks were all vertical, long-range slices, so as long as you identified where he was aiming when he attacked, it was a snap to evade, even at close range.

On Diavel's orders, the six members of team C spun into a circle surrounding the boss. This formation would not have worked against his wide horizontal swipes with the bone axe. The order was so precise and confident that you'd never guess he had nothing more to go on than a flimsy little strategy guide. Now the six could continue attacking and evading the talwar's swings until the battle was...

"...Hgk...?"

A small grunt escaped my throat.

In giving Kibaou forty thousand col and attempting to buy my weapon from me, Player X was attempting to prevent me from scoring the last hit for personal gain—or so I presumed. While I still had my sword, X's goal was essentially fulfilled at this point. I was a straggler at the very fringe of the raid, taking on these wimpy sentinels. I wouldn't get within twenty feet of the boss.

But in that case...

Would the identity of Player X be whoever was poised to land that LA now? It made no sense to pony up so much money just to keep me from being successful. The only way that kind of expenditure made any sense was if the spender wanted to finish off the boss himself.

Meaning...the mystery player who was manipulating Kibaou and knew of my beta-tester past was none other than—

"Here it comes!" Asuna cried, snapping me out of my train of thought. The Kobold Sentinel lunged forward with its halberd, and only an instant reaction with the Slant sword skill was able to parry the blow.

"Switch!"

I leapt backward and Asuna took the front line. Again, I glanced back at the main battle, a good twenty yards to our left.

The boss's invincible transition animation finished, and the combat was set to resume. First to catch his attention was the blue-haired knight, who prepared to deflect the boss's initial attack.

Was it you?

Diavel the knight...did you arrange all of this?

There was no answer to my silent question, of course. Illfang bellowed and lifted his curved blade high overhead.

Again, *something* flickered through my mind.

It was alien. Something was wrong. There was a difference between the Kobold Lord I knew and this boss monster. It wasn't his color, nor his size, nor his face or voice. The difference was not in the creature...but the weapon he held.

From my position, I could only see a vague silhouette of the blade...but was it always that slender? The gentle curve was the same shape I remembered, but the width and its luster were both different. That texture wasn't crude cast iron. It was the tempered, sharpened look of steel. I'd once seen a weapon like that...on the *tenth* floor of Aincrad. A weapon carried by the most fearsome of foes I encountered in the beta, clad in their red armor. That was a monster-exclusive weapon, something not available to any player...

"Ah...aaah!" I gasped, forcing more air into my tense lungs so I could scream with all of my voice.

"No, get back!! Everyone, jump back as far as you can!!"

But my warning was drowned out by the sound effect of Ill-fang's sword skill. The kobold's massive bulk pounced low on the ground and leapt upward. He twisted his body in midair, building momentum for his strike. As he fell, all of that accumulated power burst outward in a crimson whirlwind.

Plane: horizontal. Angle: 360 degrees.

A wide-area katana skill called *Tsumuji-guruma*—"Spiral Wheel."

The six lights that spun out from Illfang were red as sprays of blood. The readout of team C's average HP on the left side of my vision instantly plunged below halfway, into the yellow zone. I could see individual totals if I touched that bar with my finger, but there was no point to doing that. They'd clearly all suffered the same amount of damage.

It was bad enough that a wide-area attack took more than half of a player's full health, but this attack's effects did not stop there. The six members lying on the floor had blurry yellow circles around their heads. They were afflicted with temporary paralysis—a stun effect.

Among the dozen or so negative status effects in *SAO*, nothing was worse than paralysis or blindness. At most, the effects lasted only ten seconds. But because of that short span, there were no recovery methods. If a front-line member got stunned, his partners had to jump in without waiting for the switch call and try to draw the enemy's attention.

However, they were all stunned. The fight strategy had been meticulously planned out beforehand. All seemed to be proceeding well. And Diavel, the trustworthy and capable leader, was knocked flat on the ground. All of these reasons combined kept the other teams in the raid rooted to the spot. Amidst that eerie silence, the Kobold Lord recovered from his massive attack and prepared to resume fighting.

Finally I came to my senses.

"Watch out for the follow-up—" I tried to scream, as Agil and his party moved in to help. But they were not quick enough.

"Urgruaah!!" the beast howled, and swung its double-handed blade straight upward from its resting position near the floor— the sword skill *Ukifune*, or "Rising Ship." It was aimed right for Diavel, who was still lying prone on the floor. His silver-mailed body rose off the ground, as though pulled upward by the pale red arc of light. This move's damage was not so bad, but it was also not the end of the kobold's assault.

Its large wolflike mouth open in a fierce grin. The sword blade glowed red again. *Ukifune* was merely the initial move of a skill combo. The best response when lifted into the air like that was to curl into a ball and focus on maximizing defense, but it was impossible to know that upon facing it for the very first time.

Diavel pulled back his longsword in midair, hoping to fire back a sword skill. But the system did not recognize his flailing motion as the initiation of a skill. Illfang's giant sword caught the knight dead-on.

Two strikes up and down faster than the eye could follow, then a brief pause and a thrust. If I recalled correctly, this three-hit combo was called *Hiougi*—Scarlet Fan.

The blows landing on the knight's body burst with brilliant color and crashing sounds, the indicators of critical hits. His avatar flew sixty feet through the air, well over the raid party's heads, until he came crashing down right next to me. His HP gauge was down in the red and decreasing rapidly.

"...!!"

An odd squeak gurgled up from my throat. I hit the oncoming sentinel's halberd with a powerful Slant. It caught the haft of the weapon, breaking it in two and stunning the kobold. Asuna quickly darted in and delivered the fatal blow to its throat.

I spun around, ignoring the monster's explosive death animation to look at Diavel. Once I'd finally locked eyes with him at a distance of mere feet, sparks went off in my brain.

I know this player.

The name and appearance were different, but I was certain that in the old Aincrad, I had seen this player, perhaps even spoken with him. Diavel was a former beta tester, just like me. And like me, he'd kept his past hidden. In fact, he'd found himself partners, so the pressure to keep that secret hidden had to be much worse than mine.

But that former tester knowledge was poisoning him, with the crucial juncture of the end of the first floor in sight.

I didn't recognize him, but he knew me, and knew that I scored LA bonuses by the dozens in the beta test of Aincrad. He suspected I would do the same thing again this time. It was highly likely the floor boss would drop unique items, which would vastly increase anyone's stats. Now that *SAO* was deadly, increased power meant increased survivability. Diavel wanted to do anything in his power to get Illfang's rare loot in order to survive the trials of *SAO*—not as a selfish solo player but the leader of a group.

Diavel seemed to understand my conclusion. His eyes, blue as his hair, squinted angrily for a moment, then took on a serene light. His lips trembled and parted to speak words that only I could hear.

"...You have to take it from here, Kirito. Kill the...b—"

He couldn't finish his sentence.

Diavel the knight, leader of the first raid party in Aincrad, turned to blue glass and shattered.

14

A ROAR—OR PERHAPS A SCREAM—FILLED THE BOSS chamber.

Nearly every member of the raid party was clutching his weapon as though desperate for something to cling to, eyes wide. But no one moved. The idea that their leader would the first to fall, to die, was so far out of expectations that no one knew how to react.

I was no different.

Two options alternated within my head. To run or to fight?

We'd suffered two major blows: The boss's weapon and skills were not what we'd expected, and our leader was down. The group ought to retreat from the boss chamber immediately. But if we turned our backs to Illfang to run, his long-range katana skills would stun at least the ten closest to him, if not more, and lead to many more deaths at the hands of the combo that killed Diavel. On the other hand, it would be difficult to retreat while trying to face the beast and defend against unknown skills. Because of the extra time that travel would take compared to turning and sprinting, the gradual loss of HP might eventually claim just as many victims.

Most importantly of all, if we suffered that many fatalities, including our leader, and the battle ended in defeat, we might never be able to arrange a raid party of this scale again. It could spell disaster for our possibility of defeating *SAO*. The eight thousand survivors would be permanent prisoners rather than warriors, trapped on the first floor until some ultimate, unknown conclusion...

Two simultaneous sounds jarred me out of my hesitation.

One was the sound of Illfang, fresh out of his combo cooldown, beginning another attack: clanging and screaming, the sound of damage ringing through the darkness.

The other was the voice of Kibaou, slumped to his knees next to me. "Why...why? You were our leader, Diavel. How can you be the first ta go...?"

It would be all too easy to say *because he was greedy and tried to get the LA*. But I couldn't do it.

I thought back to that scene where Kibaou railed against Diavel during the first planning meeting. Kibaou demanded that the former beta testers apologize and offer up their ill-gotten loot or face ostracization. Diavel did not override his opinion—he allowed it to be discussed openly.

Perhaps that little act was Diavel's offer to Kibaou, his price in exchange. For taking on the task of negotiating the sale of my sword, Diavel granted Kibaou a public stage to air his grievances with the former beta testers. It didn't pick up steam, thanks to Agil's levelheaded response, but if all had gone to plan with this boss battle, Kibaou no doubt planned to bring up the topic again. Clearly, he didn't have a single ounce of suspicion in his mind that Diavel might actually be one of those beta testers himself. He trusted in Diavel, thinking him to be the model of an upstanding retail player, someone who would stand in contrast to the underhanded testers. Could there be a more devastating scene for him to witness?

I had to be the one to put a hand on his shoulder and force him to his feet.

"No time for disappointment!" I growled. His eyes glittered with that familiar hatred.

"Wh...what?"

"You're the leader of team E! If you lose your cool, your party will die! There might still be more sentinels on their way...In fact, I'm sure of it. You have to take care of them!"

"Well...what about you, then? You just gonna up an' run for it?!"

"Of course not. That should be obvious..."

I leveled the Anneal Blade in my right hand menacingly.

"I'm going to score the LA on the boss."

Every choice I'd made in the last month since being taken prisoner by this realm was for the sake of my own survival, nothing more. I didn't share the vast store of knowledge I'd gained in the beta test. I reaped the rewards of all the best hunting grounds and quests. I focused only on strengthening myself.

If I was going to uphold that principle, this was my chance to make a break for the exit, while many other people stood between me and the boss. I ought to secure my own safety, letting the mad Kobold Lord sacrifice my fellows, using them as shields.

But there was not a shred of that idea running through my mind now. Something like fire shot through my veins, pushing my feet onward toward the precipice between life and death. Perhaps my source of inspiration was Diavel's final message.

"Kill the boss," he was trying to say. Not "help everyone escape." He'd died because he tried to tweak the odds to give him the best chance of getting that coveted last attack on the boss, but there was no doubting the excellence of his leadership. His final order was not retreat but battle. As a member of the raid, I had to follow his plan...his last will.

There was only one concern I couldn't erase.

Before the battle, I swore to myself that no matter what happened, I would protect Asuna's life. She'd shown a glimmer of talent beyond even my own. As a fan of the VRMMO genre, I couldn't stand to see potential like that plucked before it had the chance to bloom.

I turned to Asuna, preparing to warn her to stay back and make a break for it if the front line broke down. But as though she knew what I was going to say, she cut me off first.

"I'm going, too. I'm your partner."

I didn't have time to shut her down or explain why she shouldn't. I had to simply ignore my indecision and accept.

"All right. Let's do this."

We started running toward the far side of the chamber. Roars and screams washed over us. None aside from Diavel had died yet, but the fighters at the front were all below half of their HP, and the leaderless team C was down to 20 percent. Some players had fully panicked and abandoned their positions. It would be less than a minute before the group completely lost control at this rate.

The first step was calming down the party. But a halfhearted command would be swallowed by the chaos. I needed something short and powerful, but I had no experience leading a group, and had no idea what to say…

To my surprise, Asuna irritatedly grabbed her hooded cape and ripped it off.

She shone as though all the torches hanging on the walls had been condensed into one source of light. Her long brown hair seemed to blast away the gloom of the chamber with a deep golden light.

The image of Asuna racing, hair rippling in the wind, was like a shooting star in the midst of the dungeon. Even the panicking players were stunned into silence at her otherworldly beauty. I seized upon this miraculous instant of silence and screamed out an order with all of my strength.

"Everyone, ten steps toward the exit! The boss won't use an area attack if he's not surrounded!"

When the last echo of my voice died out, time seemed to flow once more. The players at the front parted to the sides to let me and Asuna through. As though following this train of thought himself, Illfang turned to face us.

"Same order as we used against the sentinels, Asuna! Here we go!"

The fencer shot me a glance when I called her by name, but she looked back ahead just as quickly.

"All right!"

The kobold lord took his left hand off the long katana and put it to his waist. That looked like the animation for—

"…!!"

I held my breath and initiated my own sword skill. My right hand and the sword went across my body to the left side of my waist, and I bent over forward until I might flip over. If the angle wasn't sharp enough, the game system would not recognize it as the start of the skill. I pounced with my right leg from a starting stance so low I was nearly crawling, my body shining blue. It took only an instant to cross the thirty feet to the boss. This was Rage Spike, a one-handed sword charging skill.

The boss's katana took on a slick green shine and bit faster than my eye could follow in a direct, long-range katana skill: *Tsuji-kaze,* or "Cyclone." It was an instantaneous attack that struck as soon as it began, so there was no way to react once it started.

"Aaahh!!" I howled, bringing my sword up from the left into the path of Illfang's blade. Sparks exploded with a high-pitched clanging, and we were both knocked back several feet by the force of the collision.

Asuna, who'd been following close behind my burst of speed, did not miss this opportunity.

"*Seyaa!!*"

Her Linear landed deep within the kobold lord's right side. His fourth HP bar shrank—not by much, but it was enough.

Even as I felt the shudder of the impact in my right hand, I tried to calculate the risk of our situation.

When I had faced Illfang's talwar skills in the beta, I wasn't strong enough to cancel his attacks with my own. But because this katana was lighter than the talwar, I hadn't lost any HP in our clash. The tradeoff was that his moves were now much faster.

Was it even possible to deflect and parry his ensuing rush without slipping up at any point?

There was one other thing. Asuna's Linear could dispatch a Kobold Trooper with three hits and a Sentinel with four, but this boss monster's HP were far, far beyond a simple enemy's. I couldn't guess how many hits it would take her to finish off his final HP gauge. One of the advantages to players fighting a boss was that the enemy's massive size made it easier for many people to attack it at once, so ideally we'd have one more damage-dealer on either side. But all of teams A through G were heavily damaged at the moment. We couldn't call for assistance until they had healed themselves with potions.

Asuna and I had to hold out on our own. And wasn't I originally expecting to attempt it all by myself? Well, now I had double the help, so what more could I ask for?

"Here he comes again!" I cried once I was out of my post-skill delay, concentrating with all my willpower on the boss's massive blade.

In the thousand-man *Sword Art Online* closed beta test the previous August, I made it as far as the tenth floor of Aincrad but never saw the boss there.

The labyrinth of that floor was nicknamed the Castle of a Thousand Serpents, and I simply couldn't get past the spot guarded by a particularly tough kind of samurai monster called Orochi Elite Guards. They used bewildering, free-form katana skills that no player could wield. Each attack I suffered added the skill names and descriptions to my reference menu, which I consulted desperately in order to memorize the information. By the time I could finally recognize the initiation of each skill, it was August 31, the end of the test.

The Orochis and Illfang were completely different in shape and size, but they were both humanoid and their attacks were, as far as I could tell, the same. I was able to follow my memory from four months ago to cancel out all of the attacks, even the instant ones.

Needless to say, it was a high-wire act. The boss's slash attacks had a high enough basic damage that just tossing up Slant or Horizontal with the system assist would get me knocked backward. I needed to use them while pushing my body along the thrust of the skills to boost their power to the point that I could actually stop the blows.

This kind of system-independent technique could be very powerful if successful, but it was not without its risks. One wrong move might interfere with the system's automatic assistance, perhaps even cancel out the sword skill entirely.

In the two months I'd played *SAO*, both beta and release, I'd never used so much concentration for so long until now.

And after the fifteenth or sixteenth parry, I finally slipped.

"Damn!" I hissed, and tried to cancel out of my half-initiated Vertical skill. I'd read Illfang's swing as an overhead slice, but he spun it around in a half-circle to come up from below instead. This was *Gengetsu*, or "Phantom Moon," an attack that either landed high or low on a random chance, despite starting with the same animation. I brought back my Anneal Blade in a hurry, but it was too late. An unpleasant shock struck my body and knocked me still.

"Ah!" Asuna shouted next to me, but the striking katana had already caught me directly on the front. There was a sharp shock, cold as ice. My entire body went numb, and my HP bar lost nearly a third of its points.

While I fell to my knees with the impact of the blow, Asuna plunged toward the kobold king. I tried to tell her not to—*Gengetsu* had a very quick recovery period. The blade ended up high in the air after his attack on me, and now began to glimmer again. It was *Hiougi*, the three-part combo that had killed Diavel...

"Nnnraaah!!"

A bellow rumbled forth just before the katana hit Asuna. A massive, glowing green weapon swung just barely over her head, utilizing the two-handed axe skill, Whirlwind.

The katana and the whirling axe clashed. Their impact rocked the entire chamber, and Illfang was blasted backward. On the other hand, the attacker had held firm with nothing more than leather sandals and slid back only a few feet.

It was the brawny, brown-skinned leader of team B, Agil. He shot a grin at me over his shoulder while I scrambled in my coat pockets.

"We'll back you up until you finish your pots. Can't keep forcing a damage dealer to do a tank's job."

"…Thanks, man," I replied, pushing down the strange feeling that was rising in my chest with a healing potion.

Agil wasn't the only one who came forward. Several other players, mostly from team B, had finished recovering and were ready to resume combat. I sent Asuna a look that said I was okay, and shouted as loud as I could to the rest of the group.

"If you surround the boss all the way, he'll unleash his full-circle attack! I'll warn you about the trajectory of his attack, so whoever's in front can prepare to block it! You don't need to cancel it with a sword skill; just deflecting it with a shield or weapon should cut down most of the damage!"

"Okay!" the others roared in response. The Kobold Lord added his own bellow to the fray. It seemed as though there was a hint of irritation to it.

I checked on the rest of the party as I slumped back to the wall and recovered with some low-level healing potions.

As I feared when I noticed the boss's weapon had been altered, they had added extra Ruin Kobold Sentinels to the battle as well. Kibaou's team E and the relatively unharmed polearm team G were dealing with four of the creatures now. They hadn't suffered too much so far, but I had a feeling that groups of four sentinels would continue to pop at regular intervals as long as Illfang was alive. Without any help, the two parties would eventually have their hands full.

Between the back line and the front, the most grievously wounded party members, such as the survivors from team C, were working on healing. Frustratingly, potions in this game worked on a heal-over-time basis. Rather than instantly recovering, the gauge would fill up pixel by pixel. On top of that, once the potion was empty, a cooldown icon appeared at the bottom of the player's view, meaning that until the effect wore off, any extra potions would provide no benefit. To add insult to injury, the weak potions from the first-floor NPCs tasted disgusting.

Because of that cooldown timer, it took a significant amount of time to recover from heavy damage. The common strategy was therefore to switch with another member once you'd suffered a full potion's worth of damage—also known as "pot rotation"—but that pattern broke down when there were too many injured to stand in and fight. On higher floors, there would be valuable healing crystals that acted instantaneously as long as you didn't concern yourself with the astonishing price, but those weren't an option for us down here.

So the battle would be determined by how long Agil's group of six could hold out in the face of Illfang's fierce attacks. And in order to give them a fighting chance, I had to identify his skills as soon as the tell appeared.

I took a knee and focused all of my senses on the boss kobold, shouting out warnings like "flat slice from the right," or "downward from the left" as soon as I recognized them.

Agil's group followed my instructions, prioritizing guarding with their shields or large weapons, rather than gambling on a neutralizing counterstrike. As tank builds, they had excellent defense and HP, but not enough to hold the boss's sword skills to zero damage. Their HP bars shrank bit by bit with every crashing sound effect.

And between them all, one fencer danced spryly here and there: Asuna. She was careful never to pass by Illfang's front or rear, and whenever there was any delay in his movement, she delivered a powerful Linear. Over time, that would raise his aggro level toward Asuna, but the six tanks regularly performed aggro skills like Howl to draw the enemy's attention.

For nearly five minutes, this dangerous, delicate game continued, threatening to fall apart as soon as a single step of the process failed. Finally, the boss's HP fell below 30 percent, and his last bar turned red.

In a moment of relief, one of the tanks lost focus and stumbled. He lurched to the side and only caught himself when he was directly behind Illfang.

"Move!" I screamed, but I was a fraction of a second too late. The boss sensed that he was surrounded, and unleashed a terrible roar.

The large body sank to the ground, then launched itself directly upward into the air. His body and katana spun around and around, becoming a single vortex—the deadly full-circle *Tsumuji-guruma*...

"Aaah!" I howled, and forgetting that my HP hadn't been entirely healed yet, leapt from the wall.

I slung my sword over my right shoulder and pushed hard with my left foot. My back was hit with a sense of acceleration that shouldn't be possible based on my agility as my body flew like a rocket diagonally through the air. The one-handed sword thrust skill Sonic Leap had a shorter range than Rage Spike, but it could be aimed upward into the air as well.

The sword took on a brilliant neon green glow. Ahead of me, Illfang's katana was a fiery crimson.

"Get there...in...time!!"

I swung, stretching my arm as far as it would go. The tip of my Anneal Blade +6 followed a wide arc and just barely caught Illfang's waist before he could unleash his *Tsumuji-guruma*.

There were a heavy, sharp sound and the powerful, unmistakable flash of a critical hit. The kobold's large body slumped in midair, and he fell to the ground without producing his deadly whirlwind.

"*Gruhh!*" he growled, and flailed wildly in an attempt to get to his feet. I'd inflicted him with the Tumble status that was unique to humanoid monsters.

Somehow, I managed to land in balance and, without missing a beat, pushed every last ounce of air out of my lungs.

"Full attack, everybody!! Surround him!!"

"Raaahh!!"

Agil's gang of six unleashed all the frustration of their long defensive shift. They spread out around Illfang and tore into him with Vertical sword skills. Axes, maces, and hammers flashed in a spectrum of color and pounded the kobold's body. The explosion of light and sound began to bite serious chunks out of the enemy's HP gauge, which was fixed at the top of every player's vision.

It was a bet. If we could lower the Kobold Lord's remaining HP to nothing before he got back to his feet, we won. But if he recovered from his status and instantly performed another *Tsumuji-guruma*, he would slice everyone for certain this time. My Sonic Leap was on cooldown. I couldn't attack him in midair again.

Agil's group finished their skill animations and initiated the preliminary motions for the next round, when suddenly Illfang stopped struggling and abruptly sat up.

"We didn't make it in time," I hissed, when I noticed that Asuna was standing right next to me. "Asuna, get ready to do your final Linear with me!"

"Okay!"

I had to grin at how quickly her response echoed my command.

Six weapons snarled at once, and the boss was swallowed by a whirl of flashing lights again. But he did not wait for their onslaught to die down. Illfang roared and got to his feet. There was barely 3 percent left of his HP bar, but there it shone, red and prominent.

Agil was under a delay and couldn't move. Illfang was impervious to stunning or knockbacks now that he'd recovered from the tumble—he transitioned smoothly into his jumping motion.

"Gooo!!" I screamed. Asuna and I leapt together.

She slipped between the tanks and unleashed a furious Linear directly into the boss's left flank. A second later, my blue-lit sword ripped from the kobold king's right shoulder to his belly.

Only a single pixel remained on his HP bar.

The beastman seemed to grin. I returned a ferocious smirk of my own and flipped my wrist back.

"Raaaahh!!"

I raised my sword with a soul-shattering roar. The blade, pitted here and there after the fierce ordeal, tore upward to Illfang's left shoulder to complete a V shape: a two-part sword combo, Vertical Arc.

The kobold's great form suddenly shuddered weakly and faltered backward. His wolflike face turned up to the ceiling and emitted a keening wail. Countless tiny cracks appeared all over his body. His grip loosened, and the katana clattered to the floor.

Illfang the Kobold Lord, boss of the first floor of Aincrad, shattered into a million tiny pieces of glass.

As I slumped to the floor beneath some unseen pressure, a silent message in the purple system font read, *You got the Last Attack!!*

15

THE REMAINING SENTINELS WERE OBLITERATED AT the same time as their boss. The torches on the walls shifted from a dim orange to bright yellow, removing the gloom that shrouded the chamber. A cool breeze swept through the room, carrying the heat of the battle away with it.

No one wanted to break the silence that descended. Teams E and G stood in the back, the center groups of A, C, D, and F were kneeling in recovery mode, and Agil's team B, the last line of tank defense, sat on the floor, all staring around warily. It was as though they were all afraid the beast lord might come back to life at any moment.

Even I was dead still, my sword still raised at the end of the final slash.

Was it truly the end? Or would there be another surprise, another alteration from the beta?

A small pale hand touched my arm, gently pulling the sword down. It was Asuna the fencer. Her chestnut-brown hair rippled in the breeze as she stared at me.

Only now, with her familiar hooded cape removed, did I realize just how beautiful she was. No player could truly be this gorgeous. Asuna accepted my dumbstruck gaze without a complaint—something that would probably never happen again—for several moments, then quietly said, "Nice work."

Finally, it hit me. It was over... We'd finally removed the barrier that might have trapped eight thousand players on the first floor forever.

As though the game was waiting for me to make that realization, a new message suddenly popped into existence. Experience gained, col distributed... and loot.

The faces of the other members finally returned to normal as they received the same message. A rousing cheer broke the silence.

Some roared with their fists in the air. Some hugged their partners. Some put on absurd dances. Amid the storm of celebration, one man stood and approached. It was Agil.

"That was brilliant command, and even better swordsmanship. Congratulations—this victory belongs to you."

I couldn't help but notice that he spoke the word "congratulations" in English with perfect intonation. The big man grinned widely and extended a thick fist.

I thought about how to respond to this and sadly couldn't come up with anything better than a muttered "Nah..." I lifted my own fist to at least give him a bump when someone bellowed behind me.

"Why?!"

The entire room fell silent again at the agonized, tearful shriek. I tore my gaze from Asuna and Agil to look at a man with light armor and a scimitar. I didn't recognize him at first, but when the next words poured from his twisted lips, I finally understood.

"Why did you abandon Diavel to die?!"

He was from team C, one of the perished knight Diavel's friends. Behind him, the other four members were standing, their faces red and miserable. Some were even crying.

"Abandon...?"

"You know what you did! You... you knew the moves the boss was using! If you'd told us that information to start with, Diavel wouldn't have died!"

The other raid members stirred at these words, murmuring among themselves.

"Now that you mention it…"

"How did he know? That stuff wasn't in the strategy guide…"

To my surprise, Kibaou did not follow up these suspicions. He was standing to the side, his lips firmly closed, as though grappling with indecision. Instead, another member of team E stepped forward and jabbed an accusing finger at me.

"I…I know the truth! He's a beta tester! That's how he knew the boss's patterns! He knows all the best quests and hunting grounds! He's hiding them from us!!"

There was no surprise on the faces of team C. I doubted Diavel had told them himself—he would not bring up the topic of the beta test on his own, as he was hiding his involvement in it—but they'd no doubt all had the same suspicion when I identified those katana skills.

The scimitar man's eyes boiled over with hatred, and he prepared to level another accusation at my feet when a mace warrior in Agil's tank party raised his hand and spoke calmly.

"But the strategy guide we got yesterday said it was based on the boss's attack patterns in the beta. If he's really a beta tester, wouldn't all of his knowledge be based on what we learned from that?"

"W-well…"

The scimitar-wielder pressed on in anger, speaking for the rest of his teammates. "That strategy guide was all fake. Argo sold us a bunch of lies. She's a former beta tester too; there's no way she'd give away the truth for free."

Uh-oh. This was heading in a bad direction.

I held my breath. I could take whatever criticism was directed my way, but we had to avoid an outright witch hunt of Argo and the other beta testers. But how to prevent their hatred from running out of control…?

I looked down at the dark floor, where the system messages hanging in view came into sharper relief. My experience, col and items…

An idea abruptly popped into my head, followed by a terrible indecision. If I made this choice, there was no telling what might happen to me. I might even be assassinated when I least expected it, as I once feared. But at the very least, it might redirect the anger away from Argo...

Agil and Asuna had finally heard enough. They spoke up simultaneously.

"Oh, come on..."

"Listen..."

I cut them off with a gesture and stepped forward, assuming an arrogant look and staring coldly into the scimitar-wielder's eyes. I slumped my shoulders and spoke in as emotionless a voice as I could manage.

"A former beta tester? Please...don't treat me like those amateurs."

"Um...what...?"

"Think back. The odds were stacked against anyone trying to get into the *SAO* closed beta. How many of the thousand who made it in do you think were true MMO fans? They were all noobs who barely understood how to level. You guys are way smarter about this game than they ever were."

Forty-two players silently took in my disdainful words. There was a chill in the air, an unseen blade that traced the skin, just as it had before we tackled the boss.

"But I'm not like them." I grinned snidely. "I made it to a floor that no one else in the beta reached. I knew the boss's katana attacks because I'd fought mobs on a way higher floor who used the same moves. I know plenty about this game—way more than Argo."

"What...do you mean...?" rasped the man from team E who had first labeled me a beta tester. "You're...you're worse than a beta tester...You're a cheat! A cheater!"

Calls of *cheater* and *beta cheater* rang out from me. Eventually they blended together into a strange new word, "beater."

"A beater? I like the sound of that," I proclaimed loudly for the entire group to hear, fixing them all with a level stare. "That's right, I'm a beater. Don't you ever insult my skill by calling me a former tester."

It was for the best.

Now the four to five hundred beta testers still out there in the game could be broadly divided into two categories. The vast majority were "simple, amateur testers," and a select few were "filthy beaters who hoarded their information."

The hostility of the retail players would be turned upon the beaters. Anyone being outed as a beta tester wouldn't necessarily have to be afraid of retribution.

In exchange, I'd never be invited to join any front-running guilds or parties...but that was no different from the way I already played. I'd been a solo player, and I would continue to be one. It was that simple.

I looked away from the pale-faced scimitar wielder and the others from teams E and C, opened my player window, and fiddled with my equipment mannequin.

Instead of the familiar old dark gray leather coat, I put on the new unique armor I'd just received from the boss, the Coat of Midnight. Tiny lights covered my chest and the faded old gray material turned into sleek black leather. It was a long coat, too; the hem hung down below my knees.

With a flourish of my new coat, I spun around and faced the small door at the back of the boss chamber.

"I'll go activate the teleport gate on the second floor. There's a bit of a hike through the wilderness to reach the main city once you leave the exit above, so you can tag along—if you're not afraid of being slaughtered by unfamiliar mobs."

Agil and Asuna gave me appraising looks as I strode forward. Their eyes said they knew what I was doing. That, at least, was some small comfort. I gave them a hint of a smile, picked up my pace, and pushed open the door on the back wall behind the empty throne.

At the top of a narrow, spiraling staircase, there was another door. I opened it gently and was met by a stunning sight. The door opened directly from the middle of a sheer cliff, with a narrow terrace-styled downward staircase carved out of the rock to the left. For the moment, I simply drank in the sight of the second floor.

Unlike the varied terrain of the first floor, the second was a series of rocky mesas from end to end. The upper areas of the mountains were covered in soft green grasses, grazing land for large cattle monsters.

Urbus, the main town of the second floor, was carved directly into the top of one of those mesas. All I had to do was descend these stairs, walk half a mile to reach Urbus, then touch the teleport gate in the center of the city to activate it. At that point, it would be connected to the teleporter in the Town of Beginnings below, and anyone could travel between the two.

If I actually did die on the short journey—or just sat here and did nothing—the teleporter would activate automatically anyway, two hours after the boss's destruction. But word had no doubt spread to the Town of Beginnings about today's attempt on the boss, and I could imagine a crowd of players standing in the town center, waiting for the moment that blue warp gate appeared. I wanted to get to Urbus and open it up for them...but I had the right to stop and enjoy the scenery for a minute first.

I walked forward and sat down at the edge of the terrace carved out of the rock face. Beyond the many craggy mountains was a tiny sliver of blue sky at the outer perimeter of Aincrad.

How many minutes did I sit there? Eventually I heard petite footsteps coming up the spiral staircase behind me. I didn't turn around. The owner of the steps reached the door and stopped, then sighed and came to sit next to me.

"...I told you not to come," I muttered. She looked affronted.

"No, you didn't. You said to tag along if I wasn't afraid of dying."

"Oh...right. Sorry."

I ducked my head in embarrassment and glanced over at Asuna, whose face was beautiful from any angle. Her light brown eyes looked back at me briefly, then returned to the scenery below. She exhaled and said, "It's so pretty."

After a minute of silence, she spoke again.

"I have messages from Agil and Kibaou."

"Oh...what did they say?"

"Agil said we should tackle the second floor boss, too. And Kibaou said..."

She cleared her throat, expression serious, and clumsily attempted to re-create his Kansai accent.

"...Ya saved my ass this time, but I still can't get along with ya. I'm gonna do things my own way to beat this game, y'hear?"

"...I see."

The words echoed in my head a few times. Eventually Asuna coughed again and pointedly turned her head away.

"Also...I have a message from me."

"Um...yes?"

"You called out my name during the battle."

It took me a moment to remember. Yes, perhaps I had given her an order directly by name.

"S-sorry, I didn't meant to disrespect you, if that's what you think...Or...did I pronounce it wrong?"

Now it was Asuna's turn to look skeptical.

"Pronounce it wrong...? How did you even know it in the first place? I never told you my name, nor did you tell me yours."

"Huh?!" I yelled. What did she mean? We were still registered in a party, so there were two HP bars to the upper left of my vision. Beneath the lower of the two was a little label reading "Asuna"...

"Wait...are you saying...this is your very first time being in a party?"

"Yes."

"...I see."

I reached up with my right hand and pointed to the left side of Asuna's face. "Do you see an extra HP bar over here, in addition to your own? Is anything written beneath it?"

"Um..."

Asuna turned her head, so I reached out and stopped it with my fingers.

"No, if you turn your face, the readouts will move with it. Keep your head still and look to your left."

"Like...this?"

Her brown eyes awkwardly rolled left, finding a string of letters that I couldn't see. Her graceful lips sounded out three syllables.

"Ki...ri...to. Kirito? That's your name?"

"Yep."

"Oh...so it was written here the entire time..."

Suddenly Asuna twitched in surprise. I realized that I'd been holding my hand to her cheek for several seconds, almost as though I was initiating the motion for a skill.

I pulled my hands back so fast, they almost made a zooming sound. After a few seconds, I thought I heard a soft giggle. Was she laughing? Asuna the kobold overkiller, master of the perfect Linear thrust? That was a sight I wanted to see, but I resisted the urge to turn.

The laughing ended all too soon, and she followed it with a soft statement.

"...Actually, Kirito, I came up here to thank you."

"For...the cream bread and the bath?" I asked without thinking. She denied it in a mildly terrifying way, then gave it some thought and agreed that they were part of it.

"It's for...a lot of things. Thanks for everything. I think...I've finally found something here that I want to do, a goal I want to reach."

"Oh? What's that?" I glanced at her. Asuna grinned for just an instant.

"It's a secret." She stood up and took a step back. "I'm gonna keep trying. I'll try to survive, to be stronger. Until I can reach the place I want to be."

I nodded without turning around.

"I know...You *can* be stronger. Not just in terms of your fighting skill, but in a much more important, personal sense. So take it from me...if someone you trust invites you to a guild, don't turn them down. There's an absolute limit to what you can accomplish playing solo…"

For several seconds, the only sound was Asuna breathing. When she did speak, it was not what I expected to hear.

"The next time we meet, tell me how you took me out of that labyrinth."

"Sure…" I was about to say it was simple, then stopped myself and added, "You bet. In fact…there's one more thing I ought to tell you. What I was about to say before the meeting two days ago…"

That's right. I owed her an explanation. She ought to know that the deaths of two thousand and her terrible despair were at least in part my responsibility for being a self-interested beta tester… a beater.

But just as I was about to tell her this, Asuna waved it aside.

"It's fine. I get it. I know what you've been through to get here…and where you'll go on your own from here. But…someday, I'll…"

She broke off there in a whisper. After a brief silence, her voice was calm but firm.

"See you around, Kirito."

There was the creak of a door opening. Footsteps. The thump of it closing.

I stayed sitting on the edge of the terrace jutting from the mountain until the sensory information of Asuna's scent disappeared from the virtual air. I tried to figure out what she meant, but decided I didn't need to know that right now.

With a deep breath, I got to my feet, looked at the door Asuna had just passed through, then turned and started descending the steps.

As they wound down the side of the slope, I found myself counting the stairs. Every forty-eight steps, they turned back the other way in a zigzag pattern. Eventually, the meaning behind that became clear. Forty-eight was six times eight—the number of people in a full raid party. If we'd had a full complement and beaten the boss without any fatalities, we could have filled an entire flight from landing to landing, with a step for each member.

I doubted the designer of this feature imagined just a single player descending these steps. The path seemed to be foretelling my travels ahead. Looking forward or back, there was not a soul in sight. I walked on, down and down, entirely alone...

But, after the umpteenth landing of the endless staircase, I noticed a small envelope icon flashing on the right side of my view. It was a friend message, a form of communication that could bridge any floor of Aincrad. There were only two players on my friend list. My first friend, Klein—and Argo the Rat.

I opened the message to discover that it was from the latter.

Sounds like I really put you through the wringer, Kii-boy, it said. I marveled at how fast she worked. I scrolled down to read more, but the message was very short.

I'll make it up to you by giving you any single piece of info on the house.

Oh? I grinned devilishly and popped up the holo-keyboard as I continued walking down the steps, typing my reply.

Why the whiskers?

I hit the send button, smiled again, then finally set foot on the soil of the second floor of Aincrad and started walking in the direction of Urbus.

SWORD ART ONLINE PROGRESSIVE

INTERLUDE

THE REASON FOR THE WHISKERS

URBUS, THE MAIN CITY OF THE SECOND FLOOR OF Aincrad, was carved directly into the flat top of a three-hundred-yard wide mountain, with only the outer perimeter left standing.

Once I was through the southern gate, a notification reading SAFE HAVEN appeared, and the sound of a slow-paced town BGM hit my ears. Unlike the strings-heavy music from the first-floor towns, this was played by a wistful oboe. The style of clothes worn by the NPCs milling about was subtly different, reinforcing that sense of having come to a new floor.

About ten yards past the gate, I took a look around me and didn't find a single green player cursor—as it should be. I'd just defeated Illfang the Kobold Lord, boss of the first floor, barely forty minutes before. All the other raid party members who had taken part in the fight had turned back to the first floor rather than follow the spiral staircase up to the second.

Which meant that there was only one solitary player on this entire, vast floor: Kirito, former beta tester, beater.

It was a luxurious feeling, but it would not last for long. Two hours after the death of the floor boss, the teleport gate in the center of the floor's main town (Urbus, in this case) would automatically activate, linking up with the gate of the floor below. As soon as that happened, an entire flood of excited players would burst through the portal.

On the flip side, that meant that if I felt like it, I could monopolize this floor for another hour and twenty minutes.

With that much time, I could complete two or three "slaughter" quests to kill a certain number of monsters without having to jostle with other players. It was a tempting idea for a truly self-interested solo adventurer, but I didn't have the guts to hold out on the hundreds, if not thousands of players below who were waiting for the gate with bated breath.

I trotted through the main street of Urbus directly north, climbing a wide staircase to the open town center, which featured a large gate in the middle. It was not really a gate so much as a standing stone arch with no door or fence connected to it. Only by standing close to the structure was it possible to see that the space beneath the arch was gently rippling somehow. It was like a very thin, vertical film of water suspended in the air.

Only after scanning the perimeter for a convenient escape route did I reach out to the shifting, transparent veil. My fingertip, covered by black leather, brushed the water surface.

In the next instant, my vision burned a brilliant blue.

The light pulsed outward in concentric circles until it filled the fifteen-foot arch. Once the entire space was full, the teleport was complete, and the town had been "opened." The exact same phenomenon was happening at the same time down on the first floor. The players below would be preparing to dash through the finished portal, now that they realized they wouldn't need to wait the full two hours.

But I didn't wait to witness the entire show. I turned and sped toward a church-like building on the east end of the square, bursting through the door and scrambling up the stairs inside. Eventually I made my way into a small room on the third floor and set my back against the wall next to a window so I could see down into the clearing.

At that precise moment, the interior of the gate flashed, and the NPC musicians set up in the corner of the square began to play the bright and cheery "Opening Fanfare." A second later, countless players spilled out through the blue light in a jumble of colors.

Some stopped in the middle of the clearing and looked around. Some held parchment maps bought from information dealers and took off running. Some jammed fists into the air and shouted, "We made it to the second floor!"

A similar town opening had occurred nine times in the *SAO* beta test, and in each case, the raid members who had dispatched the previous floor's boss lined up facing the new teleport gate, soaking in the applause and congratulations of those who traveled upward to see the new environment. But in this case, I was the only person who had stuck around to open the town, and I'd taken off running. There would be no grand celebratory event. Perhaps those looking curiously around the square were searching for me, but I could not step forward to name myself.

Just minutes earlier, after we defeated the boss, I made a proclamation to the forty-some raid members that I, Kirito, was not just some beta tester, but a "beater" who had ascended further than any of the thousand other testers, accumulating more information about the game than anyone else.

It wasn't out of a desire to play the villain. I did it to avoid having the wrath of the new retail players focused on the former testers, but the end result was that, soon, every high-level player in the game would know of my infamy. Appearing in public would not provoke cheers but ugly booing. I didn't have the willpower to withstand that kind of open hostility.

So I decided to hide out in the third floor of this chapel until the excitement in the town square subsided. However...

"...Huh?"

I noticed something odd down in the square. One female player who traveled through the gate ran pell-mell straight to the west end of the square. She might have been rushing to find a weapon shop or quest-giving NPC, but the real issue were the two men who showed up after her. They stopped briefly and looked around for the retreating player, then raced after her. They were clearly chasing the woman.

The safe haven of town was under the anti-crime code, so normally I'd pay no attention to something like that, but it was different when the person being chased was someone I knew. Those brown curls and the plain leather armor belonged to none other than Argo the Rat.

Plenty of people hated her and her motto of "selling any information with a price," but something was wrong if they were hurtling around at that speed. I pondered the situation for a moment, then put a foot on the windowsill and leapt down to the short roof below.

I dashed across the tiles and leapt onto the next roof over, making good use of my high agility stat before anyone could spot me, and continued along the rooftops in the direction of the chase. This feat was only possible thanks to the uniform height of the buildings in Urbus.

I waved my hand to call up my menu as I ran after them, clicking the Search button in my skills tab. When a sub-menu followed, I selected "Pursuit," then entered the name "Argo" into the field. A set of green footsteps suddenly glowed on the path below me.

Pursuit was a modifier effect on the Search skill once its proficiency level was high enough. It was designed to increase the efficiency of monster hunting, but it could also be used to track a player on your friends list. My level was still fairly low, so I could only see footsteps up to a minute old. I raced alongside the trail, trying to keep up before they vanished.

If Argo, with her incredible agility, couldn't shake the two men, they were bad news. I didn't recognize them from the boss raid, but they had to be among the top players by level. Moreover, the chase was proceeding straight down the westward route and through the town gate carved into the outer perimeter of the flat-top mountain in which Urbus was nestled.

The plains to the west of town were a dangerous zone populated with large cattle monsters. The situation was looking downright grim now. I bit my lip and raced out into the virtual savanna.

The wasteland beyond the plains was deadly enough that even at my level it was too risky to go in there alone. Fortunately, the footsteps in the grass were growing brighter, meaning that Argo's pace was slowing and I was getting closer. Eventually I reached a small canyon between two rocky hills and heard a familiar voice.

"...told you a hundred times! I wouldn't sell that info, no matter the price!"

The nasal inflection was undoubtedly Argo's, but it was fiercer and angrier than I'd ever heard her before. Next was a similarly furious man's voice.

"You do not intend to monopolize the information, but neither will you reveal it. One can only assume that you seek to inflate the value of it in order to sell!"

His way of speaking was oddly archaic. I slowed down and began to climb the rock face at the side of the canyon. Even the most forbidding terrain in *SAO* could be climbed with enough persistence and cleverness. It was a secret ambition of mine to one day attempt to scale the enormous pillars that separated the floors of Aincrad in the hopes of bypassing the labyrinths altogether. But my clandestine climb in this case was not done for want of a good challenge, but to guarantee my own safety.

After about fifteen feet, I reached a narrow flat space that overlooked the canyon. I crawled forward on hands and knees. The shouting voices were almost directly below me.

"It's not a matter of price! I'm saying that I don't want to sell something if all it gets me is hatred in return!"

The second man responded, "What quarrel would we have with you? As we said, we will pay the asking price and be grateful for your service! Just sell us the information on this floor's special quest that grants the Extra Skill!"

...What?

Now I held my breath entirely. Extra Skills were hidden

abilities that could not be chosen without meeting special conditions. Only one had been discovered in the beta: the Meditation skill, in which assuming a pose of concentration increased the HP recovery rate and decreased the infliction time of negative status effects. Because of its tricky usage and very uncool look, few bothered to earn it. I had my suspicions that the katana skill used by the kobold lord and the samurai monsters on the tenth floor might be an Extra Skill as well, but the means to unlock it were still a mystery.

At any rate, Argo and the two wannabe actors were clearly not talking about Meditation. The NPC that taught that skill was up on the sixth floor. No, this was about some hidden quest on the second floor that even I didn't know about (and neither did almost any of the former testers) that unlocked an Extra Skill, and the two strange men were pressing Argo for that information.

The men's voices grew louder.

"We are not backing down—not today, you see!"

"That Extra Skill is necessary for us to complete our characters, you see!"

"You just don't get it! I'm not going to sell it to *anyone*, you see—I mean, I'm not going to sell it, period!"

The tension in the air turned electric, crackling tangibly. I leapt to my feet on the rocky ledge and jumped down the fifteen feet to the ground below, landing perfectly between Argo and the men. I didn't have quite enough agility points to jump that distance without damage, so I had to tense my knees to cushion the shock.

"Who goes there?!"

"An interloper from an enemy province?!"

A single glance at their outfits sent a powerful shock through my memory. They wore full-body cloth armor in dark gray, with light chainmail on top. I noticed small scimitars draped over their backs, and dark gray bandanna caps and pirate masks to match the armor.

Taken as a whole, these outfits could be interpreted as a creative attempt to re-create a classic "ninja" costume. I couldn't help but feel as though I'd seen people dressed in this style during the beta as well.

"Oh! You're, um, you're…let's see, the F, Fu…Food? No, Fugue—no, not that either…"

"It is Fuma!"

"We are Kotaro and Isuke of the Fuma Ninja Force!!"

"Right! That was it!"

I snapped my fingers, satisfied that my memory had been corrected. These two were members of a ninja guild feared for their incredible speed during the beta test. As to why they would be "feared"—like Argo, they raised their agility as high as possible, forming a wall of eye-popping speed on the front line, then running off when the battle grew too dangerous. When the monsters followed in pursuit, they usually wound up targeting a different party when the ninjas escaped, which earned them a very bad reputation indeed.

I didn't realize that they'd continued their adherence to the way of the shinobi even after *SAO* had become a game of death, but I didn't have any issue with their choice—for now. But chasing down a female player, ganging up on her, and demanding her trade secrets was crossing a line.

I reached back to make sure Argo was safely behind me and ran a finger along the hilt of my Anneal Blade +6.

"As a spy for the shogun, I cannot overlook the wicked deeds of the Fuma."

Instantly, Kotaro and Isuke's eyes flashed beneath their knock-off ninja hoods.

"You Iga dog!!"

"Huh?!"

It seemed my half-assed joke had struck a nerve, and they'd confused me for a member of a rival school. In perfect rhythm, they reached over their shoulders to remove the scimitars that passed for ninja blades.

They weren't going to draw on me, were they? Then again, we were out in the open, where the anti-crime code had no effect. If a player attacked another player, damage would be done. At the same time, the aggressor's cursor would turn orange, signifying them as a criminal and keeping them from entering town. Even ninjas could not fool the god that presided over this game.

I briefly considered resolving the argument with the preposterous claim that I wasn't an Iga ninja but a Koga ninja like them, when the situation was resolved in a most unexpected way.

When I snuck into the canyon, I scaled the walls in order to eavesdrop on their conversation rather than standing around near the entrance. I did this because we were out in the wilderness, not in town, and standing around in place long enough *always* led to one thing happening.

I took a careful step backward and murmured, "Behind you."

"We will not fall for your trickery!"

"It's not trickery. Look behind you."

Something in my voice convinced the skeptical ninjas. Kotaro and Isuke turned their heads and abruptly leapt backward. Right before their eyes, someone had joined the group. No, something.

It was a Trembling Ox, a giant cattle monster unique to the second floor, standing over eight feet at the shoulder. Its attack power and toughness were obvious at a glance, but what made them so dangerous was their extremely long targeting range, both in time and distance. I'd climbed the inaccessible boulders specifically to avoid drawing the notice of these fearsome beasts.

"*Brooooh!!*" the ox roared.

"G-gaaah!!" the ninjas screamed in unison. With stunning speed, two gray-clad blurs shot back toward town away from the canyon, but the ox showed surprising agility for its size. In no more than five seconds, the rumbling footsteps and screams disappeared over the horizon. Kotaro and Isuke would likely be in a footrace all the way back to Urbus.

The great ninja war averted for now, I sighed in relief and looked down at my body. Until an hour ago, I'd been wearing a boring outfit of black leather pants, cotton shirt and a dark gray leather coat. However, with the unique Coat of Midnight I'd looted from

Illfang the Kobold Lord, I was dressed in full black to match my hair and eyes. It seemed like a good way to reinforce the dirty beater persona I'd developed, but I had to admit it also made me look a bit like a ninja. I started to wonder if I should put on a different color undershirt just to avoid any rumors about "Kirito the Iga Ninja" from now on.

Once again, I was broken out of my thoughts by a very unexpected event.

Two small arms reached out and squeezed around my midsection from behind. I felt a soft warmth on my back, and heard a faint whisper.

"That was a little too much showing off, Kii-boy."

It belonged to Argo, who had been silent since I leapt from my perch. But it felt as though the sound of her voice was different somehow from the snide, obnoxious Rat I knew.

"Keep that up, and you might force Big Sister to break the very first rule of the information dealer."

...Big Sister? The first rule of the information dealer?

They were very intellectually curious words, but as a middle school game addict with zero personal skills, I had no idea how to react to the situation. I froze up, my mind racing, and eventually found my answer.

"...You owe me one, remember? I can't have anything happening to you until you explain the reason for your whiskers."

Argo the Rat had three thick black whisker lines drawn on either cheek with face paint. They were the source of her nickname, but no one knew why she painted them in the first place. She claimed the answer would cost the astonishing price of one hundred thousand col.

But in the recent boss battle, I had taken on the mantle of a "beater," distinguishing myself from the majority of beta testers, including Argo, and drawing the ire of the new retail players away from them. After that, she sent me a message of thanks, offering a single piece of information for free. I'd told her I wanted to know the reason for her whiskers.

I'd meant it to be a lighthearted joke to ease the gravity of the situation, but that only made Argo press her face harder into my back.

"...Okay, I'll tell you. Just wait so I can get the paint off..."

Huh?

The paint...meaning her whiskers? So she was going to show me her plain face, something she'd never shown anyone in-game? Was this meant to be a symbolic act with a deeper meaning?

My social anxiety rose to a dangerous peak. Before she could let go, I shouted out, "N-never mind, I've got a better idea! How about you tell me the details of that hidden skill those guys were going on about?!"

When Argo let go and came around to my front, she fortunately still had the three big whiskers on either cheek. I could have sworn that just before she let go, she'd muttered a faint "coward." Or was that my imagination?

Back to her usual impertinent glare, the Rat crossed her arms and grunted, "Well, I said I'd tell you any one thing, and a deal's a deal. But you need to promise me something as well, Kii-boy. You can't blame me for what happens, no matter what!"

"You said the same thing to those ninjas earlier. What do you mean by that? Why would someone bear a grudge against you for selling information on an Extra Skill that everyone wants?"

Argo answered my question with her familiar wry grin. "That one'll cost ya, Kii-boy."

I stifled a sigh. "All right, I promise. Swear to God—I mean, swear to the system, no matter what happens, I won't hold it against you."

Even if this quest for an Extra Skill was potentially deadly, I could determine that on my own. Argo nodded and beckoned me to follow.

The route we traveled from there would never have occurred to me without a map item, or infinite curiosity and persistence.

She took me up the side of one of the many flat-topped mountains that dotted the second floor—which was the same size as the first—then into a small cave and down an underground river like a water slide. We ran into three battles along the way, but with my careful leveling in preparation for the first-floor boss, they were no big deal. The trip took about thirty minutes, all told.

Based on our map location, it seemed we had nearly scaled the rocky mountain that loomed over the eastern edge of the second floor. We were in a small clearing surrounded by sheer rock walls all around, with nothing else but a spring of water, a single tree—and a tiny shed.

"...Is this it?"

Argo nodded. I strode up to the building. It seemed there was no danger, at least so far. Suddenly, the door before me flew open.

Inside there were a few pieces of furniture and one NPC. It was a large, elderly man, all muscle and bone, bald as a cue ball, with a magnificent beard. There was a golden exclamation mark above his head, the sign of a quest.

I looked back at Argo and she nodded.

"That's the NPC who gives you the Extra Skill, Martial Arts. This is all I can tell you. It's up to you whether to accept the quest or not."

"M...Martial Arts?"

I'd never heard that term in the beta. Argo offered a few extra tidbits, claiming they were on the house.

"Martial Arts is the catch-all term for attacks using just the hands, no weapons, I expect. It'll be useful when you drop your weapon or it runs out of durability and breaks."

"Whoa...Yeah, that actually seems useful, unlike Meditation. In that case...I guess I can see why those ninjas were so set on getting it for themselves."

Argo looked quizzical, so I shot back an explanation of my own, "on the house."

"People think ninjas use a ninja blade and shurikens, but it's a bit different in the gaming world. One good wrist chop at the neck, and the head flies off. For whatever reason, that's been the pinnacle of any video game ninja's style. So Kotaro and Isuke wanted the Martial Arts skill to round out their perfect image of a ninja. But in that case...if they didn't know where to find this place, how did they know it involved the skill, and that you knew about it, too?"

"...This one's double on the house. At the very end of the beta, an NPC on the seventh floor revealed some info about the 'Martial Arts master down on the second floor.' I'd found him long before that, of course, but I'm guessing the ninjas heard it from this fellow on the seventh floor. So once I started getting into the strategy guide business here, they came to me for details on the Extra Skill."

"Then...why didn't you just say you didn't know? Then they wouldn't be harassing you so much..."

She grimaced at my straightforward question.

"I think my pride as an information merchant prevented me from simply saying 'I don't know.'"

"...So you said you did, but that you wouldn't sell it. Well...I guess I can see why you'd make that statement..."

I stifled a sigh and looked back to the NPC, who had assumed a Zen position on a little tatami-like mat in the center of the shack.

"And you didn't sell it because you were afraid your buyer would blame you for it. Well, if you ask me, it seems like you've made more than a few enemies already..."

"Any grudge over information sold or bought only lasts three days! But this one's different! It could last a lifetime..."

Argo's petite body shivered. I pondered for several seconds, then came to a conclusion.

"So I guess I just have to find out what happens after this point for myself. All right, you've got a deal: Whatever happens, I won't hold it against you."

I stepped into the shack and stood in front of the meditating man. He was wearing a tattered outfit that looked like a robe.

"You want to follow my school?"

"... That's right."

"The road of training is long and fraught with peril."

"That's what I like to hear."

The exclamation mark over his head turned into a question mark, and the quest acceptance log scrolled before my eyes.

My new master escorted me out of the shack to a massive boulder at the edge of his stone-lined garden. He walked over and patted the stone, a good six feet tall and five across, then rubbed his whiskers with the other hand.

"Your training is simple: Split this stone with your two fists. If you succeed, I will teach you all of my secrets."

"...... Um ... timeout."

Startled by this unexpected challenge, I gave the large rock a light tap. Once you got used to the game, you could tell the durability of a target based on the physical sensation. What I felt was an ultra-hard surface just one notch below an "immortal object."

Yep. Can't do this.

I turned back to the teacher, ready to cancel the quest. But before I could speak—

"You are not permitted to descend this mountain until you break the stone. I will put the sign upon you now," the teacher said, pulling out two objects from his robe pockets. In his left hand was a small jar. In the right, a thick and magnificent paintbrush.

Suddenly I had such a bad feeling about this that the words "a bad feeling" practically popped into existence over my head. Before I could announce that I was quitting the school of martial arts, the master's hand shot out with terrific speed. He plunged the tip of the brush into the pot and whipped it across my face.

It was at that precise moment that I understood where Argo's whiskers came from.

She *had* found this old man on her own during the beta, and accepted his quest. Who wouldn't? He ordered her to break the stone and drew on her face—three thick whiskers on either cheek.

"Wh-whaaa?!" I shrieked pitifully and fell back. My glance met Argo's. Her ratty face was full of deep sadness, empathy—and the tension of one holding back the biggest gut laugh she'd ever had.

Freed from the brush attack, I tried to rub my face with my hands. But the ink was ultra quick-drying, and none of it came off on my fingers. The master nodded in satisfaction at his work, then delivered a shocking but sadly predictable proclamation.

"That sign will not vanish until you break this rock and complete your training. I have faith in your potential, my apprentice."

And he plodded back to his shed and through the door.

After a good ten seconds of standing in place, I looked at Argo, whose face was still a subtle mixture of emotions.

"I see... So you took on this quest during the beta... and had to give up. You played to the very end of the beta with those whiskers still drawn on your face. Ultimately, that helped you develop the persona of 'The Rat,' so you kept up the tradition of the paint when the retail game shipped... It all makes sense."

"Brilliant deduction!" she applauded. "Aren't you lucky, Kii-boy? You got both the reason for my whiskers and the details of the Extra Skill, packaged into one! In fact, I'll even let you in on one more nugget. That rock... is hard as hell!"

"... Figures."

I resisted the urge to fall to the ground and asked Argo one last question, my final hope.

"Hey... did he paint whiskers on my face just like yours?"

"Hmm, they're not the same."

"Oh...? Wh-what are they like?"

If they weren't too obvious, or even looked kind of cool, I'd have the option of going back to my regular life with a slightly different look. I didn't have the guts to go look at my reflection in the pond, so I let Argo stare for another three seconds.

"If I had to describe you in one word, it would be... Kiriemon."

That was the last straw for her. She fell to the ground, flailing her feet back and forth and screeching with laughter. Over and over and over.

After three solid days on the mountain and countless painful attempts, I broke that rock. I'm just glad I didn't have to hate Argo for the rest of my life.

SWORD ART ONLINE
PROGRESSIVE

RONDO FOR A FRAGILE BLADE

SECOND FLOOR OF AINCRAD, DECEMBER 2022

1

"S...S-SCREW YOU!!"

My feet stopped when the high-pitched shriek hit my ears.

I took a few quick steps to the side and pressed my back against the wall of the NPC shop. Up ahead, the path opened into a wider plaza, from which the disturbance was coming.

"P-put it back! Back to the way it was!! That was a plus-four... P-put it back to what it was!"

Another shriek. It sounded like an argument between two players. Given that we were in the protected zone of Urbus, the main city on the second floor of Aincrad, the disagreement was unlikely to lead to physical harm to either player. I certainly had no reason to hide, given that it had nothing to do with me.

But even though I understood that well enough, I couldn't help but be more cautious than usual these days. After all, Kirito the level-13 swordsman was the most hated solo player in Aincrad— the first man to be known as a beater.

Thursday, December 8, 2022, was the thirty-second day of *Sword Art Online*, the game of death.

Illfang the Kobold Lord, master of the first floor, was dead. Four days had passed since the teleport gate of Urbus went active.

In those four days, the story of what happened in the boss

chamber had spread among the game's top players, albeit with wings of its own.

A boss monster with the Katana skill, a piece of information that wasn't previously known. The death of Diavel the Knight, leader of the raid. And one beater, a beta tester who got further than anyone and used his knowledge to steal the last hit on the boss and reap the rewards.

Fortunately for me, while the name Kirito had spread like wildfire, only forty or so players had actual knowledge of my physical appearance within the game. And in *SAO*, the names of strangers did not appear on their in-game cursors. That was the only reason I could walk through town without fear of being pelted by stones. Then again, even if that happened, a purple system wall would deflect the projectiles.

Even still, I felt ashamed that I was removing my signature Coat of Midnight—my prize for defeating the boss—and wearing a wide bandanna to escape notice. It wasn't that I was so desperate for human contact that I would sneak into the city in disguise; I just needed to refill on potions and rations as well as perform maintenance on my equipment. There was a small shop at the village of Marome about two miles southeast of Urbus, but its selection was poor, and there were no NPC blacksmiths I could pay to repair my weapon.

Due to these factors, I was busy in the market on the south side of Urbus, filling my item storage with sundry goods and supplies, then making my way along the side of the street toward my next errand when I heard the shouts.

Out of reflex, I had to check to make sure the angry screams weren't directed at me first, then sighed in disappointment at my own timidity. Satisfied that it wasn't me, I resumed my trip to the eastern plaza, which was both my destination and the source of the argument.

In less than a minute, I arrived at a circular, bowl-like open space. It was relatively crowded for three o'clock in the afternoon, which was normally prime adventuring time. Most likely, the foot traffic was due to the recent opening of the town—there were plenty of players coming up from the Town of Beginnings on the first floor to visit the new city.

The flow of pedestrians slowed down in a corner of the plaza, and I could hear the same shouts coming from that area. I slipped through the crowd and craned my neck, trying to detect the source of the argument.

"Wh-wh-what did you do?! The properties are all way down!!"

I vaguely recognized the red-faced man. He was a proper frontier player, not a tourist. He hadn't taken part in the first-floor boss raid, but his full suit of metal armor and large three-horned helmet spoke to his level.

What truly drew my eye, however, was the naked longsword clutched in the three-horned man's right hand. The edge couldn't hurt anyone inside of town, but the idea that he would wave it around in the midst of a crowd was distasteful. He was too furious to think straight, however, so he stuck the tip into the pavement stone and continued bellowing.

"How could you possibly fail four times in a row? You can't have reduced my sword to plus zero! I should have left it with a damn NPC! You owe me for this, you third-rate blacksmith!"

Standing quietly in a plain brown leather apron and looking guilty through the minutes of raging insults was a short male player. He'd set up a gray carpet at the edge of the plaza with a chair, anvil, and shelf crowded together. The rug was a Vendor's Carpet, an expensive item that allowed a player to set up a simple shop in the middle of the town—a necessity for any enterprising merchant or crafter.

You could display your wares without a carpet, of course, but when left abandoned in the open like that, the items would lose durability bit by bit as time wore on, and there was no defense against thievery. In the beta test, I'd seen lively player markets along the main streets of all the major cities with carpets of every color, but this was the very first I'd noticed since *SAO*'s retail version had turned deadly. In fact, it was very first non-NPC blacksmith I'd seen.

. Now that I recognized the circumstances, the reason for the uproar was clear.

The man repeatedly slamming his sword against the ground had paid the silent, drooping blacksmith to fortify the blade. In general terms, a player of the same level would be better at augmenting weapons than an NPC. The requisite production skills had to be at a certain level, of course, but that could generally be recognized at a glance. The crafting tools used—in this case, the blacksmith's hammer—were all grouped into tiers that could only be equipped with the right level of skill proficiency. The Iron Hammer resting on the silent blacksmith's anvil required a higher level than the Bronze Hammers this town's NPCs used.

So this blacksmith should have better odds at strengthening weapons than the NPCs of Urbus—in fact, he couldn't run a business without them—which was why the three-horned man had entrusted him with his beloved sword.

Unfortunately, however, weapon augmenting in *SAO* was not a surefire success unless one's skill proficiency was quite high. With a failure rate of 30 percent, there was a 9 percent chance of failing twice in a row and a 3 percent chance of three failures. Even the tragic outcome of four consecutive failed attempts had a 0.8 chance of occurring.

The terrifying thing was that in a vast online RPG world, these odds were just high enough to happen every now and then. I played games before this that featured rare items with drop rates like 0.01 percent that made you want to scream, "You're joking!" And yet plenty of lucky players wound up with them. I prayed that such cruelly rare items did not exist in *SAO*, but a part of me knew they must and that I would spend days and days in the dungeons looking for them...

"What's all the ruckus about?" someone muttered in my ear, startling me out of my thoughts.

It was a slender fencer. She wore a white leather tunic, pale green leather tights, and a silver breastplate. Her facial features were so pristine and graceful that you might wonder how an elf wandered into the world of Aincrad, but the crude gray wool cape from her head to her waist ruined that effect.

But she didn't have much of a choice. If she'd taken off the cape and let her luscious brown hair and elven beauty catch the sun, she'd never escape the attention of the crowds again.

I took a deep breath to calm my head and responded to this person I might actually call a "friend"…one of the very few I had in this world.

"Well, the guy with the horned helmet wanted the other one to power up his…"

At this point I realized that I, like her, was in disguise. I didn't want to believe that my nondescript costume of plain leather armor and a yellow-and-blue striped bandanna was that easy to see through. Perhaps I ought to pretend that I did not know her.

"Er, well…have we met before?"

The look I got in response was like twin rapier thrusts burning holes through the center of my face.

"Met? Why, I believe we've shared meals and been in a party together."

"…Oh…Now I remember, of course. I believe I lent you the use of my bath—"

Thunk. The sharp heel of her Hornet Boots slammed down on the top of my right foot. A piece of my memory disintegrated.

I cleared my throat, pinched the edge of her hood, and walked her a few yards away from the crowd so we could have a proper conversation.

"H-hi, Asuna. Long time no see…if two days counts."

"Good afternoon, Mr. Kirito."

Two days ago, when I'd met her on the front line, I claimed that there was no need for formality between avatars. But as this was her first VR game, she seemed to have difficulty getting over that. And when I'd offered to call her "Miss Asuna" in return, she said it was a pain in the neck and totally unnecessary. I didn't understand women.

At any rate, once the pleasantries had been peacefully exchanged, I turned back to the unpleasantness with the blacksmith and gave her a brief explanation.

"It seems the guy in the three-horned helmet asked the blacksmith to strengthen his weapon, but the process failed four times in a row, returning it back to a plus-zero state. So he's furious about it—which I can understand. I mean, four in a row…"

Asuna the fencer, the fastest and most coolheaded player I knew in Aincrad (I'd add "most beautiful," but I didn't want to cross the line of my personal harassment code) shrugged her shoulders and said, "The one who asked the other had to be aware of the possibility of failure. And doesn't the blacksmith have the rates of success for different weapons posted? Plus, it says that if he fails, he'll only charge the cost of the upgrade materials, and not the labor."

"Uh, really? That's quite considerate," I muttered, recalling the image of the short blacksmith bowing and scraping repeatedly. Forty percent of my sympathy had been for the three-horned man whose weapon had been ruined, but now it dropped to closer to twenty.

"I'm guessing that after the first failure, the blood rushed to his head, so he kept demanding another attempt to make it up. Losing your self-control and paying a terrible price for it is a constant feature of any form of gambling…"

"That almost sounded like it had personal experience behind it."

"N-no, just a common-sense observation."

I avoided looking at her, sensing that telling her I'd lost all of my money at the seventh-floor monster coliseum during the beta test was not going to win me any points. Asuna gave me a piercing look for several seconds before mercifully returning to the topic at hand.

"Well…I can't say I don't feel a little sorry for him, but that kind of rage doesn't seem necessary. He can just save up the money for another attempt."

"Um…well, it's not that simple."

"What do you mean?" she asked. I jabbed a thumb at the Anneal Blade +6 strapped over my back.

"The three-horned guy's sword is an Anneal Blade, just like mine. He must have gone through that terrible quest on the first floor to get it, too. On top of that, he'd gone to the trouble of having an NPC bump it up to plus four. That's not too hard to reach. But once you get to plus five, the odds really start to drop—that's why he had a player blacksmith try it. But the first attempt failed, so now it's back to plus three. He asks for another attempt, hoping to get it back to where he started, but it fails again, down to plus two. Then the process repeats. The third and fourth attempts fail, so now he ends back at zero."

"But…there's no way to fall further from zero. Can't he just try to get it up to plus five again…?"

At this point, Asuna seemed to understand where I was going with this. Her hazel eyes widened in the shade of her hood. "Oh…there's a maximum limit to attempts. And what's the limit for an Anneal Blade?"

"Eight times. He got four successes and four failures, which put him at even and used up all his attempts. That sword can't be smithed anymore."

It was the trickiest part of *SAO*'s weapon upgrading system. Every piece of equipment that could be powered up had a preset number of possible attempts. It wasn't the maximum level you could reach with the weapon, but the number of *attempts*. For example, a Small Sword, the starting weapon at the beginning of the game, only had a single potential attempt. If the process failed, that sword could never be a Small Sword +1.

Even worse, the success rate could actually be affected by the effort of the owner. Obviously, finding the best blacksmith possible was a major part of that—and ultimately, one could master the Blacksmithing skill themselves, though at this point in the game, it was an unrealistic option. One could also increase the chances of success through better materials, either in quality or quantity.

Most player blacksmiths set their upgrading fees based on a success rate of around 70 percent. If the client wanted a better chance, they could pay extra to have more crafting materials added, or simply provide them directly to the blacksmith.

Which meant the biggest fault of the three-horned man was that he'd gotten worked up and gambled on more attempts. He should have taken a deep breath after the first failure, then paid (or provided) extra to improve his chances the next time. That would likely have prevented his tragedy of an Anneal Blade +0 with no remaining attempts.

"I see...Well, I can understand why he'd be upset. Just a little."

I nodded in agreement and offered a moment of silence to the fateful blade. Suddenly, the screaming man ceased his rage. Two of his friends had raced over and put their hands on his shoulders, offering support.

"C'mon, Rufiol, it's gonna be okay. We'll help you try the Anneal Blade quest again."

"It'll only take a week to get it back, then we can push it all the way up to plus eight."

Wow, now it takes three players a week to get it? Glad I got mine early, I thought. *And you guys...take care of your pal. Don't let him gamble it away again.*

Rufiol seemed to have recovered his cool. He trudged off out of the plaza, shoulders slumped.

The blacksmith, who'd withstood the insults in silence the entire time, finally spoke up.

"Um...I'm truly sorry about this. I'll try much harder next time, I swear...I mean, not that you'd want to bring me again..."

Rufiol stopped and looked back at the blacksmith. When he spoke again, it was in an entirely different voice.

"...It's not your fault. I'm...I'm sorry for ripping you apart."

"No. I failed at my job..."

I looked closer at the blacksmith, who was still bowing, hands clasped in front of his leather apron. He was quite young, still in his teens. His slightly drooping eyes and plain parted bangs made him look, I hated to admit, like a perfectly typical crafter. A little shorter and thicker, and he'd be the perfect dwarf. Or perhaps a gnome—he didn't have the beard.

The blacksmith stepped forward and bowed deeply yet again.

"Um, I know it's nothing in return...but do you think I could buy back your spent plus zero Anneal Blade for 8,000 col?"

The onlookers murmured in surprise, and even I grunted at the offer.

The current market price for a fresh new Anneal Blade +0 was about sixteen thousand col. So the offer was only half that, but Rufiol's weapon was "spent," fresh out of upgrade attempts. The market price for a weapon like *that* was probably halved again, down to four thousand col. It was an extremely generous offer.

Rufiol and his two friends were stunned, but after a moment's conferral, they all nodded.

The incident was over. The three partners and the crowd of onlookers were gone, and the rhythmic clanging of the blacksmith's hammer echoed through the plaza. The blacksmith—not dwarf—was producing a weapon on his anvil.

Asuna and I took a seat on the bench across the circular plaza, listening to the hammering.

Normally, I wouldn't spend this much time here—I'd get my business done and zip back outside of the Urbus town limits. There were two reasons my plans had changed. For one, the presence of Asuna, one of the few people in Aincrad who wouldn't call me a dirty beater, meant that I could actually have a conversation and practice my increasingly rusty Japanese. The other reason was on my back: I'd come to power up my Anneal Blade +6.

I'd overhead someone talking about a talented player blacksmith setting up shop in the east plaza of Urbus over in the small town of Marome just yesterday. I'd been thinking it was about time to give that +7 a shot, so I got the crafting materials in order and changed into my disguise for a trip into Urbus. The previous scene had given me pause, however.

In truth, it would be as easy as standing up and walking over to the dwa—er, blacksmith, and asking him for an upgrade. We'd never met before, and I doubted he would say, "My hammer isn't meant to work on the swords of a dirty beater!"

But the prior squabble had put some pressure onto my decision. Another Anneal Blade had gone from +4 to +0 despite a 70 percent success rate. It was mathematically possible, but a tragedy of the highest order for such a fine weapon. If the same fate befell my attempt, I might not lose my cool the same way, but I'd definitely be sulking in my inn room for a good three days.

Something told me that embarking upon my attempt with this pessimistic view would ensure that I wound up with an Anneal Blade +5. Then I'd panic, try again without providing more materials, and finish with a +4. There was no logical reason for my suspicion, but the gamble of attempted upgrades in MMOs was a topic that often defied logic…

"…Well?"

I looked over at the questioning voice, still lost in thought. "Huh? What?"

"Don't play dumb with me. Why did you force me to sit here?" Asuna glared at me.

"Er, um, oh, right. Sorry, just thinking…"

"Thinking? Weren't you coming here to have that blacksmith work on your weapon, Kirito?"

"Um, h-how can you tell?" I asked, startled. She shot me an exasperated look.

"When we were in Marome two nights ago, you said you were hunting Red Spotted Beetles in the rocky mountains to the east. That must have been for one-handed sword upgrading materials."

"Oh...yeah," I sighed.

"What was that reaction for?"

"Um...I just can't believe I'm hearing this from the girl who didn't know how to read her party companions' names just four days ago...in a good way! I'm not being sarcastic."

"..."

Apparently Asuna believed my sincerity, as her expression softened and she murmured, "I *have* been studying a lot."

For some reason, this admission made me happy. I nodded excitedly. "That's great, really. In an MMO, knowledge makes all the difference when it comes to getting results. Anything you want to know, just ask. I was a former tester, after all, so I know everything from the items sold in towns up to the tenth floor to the different sounds of all the mobs..."

At this point, I realized the terrible mistake I was making.

Just as I said, I was a former beta tester. But at the same time, I'd taken on the persona of a dirty beater who hoarded information and used it solely for his own benefit. Many other high-level players despised me for this, not least of whom were the party members of the fallen knight Diavel. Even with the leather armor and bandanna, someone who knew me would recognize my face close up, and they would assume that Asuna, sitting on the bench next to me, must be my partner. It was incredibly reckless of me to be talking about this in a crowded public place.

"Uh...s-sorry, just remembered something I need to do," I excused myself clumsily, preparing to stand and rush off.

The fencer stopped my shoulder with the lightest tap of her index finger and spoke in a low but firm voice.

"It's crazy and arrogant of you to think you can bear the burden of all the hatred and jealousy toward the former testers... but that was your choice, so I won't say anything more on the subject. But I also wish you'd respect my decision as well. I don't care what other people think. If I didn't want people to think that I was your friend...your companion, I wouldn't have spoken to you."

"......Aw, geez. You can see right through me," I muttered and sat back down on the bench.

She had identified all my motives, from calling myself a beater at the boss chamber to my attempt to get up and flee just seconds ago. No use trying to hide now. I raised my hands in brief surrender and she grinned slightly beneath her deep hood.

"If you're a pro at Aincrad, then my all-girls' academy upbringing makes me a pro at mental battles. As if I couldn't read your avatar's face like a page in a book."

"W-well...I'm sorry to have doubted you..."

"So be honest. Why are you hesitating on upgrading your weapon? I was coming here to do the very same thing, in fact."

"Wha...?"

I looked down at Asuna's fragile blade in surprise. Her green-hilted rapier in its ivory scabbard was called the Wind Fleuret. I'd looted that sword from a monster and given it to her as an upgrade when we first formed our party, preparing for the first-floor boss fight. It was a fairly rare item, with the potential to serve admirably until midway through the third floor if it was upgraded properly.

"Is that plus four right now?" I asked. She nodded. "Did you bring your own upgrade mats? How many?"

"Umm...I have four Steel Planks and twelve Windwasp Needles."

"Wow, nice work. But..." I did some mental calculation and groaned, "Hmm, but that means the chance of going to plus five is only a bit over eighty percent."

"Aren't those good odds to risk?"

"Normally, sure. But after what we just saw..."

I looked back across the plaza at the dwarfish blacksmith, rhythmically pounding away. Asuna looked at him as well and shrugged.

"The odds of a coin turning up heads is always fifty percent, no matter what happened the last time. What effect does the last person's consecutive failure have on you or me trying our hand?"

"Well…nothing…but…"

I couldn't come up with a good answer, but my mind was racing. Clearly, Asuna was a person of logic and reason, and she wouldn't accept my assertion that there were streaks and mojo when it came to gambling. Even my left brain knew that there was no proof behind the "bad feeling" I was getting.

But on the other hand, my right brain was screaming danger. It claimed that whether Anneal Blade or Wind Fleuret, the next weapon to be given to that blacksmith, regardless of extra boosts and bonuses, would end in failure.

"Listen, Asuna." I turned my body to face her directly and put the gravest possible tone in my voice.

"Wh-what?"

"You like ninety percent better than eighty percent, right?"

"…Well, sure, but—"

"You like ninety-five percent better than ninety percent, right?"

"…Well, sure, but—"

"Then don't compromise. If you already put in the work to get these materials, why not give it one more round and get those odds up to ninety-five?"

"……"

She gave me a very skeptical gaze for several long seconds, then beat her long eyelashes slowly, as though realizing something.

"Yes, it's true that I hate compromising. But I hate people who are all talk and no walk just as much."

"…Huh?"

"Since you're so dead-set on me pursuing perfection, I assume you're going to lend me a hand, Kirito. The drop rate on Wind-wasp Needles is only eight percent, after all."

"……Huh?"

"Now that that's settled, let's go hunting. I think the two of us together can take down about a hundred before nightfall."

"......... Huh?"

Asuna patted my shoulder and stood up, then squinted slightly, her shapely eyebrows knitting together, and delivered the finishing blow.

"Oh, and if we're going to hunt together, you must take off that ugly bandanna. It looks absolutely hideous on you."

2

BECAUSE OF THE "SWORD ARTS" THAT WERE THE greatest selling point of *SAO*, the game had far more humanoid monster types than any other MMORPG. This tendency didn't come into focus until the next floor, however, so there was still a wide variety of nonhuman monsters on the first and second floors. The animal and plant mobs that couldn't use sword skills were much easier for newbies to deal with, but there were exceptions, of course.

Most notable of those were monsters with dangerous side effects like paralyzing toxins and corrosive acid, but aside from that, flying mobs were surprisingly tricky. After all, there was no magic in *SAO*. The only means of attacking targets at a distance was throwing knives, and they were more like a complementary weapon, not a primary source of damage.

I had to admit there was something cool about the idea of sinking all my time into the Throwing Knife skill and terrorizing all the flying mobs, but I didn't have the willpower to dedicate to such an extreme build now that the game was deadly. On top of that, *SAO*'s throwing weapons all had a finite amount, so if you ran out of knives in the midst of battle, tragedy awaited.

Therefore, when Asuna the fencer called upon—more like forced—me to help her hunt the flying Windwasps in the western zone of the second floor, with our very limited weapon range, there was only one thought on my mind.

Ugh, this is gonna be such a pain in the ass.

Once we left the west gate of Urbus, I called up my equipment mannequin and unequipped the yellow-and-blue-striped bandanna. I looked up at the long black bangs hanging below my eyebrows and sighed in relief. My original *SAO* avatar had parted hair in an attempt to escape those loose bangs, but now that I'd been living with this for a month, it was the most comfortable and familiar look for me.

Asuna watched me removing my costume and snorted. "I can't believe you thought putting on one stupid bandanna made for a disguise. It won't work unless you hide your entire face or use face paint."

"*Urgh...*"

The latter term sent a painful shock through my memory.

My face *had* been covered in thick black paint until two nights before. And it wasn't a cool tribal pattern on the cheeks or a reverse cross on my forehead. No, it was something much, much more embarrassing—I thought. I didn't have the nerve to look for myself. The only human player who saw me described me as "Kiriemon," after the famous robotic cat character.

My face was marked against my will the moment I accepted a certain quest, and the marks would not come off until I completed that quest. I worked myself to the bone, tears in my eyes, to finish it up after three nights, when the whiskered old martial arts master finally erased the markings. There were no words to describe the joy and satisfaction of that moment. I was so happy, I even forgave him for the fact that cleaning them off was as simple as a wipe of the light brown rag from his robe pocket.

For that reason, I'd lost a good fifty hours of forward advancement since the opening of the second floor. I rushed to the village of Marome, the current front line of player progress, where I met Asuna for the first time since the boss fight.

She, of course, had no idea why I would give that odd reaction to her innocent suggestion, and stared at me suspiciously. I cleared my throat in a hurry.

"Ah, um, g-good point. Maybe I should get one of those hooded capes for myself the next time I go to Urbus. Where did you buy yours?"

"From an NPC in the western market of the Town of Begi…" She trailed off, and I felt flames pouring from her eyes. "You'd better not buy the same thing! Then people will think we're a coup…a fixed party! Wear a burlap sack if you want to hide your face!"

Asuna turned her head away in a blinding huff, opened her menu and tapped the equipment figure. The plain gray wool cape sparkled briefly and vanished, and her long, straight hair glimmered in the afternoon sun.

It was the first time I'd seen her full face in four days, not since the battle against Illfang the Kobold Lord, and it was indescribably beautiful. It almost made me wonder if Akihiko Kayaba, the ruler of our new world, had made one careless mistake and left her face in its original avatar form—but if I ever said that aloud, she'd pound me.

Marome was to the southeast of Urbus, so the southwest road was empty of adventurers. If it weren't for the whole game-of-death thing, being able to stroll with a beautiful girl in the midst of a video game would be the greatest gift God could give any teenage boy. Even if we were only going to farm wasps for a royal-pain-in-the-ass mission.

"People might confuse me for a PKer if I wear a burlap sack. Can I at least get the same cape in a different color?"

"Negative!"

"…Yes, ma'am."

I brought up my equipment mannequin again, removed the leather armor disguise and put on the pitch-black Coat of Midnight I'd looted from the boss.

Asuna seemed about to say something as she watched the long

hem of the coat flap in the wind, but when our eyes met, she turned away in a huff. I started to wonder why I was even helping her gather upgrading materials, then remembered that it had been my own suggestion.

On the other hand, Windwasps were worth the trouble thanks to their experience value. It would be a good source of points before dinner. Plus, no doubt Asuna would be generous enough to pay for dinner in place of her lodging fee. Sure, she would.

The path ahead took us through a narrow ravine that split the fields of grazing oxen into north and south. Through that canyon was where we'd find the wasps.

"As I'm sure you already know, given that you've hunted a fair number of them, the wasps' stingers have a two- or three-second stun effect. Let's keep in mind that if the other gets stunned, we should immediately go in and take over for them."

"Got it," she said, then added, "If you go too far south, you'll run into Jagged Worms, so watch out for that."

"G…got it."

Belatedly, I recalled that bit of info from the beta test.

We crossed the natural stone bridge that spanned the thirty-foot gorge, nervous despite its reasonable width, and sighed in relief once we were across.

"I wonder what would happen if we fell off," Asuna asked. I shrugged my shoulders.

"I doubt you'd die if you're over level five. But the path out of the ravine is way to the south, and there's plenty of slimy monsters down there, so it'd take a while to get out."

"Oh."

I thought I detected something other than relief in her face. As though sensing my suspicion, she turned away toward the valley and said, "I was just thinking, if we go up against a boss monster, scouting it out and leveling up, creating a strategy and all that, and still lose, that's one thing. But dying because you were careless and fell from a tall height would really suck."

"Yeah. In a normal MMO, dying from a fall would be a funny

story…but not here," I murmured. "But do you even think there's a way of dying in the real world that might make you say, 'Well, I did my best, so I have no regrets'? Whether it's a disease or an accident, I think all you'd be left with is sadness and frustration…I mean, if there's any way to die in Aincrad and feel satisfied that you did what you needed to, it would have to be…"

Sadly, my fourteen-year-old-nerd's vocabulary failed me; my fingers wriggled and my mouth opened and closed without a sound. Asuna mercilessly watched the entire sorry display, then gave a brief answer.

"Perhaps that wouldn't be so bad. Not that I'm eager to find out what that's like any time soon."

"Y-yeah."

"In which case, we ought to put our best effort into defeating the second-floor boss. And helping me power up my weapon is part of that process."

"Y…yeah."

"Since we're both in agreement, let's get started. A hundred in two hours!"

Asuna drew her rapier and headed in the opposite direction of the stone bridge—a small basin lined with low trees.

One hundred wasps in two hours. One every seventy-two seconds? For real?

All I could summon in response was a halfhearted grunt of agreement.

The Windwasps were black with green stripes and a foot and a half long, easily making them larger than any insects on earth, but among the smallest monsters found on Aincrad. Their HP and attack values were fairly low for second-floor mobs.

However, it was very difficult to suppress the brain's primitive signal to flee when a bee larger than your head approached, brandishing a stinger the size of an ice pick. Hunting the wasps therefore became an exercise in mastering one's instincts.

It was for this reason that I'd been concerned about Asuna, who did not seem to take kindly to bugs. However—

"*Haah!*"

Her rapier skill Linear burned a silver line through space, unerringly piercing the weak abdomen band of a wasp. It screeched metallically and burst into polygonal shards. A list of experience and col rewards appeared before my eyes automatically for being in her party.

"Twenty-four," she shouted, looking over with what I suspected to be confident glee in her eyes. My juices of rivalry energized, I turned toward a fresh new wasp to my right.

It had spawned with me inside of its aggro range, so as soon as the curved compound eyes spotted me, it reared up high. The wasp stopped about five yards off the ground, then buzzed down with a heavy, stomach-churning vibration. If the wasp's body stayed straight, it would lunge for a bite attack, and if it curved like a hinge, it would use its poison stinger. That was the first step to dealing with the creatures, but even after my considerable beta experience with these and the more powerful Storm Hornets, I couldn't help but recoil in fear when they lunged.

This time, I withstood the terror and noticed the bee had its abdomen exposed, signaling a stinger attack. I stood my ground.

The wasp charged right before me, then briefly stopped to hover again. The massive poisoned barb was glowing with a faint yellow light. I waited until that moment, then jumped backward. The stinger shot forward with a mechanical clank but found no purchase.

Once the wasp missed, it would fall under a delay effect for a second and a half. Without missing a beat, I unleashed Vertical Arc, a two-part sword skill. The blade carved out a V shape and hammered the wasp with satisfying sound effects. The monster's HP gauge fell nearly 60 percent.

Fresh out of its delay, the wasp flew up high again. It spun around and began another dive. This time, it hurtled body first, the sign of a bite attack. I sidestepped rather than waiting for the attack, then raced after the bee when it passed by. It stopped and briefly hovered before its next turn, more than enough for me to catch it with a clean diagonal Slant.

One more Vertical Arc would finish off the monster, but its cooldown icon was still lit at the bottom of my view. A follow-up Slant could do the job if I hit its weak point, but from behind, the wasp's large wings were in the way. If I didn't strike a critical hit, its HP bar would still have a bit left. I clicked my tongue in disappointment and launched a regular swing attack before the wasp's delay wore off. Fortunately, I hit it before its bite started, reducing the wasp to pieces of blue glass.

"Twenty-two!" I yelled, looking around for a fresh opponent.

The fact that I was losing despite the edge in level and equipment was thanks to Asuna's high rate of critical hits—in other words, she was so accurate that she could hit the wasps in their weak point every single time.

My Vertical Arc did 60 percent of a wasp's life bar with a normal hit, whereas Asuna's Linear did just over fifty for a critical blow. But because that move was a basic skill, it had a very brief cooldown time, meaning she could use it every single time the wasp was vulnerable.

I could try to follow her lead and aim for crits with my basic attacks like Slant and Horizontal, but I just didn't have the confidence in my own accuracy. If I had an excuse, it was that my Anneal Blade +6 was specced "3S3D," meaning three points to sharpness, three to durability. On the other hand, Asuna's Wind Fleuret +4 was 3A1D, meaning three points to accuracy, one to durability. That gave her an excellent bonus to critical hits, no doubt.

But even taking that into account, an extremely high level of player skill and calm concentration was necessary to land every single hit as a critical attack—to say nothing of experience.

I suspected that Asuna had spent a considerable amount of time fighting these giant wasps since reaching the second floor. Much of that had to do with farming the materials to upgrade her

Wind Fleuret, but I thought there was something bigger behind that. It was about strengthening herself as a player, not just her stats. If she learned to jab the weak points of the nimble flying enemies, landbound monsters would seem slow as molasses in comparison.

I recalled what Asuna said to me on our first encounter deep within the first-floor labyrinth.

We're all going to die anyway. The only difference is when and where, sooner...or later.

Her eyes had shone with a dim light that saw not hope but despair at the end of her battle. That she was able to strive in search of true strength now filled me with joy. I could only hope that someday she'd stand atop the entire population, a shining example and beacon of light to all.

But having said that...I was not about to lose our competition to see who could kill fifty wasps first.

Before we began battle, Asuna had proposed a chilling bet. She would provide the dinner for tonight, but whoever could hunt fifty wasps first would also get a free dessert, courtesy of the loser.

I'd accepted the challenge without thinking, and it wasn't until after we started that I realized what she was after. One of the NPC restaurants in Urbus sold a shortcake with an astonishing amount of sweet cream made from giant cow's milk, the local delicacy. And it was delicious—enough to make one forget about my favorite black bread with cream from the first floor. It was also expensive—enough to use the majority of the col I'd earn in the hunt.

That's what Asuna was after. If she bought the meal and I bought the dessert, I'd come out way, way behind. I had no choice but to emerge victorious!

"*Raaahh!!*"

I raced after the freshest new wasp, a bellow ripping through my lungs.

But the next moment, all the wind went out of my sails when I heard her call out, "Twenty-five!"

A three-point margin. That was bad news at the halfway mark. If we both continued at this pace, she'd pull away and leave me in the dust. If I couldn't find a way to kill them in two moves like Asuna, I would never make up the difference.

I didn't have any other choice.

After turning back to ensure that Asuna was looking the other way, I gave my target an appraising stare.

The black-and-green wasp hovered high, then plunged down at me. Its body was bent, the gleaming stinger extended.

I followed the proper pattern, stopping in my tracks and inviting the enemy to strike and miss before employing a Vertical Arc. Two pleasing slashes rang out, but as usual, they only did 60 percent of its health. If the wasp pulled away, I couldn't finish it off in two moves, short of a lucky critical hit.

"......!!"

I clenched my left fist with a silent scream.

Normally, I'd suffer a brief delaying effect at the end of my sword skill, but my left fist began glowing with a red visual effect when I held it to my side. Largely automatically, my body jutted forward and pounded the wasp, which was already in a knock-back state from the sword attack.

The meaty thud that resulted was unlike the sound of any blade. My fist shot forward and caught the wasp in its round, bulging abdomen: Flash Blow, a basic Martial Arts skill. The wasp lost another 20 percent of its HP.

Poised again, the wasp zipped upward and out of reach. Its second dive was another stinger lunge. I had already recovered from my delay, and I easily evaded the wasp and dispatched it with a simple Slant. The time it took to defeat this wasp was nearly the same as two hits.

At this point, depending on how quickly I could find the next monster, I had a chance. I had a chance.

Eyes wide, I scanned for the formation of a polygonal blob that signaled a new monster being generated into the environment, and raced after it.

* * *

One hour later, I sat on the grass, fifty wasps killed, burnt to a crisp by sheer exhaustion. Asuna walked over and patted me on the shoulder.

"Nice work, Kirito."

There wasn't a hint of fatigue in her voice. She circled around the front and smiled. "Well, let's go back to Urbus for our dinner. And when you buy me dessert, I'd like to hear all about that bizarre punching skill you were using."

"......"

I had no response. The beautiful fencer leaned in for the critical finish.

"I can't wait to finally try that cake. A win's a win, even if it was only by one point. A boy must keep his promises, after all."

5

JUST AS WE ARRIVED BACK AT URBUS, BELLS RANG crisp and clear from all over the town, signaling the arrival of night. It was a calm, slow melody with a hint of longing. Seven o'clock was about the time for the players out adventuring in the wilderness to make their way back home.

In the MMORPGs I'd played before *SAO*, seven o'clock was just when the game was getting going. People would begin to log in to the server around then, hitting peak traffic at about ten, with the hardiest of souls lasting all through the night until morning.

As a student of mandatory schooling age, I always logged out by two in the morning at the latest. I remembered looking on in jealousy at those who were preparing to race out for yet another round of hunting.

Ironically, now that all I wanted was to be able to go *back* to school, I could stay out well past two, until five or eight o'clock in the morning if I chose. And yet once it got dark outside, I always found my way back to town.

Many times, it was just to eat dinner and fill up on supplies before trudging out for another round of adventures until sunrise—the night I met Asuna in the labyrinth was just such an occasion. But every time I saw that red, sinking sun through the outer perimeter of Aincrad, the sky changing from purple to navy blue, I couldn't sit still. I had to walk back to civilization.

of that this urge was not solely in my own mind, there a number of players walking the main street of Urbus, all wearing smiles of relief. Lively cheers erupted from the restaurants and bars on the sides of the street, with the occasional toast or song dedicated to another day of survival.

This same scene occurred at the towns and villages of the first floor. But it had been quite a while since I'd heard such unreserved laughter—perhaps never—since we'd been trapped in Aincrad.

"This is the first time I've come back to Urbus at this time of day. Is it always like this? Or is today a special day?" I asked Asuna. December 8 wasn't a holiday. She shot me a quizzical look, her beauty hidden beneath the wool cape once again.

"Both Urbus and Marome have been like this for several days. Have you been in hiding both day and night?"

"Um…well…"

She was probably asking if I really cared that much about being seen. As a matter of fact, I couldn't visit Urbus even if I wanted to. If I was going to tell her about my Martial Arts skill over dinner, I'd eventually get to this topic, but it was not something that could be summed up briefly.

"You could say I was hiding. Or maybe I wasn't," I stammered. Asuna's stare grew even more incredulous.

"Didn't I tell you you're being paranoid? We've passed by dozens of people so far, you're not in disguise, and not a single one has bothered you in the least."

She was correct: My awesome striped bandanna was not on display. My face and hair were just like normal, though the black coat was stashed away, too. But I had a feeling that it was not a case of players recognizing me as "Kirito the Beater" and choosing to leave me alone, but that they were simply too full of relief and anticipation of dinner to bother spending any time examining one gloomy-looking swordsman out of many.

I coughed lightly, subtly maneuvering myself to use Asuna as cover.

"Ahem…w-well, perhaps. Anyway, back to the topic—is this place always this lively at night? For no particular reason?"

"Oh, I'm sure there's a reason."

I shut my mouth. She shot me another look.

"…In fact, you're responsible for about three-quarters of that reason."

"Huh? M-me?!" I sputtered. She sighed in total exasperation.

"Look…Isn't it obvious why everyone is smiling and laughing? It's because we're on the second floor."

"…Which means?"

"It wasn't a riddle. Everyone was much more nervous for the entire month we were trapped on the first floor. They were terrified that they might never see the real world again. I was one of them. But then the boss raid came together, we won on the first try, and opened up the second floor. Everyone realized that maybe we *can* beat this thing. That's why they're smiling. I'm just saying…we wouldn't be seeing this phenomenon if a certain someone hadn't stood strong during that battle."

"……"

Finally I understood the point Asuna was making, but I was no closer to knowing how to react to that. I coughed again and grasped for something to say.

"Uh, I g-guess. Well, if you ask me, that certain someone did a good enough job to deserve a free shortcake," I finished hopefully.

"That was that; this is this!"

It was worth a shot.

We turned onto a narrow path leading north from the east-west main street, then made another right and a left to reach the restaurant.

I knew about this establishment (and its infamous shortcake) from my tireless exploration of Urbus during the beta test, so I was a bit surprised that Asuna knew about it after just a few days on the second floor. We took a table near the back and ordered our food, at which point I decide to ask her how she knew.

"So let me guess, Asuna: the smell of the sweet cream—"

Those brown eyes went sharp beneath her hood. I instantly changed course.

"—did *not* guide you here. So was it coincidence? It's got a small storefront with a tiny sign. I think it would be difficult to pick this place out at random."

There wasn't anything to be lost by wandering into a business at random in Aincrad, as there were no rip-off bars that bullied you into paying up just for entering (as far as I knew), but there were some that automatically initiated an event-type quest when you walked in the door. There was no danger to one's HP within town (again, as far as I knew), but such events might come off as a nasty surprise to someone not familiar with MMOs. I figured Asuna was not the type of person to appreciate or desire unexpected thrills, but her answer surprised me.

"I asked Argo if there were any low-traffic NPC restaurants in Urbus and bought the answer from her."

Sure enough, there was no one else in the restaurant. Asuna opened her menu and unequipped the cape, letting her hair swing free with a sigh.

"Oh...I see. That makes sense..."

On the inside, I broke out into a cold sweat. I was the one who brought Asuna and Argo together. Technically, it was when Asuna borrowed the use of my bath at the farmhouse near Tolbana, and Argo had visited with perfect timing. Despite my best efforts, they ran into each other in the bathroom, much to Asuna's shock. She screamed and ran out into the main room, where I was sitting—

"You're not remembering something you shouldn't, are you? If so, I might need two cakes instead of one."

"No, not remembering a thing," I replied instantly, vigorously shaking my head clear. "Anyway, Argo might be quick and accurate with your information, but be careful around her. There's no entry for 'client confidentiality' in her dictionary."

"Meaning...I could ask her to sell me all the information she has about you?"

It was too late to regret my slip of the tongue now.

"W-well, yeah...maybe...but it'll cost you a lot. I'm sure the whole bundle would cost you at least three thousand col."

"That's actually not as much as I expected. I bet I could raise that amount without much trouble..."

"N-n-no! I'd buy all of yours in return! After all, she saw your—"

I shut my mouth so hard my teeth clicked. She grinned at me.

"My what?"

"Umm, er...what I meant to say is..."

At that moment, a miracle occurred and the NPC waiter returned with dishes of food, saving me from certain catastrophe.

The menu was simple salad, stew, and bread, but this was the finest to be found on the second floor. Asuna's eyebrows emitted a threatening aura as we ate, but it disappeared by the time the long-awaited dessert arrived.

As we agreed, Asuna paid for the dinner, while the cost of the dessert came from my own wallet. The terrifying thing was the cost of that one dish easily exceeded the three-piece dinner for two. But given that I'd busted out my secret Martial Arts skill and still lost the bet, I wasn't in any position to complain. My only option was to rue the lack of my own skill.

The triumphant winner, seemingly oblivious to my inner turmoil, looked at the green plate piled high with a mountain of cream, her eyes sparkling.

"Oh my gosh! Argo's info said you just *have* to try the Tremble Shortcake once. I can't believe the moment has finally come!"

The "tremble" in the name was clearly derived from the Trembling Cows, the female versions of the terrifyingly huge oxen that roamed the second floor. The cows were nearly twice the size of the oxen, practically bosses in their own right. The cream piled atop the shortcake came from their milk (supposedly), but now was not the time to mention that.

There was another angle to the "trembling" moniker, however: the cream was piled so high atop the dish that it shook on its own. The piece was a triangular slice from a full-size round cake, seven inches to a side, three inches tall, about sixty degrees of the whole.

That meant the total volume of the cake was $(7 \times 7 \times 3.14 \times 3) / 6$... totaling seventy-seven cubic inches of pure heaven. There had to be almost an entire quart of cream on that thing.

"So...what about this cake qualifies as 'short'?" I whined.

Asuna picked up the large fork that came with the cake and said, "You don't know? It's not called shortcake because it's short in stature."

"Why, then? Was it invented by a legendary big-league shortstop?"

She effortlessly ignored my killer joke. "It's because the crispy texture of the cake is achieved through shortening. In America, they use a tough, crispy biscuit-like cake as the base, but we have soft sponge cake in Japan, so it's not really accurate to the original meaning. Let's see which kind this is..."

She put her fork to the top of the triangular wedge and carved out a good five cubic inches, exposing golden sponge cake. It was a four-layer cake, going sponge, strawberries and cream, sponge, strawberries and cream. The top of the cake, of course, was covered in a stunning amount of strawberries—or more accurately, some kind of in-game fruit that resembled strawberries.

"So it's sponge cake. I like this style more, anyway," Asuna said. Her smile was so radiant that it was almost worth losing the bet and being forced to pay a massive dessert bill just to see it.

In truth, it didn't matter whether I came out ahead or behind. The fact that she'd gone from pale-faced despair in the depths of the labyrinth to a full-faced smile under these warm oil lamps was a very good thing, indeed.

If there was one very bad thing here, it was that there was only a single slice of cake on the table. I'd been planning to live dangerously and order two servings outright, but the price on the menu was like a bucket of ice water dumped over my enthusiasm.

I summoned up every last point of my Gentleman statistic and waved a magnanimous hand, smiling as naturally as I could. "Please, dig in. Don't mind me."

She smiled back. "Oh, I won't. Here goes."

Two seconds later, she cracked with laughter, then reached into the cutlery basket at the side of the table and handed me a fork. "I'm just kidding—I'm not that mean. You can have up to a third of it."

"…Um, thanks," I replied, a relieved smile on my face. On the inside, my brain was doing rapid calculations.

One-third means I can eat…twenty-seven and a half cubic inches of cake!

When we left the restaurant, the town was wreathed in the dark of night. Asuna sucked in a deep breath and let out a deep sigh of contentment.

"…That was good…"

I knew how she felt. That cake was probably the first honest dessert she'd tasted since we'd been trapped in this place. It was the same for me. I sighed happily as well and murmured, "It feels like that tasted even better than in the beta test…The way the cream melted in your mouth, the perfect level of sweetness that wasn't too heavy, but still satisfying…"

"Don't you think that's just your imagination? Would they really bother with such fine-tuning between the beta and the retail release?" she asked. I answered her skepticism with all seriousness.

"It wouldn't be that hard to update the data in the taste engine. Besides, even ignoring the difference in flavor, we didn't have *this* in the beta."

I pointed just below my HP bar, in the upper left portion of my view. There was a buff icon displayed that hadn't been there before, a four-leaf clover that signified an increased luck bonus.

That effect could only be gained by making an expensive offering at a church, equipping an accessory with that particular bonus, or consuming a special food item.

SAO kept its main stats exceedingly minimal, showing only values for strength and agility. However, there were a number of hidden stats affected by equipment properties, buffs and debuffs, even terrain effects. Luck was one of those stats, and a pretty important one—it affected resistance to poison and paralysis, the probability of weapon fumbling or tripping, even potentially the drop rate of rare items.

No doubt someone on the Argus development team had taken a look at the exorbitant price of the shortcake and decided that it was enough to warrant a bonus effect when the retail game launched. The effect would last for fifteen minutes. That would be a handy amount if eaten as a snack in the middle of a dungeon, but...

"Unfortunately, it's not enough time for us to make good use of it out in the fields," Asuna said, clearly following my line of thought. Even if we ran out searching for monsters, we'd barely find a handful before the buff wore off. Plus, the monsters around the outskirts of the town didn't drop any decent loot.

"Too bad...What a waste of a good buff."

I stared at the icon timer ticking away precious seconds, wracking my brain for a way to make good use of the bonus while it lasted.

We could get down on hands and knees in the street—coins and fragments of gems could be found on very rare occasions—but I didn't think Asuna would like that. We could gamble big at a casino, except that they didn't start showing up until the seventh floor. The more I pondered, the less of the effect remained. Wasn't there anything we could do to test our luck? I supposed I could turn to the fencer and ask if she'd go out with me, but I had a feeling the system's luck bonus had no bearing on my chances there...

Just as the steam was about to pour from my ears in frustration, I heard a sound.

It was the distant, rhythmic clanging of metal. *Clank, clank,* went the hammer.

"Ah…"

I snapped my fingers, finally having spotted a use for the twelve remaining minutes of good luck.

4

FIVE HOURS AFTER OUR LAST VISIT TO THE EASTERN plaza of Urbus, there were virtually no people wandering around. The only souls left were a few players standing around the NPC shop stalls that opened only at night, and two or three couples seated on benches. Of course, I hadn't brought Asuna here to sit on a bench and stare up at the bottom of the floor above in lieu of stargazing.

The short player was still there in the northeast corner, his small anvil and display case sitting atop the vendor's carpet. This was who I came to see: the blacksmith, likely the very first committed crafter since the start of *SAO*.

"Asuna, you met your quota of upgrading materials for your Wind Fleuret during our hunt, right?" I asked. She gave me a brief nod, her hooded cape back on.

"Yes. I'm a bit over, in fact, so I was planning to sell the rest and split the money with you."

"We can do that tomorrow. Why don't you try getting it to plus five right now?"

She looked upward, thinking it over. "I see. But does the good luck bonus affect weapon augmentation attempts? Isn't it the blacksmith who does the attempt, not me?"

"True. But we can't give the blacksmith some of that cake, for obvious reasons..."

Obvious meaning financial reasons. I shrugged and continued, "So I can't claim that the effect will work, but you are the weapon's owner, so maybe there's a boost to the chance of success. I'm certain it won't have a *negative* effect, so you might as well give it a shot."

The explanation had wound the buff timer down to seven minutes. Asuna nodded again and said, "All right. I was going to do it today, anyway."

She pulled the rapier from her waist and strode directly over to the blacksmith's display. I followed her without comment.

Up close, the diminutive blacksmith reminded me even more of a dwarf. He was short and squat, with a young, honest face. It really was a shame that he didn't have any whiskers. Hairstyles and facial hair were easily customizable with cosmetic items from NPC shops, so it seemed like he could draw in more customers by going with the classic look.

Asuna's voice broke me out of my pointless reverie.

"Good evening."

The blacksmith looked up from his anvil and gave a hasty bow.

"G-good evening. Welcome."

His voice was young and boyish, a far cry from that dwarven baritone. Every avatar's voice was sampled from the player's real-life voice, so while it seemed slightly different from his face, it didn't change his overall impression. As I suspected the first time I saw him, he might be a teenager close to my age.

Atop the signboard with his list of prices, it said Nezha's Smith Shop. Under Japanese rules, I supposed that to be pronounced "Nezuha"—it must have been his name. Sometimes it was difficult to tell with the alphabetized display of *Sword Art Online* player names. In our first-floor raid party, there was a trident user with the handle Hokkaiikura. After much deliberation, I concluded that it must be "Hokka Iikura," only to find out later that he called himself "Hokkai Ikura." *Nezha* itself could have some different pronunciation, but it seemed rude to ask him that on our first meeting.

At any rate, Nezha the blacksmith got to his feet and bowed again nervously.

"A-are you looking for a new weapon or here for maintenance?"

Asuna held up the rapier in both hands and answered, "I'd like you to power up my weapon. I want this Wind Fleuret plus four boosted to plus five, bonus to accuracy. I've got my own materials."

Nezha took one glance at the fleuret and his already-drooping brows looked even more troubled.

"A-all right... How many materials do you have...?"

"The upper limit. Four Steel Plates and twenty Windwasp Needles," she answered promptly. I recalculated everything in my head.

Equipment upgrade materials came in two categories: base materials and additional materials. Every attempt had a fixed, mandatory cost of base materials, but the additional materials were optional. The type and number of additional mats would have a wide effect on the chance of success.

Windwasp Needles were an accuracy-boosting additional material, which meant that they would increase her critical hit chance even more. If my memory was correct, a full twenty needles would max out the success rate of the upgrade attempt at 95 percent.

In other words, this should have been a very good thing for the player actually performing the upgrade attempt. The best customers of all would pay the blacksmith for the materials themselves, but it still had to be much better than failing with no additional mats.

And yet, Nezha looked terrified after hearing her answer. He was clearly unsettled by the request, but he couldn't find a reason to turn her down.

"All right. I'll take your weapon and materials." He bowed again.

Asuna thanked him and handed over the Wind Fleuret first. She then opened her window and materialized a sack in which she had placed all of the goods. She handed them over to the blacksmith through a trade window. Finally, she paid him the cost of the upgrading attempt.

At this point, the luck bonus effect had only four minutes left. That would not be much help in battle, but it was more than enough for a single weapon upgrade. Whether or not it actually worked in the way we hoped was another question, but that was one expensive piece of cake. Surely they could afford to bump us from 95 percent to 97.

I said a silent prayer to the god of the game system. Asuna took two steps back and sidled right next to me. She muttered, "Finger."

"Huh?"

"Stick out your finger."

Baffled, I lifted my left hand and extended the index finger. Asuna reached out with her brown leather gloves and gripped my finger in two of hers.

"Um ... what is this ... ?"

"If I do this, maybe your buff effect will be added to mine."

That seemed stupid. "W-well, in that case ... shouldn't you hold my entire hand ... ?"

I felt an icy stare emanating from her hood.

"Since when were things like that between us?"

Since when were they like this?! I wanted to yell, but the black-smith signaled that he had counted all of the materials and found them satisfactory, so I had to stay quiet and let her squeeze my fingertip, draining away all of my valuable good luck.

Asuna and I watched over the sign as Nezha the blacksmith turned and reached for a portable furnace set next to his work anvil. The number of ingots it could melt at once was very low, meaning he couldn't create large polearms or suits of metal armor, but it did the job for a simple streetside business.

On the furnace's pop-up menu, he switched it from creation mode to strengthening mode, then set the type of augmentation. Nezha then tossed Asuna's materials into the furnace.

Four thin sheets of steel and twenty sharp stingers turned red and burst into flame in seconds, and soon after, the furnace began burning with a blue flame that signified the accuracy stat. All preparations complete, he removed the Wind Fleuret from its sheath and set it down within the brazier-shaped furnace.

The blue flames enveloped the slender blade, and the entire weapon was soon glowing azure.

Nezha quickly pulled the rapier out and laid it on top of the anvil, then gripped his hammer and held it high.

At that exact moment, something prickled the hairs on the back of my neck. It was the same sensation that I'd felt earlier that afternoon, when I decided to hold off on upgrading my Anneal Blade +6.

I opened my mouth, preparing to yell, "Stop!" But the blacksmith's hammer had already made its first strike.

Clang! Clang! The rhythmic pounding echoed throughout the square, orange sparks flying from the anvil. Once the upgrade attempt had begun, there was no stopping it. Well, I *could* grab his hand and force him to stop, but that only guaranteed that it would end in failure. All I could do now was watch and pray for success.

There was no foundation for my panic; it was a manifestation of my inner worrywart, nothing more. All the materials had been invested, the blacksmith represented better odds than an NPC, and we had two players' worth of luck bonus. We couldn't possibly fail.

I held my breath and watched the hammer go up and down. Unlike with weapon creation, only ten strikes were necessary to upgrade a weapon. Six, seven—the hammer smacked the blue rapier at a steady pace. Eight, nine...ten.

The process complete, the rapier flashed brightly atop the anvil.

There's no way it can fail, I repeated to myself, gritting my teeth.

The result was far, far worse than my bad premonition could possibly have signaled.

With a fragile, even beautiful tinkling, the Wind Fleuret +4 crumbled into dust from tip to hilt.

*   *   *

No one reacted for several seconds, from Asuna, the sword's owner; to me, the emotional and luck bonus support; to Nezha the blacksmith, the one who had caused it to happen.

Perhaps if a single passerby had been watching, they might have broken the ice. But for now, all the three of us could do was stare emptily at the anvil. As the third party in this transaction, perhaps I was best suited to smooth over the situation, but my mind was occupied by one massive question, not to mention the sheer shock of what had transpired.

This is ridiculous!

The phrase echoed through my head over and over. All I could do was stare.

It was impossible. As far as I knew, there were only three negative outcomes of a weapon upgrade attempt in *SAO*: the materials disappeared and left the already-upgraded values where they were, the properties of the bonus got switched around, or the upgraded value decreased by one.

In the worst case scenario, Asuna's Wind Fleuret +4 should have decreased to +3, and that was, at most, a 5-percent chance. Of course, 5 percent put it well within the bounds of possibility for an MMO...but it should never result in the weapon just completely disintegrating.

But there was no getting around the brutal truth that the glittering shards of silver scattered about the anvil had been, until a few seconds ago, Asuna's precious sword.

I watched the entire series of events. Asuna removed the rapier from her waist and handed it to Nezha. He picked it up in his left hand and manipulated the portable furnace with his right, then pulled the sword from its scabbard and put it in the fire. Nothing in that sequence of events was out of the ordinary.

As we watched in silence, the scattered pieces around the furnace melted into the air. The weapon-damaging skills that some monsters used might melt, warp, or chip a blade but leave it in a repairable state. A weapon that had shattered into pieces represented the loss of all durability and was irretrievably gone. Asuna's sword wasn't just visibly destroyed—it had been deleted from the *SAO* server's database entirely.

As the final fragment disappeared, it was Nezha the blacksmith who moved first.

He threw aside his hammer and bolted to his feet, bowing to the both of us over and over, his parted bowl cut waving in the air. He squeaked and wailed, trying to trap the screams in his throat.

"I...I'm sorry! I'm sorry! I'll return all of your money...I'm so, so sorry!"

Asuna couldn't react to the repeated apologies. She just stood there, her eyes wide. I eventually stepped forward to speak.

"Look, um...before we talk about money, I want an explanation. I thought that weapon destruction wasn't a possible failure state of upgrading in *SAO*. How did this happen?"

Nezha stopped bobbing his head and finally looked up. The angle of his hanging eyebrows was extreme, his round, honest face screwed up in agony. It was as though his face had been designed as an expression of pure apology. I felt extremely uncomfortable, but there was no way I could tell him that it was "all right." Instead, I tried to keep my voice as calm as humanly possible.

"Listen...I played in the beta test, and I remember the player manual they put on the official website. It said there were three possible penalties for failure: lost materials, property alteration, and property downgrade. That's a fact."

As a publically outed "beater," I had no desire to bring up the beta. But this was not the time for self-preservation. I stopped there and waited for his answer.

Nezha was no longer bowing and scraping, but his eyesight was fixed firmly downward as he spoke, his voice trembling.

"Um...I think that maybe...they added a fourth penalty type for the launch. This happened to me...once before. I'm sure the probability is very low, though..."

"......"

I had no argument left. If Nezha's claim was false, then he'd somehow just accomplished a destruction penalty that did not exist in the game. That was far more unlikely.

"...I see," I murmured lifelessly. Nezha looked up and mumbled again.

"Um...I'm truly sorry. I don't know how to repay you. I'd give you a replacement Wind Fleuret, but I don't have any in stock. I'd hate to leave you without an option, so I can give you an Iron Rapier, if you don't mind the downgrade..."

That wasn't my choice to make. I looked to my left at the still-silent Asuna.

Her face was almost entirely hidden by the gray hood, but I could still make out her delicate chin moving side to side. I answered Nezha for her.

"No, thanks...We'll make do on our own."

With all due credit to Nezha's offer, the Iron Rapier was sold as far back as the Town of Beginnings on the first floor, and wasn't going to be very helpful up here. If he couldn't give us a Wind Fleuret, the Guard's Rapier that was one rank below it was the only thing that came close to a replacement.

Besides, the risks of failing in an augmentation attempt should fall upon the shoulders of the client, not the blacksmith carrying the job out. Nezha's shop sign had a list of the success rates for various jobs at his current skill level. Being unlucky enough to hit the 5-percent chance—probably less than 1 percent for this worst of all outcomes—of failure was our problem, not his. Even Rufiol, he of the Anneal Blade +0 disaster this afternoon, had eventually given in and accepted his fate.

Nezha's shoulders slumped even lower at my answer. He murmured, "I see. Well...at least let me return your fee..."

He moved his hand to start the transfer, but I cut him off. "It's all right, you did your best. You don't need to do this. There are some crafters who say it doesn't matter how you do it as long as you hit the weapon enough times, so they just whack away..."

I didn't mean anything by that, but for some reason, he shrunk his head even farther. His arms were held as close to his body as possible, trembling fiercely. Another apology shuddered out.

"...I'm sorry...!!"

After that painful, heart-rending apology, there was nothing more to say.

I took a step back, nodded to Asuna, and started to move her away.

It was only at this moment that I noticed that her hand, which had been pinching my index finger originally, was now fully gripping my palm.

I pulled the silent Asuna away from the blacksmith and out the northern entrance of the plaza. There were few NPC shops or restaurants along this stretch, only a number of buildings of unknown utility—perhaps they would be available as player homes after some later point in the game. At any rate, the street was nearly empty.

We walked on and on, the only points of interest the occasional signboard of an inn. There was no destination, not even a general direction. The cold grip of her hand on mine told me of how heavily the loss of her favorite sword was weighing on her, and the shock of its abrupt disappearance after a single upgrade attempt. But I had no idea how to react or console her. My meager life experience as a middle-school gamer left me unprepared for this. All I knew was that pulling my hand free and running away was the worst possible choice. I wanted to pray for the advent of some sudden salvation, but the good luck bonus icon below my HP bar was long gone.

First, let's stop walking.

I noticed a wider space ahead with a bench and started off for it. After a few dozen steps, I stopped and awkwardly said, "L-look, here's a bench."

The voice inside my head screamed at me for being an idiot, but Asuna sensed my intentions and turned to sit down without a word. She was still holding my hand, so I automatically took a spot beside her.

After a few seconds, her fingers eased up and left my own to land on the wooden slats of the bench.

I had to say something, but the more I thought, the tighter my throat shrank. How could I be the same person who had stood before dozens of powerful warriors and proclaimed myself a beater? And not that just that. I was the one who had spoken first when I originally found Asuna deep within the first-floor labyrinth, wearing a much harder expression than she was now. Sure, it had been an emotionless admonishment about overkill, but there was no reason I could say something then and couldn't now. None at all.

"........Um, so," I finally began. Fortunately, the words seemed to form themselves after that point. "It's a real shame about the Wind Fleuret. But once we reach the next town after Marome, they sell a weapon that's even a bit better. It's not cheap, of course...but we can manage it together. I'll help you save up..."

If mana points existed in this world, it would have cost me every last one of mine to get those words out of my mouth. Asuna responded so quietly that I could barely hear her, even at this close range.

"...But..." The word melted into the night air as quickly as it had appeared. "But that sword...that sword was my only..."

Something in her voice, some emotional resonance, pulled my gaze directly to her face. Two clear drops ran down her cheeks, glowing with a pale light under her hood.

It wasn't as though I'd never seen a girl crying up close. But the source of those tears was always my little sister Suguha, and almost all of the instances had occurred years ago, in my kindergarten and early grade-school years.

The last time I'd seen her cry was three months before I fell prisoner to *SAO*. She'd lost at the prefectural kendo tournament and cried in the corner of our backyard. I had no words to console her, only a bag from the convenience store with ice pops, the kind you sucked from a plastic wrapper. I broke one in two and stuck one of the halves in her hand.

In gaming terms, my proficiency in the Reacting to Crying Girls skill was barely above zero, if I'd even unlocked that skill in the first place. I had to compliment myself on even having the guts to stay there rather than run off.

On the other hand, an objective look showed me in a very pathetic light: frozen still and dumbfounded, watching the tears streak down Asuna's cheeks one after the other. I ought to speak or move, but I had no ice pops in my inventory, and I wasn't ready to speak to her when I wasn't entirely sure what she was crying about.

I understood the shock of seeing her favorite weapon crumble to pieces before her eyes, of course. If my Anneal Blade suddenly vanished, I'd probably get tears in my eyes as well.

But in all honesty, I didn't peg Asuna as the type to form a deep attachment to her weapon, to see it as an extension of herself and talk to it soothingly as she oiled it…That was my category, if anything.

Asuna seemed like the opposite case. She would see a sword as simply one element of battle power out of several. If she looted a slightly stronger sword from a dead monster, she'd toss aside the one she'd been using without a second thought. The first time I met her, she had a bundle of starting rapiers that she'd bought in town, throwing each one away when it was no longer of any use.

It had only been a week since then. What had changed Asuna's way of thinking 180 degrees in just seven days?

…No.

No matter the reason, there was no use wondering about it now. She was shedding tears over her partner, the blade she'd used for seven whole days. I could understand her sorrow. What else was there to think about?

"…It's a real shame," I murmured. Asuna's back shivered. She seemed even more doll-like than ever.

"But listen," I continued. "I know this might sound cold, but if you want to keep fighting on the front lines to help beat this damn game, you're going to have to keep getting new equipment. Even if that had worked, your Wind Fleuret would be useless by the end of the third floor. I'll have to replace my own Anneal Blade at the first town on the fourth floor. That's just what MMOs—what RPGs are like."

I had no idea if this was actually comforting her, but it was the best I could do.

Asuna did not react for several moments after I finished speaking. Finally, a few weak words trickled out from her hood.

"I...I can't take that." Her right hand clenched lightly atop her leather skirt. "I always thought my sword was just a tool...a bunch of polygonal data. I thought that only my skill and determination mattered here. But the first time I tried out that Wind Fleuret you chose for me...I'm ashamed to admit I was blown away. It was as light as a feather and seemed to home in right on the spot I wanted to hit...as if the sword was helping me, out of its own will..."

Her cheeks trembled, and a fleeting smile crossed her lips. For some reason, this seemed like the most beautiful expression I had seen Asuna make yet.

"I thought, *I'll be fine as long as I have her*. I'd have her by my side forever. I told myself, even if the upgrading fails, I'll never get rid of her. I'd take great care of her, for all the swords I wasted before this...I promised..."

Fresh tears dripped onto her skirt and vanished. When things disappeared in this world, they left no trace behind. Swords, monsters...even players.

Asuna quietly shook her head and whispered, her voice barely audible.

"If what you say is true, and I have to keep switching to new weapons...then I don't want to go upward. I feel so bad. We fight together, survive together...I can't bear just throwing it away..."

Something in Asuna's words brought back a memory of an entirely different scene.

A child's bicycle with a black frame. Twenty-inch tires, a six-gear shifter. I picked it out for myself on the day I entered elementary school. I treasured that junior mountain bike more than any child would. I put air in the tires once a week. If it rained, I wiped it off and oiled the moving parts. Perhaps borrowing Dad's bike care chemicals to waterproof the frame was going a bit overboard.

Thanks to all of that, the bike was still sparkling like new after three years, but that was the root of my predicament. Once I outgrew the bike, my parents said they would buy me a new one with twenty-four inch wheels. But rather than allowing me to keep my precious first bike in storage, they said I had to give it away to a younger boy in the neighborhood.

I was in third grade at the time, and I fought back like I'd never fought before. I claimed that I'd rather not have a new bike at all. I even asked the fellow at the neighborhood bike shop to store it away in secret for me.

Instead, he told me that he'd transfer the soul of my machine to the new bike. Before my stunned eyes, he took out a hexagonal wrench and removed the bolt from the right crank. This bolt was the most important out of all of them, he claimed. So as long as he stuck that on the new bike, its soul would come over with it.

Today, it was obviously a bunch of baloney meant to quiet a child, but that first bolt and another one from my second bike were currently sitting in the saddlebag of my twenty-six-incher.

With this past experience in mind, I told Asuna, "There's a way to keep a sword's soul with you when the time comes to say goodbye."

"…Huh…?"

She raised her head just a bit. I held up two fingers.

"Two ways, in fact. For one, you can melt down your inferior sword into ingots, then use them as the base for a new sword.

The other way is to just keep your old sword in storage. There are downsides to both cases, but I think there's merit to them."

"Downsides, how?"

"Well, when it comes to turning them into ingots, you have to have strong willpower when you loot good weapons from monsters. If you switch over to a looted sword, that ends the bloodline there. You could always melt down the loot and mix them together for your new sword, but it'll cost a lot. On the other hand, if you keep it in your inventory, that's using up valuable space. Again, your willpower will be tested when you're deep in a dungeon and you run out of space for items. In either case, the more practical players will probably laugh and wonder why you'd bother..."

Asuna was looking down, deep in thought, then raised her head and brushed a tear away with her fingertip.

"And do you plan to do either of those...?"

"I'm on the ingot side, but I should explain...I do it for my armor and accessories too, not just my sword."

"...Oh."

She nodded and smiled again. This one was a bit clearer than the last, but the air of sadness still had not vanished from her face.

"If only I could have kept the shattered pieces so they could be melted down," she murmured. I could only nod in agreement. The first sword that Asuna had felt a connection to was gone forever without a trace. There was no way to bring that soul back...

I was lost in silence. Eventually, she spoke again.

"...Thanks."

"Huh...?"

She didn't repeat herself. Asuna stretched her legs forward and stood up from the bench.

"It's getting really late. Let's head back to the inn. Will you help me buy a new sword tomorrow?"

"Um...yeah, of course," I nodded, hastily getting to my feet. "I'll, uh, see you to your inn."

She shook her head at my offer. "I don't feel like walking back to Marome. I'll stay in Urbus tonight. There's a place just over there."

I turned and saw that indeed, there was a gently glowing sign that said INN. Upon further reflection, it would be too dangerous to walk through the wilderness between towns without a decent weapon. Leaving her here for tonight and coming back tomorrow to help her buy a weapon seemed like a much better idea.

I walked her to the door of the inn about twenty yards away and watched her check in, waving as she walked up the stairs. I didn't have the guts to stay at the same inn with her.

Besides, there was one other thing for me to do tonight.

I headed south back down the street toward the eastern plaza of Urbus.

5

WHEN THE BELL RANG OUT EIGHT O'CLOCK, THE tireless clanging of the hammer finally stopped.

I rushed through the gate of the east plaza of Urbus and made my way across the open space, avoiding the lighting radius of the streetlamps. I reached the line of leafy trees planted at the eastern border and put my back against a thick trunk.

In my player menu, there was a shortcut icon at the bottom of the main screen that corresponded to my Hiding skill, which was set in my third skill slot. A small indicator appeared in the bottom of the view reading 70 percent—my avatar was now 70 percent blended into the tree at my back. A number of variables affected that number: my armor type and color, surrounding terrain and brightness, and of course, my own movement.

I was risking the exposure of my "evil beater" persona by wearing the Coat of Midnight, but the black leather coat's bonus to hiding would be of more use than my usual disguise. The area was dark and there was no one else nearby, maximizing my stealth efficiency. The number seventy wasn't great because my Hiding proficiency was still low. Increasing that skill was a long and boring process, so I wouldn't max it out for quite a long time.

Even at starter status, the skill was powerful enough to work easily against the mobs on the first two floors (as long as they were sight-dependent), but that number felt awfully low against a human being. A perceptive player like Asuna would probably see through 70-percent camouflage without any trouble. On top of that, hiding in town was considered poor manners, so getting revealed by other players could lead to trouble, especially if it was one of the recent "game police" type who took it upon themselves to uphold proper etiquette.

It wasn't my style to sneak around and spy on people, but this was a special circumstance. I was about to embark on my very first attempted trail of another player.

As I waited behind the tree, a player-crafter closed up his shop at the eight o'clock bell. It was Nezha, of course, the first blacksmith in Aincrad to sell his wares in the street.

He extinguished the fire in his portable forge and put away the ingots in his leather sack. His hammer and other smithing tools went into a special box. He folded up the sign and set it down on an empty spot on the carpet, then straightened out his display of weapons for sale.

Once every object related to his business had been neatly packed on top of the six-by-six-foot carpet, Nezha tapped the corner to bring up a menu screen and hit the "store" button. The carpet rolled up by itself, absorbing the countless items on top of it. In just a few seconds, the only thing left was a thin, round tube.

The short blacksmith picked it up easily and hoisted it over his shoulder. The magic Vendor's Carpet was always the same weight, no matter what items were locked within its internal storage. When I first learned about that, visions of unlimited space for potions, food, and loot in the dungeon floated through my head, but reality was not so generous. The carpet only worked in towns and villages. On top of that, it couldn't be fit into a player's inventory, meaning that the four-foot-long, four-inch-thick rolled carpet had to be carried everywhere by hand.

Normally, this item bore little use for non-merchants or crafters, but some enterprising people found unexpected avenues for fun. Back in the beta, there was a brief period where pranksters used the "items on carpet cannot be moved by anyone but the owner" rule to block off major streets with large furniture, sowing chaos left and right. This was addressed very quickly in a patch that limited use of the carpets to the corners of public spaces over a certain size.

Magic carpet on his shoulder, Nezha heaved a sigh of exhaustion and started plodding off, head down, toward the south gate of the square.

I waited for him to be at least twenty yards away, then pulled away from the tree. My hide rate indicator dropped rapidly until it hit zero, at which point the hiding icon disappeared entirely. I still stayed in the shadows, trying to cut down on any unnatural footsteps as I trailed him.

Of course, I was not following Nezha home in order to confront him about his failure to improve Asuna's weapon, or to threaten him away from prying eyes.

If anything, it was that feeling of wrongness.

As far as I knew, he had failed twice—no, five times—to upgrade a weapon over the course of the day. The destruction of Asuna's Wind Fleuret and the four consecutive tries on Rufiol's Anneal Blade, rendering it a "spent" +0. Of course, this outcome was possible from a statistical standpoint, but it struck me as a little too easy. Or a little too *hard*, depending on how you looked at it.

The only reason I'd visited the eastern plaza of Urbus in disguise in the first place was because I heard rumors in Marome that an excellent blacksmith had set up shop there. I packed up enough materials to boost my chances to 80 percent and was pondering whether to bump up sharpness or durability when I happened across the scene with Rufiol. I would have gone up to him directly afterward to have my weapon upgraded if I hadn't happened to run into Asuna at that precise moment.

Would my weapon have failed just like theirs? I couldn't help but feel that way, although I had no proof backing my suspicion.

If rumors of his skill had reached Marome, then Nezha's chances of success must be noteworthy. There was no way to test for myself, but his numbers must surely be better than the standard NPC blacksmith. However, if he was somehow able to *fulfill a condition that guaranteed failure,* there must be some hidden reason behind it. It was possible that some malicious trick lurked behind this series of events.

This was all personal conjecture—perhaps even paranoid suspicion. Even if there was some kind of knack to what he was doing, I couldn't possibly guess how it worked. He had put Asuna's materials into the forge, heated her sword in it, then moved it to the anvil and hammered it—all before my eyes. It was all according to the book, nothing out of place. Besides, what could he possibly stand to gain by downgrading or destroying other players' weapons...?

Even as the possibilities swirled through my mind, I kept a bead on his back as he walked. Fortunately, he seemed to have no idea he was being followed and didn't spin around or force me to come to an awkward halt. On the other hand, I had no experience trailing another player, so a cold sweat ran down my back the entire time. If I got my Hiding skill higher, I could follow at a much greater distance without trouble, but at this point, the only experience I could rely on was spy movies.

I darted stylishly from shadow to shadow for seven or eight minutes, a certain impossible theme song ringing in my ears. Nezha plodded his way almost to the town walls at the southeast edge of Urbus before stopping at a faintly glowing sign. I stuck close to a tree lining the street to watch. Anyone witnessing this scene would find it extremely suspicious, but I didn't realize that until later.

The sign clearly said BAR in the light of the oil lamps. Again, I felt a strange suspicion. Nothing was out of place for a hard-working player to settle down with a drink after a long day of work...but something was wrong with Nezha's demeanor. He wasn't racing up the steps in anticipation of a nice cold mug of ale. In fact, he stood still outside the swinging door for over ten seconds, as though hesitating to even go inside.

He's not going to turn around, is he? I thought in a panic. Nezha adjusted the roll of carpet on his shoulder, then set a heavy foot forward. He put out his hand and slowly pushed the door open. His small form disappeared into the bar, the door swinging shut behind him. It only took two seconds—but even at my distance, I could faintly hear what came from inside.

There were a great cheer and applause, and a man's voice shouting, "Welcome back, Nezuo!"

"…?!" I sucked in a deep breath.

This was not what I expected. My spur-of-the-moment decision to trail Nezha was only meant to find where he was spending the night. Instead, he went to a bar at the edge of town where at least four or five people knew him personally. What could it mean?

After a brief hesitation, I left the shadows and raced up to the swinging door of the inn. Unfortunately, even with my back to the wall next to the door, I could hear nothing from inside. By nature, all closed doors in the game were soundproof; the only way to hear through them was the Eavesdropping skill. Even the swinging door, with its wide-open gaps above and below, was no exception.

I swore under my breath. There were only two options here, and entering the store disguised as a customer was not one of them. I could either give up and leave, or…

I steeled my nerves and reached out to gently push open the door a crack. Five degrees, ten—there was no sound from within. Once I got it to fifteen degrees, the man's voice from earlier floated up to my ears.

"Might as well chug it, Nezuo! None of the beer in this place actually gets you drunk, anyway!"

In contrast to his statement, he seemed to be plenty drunk already. It was true that you could drink gallons of beer in Aincrad and never take in a single molecule of alcohol, but it was fairly common for players to get "drunk" on the atmosphere of the situation. The excited cheers and yelling that floated through the doorway were no different from what could be heard from groups of college students walking through a nightlife district after a few rounds of drinks in the real world.

I strained my ears and heard a hesitant "okay" in a quiet voice. The chattering died down for a moment, only to be followed by an excited cheer and applause.

Based on the evidence, I assumed that the five or so people waiting for Nezha in the bar were close friends of his. This came as a surprise to me, as in my experience, crafters tended to be lone wolves—or in Nezha's case, sheep. I was curious as to the player builds of his friends, but there was no way to identify their playstyles based on voices alone.

I decided to take another risk and peer over the top of the swinging door for just an instant. I blinked quickly, like the shutter of a camera, then pulled my head back.

As I suspected, there was only the one group in the cramped interior. If I'd tried to waltz in pretending to be a customer, I would have drawn all of their notice. There were six of them sitting at the table in the far right corner. Nezha had his back to the door. The other five all appeared to be fighters clad in leather and metal armor.

This wasn't anything out of the ordinary. It was completely normal for MMORPG guilds to have fighters and crafters mingling naturally. The official guild feature of *SAO* wasn't unlocked until a particular quest on the third floor was beaten, but many players had gathered into organized groups already. In fact, solo players like Asuna and me were already in the minority.

Having a crafter or merchant in the group made equipment maintenance and selling loot much easier for the adventurers, and the crafters could get the materials they needed for cheap, if not free altogether. So there was nothing wrong with Nezha having friends who happened to be fighters... but the lump of suspicion in my chest did not show any signs of disappearing.

Just as I was trying to figure out the exact nature of what

troubled me, one of the friends who was just entertained by Nezha's downing of an entire mug of beer said something that caught my ear.

"...So, Nezuo, how was business today?"

"Oh...um, I sold twelve new weapons...and got a few visitors for repairs and upgrades."

"Hey, that's a new record!" "We'll have to scrape together some more ingots!" two other men shouted, and there was another round of applause. It was the very picture of a close-knit band of friends with a network of support. I didn't recognize any of the other five, which meant they probably weren't front-line players, but they might rise to that rank soon with a talented blacksmith on their side.

Maybe I really am being paranoid...

I felt ashamed. If Nezha really was using some kind of bug or trick to intentionally downgrade or destroy other players' weapons, it would have to be planned and supported by his entire group, and I just couldn't see a logical motive for them doing that.

With considerable pain, I recalled that Diavel the Knight, leader of the first-floor boss raid party, had gone through a secondary negotiator in an attempt to buy my Anneal Blade +6. Only in his final moment of life did I learn that he'd done it to deny me the Last Attack bonus on the boss.

In hindsight, I did score that very last hit on the kobold lord and earned his unique Coat of Midnight for the feat, so there was a kind of logic behind Diavel's attempt to lower my attack output.

But on the other hand, Nezha and his friends were not even on the front line. They weren't in any position to be concerned with the boss's LA bonus. There was no benefit to ruining Rufiol and Asuna's weapons.

I guess it really was just a series of coincidences...

I sighed silently to myself and was preparing to let go of the swinging door and allow it to close, when something stopped my hand.

"…I don't think we can keep doing it," came the sound of Nezha's frail voice.

The men carousing inside the bar suddenly went quiet. After a short silence, the first man responded, but in a whisper too quiet for me to make out. I pushed the door in again, moving the angle to twenty degrees.

"—ust fine, you're doing great."

"That's right, Nezuo. Nobody's talkin' about it in the least."

I held my breath. I had a feeling they were talking about the failed upgrade attempts, and focused all of my attention on the words. Nezha protested against their apparent encouragement.

"It's too dangerous to keep up. Besides, we've already made back our cost…"

"Are you kidding? We're just getting started. We've got to rake it in so we can catch up with the top players while we're still on the second floor!"

Made back the cost? Rake it in…? I leaned forward, unsure of what they were discussing.

Was it really unrelated to the upgrade failures? After all, Nezha should have lost money buying back Rufiol's spent sword, and he only made the standard fee in Asuna's case, nothing more. How could that make him any money…?

No…No, there was a way. Perhaps I was looking at this from the wrong viewpoint…

Just then, a suspicious voice arose from the bar.

"…Huh? Hey, look at the door."

I closed the door as smoothly as I could and immediately jumped off to the right, flattening myself against a nearby tree and employing my Hiding skill. Almost immediately, the swinging door burst outward.

The face that emerged was of the leader-like man who'd been sitting next to Nezha and egging him on. He wore banded armor that made his already hefty form look even more rotund, and a bascinet helm with a pointed top. While the overall effect was humorous, the sharp look in his eyes was anything but. His thick eyebrows squinted, scanning the surroundings of the bar.

The moment his eyes passed over the spot where I was hiding, the indicator dropped to 60 percent. I wasn't in any physical danger within the safe zone of town, but I didn't want to alarm them—I was just starting to peel back the curtain on Nezha and his five friends' plot. The tools at my disposal were poor, but all I needed were answers.

My hide rate dropped continuously while his eyesight was fixed on the tree. If it got down below 40 percent, he would certainly detect something wrong with the tree's outline. I kept an eye on the number and slowly, slowly tried to rotate around to the back of the trunk. Inch by inch I crawled, trying to keep the fluctuating value from creeping below 50.

Once I was around the backside of the tree, he must have looked away, because the hide rate jumped back up to 70. A few seconds later, I heard the creaking of the door swinging shut, and dashed through an alley until I was a block away from the pub.

"Whew..."

I leaned against the wall and wiped away a cold virtual sweat with the sleeve of my coat. If this was what Argo the Rat did every day in her profession, then I was in no mood to follow that line of work.

I might have made a poor spy, but at least I'd succeeded at my mission. I found Nezha's base of operations—probably the second floor of that bar—discovered the existence of his partners, and even gained a little fragment of information about the mysterious trick behind the failed weapon upgrades.

That was assuming that the snippets of conversation I overheard were in fact related to such a trick. If it was true, they were somehow profiting from forcing other players' upgrade attempts to fail. Profiting enough that they were even staying in the black by buying a spent +0 weapon at twice the going rate.

If that was possible...was someone else paying them money to intentionally sabotage the orders of specific players? That was hard to imagine. It was such a roundabout way to get back at someone, and there was no guarantee that the target would ever come to Nezha for his services. If this mystery client was going to spend money, they'd be much better served following Diavel's plan and contacting the target directly.

But if that wasn't the case, what other explanation could there be?

The thoughts raced through my head so fast, I could practically feel the steam shooting from my ears. The scene from less than an hour ago replayed in my head.

Nezha taking the Wind Fleuret from Asuna. Accepting the materials and putting them into the forge with his right hand, sword in the left. When the forge was full of blue light, he pulled the sword from the scabbard and laid the blade into the fire. Once infused with that blue light, he moved it to the anvil and struck it with his hammer. A few seconds after that, the sword shone like a death scream, then shattered and disappeared.

I watched the entire string of events. I couldn't believe that there had been some sleight of hand there. If I had to assume that deception had occurred, perhaps it was in the materials. But there was no way to mimic the bright blue light that flashed out of the forge—

"Ah..."

Wait. Wait...I thought I had seen the entire thing, but there was one moment. One spot, invisible to both me and Asuna...

That meant it wasn't the materials that he'd falsified.

"Gah...!!"

My mind jumped over several logical steps and landed at a conclusion. I grunted and slapped my main menu open, checking the time readout in the corner.

The digital clock said 8:23.

There's still time!

My right hand flashed to the instant message tab, but I reconsidered and brought it down, closing the window. It was impossible to describe what I was about to do in text. I had to state it directly in person.

"There's still enough time to pull this off!" I said aloud this time, bursting out of the alleyway and racing north down the street.

The route that took eight minutes to cross during my attempt at spywork was less than three in a blazing sprint. I reached the familiar eastern plaza of Urbus but shot straight through it to the north without stopping and back into the streets of the town. Past the bench where Asuna had cried, then a hard turn shortly after. I burst through the door of her inn and raced upstairs, taking three steps at a time.

Thanking my lucky stars that I'd asked for her room number, I charged over to room 207 and slammed on the door as if to break it down. It followed the same physical rules as any other closed door, but several seconds after knocking, it would allow voices to pass through.

"Asuna, it's me! I'm coming in!"

I turned the knob without waiting for an answer and practically pushed the door down. Instantly, my eyes met those of a figure who leapt from the bed inside like a shot. Her hazel eyes were wide, and she was sucking air through her lips when I slammed the door shut.

"*Eeyaaaa!!*"

The scream was completely smothered by the closed door. I felt almost like a criminal—what I did was practically a crime—but this was all for Asuna's sake.

She clenched her fists over her chest and continued to scream. She wearing a white sleeveless shirt on top, and some kind of poofy, rounded shorts below. This didn't seem to be underwear, so I gauged that it was safe to walk over and grab her shoulder.

"Asuna, this is an ultra-emergency! There's no time, just do as I say!"

She finally stopped screaming, but I could see in her face that she was simply deciding whether to resume screaming even louder, or to start attacking me directly. But there was truly no time for anything else—I had to get to the point immediately.

"First, call up your window and set it to visible mode! Now!"

"Wha...wha...?"

"Just do it!"

I grabbed her hand, still clutched in front of her chest, and moved it in the appropriate motion, pushing out two of her fingers and sliding them through the air. A purple window materialized with a soothing sound effect, but it only looked like a blank, flat board to me. I guided her finger over to the general location of the button that would display the contents of the window to other players.

"But, um, I...I thought I locked the door..." she murmured. I answered without thinking.

"You're still partnered up with me, remember? The default setting on inn room doors is to allow guild and party members in."

"Wh...what? Why didn't you tell me that—"

I swiveled around next to the fencer, peering at the now-visible contents of her main menu. It was arranged just like mine but with a floral pattern skin selected. For a moment, I was surprised, remembering that my own window was still in the default setting, then scolded myself for getting distracted.

The right side of the window featured a familiar equipment mannequin. It was mostly empty, as she was not wearing any armor. I scrolled past the something-or-other camisole and whoopty-doo petticoat to look at the right-hand cell: no item selected. Meaning that Asuna had not equipped a new weapon since giving her Wind Fleuret to Nezha.

"Okay, first condition complete! Now the time..."

The clock in the bottom right corner read 20:28, despite how fast I'd run.

Asuna and I had returned to Urbus after our Windwasp hunt at 19:00. We had finished eating dinner around 19:30. Immediately afterward, we had moved to the plaza and asked Nezha to upgrade her weapon...meaning there was only a minute or two to spare!

"Crap, we gotta make this quick. Just hit the buttons as I tell you. Move to the storage tab!"

"Uh...um, okay..."

Asuna faithfully followed my order, perhaps so confused by the sudden turn of events that she had no time to resist.

"Next, the settings button...search button...now there should be one that says Manipulate Storage..."

Her slender finger flashed over the buttons, diving deeper and deeper into the menu. After three or four selections, we finally reached the button I wanted.

"There, that's it! Materialize All Items! Hit it!!" I screamed. She hit the tiny button, bringing up a yes/no prompt. At maximum volume,

"Yesssss!!"

Click.

Asuna muttered to herself as she hit the button. "Hmm...mm? Materialize all items...? When it says all items...does it mean...?"

With the satisfied smile of a man who did his job, I replied, "All, everything, the entire shebang, the whole nine yards."

The next moment, all of the rows of text in Asuna's inventory vanished.

And then—

Clunkclankthudwhamwhudclinkflopflipfwapswishfwuf came a cavalcade of sound from hard and heavy to light and airy. Every single item contained in Asuna's player inventory had been materialized into the game world to fall onto the floor in a great messy pile.

"Wha...wha...wha-wha-wha?!"

The mess's owner couldn't contain her shock at what had just happened, but I knew it was coming—this was what I'd run all the way from the other side of Urbus to do. The only hitch was my slight underestimation of the volume of her inventory—just a mere two or three times what I'd expected.

The amount of space for storage varied depending on the player's strength, Expansion skill, and the presence of certain magical items. For a moment, I marveled at how Asuna, a low-level player with no Expansion skill and an agility-heavy fencer build, could have packed so many items in. The answer soon became apparent.

Capacity was determined not by volume, but weight. Metal armor and weapons, liquids such as potions, and stacks of coins all put a major dent in item storage. On the other hand, lighter items such as leather armor and accessories, rolls of bread, and parchment scrolls could be packed in there with ease. The majority of Asuna's inventory was taken up with those loose effects, big and small...meaning clothes and undergarments.

I stared at the four-foot-tall pile of stuff, feeling slightly self-conscious. The heavier items had fallen out first, so the metal equipment was on the bottom, followed by leather goods, then various clothes and finally, resting on top, a small mound of frilly white and pink underwear. What was the point of keeping so many of them? Avatars in Aincrad had no bodily waste functions, and the only thing that took durability damage in battle was the outer armor. You only truly needed one set of underwear. I had three, for battle, everyday use, and sleeping, but that was probably on the high side for a male player.

And yet.

I couldn't stop here. If my suspicion was correct, and we'd hit the command in time, it would be here...piled at the bottom of this mountain.

"Pardon me!" I said, ever the gentleman, and started shoving the piles of cloth out of the way. I heard a trembling voice over my shoulder.

"Um, excuse me...Do you have a death wish? Are you one of those people who dream of dying in battle...?"

"No way," I said in all honesty, still scrabbling through the pile.

I got through the clothes to the leather armor, gloves, and small boxes, and finally reached the metal layer at the bottom.

With great effort, I pushed them aside and got to the very last section of the little mountain. The heaviest item Asuna owned—though light as a feather compared to what I had slung over my back—a single rapier.

Wind Fleuret +4.

I grabbed the green scabbard and lifted it out of the pile, then turned around to face Asuna. Her eyes had the look of one deciding a suitable means of execution, but they grew wide when she saw the sword she'd thought was gone forever. Her lips trembling, a tiny little squeak escaped her throat.

"......No way..."

6

LATER—MUCH, MUCH LATER—ASUNA SMILED ANGEL-
ically and told me that if I hadn't found her sword at that
moment, she would have thrown me through the window of
the inn.

In truth, I hadn't spared a single thought for what might have
happened if my suspicion had been false. It wasn't confidence in
my logic as much as it was panic, knowing that there were only
seconds to spare before the time limit hit. So when I barged into
Asuna's room without asking, forced her to open her window,
and yelled at her to press those buttons and eject all of her stuff, I
wasn't acting in my right mind. At least, I hoped I wasn't.

Order finally returned out of chaos three minutes after I held out
the Wind Fleuret +4 to Asuna.

All of the many items spilled over the inn room floor were
back in item storage. Asuna sat on the side of her bed, dressed
in her normal tunic and leather skirt. She silently cradled her
precious, miraculous weapon in her hands, her face a mixture
of emotion—probably caught between the polar extremes of joy
and rage.

As for me, I sat in a guest chair in the corner of the room, breaking into a cold sweat as I reflected on what I'd actually just done.
There was no time to explain anything until I got her to press that

Materialize All Items button several layers deep in the menu. But once that step was complete, there was no more time limit, which meant I had no reason to search for the sword myself.

Perhaps I had gone a step too far by ransacking the crown of delicate snow that was Asuna's undergarments on top of the pile. On the other hand, I still couldn't fathom why she would need so *many* of them. If my hazy memory served, there were enough of them that she could change every day for two weeks without reusing any. Yes, they were light enough that you could store a nearly infinite supply, but those weren't cheap. The silky smooth ones cost quite a pretty penny at the NPC shops, and surely that kind of scratch was better spent raising one of the properties of her armor—

"So, I've done some self-examination," came a voice from the other side of the room. I hurriedly sat up straight.

"Y-yes?"

"If the anger I'm feeling represents ninety-nine g, then my joy is a hundred g. Therefore, the one leftover g represents my gratitude to you," she said, light flashing in her eyes.

"So, um…why is it represented in g?" I asked.

"Isn't it obvious? If my anger had been the greater force, I would have pummeled you to make up the difference."

"Oh…so you're talking about g as in gravity, not gold? I… guess that makes sense."

"I'm glad you understand. Now, will you please explain? Why was my supposedly shattered sword left in my inventory…and why did you barge into my room like this?"

"O-o-of course. But it's a very long story. And I'm not even sure exactly how it works, myself…"

"I don't mind. We've got all night."

And the fencer, her beloved sword back in hand, finally cracked a menacing smile.

I went down to the check-in counter and bought a small bottle of herb wine and a mysterious bag of assorted nuts. When I got back to the door to room 207, I politely knocked and waited for an answer before opening.

Once the wine was poured, we shared a toast to the recovery of her fleuret, though there was still a dangerous air to her attitude. I moistened my tongue with a sip of the sweetly sour nonalcoholic wine and decided that getting right to the point was in my best interest.

"A minute ago, you asked why your shattered sword was in your item storage."

"Yes...and?"

"That was the hitch...the trick...the centerpiece of an upgrading scam."

Her eyes narrowed at the clear direction of the conversation after that last word. She nodded silently, pressing me onward.

"It might be faster to show you than to explain," I said, swinging my hand to call up my own menu and hitting the visibility button. I touched the top and bottom of the screen and flipped it around until I got it to an angle that was easily visible to the both of us, then pointed out a spot.

"Right here. See how the right-hand cell in my equipment mannequin has an icon for my Anneal Blade plus six?"

Her hazel eyes glanced at the sword grip poking out over my back, and she nodded. I reached backward and removed the entire scabbard, which was affixed to my coat, and dropped it to the floor with a heavy thud. A few seconds later, the icon on my menu was grayed out.

"This indicates that the equipped weapon has been dropped. It happens if you fumble the weapon in battle, or an enemy uses a disarm attack on you."

"Yes, I'm familiar. It can be quite alarming if you're not used to it."

"You can always stay calm and pick it up once you evade the next attack, but it's tricky at first. The Swamp Kobold Trappers in the middle of the first floor were the first to use disarms. I hear there were quite a few casualties around then..."

"In Argo's strategy guide, she warns not to attempt to pick it up right away... When I had to fight them, I dropped a spare rapier first, almost like a good luck charm."

"Ahh... that's a good idea. You can do that if you've got plenty of the same weapon."

I was impressed. It wasn't the kind of idea you expected a new player to implement... although maybe her lack of experience gave her greater creativity in tackling the game's challenges.

"But I digress. If you don't pick up the dropped weapon, it eventually goes into an Abandoned state, which gradually decreases its durability rating. Asuna, go ahead and pick up that sword."

She raised an eyebrow but dutifully stuck the Wind Fleuret onto her waist attachment point and bent down to my scabbard. Asuna lifted the simple one-handed longsword with both hands, grunting, "This is heavy. Am I doing it right?"

"That's good. Now take a look." I poked at my window, still floating above the table. The cell with my Anneal Blade grayed out had gone empty the moment Asuna picked it up.

"In combat, this is called weapon-snatching. Unlike a disarm attack, snatching enemies don't show up until much later in the game. For a solo player, that can be deadly. There's a weapon skill modification called Quick Change that you'll have to get before you fight them... but that's not the point."

I cleared my throat and attempted to get back on topic again. "You can give your equipped weapon to your friends, even when you're not in battle. Instead of a 'snatch,' that's called a 'handover.' So anyway... if someone picks up your weapon or you hand it to them, the weapon cell in your menu goes blank. Including situations like the one where you gave the blacksmith your Wind Fleuret."

"...!"

She must have seen where I was taking this at last. Her eyes went wide, then filled with a sharp light.

"But here's the thing. The equipment cell might be empty, as though you're not equipping anything... but that Anneal Blade's equipper info hasn't been deleted. And the equipment rights are protected much more tightly than simple ownership rights. For example, if I take an unequipped weapon out of storage and give it to you, my ownership of that item disappears in just three hundred seconds—that's five minutes. As soon as it goes into someone else's inventory, it is owned by that player. But the length of ownership for an equipped item is far longer. It won't be overwritten until either three thousand six hundred seconds have passed, or the original owner equips a different weapon in that slot."

Asuna's eyelashes dropped as she mulled over this information. Her response caught me by surprise.

"Meaning that if your main weapon gets snatched and you do a Quick Change to a backup weapon, you should put it in your left hand rather than your right?"

"Eh…?"

I was momentarily taken aback, but I eventually understood her point. It was indeed true that if a monster stole the player's weapon and they put a backup in the same hand, the equipment right of the stolen weapon would vanish. If the player had to retreat for survival and couldn't immediately kill the monster to retrieve the weapon, the results could be disastrous. Once the player was back in the safe haven of town, there would be virtually no way to get it back.

"Ah, I see…Yes, that's a good point. But it's a lot harder to swing a sword with your non-dominant hand." Even as I said it, though, I made a mental note to practice sword skills with my left hand.

"And one other thing. When you barged into my room and forced yourself a peek at my equipment mannequin, that's what you were checking, yes? That I hadn't equipped another weapon in its place. So if that was the very first condition…"

I nodded slowly as she stared directly into my eyes. "Yes, that's right. The second condition was that it had to be within three thousand six hundred seconds of letting go: one hour. As long as those two conditions were fulfilled, we had a shot—one ultimate method of pulling back your equipment, no matter where it happened to be. Remember that you asked me how your supposedly shattered sword was in your item storage?"

"In reality, my sword wasn't shattered, and it wasn't in my inventory, either. So that's why…" She took a deep breath and resumed glaring up at me. "And your last-ditch method of bringing back my sword was the Materialize All Items command. And because there was not a second to spare, you had no choice but to invade my room and force me to flip through my menu. Is that what you're claiming?"

"Umm, I think that sums it up…I guess?" I trailed upward at the end in an attempt to sound innocent, but Asuna only snorted, unconvinced. Fortunately, she seemed more interested in getting to the bottom of the situation than holding me responsible. She handed back the Anneal Blade and changed topics.

"So anyway…why was that materialize button buried so deep in the menus? It's almost like they don't want you to use it…And why does it have to be *all* of the items? If you could just select the items that aren't on hand already, there would be no need for that pile of my und…my other equipment."

"You just said the answer yourself. They want to make it harder to use."

"Huh…? Why would they do that?" she asked, shapely eyebrows squinting in suspicion. I shrugged.

"It's basically a last-resort option. If you drop your weapon, leave it behind, or lose it to a monster and have to run away, those are all the player's fault. In a sense, you should probably just accept your loss and move on. But they probably decided that it would make the game a bit too hard, so they added this option in case of an emergency. They just made it less convenient so you can't use it like a crutch. Hence, it's stuck under a pile of menus and you can't just pick and choose what to materialize. Boy, you should hear this story from the beta test…"

I grabbed a star-shaped nut from the dish on the table, flipped it into the air, and caught it in my mouth. Even this trifling action was affected by agility, the brightness of the surroundings, and the hidden influence of luck.

"So, the first snatching mob appears in the fifth-floor labyrinth. A guy loses his main weapon and doesn't have a backup for a quick change. So he turns tail and manages to escape the monster. However, he doesn't feel like trekking all the way back to a safe room. Instead, he finds a spot he thinks is safe, then does the Materialize All Items trick. Sure enough, in the pile is his stolen sword. The problem is, the snatch mobs aren't the only guys to watch out for there...there are also looting mobs! All these little gremlins come pouring out of the woodwork and grab everything off the floor, stuff it into their sacks, and scamper off."

"That *does* sound awful...But couldn't he just find an actual safe haven and do that same trick again to get it all back?"

"That's the thing. Most looter mobs have the Robbing skill, which immediately rewrites the item's ownership. Fortunately for him, nobody else had been to that area yet, so he crawled the entire dungeon to hunt down all the gremlins and managed to get his stuff back by hand. I tell you, it brought tears to my eyes..."

I flipped another nut into the air, sighing in exasperation.

"That story sounded like there was some personal experience behind it," Asuna noted wryly. My internal panic system must have kicked in, because the nut landed in my hair rather than my mouth. I shook my head and tried to look aggrieved.

"It's...just a story I heard, nothing more. Anyways, where was I..."

"You were explaining how the Materialize All command is useful but has its limitations," she sighed, and reached out to pluck the star-shaped nut off my head. Before I could ask what she planned to do with it, she flicked it with a finger directly into the open crack of my mouth. I crunched it with my teeth, marveling at her accuracy.

"At any rate, now I understand the logic of how my sword came back," she said, taking a sip of her wine. When the glass left her lips, that dangerous light was back in her eyes. "But that's only half of the story, isn't it? After all, I saw the sword I gave the blacksmith shatter on top of that anvil. If the Wind Fleuret that came back was my original sword…what sword was it that broke into pieces?"

A very good question. I nodded slowly, trying to piece together the fragments of information and suspicion into an easily explainable form.

"To be honest, I don't have a full explanation of that train of logic. What I can say for certain is this: At some point from the time you handed your Wind Fleuret to Nezha, to the time it shattered into pieces, he switched it out for another item of the same type. At first, I suspected that he'd found a way to intentionally destroy other players' weapons, but that wasn't it. He's the first blacksmith in Aincrad, and the first upgrade scammer…"

Upgrade scams, enchantment scams, forging scams, refinement scams.

The name varied depending on the title of the game, but it was a classic, traditional means of deception that had been around since the early days of MMORPGs.

The method was simple. The blacksmith (or other type of crafter) put out a sign advertising his weapon upgrade service, charged his clients expensive fees, then embezzled the funds by pretending the upgrade attempt destroyed the item. In games where weapon destruction wasn't one of the failure states, they had a variety of other options to fool clients, such as replacing the item with the same one a single level lower, or just keeping the crafting materials for themselves without attempting to upgrade.

In the original pre-full-dive games played on a monitor, the player's weapon was completely lost from view as soon as they handed it over to the blacksmith. The entire process happened on the other player's screen, so there was no means of telling whether any fraud had taken place.

Leaning too heavily on such deception would quickly lead to the kind of bad reputation that kept any more players from using their services, but rare gear in MMOs could be incredibly valuable. Even the occasional bit of trickery might reap huge benefits. There were almost no bad rumors about Nezha, so the rate of his fraud must still be quite low. However...

"The problem is, this is the world's first VRMMO. Even after handing over the weapon, we can see it. It can't be easy to switch it out—in fact, it must be incredibly hard."

My long explanation finally concluded, Asuna frowned and murmured, "I see...I thought I kept the sword in my sights the entire time after giving it to him. The blacksmith held my sword in his left hand and did all of the controls and hammering with his right. He couldn't possibly have opened a window, put my sword into storage, and brought out a fake."

"I absolutely agree. He had a number of pre-forged weapons on his store display, but the best ones were Iron Rapiers, and none were Wind Fleurets. So he couldn't have just switched them like that. However..."

"However?"

"However, there was a brief point where my eyes left the sword. The time when Nezha tossed your materials into the forge and it started glowing blue. It was three seconds at the most. I wanted to make sure that he used all of the materials we spent so much time collecting..."

I trailed off. Asuna's hazel eyes went wide.

"Oh! I...I think I was watching the furnace the entire time... but only because I thought the blue flames were pretty."

"Um, okay. Anyway, we weren't watching the sword in his hand while it happened. I think anyone would be staring at the flames. The materials burn and melt and change into the color of the property, so it's a big show to those watching. I think he might be using that as misdirection, the way a magician would…"

"So he switched out the sword in the three seconds we were watching the forge? Without opening his menu?" She started to shake her head in disbelief but stopped just as quickly. "On the other hand, that's the only moment it could have happened. He must have pulled off some kind of trick in those three seconds. I can't imagine what it is, but if we can just witness him doing the same thing again…"

"Agreed. Then we can watch his left hand the entire time. But that'll be difficult…"

"Why?"

"Nezha must have noticed by now that the Wind Fleuret plus four he supposedly stole is gone. Meaning that the player he tricked—in this case, you—utilized the Materialize All command, because you probably saw through his deception. He'll be spooked, and either not set up his shop for a while, or if he does, he won't attempt that scam again."

"…I see. He didn't seem to be that excited about it to begin with…In fact…"

Asuna paused, but I knew exactly what she was about to say. *In fact, he didn't seem like the kind of person to commit fraud.*

"Yeah…I agree," I said. She glanced over at me and smiled shyly. I went on, my voice quiet. "We'll lay low and gather information. Both on the switch-out trick and on Nezha himself. Either way, we've got to get back to the front line tomorrow."

"Yes, you're right. From what I heard in Marome today, they're going to challenge the last field boss tomorrow morning, then enter the labyrinth in the afternoon."

"Wow, that's quick…Who's leading the battle force?"

"Kibaou and someone else…named Lind."

I recognized the first name she said, of course, but the second was unfamiliar.

"Lind was in Diavel's party during the first-floor boss fight. He used a scimitar." Her words seemed to be coming from miles away.

The instant the words hit my brain, I heard his tearful scream in my ears. *Why did you abandon Diavel to die?!*

"Oh...him."

"Yes. It seems like he took over in Diavel's place. He even dyed his hair blue and his armor silver, just like Diavel's."

I shut my eyes, envisioning the dead knight in his blue-and-silver finery.

"Between Kibaou and the other guy as leader, I'm guessing they won't save a space for me in the boss fight. Will you participate, Asuna?" I asked her. She was a solo player, just like me. Her long brown hair shook left and right.

"I took part in the scouting of the boss, but it was just a big bull. Didn't seem like it needed too many, as long as they were well coordinated. Plus they started getting really bossy about who would get the last attack bonus, so I told them straight out that I wouldn't be in the battle."

I grimaced to myself; I could practically see the scene floating before my eyes.

"I see. You're right; that boss isn't anything to worry about. The real problem is the floor boss..."

"It's a problem?" she asked, to the point. I grimaced again.

"Of course. I mean, it stands to reason that the second-floor boss would be tougher than the first."

"Oh...right. Of course."

"His attack isn't all that high, but he uses special skills on you. It's possible to practice a defensive strategy on the auto-generating mobs in the labyrinth, but..."

If Diavel—secretly a beta tester—was still alive, he'd make sure that information made it to all the other front-line players. But without him, the only reliable source of beta info was Argo's strategy guides, and that was a problem. As we learned in that terrible battle four days ago, the boss's attack patterns could have been altered since the beta.

"Let's ignore the blacksmith for now and spend tomorrow on practice," she suggested.

I nodded automatically, lost in thought. "Yeah, good idea..."

"South gate of Urbus, seven o'clock tomorrow morning?"

"Sounds good..."

"And make sure you get a full night's sleep tonight. If you're late, you go back to a full hundred g."

"Yeah, I know—wait, what?"

I tuned back in to the conversation and raised my head. Across the table from me, her normal spirits recovered with the return of her sword, Asuna set her morning alarm.

7

SCATTERED IN THE WILDERNESS OF EACH FLOOR OF Aincrad were unique named monsters called "field bosses" that acted as gatekeepers of sorts along the route to the labyrinth.

Field bosses were always found in tight areas adjacent to sheer cliffs or river rapids, natural chokepoints that couldn't be passed without defeating the guardian. What this meant, in practice, was that while each floor might be circular in shape, it was broadly divided into multiple discrete zones.

The second floor was split into a wide northern area and a cramped southern area, which meant there was only one field boss on the entire floor. It was named the Bullbous Bow, a combination of "bull" and "bulbous bow," the protruding bulb at the front of many large ships. As the name suggested, it was a massive bull with a bulging, rounded forehead that it used for powerful and deadly charging attacks.

I watched the distant, twelve-foot-tall monster paw at the ground with powerful legs and lower its four-horned head. "Since his fur is black and brown, does that make him a Black Wagyu?" I wondered.

"You'll have to ask them to share any meat it drops in order to find out," Asuna responded, disinterested.

"Hmm…"

I actually gave that option serious thought. Many of the animal-type monsters in Aincrad dropped food items like "so-and-so meat" or "so-and-so eggs" that could actually be cooked up into meals. The flavors varied far more widely than the offerings available from the NPC restaurants in town—meaning that some of them tasted much better than what you could buy, while some were much worse.

The Trembling Oxen that roamed the second floor had such unfortunately tough meat that you could chew it forever without softening it up. On the other hand, the Trembling Cows weren't bad at all. Therefore, you'd expect the boss of all the cattle on the level would taste better than any of them. I rued my lack of foresight in not testing that theory during the beta.

"Forget about that. They're starting."

Her elbow snapped me out of my reverie, and I concentrated on the sight below. I, Kirito the swordsman, and my companion for the last two days, Asuna the fencer, were in a position atop one of the mesas that looked down on the field boss's lair. Some low trees growing right at the lip of the mountaintop made for excellent camouflage that kept us hidden from those below.

The basin was about two hundred yards long and fifty yards wide. The Bullbous Bow stood its ground, ready to turn aggro at any moment, as a neatly organized attack party inched toward it. The group was made of two full parties and three reserves—fifteen players in total.

It didn't seem that impressive in comparison to the forty-some warriors that tackled the kobold lord on the first floor, but field bosses were generally designed so that even a single party of a decent level could emerge triumphant. Fifteen was more than enough to do the job, but that depended on their knowledge of the boss's patterns and their ability to work seamlessly as a team.

"Hmm?" I muttered to myself, watching the raid closely.

Asuna whispered, "Which ones are the tanks, and which ones are the attackers?"

"I was just noticing that...Both parties look awfully similar from up here."

The Bullbous Bow was the size of a small mountain, but its attack pattern was quite simple: charge, turn, charge, turn. With two parties, the orthodox strategy said that the tanks should hold its attention and absorb its charges, while the attackers did all the damage at its flanks.

But from what I could tell, there was no real difference in the equipment of the two parties of six. Both had roughly the same number of heavily armored tanks and lightly armored attackers.

I continued to squint down at them from our height of three hundred yards and eventually noticed a subtle detail.

"Wait...look at the cloth they're wearing under their armor."

"Huh? Oh, you're right. Each party has its own color."

It was hard to tell beneath all the metal and leather armor, but Asuna was correct. The right-hand part wore royal blue doublets, and the six on the left were clad in moss green.

If the colors were meant for easy visual identification of either party, it made more sense to wear brightly colored sashes on top of the armor. Also, blue and green weren't the most distinct opposing colors. No, those were not temporary colors arranged for this fight—they were probably the original uniform designs of their parties.

"They didn't reform into new parties based on battle roles," Asuna noted, her voice hard. "The blue party on the right is Lind's—they're all Diavel's friends. And the green party on the left is Kibaou's. I suppose they weren't the type to get along..."

"Maybe they just figure that they'll perform better if each team is made up of familiar faces."

"But that will make coordination across the parties worse. It seems obvious that against that boss, you want one team to pull aggro from him, and another to deal all the damage."

"You're absolutely right," I agreed. The slowly advancing twelve below had finally breached the boss's reaction zone.

"*Bullmrooooh!!*" it roared. Even the ground up here seemed to shake. White steam puffed out of the Bullbous Bow's nostrils, and it lowered its four horns and began to charge.

There were still nearly five hundred feet between the boss and the raid party, which left plenty of time to react before it reached them, but that was easy to say from my safe vantage point. Those fighters down on the ground no doubt felt like the bull would reach them in no time at all.

After a pause long enough to make me feel nervous, the two leaders finally issued commands to their companions. I couldn't make out their voices from here, but the orders were obvious. On either side, heavily armored fighters stepped forward, raised their shields, and roared.

That was not bluster but a skill called Howl that increased the target's aggression and made it focus attacks on the user. At least, it was supposed to.

"Wait a second...why are they *both* trying to pull aggro?" I wondered. The Bullbous Bow looked back and forth between the two in indecision, then ultimately settled on the blue party. The fighter who had howled and one other shield user inched forward and stood their ground, crouching.

Two seconds later, *thwam!* The giant bull collided with the two fighters. If their defense was not up to the task, they'd be thrown into the air and take massive damage, but fortunately they managed to stay on their feet, despite being knocked ten yards backward. The other four members of Lind's party descended on the beast, unleashing sword skills on its open flanks.

"I feel nervous watching them...but it seems like they might manage to win," Asuna murmured, unimpressed. I hesitantly agreed.

"Yeah, I guess. It's supposed to be beatable by a single party. But..."

Kibaou's green party was standing off to the side rather than joining the fray. In fact, the tank was still up front, tensing himself for another Howl once the cooldown timer expired.

"Seems to me like there was no point to forming a raid party in the first place. They're more like parties competing for the same mob. Maybe it's working for now, but who can say if that will last?" I sighed.

At this point, I began to wonder about the three reserve members who weren't in the equal camps of Lind and Kibaou's men. Were they aligned with either side? I took my eyes off the fight and examined the backup adventurers standing far to the rear.

"Hng—?!" I grunted. Asuna gave me a questioning look, but I didn't have the presence of mind to answer her. I leaned forward.

Standing at the center of the three was a burly swordsman. He wore dark banded armor and a pointed bascinet helm that look like an onion sprout—the leader of the five men I saw last night after trailing Nezha to the bar.

His outfit was humorous, but I would never forget the sharpness in his eyes when he noticed me listening in on them. It seemed likely that the other two reserve members with him were also in Nezha's party.

"What are they doing here?!" I muttered. Asuna shot me another suspicious look. I pointed down at the rear of the battleground. "Do you know the names of those three guys on standby? Particularly the middle one in the bascinet."

"Bassinet...? Aren't those baby cribs?"

"Huh? N-no, I mean the guy in the pointy helmet with the visor that looks like a duckbill. That's called a bascinet helm..."

"Oh. Maybe they're spelled differently. You know, it's really irritating that being stuck in this world means I can't open a dictionary. Maybe someone will make one."

"I think it would be nearly impossible to craft an E-J dictionary, writing by hand. On the other hand, Argo did say that some folks were looking to create a simple game encyclopedia of sorts. Wait, why are we talking about this?"

I pulled us back to the topic at hand by pointing down at the rear of the basin. "That round guy in the middle of the reserve members. Ever seen him before?"

"I have," she said easily. I froze for a moment, then turned on the fencer, the questions flowing out of me.

"W-when did you see him? Where? Who is he?"

"Yesterday morning, exactly where he's standing now. He was at the Bullbous Bow scouting session. Remember how I told you about that? His name is...Orlando, I think..."

"Orlando...? First a knight, now a paladin," I muttered to myself. Asuna raised a questioning eyebrow. I added a quick explanation as the three men continued to survey the battle before them. "Orlando was the name of a knight who served King Charlemagne of France and bore the legendary blade Durendal. He was an invincible hero."

"A knight...I see."

Something in her voice made me curious, and it was my turn to cast her a quizzical look. She extended a slender finger to point to the short warrior with the two-handed sword to the right of the onion-headed paladin.

"When we did introductions, he called himself Beowulf. That's another legendary hero, right? From England. And the skinny spearman on the other side was Cuchulainn. That name sounded familiar, too..."

"Ohh...Yes, that's another legendary hero. I think he's Celtic," I added. Asuna shrugged her shoulders.

"Apparently they already decided on their guild name. I think it was Legend Braves."

"...I see...Hmm...Hmmmmmm!" I couldn't think of anything better to say.

A player was free to choose any name they wanted to attach to their MMO avatar—as long as it didn't violate the game's terms of service, that is. If they wanted to name their guild Legend Braves and pretend they were all legendary heroes, that was their right. In fact, it was probably fairly rare for names like those to go unclaimed in an MMO.

But I couldn't shake the feeling that it was a much harder sell in a VRMMO, where you literally became your avatar. That took guts. But…what if their choice of names was a statement of intent?

Perhaps they meant to grow into the heroes their names suggested. You couldn't just write that off as youthful exuberance. Orlando, Beowulf, and Cuchulainn were currently standing just behind the front line of player progress in *SAO*. In terms of pure distance, they were two hundred yards closer than I was.

Before I could ask the question, Asuna said, "They just showed up in Marome yesterday morning, where all the frontier players were gathering, and asked to take part. Lind checked out their stats and said their levels and skill proficiency were a bit below average for the group, but their equipment was good and powered up. So instead of putting them in the main force, he let them join as reserve fighters. Part of the reason I didn't join in is because they showed up to round out the group."

"I see…That makes sense." I nodded slowly and gazed down at the three heroes, feeling conflicted.

I hadn't explained to Asuna yet that they were Nezha's friends. Based on this new information, he must be another member of the Legend Braves. Perhaps the reason he had the name Nezha and not another knight or hero was because he was a crafter, not a fighter.

This also led me to a new conjecture. One that explained how three men that neither of us had seen until a day ago, who hadn't taken part in the first-floor boss raid, could be right here with the other front-line warriors…

"Bullmrrrroooh!!"

Another ferocious roar redirected my attention to the far end of the basin. For the second time, I was stunned.

Now both Lind and Kibaou's parties, a confusing mishmash of blue and green, were tangled together in one unorganized mass. They'd been squabbling over who was drawing the Bullbous Bow's aggro and collided in an attempt to get into the proper position to defend his charge. The shield-carrying tanks had lost their balance—it took quite a long time for heavy warriors to recover from a Tumble status—and no one was able to defend.

"Watch out!" Asuna hissed.

"Attackers, dash outta the way!" I shouted. They couldn't hear me, of course, but Kibaou and Lind finally raised their hands and the eight light warriors darted left and right.

But they weren't quite fast enough. The raging ox passed right through the line of shield-bearing warriors, who were only just now getting back to their feet, and caught two swordsmen with his four horns. With a vicious toss of his head, they flew high into the air.

"...!!"

Asuna and I both gasped. I had a momentary premonition of both men shattering into glass, either in midair or when they crashed to earth. Fortunately, perhaps because of the soft grass, they recovered and got their feet after only a few bounces. They had trouble keeping their footing, however; they'd suffered quite a mental shock.

Lind swung his arm again—probably the signal for retreat and potion recovery—and at the same moment, Kibaou looked back to the rear of the battleground and waved his sword.

As the bull dashed back to the far end of the basin, the two wounded members retreated, and two of the reserves stepped forward to take their place: Orlando the bascinet-wearing paladin and Beowulf with his two-handed sword. They ran forward a few yards, then stopped in apparent hesitation. The pair unleashed roars so loud that even Asuna and I could hear them, and resumed dashing toward the battle.

Orlando reached behind his round shield and pulled out a longsword of black iron that was unmistakable to me—the very same rare Anneal Blade that was only available as a reward for a quest on the first floor. The paladin brandished his sword high, glowing with the light of a highly upgraded weapon, and valiantly charged at the massive boss.

* * *

The Bullbous Bow, the only field boss on the second floor of Aincrad, exploded into a small mountain's worth of polygonal shards about twenty-five minutes after the start of the battle.

Based on the scale, level, and gear of the raid party, that was quite a long time, but it was easy to say that from my vantage point, safely removed from danger. And above all, there was one new, ironclad rule that never existed in the beta: Even a single fatality was an unacceptable result.

In that sense, the three from the guild (technically, still just a team) Legend Braves performed admirably. Compared to the first-string members who had fallen into the yellow danger zone, their movements were a bit awkward, but they upheld their duty well.

"Well, that was nerve-wracking…but at least it all ended safely," Asuna said. She took two steps back from the lip of the flat mountaintop, sat down on a rock, and looked up at me, crossing her legs.

"Well? What is it about those heroes?"

I nervously looked back down at the far end of the basin, where the fifteen combatants were gathered together and raising a victorious cheer. However, there seemed to be differing degrees of celebration—Lind's royal-blue team and the colorless Braves were truly rejoicing, while Kibaou's moss-green team was a bit muted. Probably because it was Lind's scimitar, Pale Edge, that had scored the last attack on the boss. I couldn't tell how much it was powered up at this distance, but the strength of its glow suggested that a considerable amount of work had gone into it.

I fixed Orlando the paladin with another gaze before I turned back to Asuna. He was standing boldly right next to Lind, sword raised in the air.

Asuna's cape hood was off, and the morning light shone dazzlingly in her light brown eyes. It was as though they stared right through my avatar and into my soul. There was no use hiding anything at this point. I summoned my courage and began to explain.

"...Nezha the blacksmith is one of the Legend Braves."

"Wha...? So...you mean..."

I nodded. "Nezha's upgrading fraud was done at the order of their leader, Orlando. I think. Do you know exactly when Nezha's Smith Shop first set up in Urbus?"

"Umm...I think it was the very day that the second floor was opened."

"So it's only been a week. But even bilking one or two high-powered Wind Fleurets or Anneal Blades a day would make them a ton of money. At least ten—no, twenty times what you'd make in a day from farming monsters. Remember what you said earlier? Orlando's group was weak, but they made up for it with good gear. Weapon skills have to be raised through experience in battle, but weapon upgrades..."

"...are easy if you've got the money. So that's what's going on," she said, her voice hard. Asuna bolted to her feet and glared down at the battlefield, then turned to the path that wound down the mountainside. I rushed to stop her.

"W-wait, hang on! I know how you feel, but we have no proof yet."

"So you're just going to let them get away with it?"

"If we don't at least figure out how exactly they're performing the trick, people will accuse us of defamation. There are no GMs in this world, but you don't want the majority of people treating you like an enemy. It's too late for me, but I'd hate to see you slapped with the beater tag and—"

A finger jabbed right at my face stopped me mid-sentence.

"We're about to go adventuring in the dungeon together, and *that's* what you're trying to protect me from? Anyway, your point is taken. If we don't have any proof or explanation, the only thing we're producing is empty accusations..."

She pulled her finger back to her chin and looked down, her voice softening. "I'll try to come up with some ideas of my own.

Something that won't just expose how their weapon-switching trick works but also give us solid proof."

There was a different kind of fire blazing in the fencer's eyes now, and I had no choice but to agree with her.

Once the victorious battle party turned and headed back to Marome to restock supplies, we descended the mountain and stealthily raced across the narrow basin. The right to set the first footprint on the southern side of the second floor belonged to Lind or Kibaou, but we didn't have the patience to sit around and wait for them. Plus, they seemed competitive enough that they'd waste time arguing about who got there first.

The far end of the basin turned into a narrow, winding canyon. The walls were nearly vertical and so sheer that not a single hand-hold could be seen. There was no climbing them.

We took a breather in the empty gorge after our sprint, then headed through the exit to a brand-new sight—well, for Asuna, at least.

The flattop mountains with two or three levels were the same, but the gentle grasslands of the northern area were replaced by thick jungle. Vines and ivy crawled up the sides of the moun-tains, and clumps of fog here and there made visibility poor.

There was one thing clearly visible through all of the fog, how-ever, looming over everything on the far side of the jungle. The labyrinth tower of the second floor stretched all three hundred feet to the bottom of the floor above. It seemed thinner than the first-floor labyrinth, but it was still a good eight hundred feet across. It was really more like a coliseum than a tower.

We stared at the shape in the distance until Asuna finally broke the silence.

"...What's that?"

I suspected that she was referring to the two protuberances extending from the upper half of the tower.

"Bull horns."

"B-bull—?"

"When we get closer, you'll see a huge relief of a bull on the side of the tower. It's kind of the theme of the second floor."

"I just figured that giant one they killed was the last of the ox things…"

"Not even close. The Moo-Moo Kingdom is only getting started. The ones ahead are certainly beefy, but they don't look very tasty." I coughed to hide my embarrassment at that terrible pun and clapped my hands to switch gears. "Well, let's get going. The last village is about half a mile to the southeast, and beyond that is the labyrinth. We could do all the quests in the village and still reach the tower before noon. It's actually safer and quicker to take the detour to the left, rather than going straight through the forest."

Just as I was getting ready to start hiking, I noticed that Asuna was watching me with a strange expression.

"…What is it?"

"Nothing…" She coughed as well, then looked serious again. "This isn't meant to be sarcastic, it's an honest opinion."

"…Y-yes?"

"With all that knowledge, you're very handy to have around. Everyone should have one of you."

I had no idea how to respond to that comment. Asuna strode past me and turned her head.

"Come on, let's go. I want to get into that tower before Lind's group catches up."

8

"EEK...NO! STAY AWAY!"

The beautiful girl's eyes were wide with fear as a menacing silhouette plodded closer.

It sounded like a scene from a suspenseful horror film, but it would not be following the Hollywood template for much longer.

"I told you...to stay the hell away!" she roared, and dashed forward rather than backward. The large attacker reacted by waving its crude two-handed hammer, but her right hand shot forward like lightning before it could hit the target.

The rippling thrust caught the attacker directly on its exposed chest. Brilliant beams of light exploded outward, and the hammer's progress slowed. Normally at this point, the player should dart backward and evade, but the girl plunged farther onward, pulling her rapier back and unleashing another attack. Two strikes hit the thick chest high and low, and the half-naked body writhed in pain.

"Brmooooh!!"

It leaned back and emitted a death cry, short horns and ring-pierced snout in clear profile. The massive body tipped backward, then stopped in mid-fall. The rippling muscles turned to hard glass and cracks trickled down the surface, emitting blue light until it finally exploded.

The combo was Linear and the two-strike Parallel Sting, and

the creature was a Lesser Taurus Striker, a humanoid with the head of a bull. The fencer bent over, panting heavily, and turned to fix me with an angry look.

"That...was *not* a bull!"

Two hours had passed since Asuna and I reached the second-floor labyrinth, the first players in Aincrad to set foot inside of it. Kibaou and Lind's parties were probably down on the first level of the tower, gnashing their teeth over the ransacked chests they found, but if I had to be stuck with the "evil beater" role, I might as well reap the benefits. The initial locations of the treasure chests were about 80 percent unchanged from the beta, so I steered us from one to the other, with the occasional battle in between. Once we reached the second floor, we finally met one of the true masters of the labyrinth—a Taurus.

"Well, I guess they're closer to human than bull," I admitted. I had no idea why Asuna was so upset about this. "But this is pretty much what minotaurs are like in every MMO. So people call them 'bulls' or 'cows' as a nickname..."

"...Minotaurs? Like from Greek mythology?"

The anger in her eyes subsided slightly. It seemed that she had a fondness for topics related to studying and learning. I wasn't particularly well versed in mythology, but my little sister had always liked the stories, and I had read them to her when she was young. I nodded and tried to recall some nuggets of information.

"Y-yeah, that's the kind. The legendary minotaur lived in a dungeon on the island of Crete—they called it the *labyrinthos* in Greek. Anyway, the hero Theseus delves into the dungeon and kills the minotaur. It's a very game-like scenario, so the minotaur has been a classic RPG enemy type for years and years. In this game, they take out the 'mino' part and just call them tauruses."

"Well, that makes sense. Isn't the mino in minotaur from King Minos of Crete?"

"Huh? So you're saying that calling it a 'mino' for short would be incorrect?"

"Of course. After Minos died, he became the judge of the dead in Hades. So it's probably best that you don't call them that."

This discussion seemed to have taken the edge off of Asuna's anger, so I tried to take advantage of the opportunity.

"So, erm…Miss Asuna, what was it about that mino—I mean, taurus, that didn't meet your approval…?"

She glared at me side-eyed. "It wasn't wearing, well…hardly anything at all! Just a tiny little scrap of cloth around the waist. It was practically sexual harassment! I wish the harassment code would kick in and send it to the prison of Blackiron Palace."

"Ah…I see."

The lower tauruses did indeed feature minimal clothing compared to the kobolds and goblins of the first floor. If you removed the bull head, they were basically nearly naked muscle men—quite a shock to (I assumed) a pampered rich girl from an all-girls' school.

But that left one big problem. One of the chests I'd just opened had a set of armor called Mighty Straps of Leather. Not only did it have excellent defense, it also granted a strength boost. However, when equipped, it turned the wearer's torso naked except for a few strategically placed leather straps. No other clothes or armor could be worn over or under it. I figured the dungeon was a discreet enough place for it, and was planning to change the next time we found a safe room, but Asuna's reaction to the taurus was causing me to reconsider. Still, it was a shame to waste such a great piece of loot. Should I offer it to her, or banish it for having no value to the party?

"Hey, Asuna…I got a strap-style armor with magical effects from a chest back there."

Suddenly, her eyes were three times as frosty as when she had dispatched the taurus.

"Yes, and?"

"……Um…Just thinking, not many people will look good in that. Maybe *he* would. You know, the tank leader from the first boss raid…"

"Agil? Yes, I suppose he would look the part. I met him at the reconnaissance mission for the Bullbous Bow yesterday."

I hid my surprise with an expert poker face, secretly relieved that I had avoided stepping on a landmine.

"O-oh really? But he wasn't in the actual battle today, was he?"

"I don't think he really gets along with Lind or Kibaou. But he did say he'll be there for the floor boss, so you'll see him there. Why don't you give it to him then?"

"G-good idea. So anyway, do you think you can handle the mino...I mean, taurus's Numbing Impact?"

"Oh, just call them minos already. I think I'll be fine after another two or three encounters."

"Okay. The boss's numbing effect is way wider than the normal ones, but the timing works the exact same way. Anyway, shall we go to the next block?"

She nodded without a hint of fatigue, got to her feet, and started marching off toward the exit.

We defeated four more tauruses after that, but they were timed to pop at set intervals, so you couldn't hunt tons of them even if you wanted. Our inventories were bulging with loot from the monsters and chests we'd run across, and luckily for us, we were able to leave the labyrinth without running into any other players.

At a safe zone near the entrance, I flipped open my map tab and found that we'd almost entirely filled in the blank space for the first two levels. If I turned that data into a scroll and sold it, I could make some pretty good cash, but the evil beater wasn't enough of a merchant to make a business out of map data. I decided to offer it to Argo the Rat free of charge.

In a way, it didn't seem fair. By tomorrow, Argo would be selling the latest strategy guide out of the nearest town, based on intel provided by me and the other former beta testers, and I'd have to spend five hundred col for it. But I couldn't complain too much. She claimed that the funds she earned selling the guide to the top players went into producing a free version for middle-zone folks who were still catching up.

I switched tabs and shot her an instant message with the map data, then yawned widely and looked up at the sky. Looming over the overgrown jungle was not actual sky, but the bottom of the third floor. Yet the sunset rays coming from the outer perimeter of Aincrad cast that lid overhead in a brilliant, beautiful orange.

"Today is December ninth…a Friday. It's got to be winter on the other side by now," Asuna murmured. I gave that some thought.

"I read in some article that, depending on the floor, some places in Aincrad are actually modeled after the current weather conditions. Maybe if we climb a little bit higher, it'll really be winter."

"I don't know whether I want that or not. Oh, but…" She trailed off. I turned to look at her. Her lips were pursed, but I couldn't tell if she was feeling angry or shy. "It was just an idea. What if we reach a floor with proper seasons by Christmas, and it snows that day?"

"Oh…good point. It's already December. By Christmas would mean…fifteen days left. I sure hope we finish this floor by then…"

"Well, that's not very ambitious of you. I want to be through here within a week—no, five days. I'm exhausted from all these cows."

"Oxhausted?"

I couldn't help it. She stared at me blank-faced for several seconds, then her cheeks went bright red, and she stomped on my foot just softly enough not to cause damage. The fencer promptly turned and stormed off toward the town, forcing me to run after her.

We walked for twenty minutes down the stone path through the jungle, evading battles whenever we could, and only stopped for breath once we reached the limits of Taran, the village that would serve as base for the boss raid.

As I suspected, the main street was already packed with players. Once the Bullbous Bow that blocked the path was defeated, many who'd been staying in Marome made their way here. I carefully removed my black leather coat and covered half my face with the bandanna that Asuna loved to hate.

She couldn't complain, though; she was wearing her own hooded cape low over her face. Unfortunately, her reason and mine were almost polar opposites.

"So, um...I'm going to go meet Argo in a little bit," I muttered as we walked along the side of the street. Asuna's nod was barely visible beneath her hood.

"That's perfect. I have my own reason...my own business to do with her. I'll join you."

"A-ahh."

I had no reason whatsoever to be afraid of Asuna and Argo in the same place, which made it very strange that I felt a sudden panic. I tried to hide the shiver that ran down my back by showing her to the bar where we'd meet up.

But before I could, a sound hit my ears. I nearly missed it at first, so I focused and caught it directly.

The regular clanging of metal on metal. Not as melodious as a musical instrument—tough and hardy, like a tool.

"—!!"

Asuna and I shared a look and turned together in the direction of the sound: the eastern plaza of Taran. We proceeded quickly toward the plaza, stifling the urge to sprint. When we got there, our expectations were not betrayed.

A carpet was laid out with an array of metal weapons and a simple wooden sign. A portable forge and anvil. Seated on a folding chair, swinging away with his hammer, was a short blacksmith. It was Nezha. A member of the Legend Braves, and Aincrad's first upgrade scammer.

"The nerve he's got. You saw through his deception yesterday, and instead of laying low, he's set up in the latest town," Asuna whispered with distaste from the shadow of a pillar. I was going to agree but changed my tack at the last second.

"Actually...Maybe the fact that he's here in Taran is a sign of caution. I mean, he has no way of knowing that we'd be here at the same time. Maybe he's just avoiding Urbus for now, since that's where his fraud was discovered."

"It doesn't change the fact that he's got nerve. I mean, if he's going to change towns just to set up shop again...it means he's still going to do his weapon-switching trick, right?"

She silently mouthed the words "weapon-switching," then bit her lip. There was anger in her face, of course, but also a number of other emotions. My skill at reading expressions was near zero, so I had no way of knowing exactly what was on her mind. But it seemed to me that there was something like sadness shining in those eyes, within the darkness of her hood.

I turned to look back at Nezha, who was a good sixty feet away, and said, "He probably will. He'll just be more careful about choosing his victims..."

"What do you mean?"

"If the Legend Braves are trying to leapfrog their way up to the ranks of the front-line players, they're not going to target those players for their scam. There's no point trying to reach that rank if no one else trusts you."

But then I gave voice to a suspicion that had just popped into my head.

Unless Orlando and his friends intend to cut Nezha loose.

After all, they might be friends in the same party, but the guild feature hadn't been unlocked in the game yet. There was no guild emblem showing up on his player cursor to identify him, no proof that he was connected to Orlando and Beowulf. They might be forcing him to use his sleight of hand to bilk other players out of money and equipment, and if the word got out that he was cheating customers, they could cut him out of the team and avoid any blowback.

"But…no…"

I dispelled that depressing thought with a sigh.

The camaraderie I had witnessed after trailing Nezha back to that bar did not signify a group that met in an online game for the first time. They seemed to have been friends since long before *SAO* came along.

So that theory was impossible…I didn't want to believe it could happen.

I felt a gaze on my cheek and turned to see Asuna staring at me. If she was annoyed by my solitary muttering, she did not dig deeper for clarification.

"So I suppose that means they didn't classify me as one of the top players, since they weren't afraid of stealing my sword," she said bitterly. I hastily tried to do some damage control.

"N-no, I didn't mean it like that. When I say front-line players, I mean organized parties like the guys in green and blue earlier. You can't tell someone's like that unless they have some visual identifier—I bet Nezha didn't think I was a top player, either. And who's to say he wouldn't be right?"

"Are you kidding? Aren't you getting ready to fight the next floor boss?" Asuna shot back. I nodded out of habit but needed to clarify a bit.

"W-well, I'd like to…but if Lind or Kibaou say they don't want me, that's that. In fact, I feel like there's a high probability of that happening…"

Her eyebrows shot up at an extremely dangerous angle; fortunately, they soon returned to normal. Her voice was troubled, but fairly calm.

"I don't know about Lind, but Kibaou has to understand how crucial your strength and knowledge are in defeating the boss."

"Huh? Really?"

"He sent me a message after we beat the kobold lord. It said, 'ya really saved my ass today.'"

I tried not to smile at her faithful re-creation of his Kansai accent, and decided I should join in. "Yeah, but he also said, 'I still can't get along with ya. I'm gonna do things my own way...'"

"'...to beat this game.' If that's his ultimate goal, then he won't let his petty pride get in the way of beating a floor boss."

"Let's hope not," I muttered, unable to shake the image of the chaotic, frantic scene at the battle against the Bullbous Bow.

I had only talked once to the scimitar-wielding Lind, leader of the blue squad, at the end of the kobold lord battle—and it wasn't a conversation as much as an excoriation. But I could easily imagine what he wanted. He sought to lead his fellow companions of Diavel and raise them into the greatest force in the game. His strength of will was apparent from his fixation on scoring the LA bonus, even against mid-bosses. I had no doubt that when we reached the third floor, he'd be the first to complete the guild establishment quest and start his own guild, decked out in Diavel's silver and blue.

The more complicated matter was Kibaou, who I'd spoken to on several occasions.

There was no doubt that the engine driving him was a hatred of all former beta testers. He'd singled me out as an enemy immediately and supported Diavel for taking charge as a non-tester. He might have even hoped to join Diavel's party ranks after that boss battle.

But even if Diavel had survived, that wish would not have come true. Diavel was secretly a former tester himself. It was possible that Kibaou realized it when he saw Diavel's drive to seize the boss's LA bonus. And when the battle seemed on the verge of breaking down, it was I, with my "dirty" beta knowledge, who set things right again.

So Kibaou followed his determination not to rely on the help of testers, and started his own group, rather than seeking to join Lind and the other companions of Diavel. That team was the one wearing moss green. He must have put a lot of work into it, because they seemed to be about equal strength during the fight against the bull. But they would never see eye-to-eye.

The top two teams—let's just call them guilds—would clash and compete, thereby raising the pace and power of all the frontier players, but that competition would also wreak havoc during the raid battles, when teamwork was paramount. It was just a question of whether the good would outweigh the bad. And the next question was how Orlando and the Legend Braves would affect the makeup of the front line...

"Oh, speaking of which," I said to Asuna, who was watching the blacksmith work, "did Lind and Kibaou's parties have names yet?"

"Um...I'm not sure about Lind's. But I did hear a name for Kibaou's group." She grinned. "It's kind of crazy. The Aincrad Liberation Squad."

"W-wow..."

"In fact, they've got some grand plans."

"Is that so?"

"He said they were going to set up base in the Town of Beginnings on the first floor and aggressively canvass for more members out of the thousands still down there. He'll provide them with equipment, give them organized battle training, and hopefully increase the number of front-line players as a result."

"...I see. So that's what he means by his own way." I nodded, and pondered this idea.

It was a valid choice. The more players there were advancing the front line, the quicker we'd progress through the game. But that also created a massive dilemma. An increased number of people also unavoidably increased the chance of fatalities...

"There's something else that bothers me," Asuna said suddenly. I blinked.

"Huh? What is it?"

"The term. Everyone has their own version: front-line players, frontier players, clearers. I get what they mean, but it's all so arbitrary. Lind's group were calling themselves 'top players.'"

"Oh...yeah, it's true. Argo likes to call them 'front-runners'... Oh, crap!"

I hurriedly opened my window and checked the time. I was supposed to meet Argo the Rat in just two and a half minutes.

"Um, so...you're coming too, Asuna?"

"Yes, I am. Why?" she responded coolly. I took one last look at the small blacksmith, swinging his hammer.

"Let's make the visit with Argo as short as possible so we can watch Nezha a bit longer. Maybe we'll figure out how his trick works."

9

"HMMM," SAID ARGO.

"It's not like that," I replied.

If the unspoken parts of those statements were to be filled in, they would look like this:

Hmmm. Kirito the former tester and Asuna the solo player are working as a team. How much can I sell that nugget for?

It's not like that. We're only temporarily traveling together, and not as a team or whatever.

Of course, denying the intent or definition did not change the fact that we were indeed working together. And that activity had begun when we met at the east plaza of Urbus the previous afternoon—twenty-seven continuous hours of companionship.

I couldn't blame her for assuming there was something deeper going on, but in my personal dictionary, a "party of two" and a "team" were very different things.

A party could come together spontaneously for the sake of a battle or two, then be disbanded and never return, but a proper team was designed to work together, each player fine-tuning their skills based on the presence of the other. This translated to choosing a particular equipment loadout and skillset that made up for the weaknesses of the other player so as to create attack combos that could take down difficult mobs—not so we could each attack our own targets (as Asuna and I did against the wasps).

It was only once you reached that step that I considered it to be a team, and by that definition, Asuna and I would probably never be a team. Even ignoring all of the beater baggage, Asuna put an incredible amount of craft and pride into her fencing skills, and I couldn't see her abandoning that fine-honed technique to prioritize her teamwork with me.

I had no idea how much of that explanation—more like excuse—got through, so I sat down across from Argo with an innocent look on my face, waited for my temporary party companion to sit down, then ordered a black ale. Asuna ordered a fruit cocktail cut with soda water, and the NPC waiter left for ten seconds before returning with the drinks. With that kind of speed, it felt as though they should dispense with the employee altogether and have the glasses just appear on the table, but I supposed the game's creator felt it was a necessary touch. NPC employees didn't cost real money, anyway.

We lifted our drinks, as did Argo, who shot me an encouraging look. I cleared my throat and announced, "Erm...to reaching the second-floor labyrinth!"

"Cheers!"

"...Cheers."

The enthusiasm was not quite shared by all, but at least we were on the same page. I drained half of my mug of beer—they called it ale in the game, but I didn't understand the difference. It was the same sour, bitter carbonated drink I remember tasting at my mother's permission in real life, but it was strangely satisfying after a long day of racing around the wilderness and dungeons. Though from what I understood, the adult players of *SAO* thought there was no reason for alcohol that didn't get you drunk.

In that sense, it seemed obvious that Argo, who gulped down her entire mug of foamy yellow liquid and exhaled with satisfaction, was probably another teenager who wasn't fixated on the alcohol part of the drink. But there was no way to be sure. In fact, it was nearly impossible to guess her age, even if there were no familiar whisker stripes painted on those cheeks.

Argo slammed her empty cup onto the table and immediately ordered another.

"Five days from the opening of the gate to reaching the labyrinth. That was quick."

"Compared to the first floor, sure. Plus, we had lots of players over level 10 because it took so long the first time. The original level required to beat the second floor was more like 7 or 8, right?"

"Well...maybe from a numerical standpoint. But that's just the point at which it becomes beatable." She lifted the second mug of ale to her lips, and Asuna filled the silence.

"How many attempts did it take to defeat the second-floor boss in the beta?"

"Hmm. We got wiped out at least ten times, and that was only the attempts that I participated in...But the first time was pure recklessness. I was only level 5."

I didn't mention that I did it hoping to score the LA bonus.

"I think when we actually did succeed, the raid's average level was over 7."

"Ahh...But this time, it'll be at least 10."

I checked the party HP gauge. I'd earned a level-up thanks to our hunting of the minos—er, tauruses—in the labyrinth, so I was up to fourteen. Asuna claimed to be twelve. Most likely Lind and Kibaou's teams, the main muscle of the raid party, would be about the same.

"Yeah...I bet it'll be over 10. Statistically, that's a high enough level...but floor-boss battles don't follow the same rules as wimpy mobs."

The battle against Illfang the Kobold Lord seemed like it had happened ages ago by now. Our average level was far higher than it had been during the beta test. Our leader, Diavel the knight, was level 12, just like me.

That did not stop the kobold king's katana skills from draining all of Diavel's HP. The sheer firepower of a boss's attacks rendered the "safe range" of levels meaningless.

Asuna and I thought in silence as Argo emptied three quarters of her second mug and said, "Plus, this boss is more about having good equipment than a high level."

"Yeah, that's the thing," I agreed with a sigh. The second-floor boss had a special sword skill called Numbing Detonation that wasn't primarily about dealing damage. But because of that, increasing the player's HP wasn't an adequate defense. Careful raising of debuff prevention via equipment upgrades was crucial.

That would all be covered in the next edition of the info dealer's strategy guide series, no doubt. All the front-line players would eagerly delve into the upgrading system, and Nezha would do a booming business here in this town.

"...Ugh..." I grunted without realizing it.

What if Nezha hadn't moved from Urbus to Taran in order to wait out the storm...but because he foresaw that there would be high demand for his services here? He might bilk players out of their hard-earned rare gear without a care for his reputation, making the Legend Braves the top guild in the game, surpassing even Lind and Kibaou's teams. And what would happen to Nezha the blacksmith?

"...Argo." I brushed off the crawling sensation going up my arms and opened my window over the table. "Here's the map data for the first and second level of the labyrinth."

I turned it into a scroll and plopped it down before her. She picked it up and made it disappear faster than a parlor magician.

"Thanks again, Kii-boy. Like I always say, if you want the proper value of this information..."

"No...I'm not trying to make a business out of map data. I couldn't sleep at night if I knew players were dying because they couldn't afford maps. However, I do have a job with a condition I want you to do for me in return."

"Ohh? Why don't you tell Big Sister what you want?"

She cast a sidelong glance at me. I could feel some kind of waves radiating off of Asuna, but I was too afraid to look, so I focused my eyes on Argo.

"I'm sure you're aware of them already..." I lowered my voice and looked around the bar. The entrance was at the end of a narrow alleyway, and no other players had come in. "I want info on a team called Legend Braves that took part in this morning's fight against the Bullbous Bow. All their names and how they got together."

"Ahh. And...your condition?"

"I don't want anyone to know that I'm looking for information about them. Especially the people in question."

The scariest thing about Argo the Rat is that not only did she not practice client confidentiality, she actually made it her motto that every buyer's name was another product to sell. So normally, there was no way I could buy information on the Legend Braves in total secrecy. Argo would follow her own rules and go straight to the Braves, asking if they wanted to buy the name of the person snooping into their business. Of course, I could pay her more than what they offered in order to keep my name out of it, but it would still let them know that *someone* was asking about them. That was what I wanted to avoid.

My condition was that I wanted her to collect information on the Braves without making any kind of contact. It was in direct conflict with Argo's motto and principles.

"Ahh...Hmmmm."

She twisted her curly hair with a finger as she mulled it over, then shrugged and said okay with surprising ease. But my relief only lasted a split second.

"Just remember this: Big Sister prioritized her feelings for Kii-boy over her rules of business."

Again, I felt a burning sensation emanating from the right, and froze solid. Argo never let the smile leave her face.

"Now, what did you want with me, A-chan?"

Ten minutes later, Asuna and I were back at the eastern plaza of Taran.

As a village, the scale of Taran was much smaller than the main town of Urbus. However, it shared the same basic construction in being carved down out of a flat mountaintop, with only the outer walls left standing. Therefore, it had at least twice the vertical space of any village built on flat plains.

The circular plaza was no exception, surrounded by tall buildings in every direction. But most of them were not NPC shops like inns or item stores, and there were no player-owned homes yet, so anyone could walk in or out.

More than a few players used these empty houses as squats instead of paying for an inn. The biggest difference was that an NPC-run inn offered full system protection on its rooms.

Of course, while it was impossible to hurt anyone in one of these places, there was always that uncertainty about sleeping without a lock, and the beds were painfully hard. I'd tried them out a few times when trying to skimp on expenses, and barely got a wink of sleep—I bolted to my feet every time I heard a noise inside the room or outside in the street. It was truly unfair; my real body was probably in some safe, sanitized hospital, with all of my senses disconnected from their external organs, but I was still terrorized by awful beds and outside noise in this virtual world.

After I'd suffered enough, I finally swore off of such frugality, and had been staying in proper inns or NPC homes ever since.

But there were other uses for an empty home than just sleeping. You could have a meeting in private, divvy up loot—or spy on someone.

"This is a good angle," Asuna said from the chair in front of the window, looking down at the plaza below, but careful not to get too close.

"It's probably the best spot you can get. Straight behind him, the angle would be too extreme to have a good idea of what's happening. I'm gonna set the dinner down here."

I placed four steamed buns of uncertain filling I'd bought from a street vendor on top of the round table. Their skin was the usual milky white, and nothing seemed out of order with the scent of the rising steam. In fact, they looked good. The official item name was "Taran Steamed Bun."

Asuna turned away from the source of the clanging outside and cast a doubtful look at the steamed buns.

"What's…inside of those?"

"Dunno. But it's a cow-themed floor, so I'd guess it's probably beef? By the by, in western Japan, when they talk about steamed meat buns, they mean beef. It's in eastern Japan that the generic term means pork."

"And is this town western or eastern?" she asked exasperatedly. I apologized for my pointless trivia and pushed the pile toward Asuna.

"Go on while they're hot."

"…Very well."

She removed the leather glove from her hand and took the bun from the top of the pile. I hurriedly grabbed one of my own.

We'd been in the dungeon since this morning, and hadn't had time to stop for a snack, so I was nearly starving. If our avatars exhibited biological processes other than emotion, my stomach would have gurgled all through our meeting with Argo. I opened my mouth wide and was about to stuff the steaming treat into my mouth, when—

"*Nyaak!*"

A strangled shriek hit my ears and I looked over in surprise. Asuna was sitting frozen in her chair, the steam bun held in both hands. The large, five-inch bun was missing one small bite—and the opening had squirted a thick cream-colored liquid across her face and neck.

She stayed dead still, properly chewing the bite she already took while resisting the impulse to cry, then finally spoke in a soft voice.

"…So the filling is warm custard cream…and some kind of sweet-sour fruit…"

"…"

I slowly lowered the Taran steamed bun from its position an

inch away from my face, down to the table. The moment I let go, her voice struck again, sharp as a rapier.

"If…if it turns out you ate this during the beta test and knew what was inside, and intentionally didn't tell me what it was… then I may not be able to stop myself from what comes next…"

"I swear to you that I did not know. Absolutely, positively, categorically."

I took a small handkerchief out of my belt pouch and handed it to her. Fortunately, "mess" effects here would disappear in only a few moments, even if left alone, and wiping them with any item categorized as cloth made them disappear entirely. With each mess, the durability of the cloth would fall, but I'd heard rumors of a magic handkerchief that could be used forever. Mess effects caused by mobs or special terrain often contained their own debuff effects, so an unlimited handkerchief would be really handy to have. If only it weren't such a rare piece of loot…

"Mm."

I was shaken from my reverie by the return of my handkerchief. After a few seconds of wiping, Asuna's face was free of cream.

She gave me one last glare, turned back to the window, and announced, "I'll cook my own food the next time we have a stakeout. I'd rather not have to eat something terrible like this again."

I felt tempted to point out that with a Cooking skill of zero, she couldn't make anything that *wasn't* terrible. But even as a fourteen-year-old, I was smart enough to know I shouldn't. Instead I gave her a forced smile and opined, "Th-that sounds great."

Two arrows shot forward and wiped the smile off my face. "When did I say, 'I'll cook my own food…for both of us'?"

"You didn't," I admitted sheepishly. When I actually tried the cooled-off Taran steamed bun, it wasn't bad…It was pretty good, actually. But only as a dessert.

The outer skin was soft and chewy, and the cream inside was smooth and firm and not too sweet, the perfect match for the sour, strawberry-like fruit inside. I suspected that the preset flavor values for the bun were meant to resemble a strawberry cream pastry, but through developer error or some whim of the system, it was sold heated. Asuna's mood improved eventually—she even ate two of the buns.

That was all well and good, but unlike the buns, the actual purpose of our stakeout was turning out to be fruitless. The entire point of doing this, of course, was to monitor Nezha the blacksmith and attempt to discover the means of his weapon-switching trick.

His business was thriving, but nearly all of the requests were maintenance repairs, and only two players in the hour that we watched asked him to upgrade their weapons. Both of those attempts were successful. I suspected that it was because they were only mid-rank weapons, but it was starting to make me doubt the possibility that there was any deception at all. What if Asuna's sword breaking and then reappearing thanks to the Materialize All Items button were just freakish errors, bugs in the system...?

"No, that can't be it," I muttered to myself, trying to shake aside my self-doubt.

The means of the weapon-switching trick were still a mystery, but we knew how it was that the Wind Fleuret was destroyed on the first attempt—it was the very piece of information that Asuna bought from Argo.

When Argo had asked Asuna what her business was, the answer surprised me. She said, "I want you to find out if destruction is one of the possible penalties for an unsuccessful attempt at upgrading a weapon."

Argo's answer was just as unexpected as the question. "I don't need to look it up. I already know the answer."

We were stunned. Argo said up-front that she'd give it to us for the cost of her drinks, and explained.

"Strictly as a failure penalty, weapon-breaking will never happen. However, there is one way to ensure that a weapon will break with absolute certainty: when you *attempt to upgrade a weapon that is out of upgrade attempts.*"

Meaning this. Last night, the Wind Fleuret that crumbled to pieces before our eyes was in fact switched in at some point... and it had already used all of its allotted upgrade attempts. It was a "spent" weapon. But the Wind Fleuret +4 hanging from Asuna's waist still had two chances left. So even if the attempt had failed, it could not have caused the sword to crack.

Now that the spent-weapon concept had entered the picture, I thought back to Rufiol, the fellow who tried out Nezha before Asuna did.

I couldn't determine if Nezha had indeed switched out his Anneal Blade with a different one. But the result was three straight failures, not destruction. Perhaps he couldn't do his normal trick because there were so many people around, or perhaps he just didn't have a spent Anneal Blade to switch it with.

If that was the case, it explained why Nezha offered the crestfallen Rufiol a sum of money much higher than the going rate for that spent +0 Anneal Blade. He wasn't compensating the man for his loss, but stocking up for the next attempt...

"Kirito."

I blinked, snapped out of my speculation. My eyes focused and saw that the plaza below was shrouded in night, and few players were still going to and fro.

One player walked directly across the circular plaza. He wore metal armor that reflected the light of the lampposts, and a dark blue shirt—clearly the uniform of Lind's group, the top team among the front-line players.

Asuna and I watched with bated breath as he approached Nezha's smith shop and removed his sword from his waist attachment. Its length and shape identified it as a one-handed longsword.

But it was slightly shorter and wider than my Anneal Blade. I couldn't be sure because of the distance and darkness, but the large knuckle guard appeared to be that of a Stout Brand. That was a broadsword, a sub-category of one-handed swords that prioritized attack strength over speed. It was about as rare as a Wind Fleuret, if not slightly higher.

"Certainly good enough to be a target for his switcheroo," Asuna whispered. I was surprised that she'd identified it at a glance, but I didn't let it show.

"Yeah. Now, whether he asks for maintenance or an upgrade…"

There was at least fifty feet in between us at the southwestern side of the plaza, and the outdoor blacksmith shop at the north-west edge. The Search skill's parameter adjustment brought several details into focus, but it was much too far to hear a con-versation at normal volume.

"Do you know that guy's name from the Lind team?" I asked. Asuna thought it over.

"I think his name is Shivata."

"With a V? Not Shibata?"

"It was spelled 'S-h-i-v-a-t-a.' Seems pretty clear to me."

"…All right, then."

We both practiced the foreign sound of the letter V by biting our lower lips. Meanwhile, Nezha and Shivata had finished their negotiation, and the Stout Brand changed hands, sheath and all.

This was the important point. We craned as close as possible to the window without being visible from the plaza and focused on the blacksmith's hands. Inevitably, our shoulders and even hair brushed up against each other, but the proud fencer would cer-tainly understand, given the circumstances.

If it was a maintenance request, Nezha would remove the sword and place it against the small grindstone affixed to the side of his anvil. But he turned away from his client and reached out with his right hand to one of the many leather sacks on the car-pet. Those sacks presumably contained different types of crafting materials. Meaning…

"An upgrade!" I hissed.

Asuna nodded vigorously and whispered, "The left hand! Keep your eyes on his left hand!"

She didn't have to tell me. I kept my eyes fixed on that left hand, fighting the natural urge to follow the movement of his right.

Shivata's broadsword hung from Nezha's hand, still in the sheath. There was nothing unnatural about the position or angle of his arm.

Very close to the sword was a display of premade weapons for sale, but there was no way he could switch them. All of the display weapons were common iron weapons; there was not a single rare weapon among them, and certainly not another Stout Brand. Besides, dropping the sword onto the carpet and lifting a nearby weapon would draw too much attention. I couldn't imagine that we'd have missed such an action when the Wind Fleuret was nearly stolen...

Nezha's left hand was completely still, holding the broadsword, while the right hand did all the work. He picked out all of his materials from the leather sacks and tossed them into the forge next to the anvil. The dozen or so items burst into flame and eventually melted into one big lump—I assumed. I wasn't actually watching. At any rate, it was the highlight of the upgrading process. For an instant, the deep red light that signified a Heaviness upgrade shone from the forge, then subsided into the waiting state.

"...!"

Every muscle in my body twitched.

At the same moment the red light flared, Nezha's left hand did something. Asuna must have sensed it as well, because our shoulders jumped.

"Did he...?"

"The sword..."

We kept staring but couldn't finish our sentences. That brief flash of light, barely half a second, was enough to blind us from the exact sight we needed to witness.

As I watched, teeth grinding, the blacksmith gingerly raised the Stout Brand. If he had indeed done something to it, the sword looked absolutely identical to the one Shivata gave him.

He grabbed the hilt with his right hand and slowly pulled the sword out, then placed the thick blade into the red flames of the forge. After a few seconds, all of the light transferred to the weapon. He placed it on the anvil, picked up his smithing hammer with his right hand, and began striking the sword. Five. Eight... Ten.

Just as we feared, the dark gray blade of the Stout Brand shattered into pieces. This time, neither of us missed it.

"... What now?" Asuna asked, watching the quiet plaza from the windowsill.

It was clear what she was referring to. Shivata showed remarkable restraint in bottling up his anger and disappointment, and left with minimal complaint to Nezha. Asuna was wondering if we should track him down and reveal the existence of the deception.

From a sympathy standpoint, I wanted to tell him, because within an hour, he could use the Materialize All Items button to retrieve his sword. But from a more practical standpoint, Shivata would not be happy just to get his sword back. He would surely return to the plaza and confront Nezha with this evidence, and I could not predict what would happen after that.

Nezha's actions were evil—of that there was no doubt. He ought to suffer proper punishment for his misdeeds. But without a GM holding court in this virtual world, who would determine what was "proper"?

Even a crafter could not just hang out in town all the time. What if, when he left the safety of the village limits, some player attempted to punish him through means within their control? What if they took it to the ultimate conclusion?

If we told Shivata now, it could ultimately lead to the very first PK in Aincrad. That concern was the driving force behind Asuna's question, and I did not have an easy answer in mind.

As I sat wracked by indecision and unease, I heard the calming ringing of bells. It was eight o'clock. At the same moment, the hammering outside stopped. I moved next to Asuna and looked to see that Nezha was closing up his shop. He extinguished the forge, put away the tools and materials, folded the sign, and began laying them all on top of the carpet. His back looked so very small and unassuming.

"Why did Nezha and the Legend Braves decide to start doing this fraud, anyway...? And how?" I murmured to myself. Asuna shrugged. "I mean, even if they came up with the idea to switch the weapons, there's a huge hurdle between something that is theoretically possible within the system, and actually doing it. *SAO*'s not just a normal VRMMO. Our lives are on the line now. Surely they have to realize what might happen if they steal other people's weapons..."

"Maybe they do realize...and decided to kick over the hurdles anyway."

"Huh?"

"Ignoring the ethical side of it, the actual hurdle is just knowing that you could risk your life if you get exposed, right? So they can eliminate that issue if they just get far stronger than anyone else before anyone finds out what they're doing. That way they can fight off any attempts to take their lives in the wilderness. The six—er, five members of the Legend Braves probably aren't that far off from their goal."

When Asuna's words sank in, I felt my virtual skin crawl.

"C-come on, don't tell me that. A team of guys that doesn't shy away from wicked acts, strong enough to destroy any front-line players? I mean..."

My throat became so constricted that even I could barely make out the next words I said.

"...They'd rule the world."

While I wasn't inclined to think that this weapon scam wasn't my problem in any way, I also assumed that I wouldn't have to suffer from it. I just had to make sure I didn't ever give Nezha my sword.

But that was a terribly shortsighted view of the situation.

Thirty-three days before, the moment we were trapped in this game permanently, I left behind my first and only friend in the game, Klein, and abandoned him back in the Town of Beginnings. I avoided the wilderness zones, which I expected to be bled dry in no time, and headed straight for Horunka, the next town. In other words, I prioritized the quickest and most efficient way to upgrade my equipment and stats so that I could maximize my chance of survival.

Using all the knowledge from my beta experience, I tore through countless quests and mobs, racing onward and onward. From the moment I chose to sprint out of the gates, I'd never slowed in my progress.

But the speed of my advancement was always based purely on the rules of the game (if not personal morals). If I were to ignore those rules, there were far more efficient ways to advance than what I did now—for example, monopolizing the best hunting grounds, or stealing rare loot from other players.

Of course, swindling weapons only earned them col and the item itself, not experience or skill points. But as Asuna had said, with enough money, there was no limit on how much you could power up your gear.

I had bumped my main weapon up to +6, but my armor was currently averaging around +3. Against a player with fully upgraded armor, even at a lower level, there was no way I could win.

In other words, allowing the Legend Braves to continue in their weapon fraud would be tantamount to allowing the creation of a group of players stronger than me and unbound by rules or morals.

"...I'm sorry. It took me until just now to realize how serious this is," I murmured. The fencer looked at me suspiciously.

"Why would you say sorry?"

"Well, you almost had your sword stolen, right? And this whole time, I've only been half-concerned, as if it was someone else's problem..."

The words emerged naturally, without thinking, but for some

reason, Asuna scowled even harder, blinked a few times, then yanked her head in the other direction, angrily.

"There's no need to apologize. It's not as though you and I are total strangers...I mean, um, we know each other and we're party members, but there's nothing more than...arrgh! Look what you did! You're acting so weird, I'm all confused!"

I thought I was more confused than she was, but before I could respond, she looked out the window and her eyes narrowed.

"That carpet..."

"Huh...?"

"So keeping your items from wasting away isn't its only function."

I turned to look at the east plaza of Taran. In the northwest corner, Nezha had finished packing away all his tools and was now fiddling with the pop-up menu on his Vendor's Carpet. It started rolling itself up, and the assortment of objects on top of it was automatically sucked into storage.

"Hey...Do you suppose he's using that function to switch the weapons?"

I shook my head instantly. "No, that's not possible. The carpet's absorption ability has to be activated via the menu, like he's doing now, plus it swallows up everything on top of the carpet. You couldn't have it take just one sword and spit another one out...in...exchange..."

I trailed to a stop.

The Vendor's Carpet's ability to store items could not be used to exchange them.

However, what if he used his own storage...meaning, the inventory tab of his main menu? I rolled away from the window and slumped to my knees.

"Wh-what are you doing?" Asuna asked. I didn't reply. I brought up the menu with my right hand and switched to the item list. As I had done the last night when I showed Asuna the equipment mannequin, I tapped the top and bottom edges of the window to make it adjustable, then lowered it down until it was almost stuck to the floor—right below where my left hand would dangle if I let it hang.

Lastly, I pulled the Anneal Blade, sheath and all, off my back and held it in my dangling left hand. I didn't have a folding chair, but I was about the same distance off the ground as Nezha was when he accepted the weapon from his customer.

Asuna held a deep breath, understanding what I was about to try. I looked up at her face and said, "Watch close and count the time."

"Okay."

"Here goes... Three, two, one, zero!"

I dropped the sword directly onto the window. Just as it touched the surface, the sword vanished in a puff of light and turned into text in the menu. I promptly touched the item name. When the sub-menu appeared, I selected "materialize." With another splash of light, the sword reappeared and I picked it up again.

"... How was that?"

I looked up and met the fencer's wide-eyed gaze. Her hazel eyes blinked slowly, moved to my left hand... and she shook her head.

"It was a similar sight. But much too slow to be the same thing. It took well over a second for the sword to disappear and reappear."

"Maybe if I practice, I can do it faster..."

"There were other differences. There are big fancy effects when you put it in and take it out of the menu. Even timed to happen at the same time the upgrading materials flash in the forge, you can't hide that kind of effect. Plus, it shines twice."

"...I see..." I sighed, and tapped the window on the floor to make it disappear. I stood up and slung the sword back into position.

"I thought I was onto something. I figured all the stuff stacked on the carpet could hide his menu..."

"Wouldn't that be impossible, too? I mean, if you put something on top of a window set to the inventory tab, wouldn't it all sink into it?"

"...Urgh."

She was right. I nodded and looked out the window again. Nezha was just leaving the plaza, rolled-up carpet balanced on his shoulder. His head was down, as though feeling the weight on his shoulder, and plodded heavily away. It was not the image of a man who had just scored himself a rare and valuable Stout Brand.

"If we can't expose the trick he's using, I suppose we'll just have to go reveal the truth to Shivata," she said.

"If the sword returns to him, that will prove that there was a deceptive attempt to steal it. But if that happens, all the blame will fall on Nezha's shoulders, and the other five Braves could get away scot-free. Obviously, what he's doing is wrong. But... I just get this feeling..."

I trailed off. Asuna fixed me with a direct stare. For a moment, it seemed as if the powerful light in her eyes softened just a bit.

"You can't imagine that Nezha is doing all of this entirely of his own volition... Am I right?"

"Huh...?"

My eyes widened. She'd hit the nail on the head. Asuna turned away and leaned against the wall, looked up at the dark ceiling and spoke in a slow cadence.

"Do you remember what he said yesterday, when I went to ask him to upgrade my Wind Fleuret? He asked if I wanted a new weapon or to repair my old one. It was as though he left out the option of upgrading, hoping he didn't have to do it..."

"I see... Good point. That would explain why he made such a sour face when you asked him to upgrade."

"Honestly, if Shivata was able to expose his fraud and all the Legend Braves stood up for Nezha and said they were false charges, I wouldn't mind that much. But... if they abandoned him and tried to pin all of the responsibility on his shoulders..."

In a worst-case scenario, all the rage of the player population would be focused on Nezha, and he might be executed. In fact, the probability was fairly high. After all...

"The five warriors all took the names of legendary soldiers and heroes, and they didn't include Nezha the crafter in that pattern..."

"Oh, about that." Asuna held up a finger as though just remembering something.

"What?"

"Something's been bugging me ever since you told me he was a member of the Legend Braves. His name...Nezha. So I asked Argo..."

At that precise moment, a purple icon started blinking on the right side of my vision, and I held up a hand to cut her off. I clicked the icon and it opened a long private message. Speak of the devil—it was from Argo.

FIRST REPORT

Beneath that header was all the information I'd requested about the Legend Braves: names, levels, rough character builds. It was an impressive amount of info to compile in such a short time.

I set my window to visible mode and beckoned Asuna over to look at the message. At the top was Orlando, their leader. Level 11, used a longsword and shield, heavy armor.

Along with these data was a simple sentence explaining the source of his name. That part was requested by Asuna. As my uncertain memory recalled, he was indeed based on one of the Twelve Peers of Charlemagne, his paladin knights. But Orlando was the Italian styling of his name, while in the original French, he was Roland.

"Where do you suppose Argo got this information?" I noted wryly. Asuna giggled.

"She must know someone who's a major history buff...So Beowulf was Danish, not English. Cuchulainn was from Celtic mythology, like we guessed."

We went down the list, ignoring the character info and reading the sources of their names. When we reached Nezha's name at the bottom, I let out a long breath.

His level was 10, a fairly high number thanks to the fact that crafting gave experience points on its own. But it didn't help his combat skill proficiency, which would make fighting on the front line difficult for him. Naturally, his player build was tuned to be a blacksmith. And at the end, the source of his name...

"Huh?!"

"What...?"

We yelped together. The answer was totally unexpected.

"Does this mean... we were pronouncing it wrong?"

"B-but I remember the other Braves were calling him Nezuo..."

We looked at each other, then back to the message. If what was written in his lengthy name background was true, I had terribly misunderstood him.

A moment later, several pieces of information stored in my brain as separate clumps suddenly began to rearrange themselves, linking together and shining bright.

"Oh...!"

I lifted my left hand and squeezed it, watching closely. Opened again, and closed.

In that instant, I knew that I had finally grasped the secret of Nezha's weapon-switching trick for good.

"Of course... That's what it was!!"

10

"UPGRADE, PLEASE."

I roughly thrust my sword and scabbard forward. Nezha the blacksmith looked up at me doubtfully.

He was suspicious because he wasn't looking at my face, but the great helm that completely covered it. The only thing it featured were narrow slits at the eyes. Such helmets were excellent in terms of defense but terribly limited the player's vision. It was one thing for a tank in the midst of a group battle to use it, but hardly any player would bother to wear such a thing in town.

As I was a vowed disciple of light, versatile armor, the only reason I'd ever wear this great helm was for disguise. And because I'd been present for the destruction of Asuna's Wind Fleuret three days earlier, I couldn't use my favorite bandanna instead, or Nezha would recognize me.

Perhaps this disguise was not that much better, but Asuna insisted that if I didn't want to stand out because of the funny helm, I should commit to the full outfit, and simply play one of *those* people.

So the great helm was only part of the costume. I was covered in thick plate mail all over and held a tower shield the size of an entire door. All the items were the cheapest of that type available at NPC shops, and the equipment weight was just light enough not to send me into the red, but the cramped, closed-in sensation threatened to make me go claustrophobic within half a day.

Feeling a newfound sense of appreciation for those tanks who'd taken part in the boss raid, I handed over my sword—the Anneal Blade, my only truly rare piece of equipment right now.

"I'll take a look at its properties," he said quietly, tapping the hilt. When he saw the contents of the window, his downcast eyebrows shot upward.

"Anneal plus six…two attempts left. And its upgrades are S3, D3. A challenging sword, but a very good one…"

I watched his lips creep into a tiny smile, and I confirmed that my initial suspicions about him were correct. This blacksmith wasn't an irredeemably evil person.

But just a second later, Nezha's smile of admiration disappeared, replaced by a grimace of pain. Through gritted teeth, he murmured, "…Which value did you want to upgrade?"

Sunday, December 11, just before eight o'clock in the evening.

A chill wind blew through the eastern plaza of Taran. There were no other players or NPCs in sight. There were only Nezha the blacksmith, just before he closed up his streetside shop, and me, his mystery customer. Somewhere in the empty houses lining the plaza, Asuna was watching our encounter, but I couldn't feel her gaze for all the thick metal armor.

It was the preceding Sunday that we defeated the first-floor boss and opened the teleport gate to the main city of the second floor, so today marked a full week since then. I had run into Asuna in the eastern plaza of Urbus three days ago, and it was two days before that I had discovered the truth behind Nezha's upgrade fraud.

Technically, I hadn't identified the trick, only been "certain" that I had, but there was a reason that I'd waited a full two days to attempt to ascertain the truth of the matter. I needed to master the technique Nezha was using to switch out weapons.

Of course, this all depended on Nezha accepting my work

request. Telling myself that the hassle of all this full plate armor had succeeded in convincing him, I murmured an answer to the blacksmith.

"Speed, please. I'll pay for the materials. Enough for a ninety-percent chance."

Nezha had heard my voice three days ago, but the distorting effect of the great helm helped disguise it enough to keep him from realizing that I'd been the companion of the woman with the Wind Fleuret.

"Very well. For enough to boost the chances to ninety, that will be…two thousand seven hundred col, including the cost of labor," he explained, his voice tense. I agreed in as flat a tone as I could muster.

Beneath the thick breastplate, my heart was already racing, and my gauntlets were clammy with sweat. If my suspicions were all entirely wrong, and Nezha wasn't in fact a fraudster, and weapon destruction had indeed been added as a possible failure state, then my beloved Anneal Blade +6 might be gone forever in a manner of minutes.

No.

That was not all. After all, we had retrieved Asuna's Wind Fleuret through the use of the Materialize All Items command. Even if my theory about the trick was wrong, I could still get the sword back within an hour by using that button.

So all I had to do was stay calm, watch everything that happened, and hit one icon at the proper moment. Nothing more.

I waved my left hand to bring up the menu, flipped to the trade tab, and paid Nezha his price. Normally I might have closed it after that, but this time I left it open on the top screen. Fortunately, Nezha did not seem to find this suspicious.

"Two thousand seven hundred col, paid in full," he muttered, and turned to the forge. Very naturally, he let the end of the sword in his left hand dangle just inches above the many products crammed on top of his carpet.

It all started here.

My concentration had been sucked toward the portable forge the last time, so I kept my gaze directly fixed on his left hand. My field of view was greatly limited by the helm's eye-slits, but that helped me ignore any misdirection he attempted through the flashy forge display.

Nezha must have tossed the upgrade materials straight from his stock into the forge, because everything flashed bright green for a second. If I'd had a view of the forge, my eyes would have been dazzled by the light for just a second.

But the next moment, Nezha's left index finger stretched and lightly tapped between two swords on the carpet. For just the briefest of instants, the Anneal Blade blinked.

That was it. The switch was complete. Such a brilliant, perfect trick. He could do this in front of a crowd of a hundred in broad daylight, and not a single one would notice.

Like Nezha when he saw the detailed properties of my sword, I let out a sigh of admiration. But I said nothing—I let the blacksmith finish his upgrading process.

Once the green light filled the forge like a liquid, Nezha lifted the sword in his left hand and pulled it from the scabbard with his right. The blade was the darkened steel color unique to the Anneal Blade. But to my eye, its shine was just a bit duller than usual.

The sword Nezha was holding right now was not my +6 sword, but the spent +0 blade he had bought from Rufiol three days before. It was only a guess, but I was sure of it.

The blacksmith laid the weapon in the portable forge, suffusing the blade in its green glow. He moved it to the anvil and started striking it with his smith's hammer. *Clang, clang,* the same crisp sound I heard when he upgraded Asuna's fleuret.

When the fleuret broke and Nezha offered to return the cost of his labor, I'd said, "It's all right, you did your best. There are some crafters who say it doesn't matter how you do it as long as you hit the weapon enough times, so they just whack away."

However, the reason these strikes sounded so heartfelt was not because he was praying for the operation to be a success through them. Nezha was mourning the loss of the weapon he was about to break for the sake of his deception.

Once a piece of gear was spent—no more upgrade attempts left—it would break without fail when the process was initiated again. Argo had confirmed that for us two nights ago. That phenomenon was about to happen right before my eyes.

…Eight, nine, ten.

The last hammer strike rang loud and high.

The sword burst into shards atop the anvil.

Nezha's back shivered and shrank. His right hand with the hammer slumped downward, and the sword-bound sheath in his left hand disappeared.

Hunched over, Nezha took a deep breath, screwed up his face, and was about to shriek an apology—until I cut him off.

"No need to apologize."

"…Huh…?"

He froze. I went up my equipment mannequin from the bottom, switching out armor. Giant ski-boot greaves, plate leggings, gauntlets, plate armor, heater shield…The items that made up my disguise vanished one by one.

When the great helm came off, my bangs flopped down over my forehead. I pushed them back and heaved a deep breath. Finally, I equipped the Coat of Midnight, its black hem swaying.

Nezha's narrow eyes went wide.

"…Y…you're…the guy…from…"

"Sorry for dressing in disguise. But I figured you would refuse my request if you recognized me."

I meant to say this in my most friendly, understanding tone of voice, but the moment he heard it, Nezha's shock morphed into fear. In that moment, he knew that I'd discovered the existence of his scam and even how it worked.

Without taking my eyes off the frozen blacksmith, I pushed an icon on my main menu—the weapon skill mod activation button.

With a quiet *swish*, another sword appeared in my right hand,

heavy and wrapped in a black leather sheath. It was my partner in battle since just after this game of death began: my Anneal Blade +6.

Nezha grimaced. It almost pained me to see that expression.

"No one would suspect another player of having the Quick Change mod so early, especially not a blacksmith... And hiding the menu to use it between the wares lined up on your carpet? Brilliant. Whoever thought that up is a genius."

Nezha's shoulders slowly sank, until he finally slumped over and hung his head.

A skill mod—short for modification—was a skill power-up available to the player at certain intervals of proficiency in a particular skill.

For example, when the Search skill reached a level of fifty, the first mod became available to the player. You could then choose from a number of options, such as a bonus to search for multiple targets, a bonus to increase search range, or the optional augmentation ability of Pursuit. There were tons of useful mods, and choosing between them was as hard as it was enjoyable.

Mods could also be applied to the numerous weapon skills in the game. Quick Change fell into that category. It was a common mod available at the very first choice for most one-handed weapons, but very few players ever picked it first. There was no need for anyone to make use of it until at least the fifth floor of Aincrad.

Following that theory, when my One-Handed Sword skill reached fifty halfway through the first floor, I chose the "shorten sword skill cooldown" mod. When I reached one hundred, I would choose "increase critical hit chance," and only at one fifty would I go for Quick Change.

Quick Change was an active mod, not a passive one. By pressing a shortcut icon on the front page of the menu, my equipped weapon would switch out instantly.

The regular method of changing weapons was a five-step process: (1) opening the window, (2) tapping the right- (or left-) hand cell in the equipment mannequin, (3) selecting "change weapon" from the list of options, (4) selecting the desired weapon from the available items in storage, and (5) hitting the OK button. When faced with a monster that had the Snatch ability, it was a long enough process that anyone would take at least one defenseless hit while trying to equip a backup weapon.

But with Quick Change, several steps were removed: (1) opening the window, and (2) hitting the shortcut icon. With enough practice, it could be done in half a second. The instant after you lost your weapon, you could have another one in hand and ready for battle.

On top of that, Quick Change had a great variety of options to specify exactly which hand received exactly which weapon when the icon was hit. You could set it to pull up a specific weapon, tell it to make you empty-handed—even *allow you to automatically pull the same type of weapon as the one you were equipping, if you had a spare.*

That last part was the secret at the heart of Nezha's weapon-switching trick.

He held the customer's weapon in his left hand, temporarily creating the condition in which it was "equipped" there. The ownership right was still with the client, but it was the same as the hand-over feature that made it possible to toss weapons to each other in the middle of battle. He could still use that weapon to activate sword skills...even Quick Change.

Next, Nezha extended the pointer finger of the hand holding the weapon to touch the shortcut icon on his window, which was cleverly hidden beneath his tightly packed wares. At that instant, the client's sword in his hand went into his storage, and a sword of the same type was automatically pulled out. Except this weapon was spent, guaranteed to break into pieces as soon as he attempted to upgrade it.

The only outward signs of this elaborate trick were a momentary blink of the weapon and a faint swishing sound. Given that it happened at the exact same time that he tossed the upgrading materials into the forge with a bright flash and bang, you'd have to be watching for that precise action to even notice he was doing it.

And if the customer realized he was switching weapons and tried to confront him about it, Nezha could simply employ the same trick just as quickly and get the client's original weapon back. Plus, once he shattered the spent weapon on his anvil, there was no proof of anything.

In other words, to prove Nezha's upgrade fraud was happening, I either had to utilize the Materialize All Items command to spill all of my belongings onto the ground here, or use Quick Change myself, thus pulling the sword directly out of Nezha's storage whether he liked it or not.

It was following the latter choice that had taken me two days from the time I noticed the trick to actually attempting it myself. I had spent all of the previous day and today in the second-floor labyrinth fighting endless hordes of half-naked bull-men tauruses to get my One-Handed Sword skill to one hundred so that I could take the Quick Change mod earlier than planned.

As a side benefit of this activity, I got some rare loot and mapped much farther into the twenty-level labyrinth. As usual, I offered the map data to Argo at no cost, and this generosity was apparently rankling both the Lind and Kibaou squads.

They were upset because someone else was always one or two levels ahead of them in the tower, but they hadn't realized yet that it was Kirito the evil beater. It was only a matter of time before they knew the truth. If there was one reassurance, it was that our relationship couldn't possibly get any worse.

At any rate, the two days of trouble were worth it, as I had finally uncovered and proven Nezha's upgrade fraud trick. I looked down at the curled-up blacksmith and sighed in satisfaction.

My goal was complete. It was not a quest, so there was no reward or bonus experience. On the contrary, it had cost me the 2,700 col for labor and ingredients, but all I really cared about was making sure that Nezha didn't attempt this dangerous scheme anymore.

The trick itself was brilliant, but if he kept filching valuable weapons from other players, someone was going to notice. Depending on who that person was, Nezha might find himself on the wrong end of an ugly lynch mob.

The worst possible outcome was if all the players decided he ought to be executed and it became a precedent for how to deal with such crimes.

I wasn't of the mind that Nezha should be forgiven for his part in this. Rufiol and Shivata had lost their beloved swords… and even though it was returned in the end, Asuna cried at the loss of her Wind Fleuret. They deserved to see some kind of justice.

But that punishment must not be the murder of another player. If that was allowed once, it would lead to pure anarchy—squabbles over hunting grounds and loot would be solved with violence rather than words. I'd taken on the scarlet letter of the beater to prevent the retail players from purging the former beta testers. That sacrifice couldn't go to waste.

My solution to this was to demand that Nezha either function as a proper, honest blacksmith from now on, or to give up his smithing hammer and become a warrior. Asuna and I had talked it over and decided on this choice. Once the source of their ill-gotten wealth dried up, the Legend Braves would sink back to a level appropriate to their skill.

I stood there, lost in thought, sword dangling from my right hand, when the blacksmith spoke in a tiny voice.

"…I suppose this isn't something that a simple apology will atone for."

Nezha's body and voice were scrunched up in such a compact form that it seemed as though he were trying to disappear entirely.

"…It would be nice if I could return the swords I stole from all those people…but I can't. Nearly all of them were turned into money. The only thing I can do now is…is this!"

His voice reached a shriek by the end. He unsteadily got to his feet. The smithing hammer fell from his hand, and he took off running without a backward glance.

But he didn't get farther than a few feet. A new player descended upon his exit path, long hair gleaming in the streetlamps beneath a wool hood: Asuna the fencer.

She'd jumped out the second-story window of an empty house and blocked his path, lecturing sternly. "You won't solve anything by dying."

This time, Nezha recognized the face within the hood immediately. She was the female fencer whose Wind Fleuret he'd (temporarily) stolen three days earlier.

His already-timid face crumpled even further. I was the very model of an imperceptive dunce, and even I could feel the powerful guilt, despair, and abandon raging within him.

Nezha turned his face down and away from Asuna, as though trying to escape her gaze. His voice was strained.

"…I decided right from the start…that if someone discovered my fraud, I'd die in atonement."

"Suicide is a heavier crime than fraud in Aincrad. Stealing weapons might be a betrayal of your customer, but suicide is a betrayal of every player working to defeat this game."

Her eloquence was every bit as sharp and piercing as her Linear. Nezha trembled and tensed—and his face shot upward as though on a spring.

"It'll happen anyway! I'm such a slow, clumsy oaf, I'll die eventually! Whether I get killed by monsters or kill myself, the only difference is whether it happens sooner or later!"

I couldn't stifle a small chuckle at those last words.

Asuna glared daggers at me. Nezha's teary face looked hurt among the desperation, so I put up both hands and tried to apologize.

"Sorry, I wasn't laughing at you. It's just that it was the exact same thing this lady here said just a week ago…"

"Huh…?"

Nezha, wide-eyed and bewildered, looked at Asuna again. He took several breaths, then finally worked up the will to ask, "Um…are you…Asuna, from the front-line fights?"

"Huh…?" Now it was Asuna's turn to blink in surprise. "How did you know?"

"Well, the fencer in the hooded cape is pretty well-known around here. You're the only female player on the frontier…"

"…Oh…I see…"

She sounded very conflicted and shrank back beneath her hood. I took a few steps closer and offered some advice.

"Sounds like your disguise is actually starting to identify you. Maybe you should try something else, before you get stuck with a nickname like Little Gray Riding Hood."

"Mind your own beeswax! I happen to like this hood! Besides, it's nice and warm!"

"Oh…I see."

I wisely chose not to ask her what would happen when the weather got warm again. Instead, I glanced at the stunned Nezha. I couldn't overcome the urge to ask him a follow-up question.

"So, erm…Do you know who I am…?"

It wasn't because I was interested in finding out how famous I was around the game. This was purely research to see how far the stories about "the first beater" had spread from that initial front-line squad.

"Um, well…I-I'm afraid I don't…"

My reaction was equal parts relief and shock. That conflict must have showed on my face, for Asuna patted me on the shoulder. "There, what have I always told you? Stop worrying about it so much."

"But…I really like that bandanna."

"Tell you what—I'll give you your own nickname. How about the Ukrainian Samurai?"

"Wh…why Ukrainian?"

"That bandanna's got blue and yellow stripes, just like the Ukrainian flag. I guess you could also be the Swedish Samurai, if you prefer."

"…Sorry, can I choose neither?"

Nezha listened to our back-and-forth in timid silence, then worked up the nerve to interject.

"Um, pardon me…Is what you said true? Did Asuna really say she would die eventually…?"

It was obviously a difficult thing for her to answer. I tried to smooth things over by answering for her in as light and breezy a tone as I could.

"Oh, yeah, yeah. It was wild, she just passed out right in front of me during a four-day camp-and-hunt expedition in the labyrinth. I couldn't just leave her there, and I didn't have the strength level yet to carry a player, so I had to take a sleeping bag and—"

Shunk.

Asuna slammed her heel down hard on my toes to shut me up. She composed herself and said quietly, "To be honest, that feeling hasn't disappeared. We're only on the second floor, and there are a hundred. There's a constant conflict inside me between my desire to get that far, and resignation that I'll probably fall along the way. But…"

Her hazel eyes shone bright from the shade of her hood. While the brightness of that shine was no different from what I saw that first day in the labyrinth, it seemed to me that the nature of it had changed.

"…But I've decided that I'm not fighting in order to die. Maybe I'm not quite optimistic enough to say that I'm doing it to live, to beat the game…but I've found one simple goal to strive toward. That's what I'm fighting for."

"Oh…really? What's your goal, to eat an entire cake of that Tremble Shortcake?" I asked earnestly.

Asuna sighed for some reason and said, "Of course not." She turned to Nezha again.

"I'm sure you can find your own reason. It's already inside of you. Something you ought to fight for. I mean, you left the Town of Beginnings on your own two feet, didn't you?"

"..."

Nezha looked down, but his eyes were not closed. He was staring at the leather boots on his feet. I realized that they were not non-functional shoes for wearing in town, but actual leather armor.

"...It's true. There was something," he mumbled. Amid the resignation, it sounded like a tiny kernel of some kind, a burning ambition. But he shook his head several times, as if trying to extinguish the flame. "But it's gone now. It was gone before I even got here. That happened the day I bought this NerveGear. When I...when I tried the first connection test, I got an FNC..."

FNC. Full-Dive Nonconformity.

The full-dive machine was an extremely delicate apparatus that sent signals back and forth to the brain with ultra-weak microwaves. It had to be finely tuned to work with each individual user.

But of course, they were producing thousands and thousands of units for mass-market use, and they couldn't spend ages of time on fine maintenance. The machine had an automatic calibration system that went through a long and tedious connection test on first use. Once that was done and it knew the player's settings, you could dive in just by turning on the unit.

But on very rare occasions, a person received a "nonconforming" response during that initial test. Perhaps one of the five senses wasn't functioning properly, or there was a slight lag in the communication with the brain. In most cases it was merely a slight obstacle, but there were a few people who simply could not dive at all.

If he was here in Aincrad, Nezha's FNC couldn't have been that serious—but he would have been luckier if it had prevented him from playing. He wouldn't be trapped in this game of death.

We packed up all the tools and items into the carpet and moved to an empty house near the plaza to continue hearing out Nezha's story.

"In my case, I have hearing, touch, taste, and smell, but there's an issue with my sight..."

As he spoke, Nezha reached out to the cup of tea Asuna left for him on the round table. But he did not immediately grab it—he reached his fingers closer, and only when his fingertip brushed the handle did he carefully lift it up.

"It's not that I'm entirely blind, but I have a binocular dysfunction. It's hard for me to grasp distance. I can't really tell how far my avatar's hand is from the object."

For an instant, I thought this didn't seem so bad...but I soon reconsidered.

If *SAO* was an orthodox fantasy MMORPG, Nezha's disability wouldn't be such a big deal. There were classes that had auto-hitting long-range attacks—a mage, for example.

But *SAO* didn't even have archers, much less mages. Every player who fought in the game did so with a weapon in his hand. And whether sword, axe, or spear, the ability to judge distance, to tell exactly how far away the monster was, made all the difference in the world. The very cornerstone of combat here was understanding, on a physical level, how far your weapon could reach.

Nezha took a sip of tea and carefully returned the cup to the saucer. He smiled hollowly.

"Even hitting a stationary weapon on top of an anvil with my short little hammer is extremely difficult..."

"So that was why you carried out the steps of the process so painstakingly."

"Yes, that's why. Of course, I did also feel apologetic toward the swords I was breaking...but..." He looked back and forth at me and Asuna, smiling weakly. "It might not be right for me to say this, but...I'm impressed that you saw through my switching trick. But it wasn't just today...you remotely retrieved Asuna's

Wind Fleuret plus four three days ago. So you must have known then…"

"Oh, at that point it was just a suspicion. At the time I noticed, the hour limit to maintain ownership was nearly up, so I had to burst into Asuna's bedroom and force her to use the Materialize All Items command, then—"

I felt a piercing stare from the right and narrowly avoided spilling the beans on what her inventory contained.

"—the Fleuret came back. That was when I knew you'd committed fraud…but it was two days ago that I figured out you were using Quick Change to pull it off. The key was in your name, Nezha…or should I say, Nataku."

"…!!"

Nezha (or Nataku) sucked in a sharp breath. His fists clenched and he even lifted up out of his seat for a moment. When he sat again, he looked straight down in shame.

"…I had no idea you'd figured that out, too…"

"Well, that required an information dealer to discover. I mean, even your friends in the Legend Braves were calling you Nezuo. It means they didn't know either, did they? Why you're named after Nataku."

"Just call me Nezha. I picked that spelling because I wanted people to call me that," the blacksmith said. He nodded and began to explain. "Yes, you're correct…"

Nataku. Also known as Na-zha, or Prince Nata.

He was a boy god in the Ming period fantasy novel, *Fengshen Yanyi*. He used a variety of magical weapons called paopei and flew through the sky on two wheels. He was every bit the legendary hero as Orlando or Beowulf.

In the Western alphabet, the Chinese name was transliterated to "Nezha," but only a true fanatic of Eastern mythology would recognize that as a reference to Nataku. It would be especially difficult here in Aincrad, without any Internet search engines. I couldn't help but wonder what kind of brain trust Argo had in her network of contacts. At any rate, when I saw the blacksmith's true name at the end of her write-up on the Legend Braves, I finally had an epiphany.

He did not join this game intending to be a crafter. He tried to be a fighter, but due to his circumstances, he was eventually forced to become a blacksmith.

However, that meant that despite playing as a smith now, his weapon skills might already be above a certain level. Following that line of logic, I eventually hit upon the possibility that he was using the battle skill mod Quick Change to switch out weapons, and the rest was history.

"The Legend Braves are a team we formed for a different Nerve-Gear action game, three months before *SAO* came out," Nezha explained after another sip of tea. "It was a very simple game, where you used swords and axes to fight off monsters in a straight-line map, and tried to get the high score...but even that was difficult for me. Because I had no perspective, I'd swing when the monsters were too far away, and then they'd come in close and hit me. The team could never get into the top ranks because of me. It wasn't like I knew Orlando and the others in real life, so I probably should have left the team or quit playing the game... but..."

He clenched his fists again, his voice trembling. "...No one told me to leave the team, so I used that as an excuse to stick around. It wasn't because I liked that game. It was because we decided that we'd all switch over to the very first VRMMO, *Sword Art Online*, when it came out in three months. I really, really wanted to try out *SAO*. But because of the FNC, I didn't have the guts to start it up on my own. I was...weak. I figured, if I got to be in Orlando's party in *SAO*, I might be able to grow stronger...even if I still couldn't fight that well..."

We could only sit in silence as we listened to his painful confession. It would be easy to say that I understood how he felt. The moment I saw the very first trailer for *SAO*, I swore to myself that

I would play this game. Even if I'd had a worse FNC than Nezha, I'd have gone in headfirst, as long as I was able to dive.

But I couldn't say that aloud. I abandoned my very first friend back in the Town of Beginnings—someone seeking help, just like Nezha.

However he interpreted my silence, the blacksmith smirked in self-deprecation and continued his tale.

"I went by a different name in the previous game...I used a name that anyone would recognize as a hero, like Orlando or Cuchulainn. The reason I changed it to Nezha was a sign of humility, or flattery. I was trying to say, 'I won't call myself a great hero like you guys, so can I still stick around?' When they asked what it meant, I said it was based on my real name—that was a lie, of course. Every time they call me Nezuo, I want to say that it's still a hero's name. I don't know...It's silly..."

Neither I nor Asuna denied or agreed with Nezha's self-flagellation. Instead, a quiet question emerged from her hood, which was still up, even indoors.

"But then things changed when we got trapped in here, didn't they? You stopped venturing into the fields and switched to crafting. As a blacksmith, you can still support your friends without fighting. But...why would you make the jump to swindling people? Whose idea was it in the first place? Yours? Orlando's?"

She leapt to the point as quickly and accurately as if she were in battle. Nezha had no response. When he did answer, it was a surprise.

"It wasn't me, or Orlando...or any of us."

"Huh...? Then, who?"

"For the first two weeks, I tried to cut it as a fighter. There's one skill, just one, that allows you to fight remotely...I thought I might be able to hack it that way, even without being able to judge distance..."

That didn't seem like it would work to me, but I explained for Asuna's sake. "Ahh, the Throwing Knives skill. But that's kind of..."

"Yes. I bought as many of the cheapest throwing knives as I could in the Town of Beginnings, hoping to train up my skill, but once I used up my stock, there was nothing I could do. Plus, the stones out in the field you can throw hardly do any damage. So it wasn't really much use as a main weapon skill...I gave up once my proficiency reached fifty or so. And because the other Braves stuck around to help me with that, we ended up getting off to a slow start..."

The Legend Braves' slow start was probably not due to them helping Nezha train with throwing knives, but because the other beta testers and I rushed off at top speed on the very first day and left everyone in the dust. I had a feeling Asuna would throw me some very dirty looks if I mentioned that, however, so I kept it to myself.

"Things got very...tense when I said that I'd give up on learning how to use throwing knives. No one said it out loud, but I'm sure they were all thinking that the guild got off to a slow start because of me. Even after becoming a blacksmith, training a crafting skill takes a lot of money...It seemed like the other guys were just waiting for someone to suggest that they cut me loose and leave me back in the Town of Beginnings."

He bit his lip before continuing, "Really, I should have offered on my own...but I just couldn't say it. I was afraid of being alone...Anyway, in the corner of the bar where we were talking, someone I thought was just an NPC came up and said, 'If you're going to be a blacksmith with some weapon experience, there's a really cool way to make more money.'"

"...!"

Asuna and I shared a look. It hadn't occurred to us that the idea for the Quick Change weapon trick came from someone outside of the Legend Braves altogether.

"Wh-who was it...?"

"I don't know the name. They only told me how to switch the weapons, and left immediately after that. Haven't seem 'em since. It was a very...strange person, too. Funny way of talking...

funny outfit. Wore a hooded cape like a rain poncho—glossy and black…"

"Poncho…?" Asuna and I repeated together.

Hooded capes were a fairly common item in fantasy-styled RPGs like *SAO*—practically a staple of the genre. Asuna herself was wearing one of her own at this very moment, though it was on the shorter side.

Just minutes earlier, she had claimed she wore it for its warmth, but the real reason for those hoods was not the ability to keep out the cold and rain but to hide her face. And whoever this man in the black poncho was, he likely wore it for the same reason…

Asuna seemed to read my mind, and she pulled back her gray hood with a snort. Even in the empty room, lit only by a single lamp, her gleaming chestnut-brown hair and pale skin seemed to give off a light of their own.

Upon seeing her face clearly, Nezha's wide eyes squinted, as though staring into the sun. Given that player names were not displayed by default in *SAO*, the main means of recognizing a person was the face, followed by the body. Eventually, the equipment and fighting style of a player might become part of their persona, but at this point in the game, everyone was rapidly switching to newer gear and even changing their main weapon skill. Someone playing a knife-wielding thief in leather armor one day might be a heavy warrior decked out in full plate armor the next.

Essentially, with an average build and a concealed face, pretty much anyone could pass anonymously. Even voices could be altered using a few special means, such as the great helm I was wearing when I approached Nezha.

But there might be a way to learn more identifying features of this man that taught Nezha how to swindle others. He was still staring at Asuna, so I brought him back to the topic at hand.

"About the guy in the black poncho…"

"Ah…y-yes?"

"How did he demand the margin be paid? I mean, how did

he want you to hand over his share of the money you made?"
I asked. Asuna nodded in understanding. If they were making
cash handoffs, we could stake out the place and catch a glimpse
of the man.

But Nezha's answer blew that possibility to smithereens. "Um,
actually, he didn't really say anything…"

"Huh? What do you mean?"

"Well…like I said, he taught me how to use Quick Change and
the Vendor's Carpet to pull off the weapon-switching trick, but
he didn't say a word about a share, or the payment for his idea,
or anything."

"…"

Asuna and I stared at each other again, dumbfounded.

The trick was brilliant and nearly flawless. I made sure Nezha
knew my opinion of it. The trick was certainly possible back in
the beta test, but not one of the thousand testers had come up
with the idea. Whoever devised it was a creative genius. If Nezha
had chosen a player handle based on his own given name, or
Asuna hadn't asked Argo for info on "Nataku," I would never
have figured the trick out.

But because of that, it was very jarring to hear that the poncho man who devised this brilliant idea would hand it over
without asking for anything in return. If he hadn't asked for
col…what did he stand to gain from giving his idea to the
Legend Braves?

Clearly it wasn't out of sheer altruism. It was fraud, a means of
ripping off other players.

"So you're saying…he just butted into your conversation,
explained how to switch weapons like that, and then disappeared?"
Asuna asked. Nezha was about to agree, but he stopped before
committing.

"Well…Technically, he did say a bit more. A scam is a scam, so
Orlando and the others weren't into the idea at first. They knew it
was a crime. But then he just laughed. It wasn't put on or menacing. It was just a really pleasant laugh, like out of a movie."

"Pleasant...laugh?"

"Yes. It was like—like just hearing it made everything seem so unimportant anymore. The next thing I knew, Orlando, Beowulf, all of us were laughing with him. Then he said, 'We're in a game, don't you know? If we weren't supposed to do something, they'd outlaw it in the programming, right? So anything you can do... you're allowed to do. Don't you think?'"

"Th-that's total nonsense!" Asuna exploded before Nezha had barely finished. "That would mean you could butt in and attack someone else's monster, or create a train that attacks someone else, or any other thing that's completely against proper manners! In fact, since the anti-crime code is turned off outside of towns, that would mean it's totally okay to—"

She stopped mid-sentence as if afraid that saying it out loud might cause it to come true.

Without thinking, I reached out and brushed Asuna's arm, the white skin even paler than usual. In most cases, she would pull several feet away in disgust, but now, that contact grounded her emotions, and the tension drained out of her.

I pulled my hand away and asked Nezha, "Was that all the poncho man said?"

"Er...yes. We nodded to him, he stood up, said 'good luck,' and left the bar. I haven't seen him since," he said, his eyes wandering as though searching his memory banks. "Now it all seems very mysterious...After he left, the guild most certainly changed. Everyone seemed very gung ho on the idea. I'm ashamed to admit that I decided I would rather be the centerpiece of the money-making scheme than be relegated to useless baggage, dragging everyone down. But..."

Expression flooded back into Nezha's face. He squeezed his eyes shut and grimaced.

"But...the first time I tried the trick...when I broke that substitute weapon and saw the look on the customer's face, I knew. Just because it was possible within the game didn't make it right. I should have given the real sword back and explained everything...but I didn't have the guts. When I went back to the hangout bar, I was going to say we should call it quits, but...but when they saw the sword I stole...they were so, so happy, and they said how great I was, and...and...and I just couldn't—!"

Wham! He suddenly slammed his forehead down straight onto the table. Purple light flashed off the walls of the room. He did the same thing again, then again, but his HP were protected by the game code in town.

He didn't know what to do. We'd prevented him from attempting suicide, he had no means of replacing the victims' belongings, and he couldn't even return to his friends.

If there was one way to atone for his sins, it would be to publicly admit his actions and apologize to the playerbase. But I couldn't demand that he do it. I couldn't guarantee that all of the honest, upfront players fighting to free us all from Aincrad, some of whom were his victims, would forgive Nezha for his actions. And I couldn't imagine the punishments they might devise for him if they didn't.

The only realistic solution I could come up with was to have him go through the teleporter back to the Town of Beginnings and hide himself in that vast city. Or perhaps he could reverse course, going back to fighting, and find some way to contribute through battle. The problem with that was that throwing knives were a total sub-skill, better for nothing more than distracting enemies...

But then I remembered a rare piece of loot I had gotten from a difficult Taurus Ringhurler in the labyrinth just earlier that day. It was rare but not particularly valuable, and of no use to me— something very eccentric and long-ranged.

"...Nezha."

He raised his forehead off the table an inch. I saw cheeks wet with tears.

"What's your level?"

"...I'm level 10."

"Then you've still only got three skill slots. What are you using?"

"One-Handed Weapon Crafting, Inventory Expansion…and Throwing Knives…"

"I see. If I told you that I had a weapon you could use…would you be prepared to give up on crafting? On your Blacksmith skill?"

11

WEDNESDAY, DECEMBER 14, 2022.

The tenth day since we had beaten the boss of the first floor, and the thirty-eighth day since we'd first been trapped inside this game of death.

The collective "front-line players," including me and Asuna, had finished progressing through the massive labyrinth tower brimming with muscled bull-men, and finally reached the chamber of the second-floor boss.

Our raid, made up of eight different parties, was at a total of forty-seven, just under the limit allowed by the game. Despite the loss of Diavel the knight and those too shocked by his death to take part, the group had grown, thanks to the addition of the five warriors from the Legend Braves.

Lind the scimitar user, formerly Diavel's right-hand man, led his blue group with three parties totaling eighteen members. Once we'd cleared the second floor and they initiated the guild quest on the next floor up, they were planning to establish the Dragon Knights guild. The *knights* part was clearly an homage to the spirit of their fallen leader, but I didn't know where the "dragon" came from.

With another eighteen was the green group, gathered around their opposition to beta testers. Led by Kibaou, who swung a one-handed sword just like me, they'd already decided on their own guild name: the Aincrad Liberation Squad.

That accounted for six parties and thirty-six members. Next was Agil, the massive axe-wielder and his three friends (all muscled like he was, for some reason), Asuna the fencer, the only female in the group, and then Kirito the evil beater. That made forty-two. With the five added members of the Legend Braves, that made a total of forty-seven, just one under the limit.

I sat in the corner of the large safe zone just outside the boss chamber, watching the separate groups check their equipment and distribute potions. I leaned over to Asuna, who was once again wearing her trademark hood, and whispered, "Just one more and we'd have a full raid."

"True... I guess he didn't make it in time."

"We got to the boss chamber a lot faster than I expected... It's a tough quest to beat in just three days," I bemoaned. Asuna shot me a dirty glare.

"Well, from what I hear, it even took a certain *someone* three days and two nights to finish it."

Three days earlier, in the village of Taran near the labyrinth, I had given Nezha a special kind of ranged weapon and a map.

The map pointed out the location of an NPC hidden in the rocky mountains along the outer perimeter of the second floor, and the secret passageway to reach him. This NPC was none other than the bearded Martial Arts skill master who had drawn the whiskers on my cheeks that turned me into Kiriemon.

I asked Nezha if he was prepared to give up on the weapon-crafting skill he'd spent so much time on, and take up Martial Arts instead. The weapon I'd picked up in the second-floor labyrinth required both the Throwing Knives and Martial Arts skills to use.

Abandoning a skill was not an easy decision to make, even when it was only a day or two of experience being lost. In the case of a blacksmith, working the skill upward was both a matter of time and considerable money. In other MMOs, it was as easy as rolling an alternate character, but now that *SAO* was a "one character per account" system by virtue of our predicament, that wasn't an option. The most rational choice was to wait until he reached the level that would open up another skill slot. Another choice might be to remove the Inventory Expansion skill that gave him extra room for items.

But instead, in exchange for the weapon and map, I demanded that Nezha remove his blacksmithing skill.

In *SAO*'s current state, attempting to balance crafting and combat was too dangerous. A player venturing into the field needed to focus everything under his control on maximizing the chances of survival, from his skill choices, to his equipment, to his inventory. Plenty of even the most well-prepared players had lost their lives because they were missing that last bit of attack strength, or armor value, or one more potion.

Nezha took just one deep breath before accepting my harsh demands.

"As long as I can be a swordsman here, I don't need anything else," he said, then smiled and added, "but I suppose using this thing won't make me a swordsman."

Surprisingly, it was Asuna who answered, "Everyone fighting to help beat this game is a swordsman. Even a pure crafter."

We had guided Nezha past the battles to the entrance of the secret passage and left him there. His level was high enough, and I considered inviting him to join the boss battle if his Martial Arts training finished in time, but it seemed three days wasn't enough for him to break that rock. There was no need to rush. Nezha wouldn't be risking danger by attempting weapon fraud again.

"He'll be a big help in beating the third floor, I'm sure. It's a pretty good weapon if you can master it, and he'll be able to find a spot in some guild or other. One aside from the Braves, I'm guessing..."

"Yes...I hope so," Asuna agreed. We looked across the safe zone at a group of five. Orlando was wearing his usual pointed bascinet helm and Anneal Blade. Beowulf was the short man with the double-handed sword next to him, and the skinny spearman was Cuchulainn. There were also two others that weren't present during the battle against the Bullbous Bow: Gilgamesh, who fought with a hammer and shield, and Enkidu, who was outfitted with leather armor and daggers.

At this morning's meeting, I detected a mixture of unease and discontent among the Legend Braves. I had to assume it was the disappearance of Nezha, their sixth member. If they had been an established guild, they could use location trackers to find him, but here on the second floor, guilds were nothing but names.

I could understand their concern, but I was under no obligation to explain the situation to them. After all, they'd forced Nezha to undertake a weeklong string of dangerous scams that easily could have led to his execution if anything was exposed to the public.

"That's all nice and good, Kirito, but we shouldn't be spending our time worrying about the state of other parties."

"Oh? Why?" I blinked. She sighed in exasperation.

"Lind said we'd put the raid group together just before the boss fight, but think about it. There are three parties for the blue team, three parties for the green team, one for the Braves, and probably one last one for Agil's group. That makes eight."

"Oh...g-good point."

I hadn't given it any thought since she mentioned it, but eight parties was the maximum for a raid. In the first boss fight, we'd had a lower number, and Asuna and I got to be in our own leftover party, but that wouldn't be an option this time.

Without any magic, *SAO* didn't have the usual full-raid heals and buffs, so it was quite possible for extra people to take part in the battle outside of the raid. The problem was that being outside the group meant you couldn't see the HP of the other members, and they couldn't see yours. It made gauging the proper timing of potion rotation very tricky.

I had to make sure that Asuna at least made her way into Agil's party. I looked around for the axe-warrior's distinct shape.

"Hey, you two. Good to see you again," came a baritone voice from behind me. I turned around to see the very man I was looking for.

His craggy face split into a grin, the light shining off his bald head. "I hear you two have paired up. I guess I should congratulate you."

"Um…we're…"

Not a pair, I tried to say, but Asuna set the record straight.

"We're not a pair. It's just a temporary partnership. Nice to see you, Agil."

Agil smiled again and looked at me, raising an eyebrow. It was a cool gesture, but it felt as though he meant it in a consoling way. I hastily cleared my throat.

"Y-yes, well, um…that's right. So I'm guessing we're about to finalize the raid structure, since we're almost at the absolute limit for eight parties…"

I was planning to ask them if they would take Asuna in their party, but again, I didn't get the chance to finish.

"Yeah, that's what I came to ask you about. There are four of us, so why don't you two join our group?"

It was such a breezy, careless invitation that I couldn't help but hesitate.

"Um…well, that's really generous of you, but are you sure? I mean, given my standing…"

Asuna sighed and Agil shrugged his shoulders and threw up his hands. That gesture, combined with his appearance, was clearly not Japanese, but his command of the language was perfect, so there was a strange mixture of exoticism and familiarity about the man that made him both fascinating and charismatic.

"What do they call you, a beater? It's only a tiny percent of people who actually call you that."

Even the word *beater* sounded fresh and new coming from his lips. Most people, including me, pronounced it with a flat intonation, like *cheater*, but he stressed the *bee* and softened the *ter*, which made it almost sound like a cool title to have.

"We actually have our own nickname for you."

"Really? What is it?" Asuna asked. Agil glanced at her and grinned.

"The Man in Black. Or Blackie."

She snorted. I wasn't exactly thrilled with that epithet—I hadn't chosen the color of the coat I looted from the kobold boss—but even more startling to me was that she'd actually laughed. I peered into her hood in curiosity.

Asuna quickly composed her expression and gave me a familiar glare before continuing, "Thanks for the offer, Agil. I suppose we'll take you up on it—me *and* Blackie."

"Oh, come on, you're not going to run with that, are you?" I protested.

Asuna replied, "Blackie, as in the prompters who wear all black during a play, right? Sounds perfect for a guy who hates being in the spotlight."

"…Oh…I see. But that's not exactly the same…"

"I mean, if you'd prefer that I just call you Mr. Kirito all the time, I can do that."

"…Like I said, that's not exactly the same…"

Agil, who grinned as he watched our bickering, burst out laughing at that point. "If you two are that in tune, then I'm leaving the switch timing up to you. The four of us will focus on tanking, so you guys do the damage."

He held out both hands, and Asuna shook his right, while I took the left. I bowed briefly to the other three behind him and received waves and thumbs-up in return. I hadn't talked with them much at the first-floor boss battle, but they all seemed to be as good-natured as Agil.

I accepted Agil's party request and noted the six HP bars lined up on the left side of my view, just as we hit fifteen minutes until the battle would begin. The noise of conversation died down toward the front, so I turned to see that two players were now standing before the massive doors to the boss's chamber.

One of them was Lind, decked out in silver armor, blue cape, and scimitar at his waist. The other was Kibaou, with his dark armor and moss-green jacket.

"Ugh, not another double-leader situation," I groaned.

"Isn't there only one leader by definition within the system?" Asuna asked.

"That's a good point..."

As if sensing our confusion, Lind raised a hand and spoke loudly to the group. Unlike the area outside the first-floor boss chamber, this was a safe zone, so there was no fear of tauruses coming to investigate the noise.

"Well, it's time. Let's start forming the raid! First, an introduction: I'm Lind, chosen to be your leader today. Greetings, everyone!"

Before I could even wonder how Kibaou would willingly give up control, the cactus-headed man interjected, "Only chosen 'cuz ya won a coin flip."

Half the gathering laughed at this, while the other half looked upset. Lind shot Kibaou a dirty glare, but he did not respond to the bait.

"...The fact that we're already here, just ten days after opening this floor, is a testament to your skill and dedication! If you lend me your help, there's no way we can fail to beat this boss! Let's finish the day on the third floor!"

He raised a fist, and all of those who didn't laugh at Kibaou's jibe roared in approval.

With his rousing speech and long hair, formerly brown but now dyed blue, Lind seemed to be fully accepting the role of Diavel's heir. I couldn't help but feel that here and there, hints of self-consciousness that his predecessor never displayed peeked through the facade.

"Now let's form the raid! Of the eight parties, the Dragon Knights will form teams A, B, and C. Kibaou's Liberation Squad will make up teams D, E, and F, and team G will be Orlando's Braves. And team H…"

He looked to us in the very back. For an instant, his breezy smile seemed to vanish when his eyes met mine, but he looked past me just as quickly.

"…will be the rest of you. Teams A through F will concentrate on the boss, while G and H handle the mobs…"

This news did not come as a surprise to me. What was surprising, however, was the voice that spoke up in response.

"Hang on just a moment."

It wasn't Agil and certainly wasn't Asuna. It was the leader of the group of five on the far wall: Orlando.

When he spoke, the eyes staring out from beneath his bascinet visor were just as piercing as when they'd nearly seen through my hiding ability outside the bar.

"We're here to fight the boss. If you want us to rotate around, I might understand, but we're not going to just hang back and deal with mobs."

His brassy voice echoed off the walls and died out, the ensuing lull filled by the fevered murmuring of the blue and green players. I could make out mutters of "Who do they think they are?" and "Bloody newcomers."

Then it all clicked into place for me.

With the disappearance of Nezha, Orlando and his team had just lost a huge source of income. This was their chance to leap out to the head of the clearers. The money earned by the raid party was equally shared between all members, but the experience points and skill boosts were not. The enormous store of experience points the boss was worth would be distributed by the amount of damage done (or blocked), and the skill proficiency gained by attacking a powerful enemy was far beyond that of a normal foe. None of that went to them if they didn't attack the boss directly.

The five Braves had upgraded their equipment to about the maximum it could be at this point, but their player levels were below the average of the raid. They probably saw this boss battle as the best chance to close that gap.

And yet, disagreeing with the raid leader's orders wasn't going to get them anywhere. The scene could have easily turned into an ugly shouting match, but the blue and green players didn't let it get any worse than whispers.

I suspected that was due to the powerful aura the Legend Braves were exuding. Level, stats, and skill proficiency were all hidden variables not exposed to the public—but equipment power was different. Weapons and armor augmented close to the limit began to glow with a depth that reinforced their value.

At the present moment, the best any player—including me—could do was upgrade their weapon, and perhaps their shield, to that glowing state. But the Braves were a different story. With the massive sum of col they reaped in the past week, they'd been able to buy full sets of excellent equipment and power it all up. All of their gear was glowing as if under a powerful buff spell, and it created the strong impression that these five men were not to be trifled with.

Of course, equipment strength was not all there was in the game. More important than anything in *SAO* was personal experience and the ability to react and adjust. But in the battle ahead against Baran the General Taurus, every value was important—especially armor strength.

This was because General Baran used an elite version of the taurus race's special attack...

"All right. In that case, team G can join the fight against the boss," Lind said stiffly. I looked up and found myself staring right into the blue-haired man's eyes again.

While his hairstyle might have been the same as the one worn by breezy, affable Diavel, Lind seemed to have a significantly more obstinate side to him. He held my gaze this time and said, "According to our prior intelligence, the boss only has one accompanying mob that does not re-pop. I trust team H will be able to handle that alone?"

Asuna and I sucked in a sharp breath, our hackles raised, but team leader Agil waved a hand to calm us. His voice and manner stayed perfectly calm.

"It might be one monster, but the intel says that it's not your average mob, but more of a mid-level boss on its own. Plus, maybe it's only the one, but we don't know that for sure. That's a lot to ask of a single party."

The prior intelligence they were referring to was, of course, the second-floor boss edition of Argo's strategy guide, which appeared just yesterday in Taran. It held the attack patterns and weak points of the boss and its attendant mob, but as the disclaimer on the cover said, all information was based on the beta test.

The first-floor boss used katana skills that hadn't been there in the beta, and it led to the death of Diavel the knight. We had to assume that there were alterations since the beta here, as well. In a worst-case scenario, there might be two or more of "Nato the Colonel Taurus" accompanying Baran instead of just one.

But Lind actually agreed with Agil's rebuttal.

"Of course, I have no intention of repeating the mistakes of the first floor. If we spot any difference in the patterns listed in our prior intelligence, we will immediately retreat and rethink our plan. If the attendant mob is too much for one party to handle, we'll send another team to help. Will that do?"

It was about as much as we could hope for at this stage. Agil murmured in the affirmative, and Asuna and I let out the breaths we'd been holding in.

Next came a review of the boss's attack patterns and a final check of each team's individual strategy, leaving just two minutes until the scheduled fight time of two o'clock. That was only a general guideline, so nothing was stopping us from beginning the fight slightly before or after the hour.

Lind raised his hand and said, "All right, it's a bit early, but…"

Suddenly, he was cut off by a familiar phrase from Kibaou, who had, somewhat surprisingly, kept quiet this entire time.

"Now, hang on just a sec!"

"…What is it, Kibaou?"

"You been basin' everything on this strategy guide so far, Lind. Now, all this info is comin' from the info dealer who ain't even been in the boss room, right? Is that really good enough for us?"

Lind's mouth twisted in displeasure. "I won't claim that it's perfect, but it's better than nothing, isn't it? What's your alternative? Are you going to walk in there to check out the boss for yourself?"

Now it was the green-clad Liberation Squad that bristled in anger, but Kibaou simply smiled confidently.

"What I'm sayin' is, we know we got at least one person here who's seen this boss for himself. So why don't we get his take on it?"

What?

I took a step back and to the left, to hide behind Asuna. But Kibaou lifted his right hand and pointed straight at me. Dozens of eyes turned in my direction, and Asuna callously stepped aside to avoid them.

"Whaddaya say, Black Beater? Why don'cha offer us some advice on this boss battle?" he bellowed. I couldn't read his expression to see what he was really thinking.

"…What does he think he's doing?" I muttered quietly, but Asuna could only shrug.

I'd heard that Kibaou's Aincrad Liberation Squad rallied around a resistance to the former beta testers. As a means to compete with the testers who rushed out to monopolize the game's best resources, they aggressively recruited new members from the thousands left down in the Town of Beginnings, distributed money and items fairly, and planned to conquer the game through sheer numbers. At least, according to Kibaou's theory.

So what did he stand to gain by giving a known ex-tester a platform? You'd think it was clearly some kind of trap...but there was something in the cactus-haired swordsman's eyes that could be taken as honest fervor.

If that look's an act, yer one helluva actor, I muttered to myself. One, two, three steps forward, and I had a proper view of every face in the raid.

"Let me just make this clear. I only know the boss from the beta test as well. So it's totally possible that something...or everything about this boss has been changed."

As I spoke, the muttering players eventually fell silent. Even Lind, who I figured would interrupt, did not speak.

"But I can say that the regular tauruses in the labyrinth use the exact same attacks that they did in the beta. So I think it's a certainty that the boss will use sword skills that are an extension of that pattern. As you just discussed, you want to evade when he goes into his motion, but what's most important is how to react when you take the first hit. Avoid getting hit with double debuffs at all costs. In the beta, every player that got stunned and then paralyzed..."

Pretty much died, I stopped myself from saying.

"At any rate, if you stay calm and watch his hammer, you can avoid the second hit. As long as we all take that into account, this lineup can beat the boss without any casualties."

Nothing I said couldn't be found in Argo's guide, but virtually all the players present nodded in understanding when I was done.

As usual, Kibaou's expression was a cipher to me, but Lind had a look of surprise. He clapped his hands briskly. "All right, everyone: Avoid the second hit! Now let's get started!"

He turned around and faced the giant set of doors and loudly drew his scimitar, holding it aloft.

"We're going to crush the second-floor boss!!"

The dim corridor shook with the roar of the gathering.

Blue hair waving, his left hand pushing the door open, Lind looked very much like Diavel had in that same exact moment back on the first floor.

12

MONSTER ATTACKS AGAINST PLAYERS FELL UNDER two general categories. One was direct attacks that dealt HP damage.

The other was indirect attacks that did not cause direct damage but occasionally posed a significant threat—in other words, debuffs.

Akihiko Kayaba, the designer of this game of death, at least had a minimum of sympathy for new players, for he did not grant any of the kobolds in the first-floor labyrinth debuff attacks. The delay effect that led to Diavel's death was a debuff, in a way, but it was an effect that occurred at a high likelihood when suffering multiple consecutive attacks, and wasn't a special skill that the kobold lord could use at will.

Which meant that the tauruses that dwelt in the second-floor labyrinth were the player's first real experience with serious, regular debuffs.

"Here it comes!" I cried, recognizing that the double-handed hammer was being lifted straight aloft.

The rest of my party called out their acknowledgment and jumped backward. The hammer stopped high overhead for an instant, its wide surface glowing with brilliant yellow sparks.

"*Vrrrooooooo!!*"

With a roar so fierce, it might as well have been a long-range attack of its own, the beast brought down the hammer. The mass of metal, rippling with lightning, slammed against the dark stone floor. It was the taurus race's special debuffing skill, Numbing Impact.

No one was standing within the direct damage range of the blow, of course, but there were also narrow sparking tendrils that extended out from the impact point. One of them shot toward me along the floor, fading out, until it just barely licked the end of my boot.

Instantly, I felt an unpleasant prickle at my toes. Fortunately, I was just outside of the debuff range, so there was no stun icon showing beneath my HP bar. Everyone else kept farther away from the shockwave, so none of them were affected.

"Full-power attack!" I shouted, and the six of us fanned out in a semicircle around the taurus and closed. Each person unleashed the strongest sword skill in their weapon's repertoire. Agil's two-handed axe, his crewmates' similar weapons, Asuna's Wind Fleuret, and my Anneal Blade blasted the beast with an array of colored lights. The bull-man's three-part HP gauge finally emptied its first bar and opened the second.

"I think we can do this!" Asuna shouted from her familiar position to my left.

"Yeah, just don't get overconfident! Once we get to the third bar, he'll start using consecutive numbing attacks! Plus," I raised my voice to ensure that Agil's group heard me, "based on the first-floor battle, we should assume there might be a new attack when we hit that last bar! If that happens, we all pull back!"

"Got it!"

The taurus recovered from its delay at the same time our skill cooldown ended. Agil's tanks recognized that the next attack would be a sideways blow and took defensive stances along its trajectory. Asuna and I hung back, waiting for the right moment to counter.

Just over five minutes had passed in the battle against the boss.

So far, our team was performing well. None of us had suffered the Numbing Impact effects yet, and none had taken heavy damage. The four tanks were losing HP with each attack they blocked, of course, but the pace of damage was slow enough that we were making do with just a one-man pot rotation so far.

And yet, the fact that our battle was going well meant hardly anything.

The blue-skinned, bull-headed beast that team H faced right now was only Nato the Colonel Taurus, an extra thrown into the boss monster fight...a distraction at worst.

"Evade! Evaaaade!" came a somewhat panicked scream from the other side of the vast boss chamber. When I had the chance, I glanced over the heads of the dozens of players to see a frightfully large shadow.

A bristly, crimson red pelt enveloped rippling muscles. His waist was covered with a luxurious golden cloth, but in keeping with taurus tradition, his upper half was bare. The chain dangling over his shoulders was also made of gold. To top it off, the golden battle hammer in his hands shone with a dazzling brilliance.

Coloring aside, Colonel Nato might as well have been a body double of Baran, but there was one other major difference: size. General Baran, the boss of the second floor, was at least twice the size of Nato.

Because of the physical height limit of the ceilings in the labyrinths of Aincrad, Baran was not as tall as the mammoth Bullbous Bow that prowled the landscape, but there was no escaping the primal fear inspired by a sixteen-foot beastman. Even the kobold lord from the first floor felt huge, and he was only seven feet tall and change.

Naturally, General Baran's golden hammer was massive as well, its powerful head the size of a barrel. When he lifted it, the surface shot golden sparks. The tanks and attackers pulled back as one, in accordance with Lind's order.

"*Vrrruuuuvraaaaa!!*"

Baran's roar was appropriately twice as fierce as Nato's, and he smashed the floor. Even at our distance, we could feel the shockwave, which was followed by a burst of sparks. Again, the effective range was twice that of his subordinate. It was Baran's unique skill, Numbing Detonation.

The queuing-up motion was very easy to identify, but the blast radius was so wide that two members failed to get to a safe distance, and their feet were swallowed by the golden sparks. The lightning wrapped around their limbs and demobilized them— the stun effect, one of the most common debuffs of the many in the game, though not one to be overlooked. The stun effect caused by the taurus's numbing attacks lasted three seconds, and unlike many debuffs, it wore off automatically.

But while three seconds might not feel long against garden-variety mobs, it was a lifetime against a deadly floor boss. Even at this distance, I was keenly aware of the fear and panic those stunned warriors were feeling.

One second, two seconds…and just before the third, one of the stunned fighters dropped his short spear to clatter onto the ground. It was a fumble, a secondary debuff that sometimes occurred in the midst of a stun. In the next instant, the soldier was free, and the blue-shirted member of Lind's group bent over to pick up his weapon.

"No—"

Get back, here comes the next one! I wanted to yell, but I held it in. He wouldn't hear me at this distance, and my companions in team H would confuse it for an order directed at them. After a brief but powerful Slant to Colonel Nato's ribs, I looked to see General Baran raising his hammer again.

Thwam! A second Numbing Detonation.

The hammer struck the same spot as the last one, and more yellow lightning shot forth. Again, they swallowed the spearman attempting to pick up his weapon.

But while he'd been standing upright last time, he fell down to the floor in this instance. The visual effect that surrounded his avatar was not yellow, but pale green. This was not a stun but a more powerful and dangerous debuff, paralysis.

It was the true terror of the tauruses' numbing skills—the second hit in succession would turn the stun to a paralyzing effect.

Unlike a stun, paralysis did not disappear after a few seconds. It wasn't indefinite either, but even the weakest effect would last ten minutes...a full 600 seconds. Obviously, no one could survive a battle while prone for that length of time, so healing items were necessary.

The main methods of recovery were healing potions or purification crystals. The latter were impossible to find until later in the game, so potions were the only choice. However, paralysis left only the dominant hand of the player able to move—and slowly, at that—so even pulling a bottle out of a pouch was a trial. Crawling out of the boss's attack range was completely out of the question.

I told them not to pick up their weapons but wait until they were sure the boss wasn't going to attack twice!

But there was no use complaining to myself. Besides, picking up a dropped weapon was just human instinct. I couldn't count the number of times I'd done the same thing and suffered additional hits during the beta. I only learned to deal with that particular challenge with a cool head once I gained the Quick Change mod so that I could call up a replacement from my inventory.

Baran callously targeted the paralyzed spearman and prepared to stomp him with a massive foot. Fortunately, his party members quickly intervened to pull him out of harm's way.

I heaved a sigh of relief, but when I saw where they were taking him, my eyes bulged.

Lined up along the back wall were already seven or eight players, clutching green potions in their stiff hands and waiting for the effect to wear off. The entire time that we'd been carefully chipping away at Colonel Nato, a large number of the main force was suffering from secondary numbing.

"Things aren't going well in the main fight," Agil rumbled as he returned from his potion rotation.

I quickly responded, "Yes, but the more they fight, the more they'll get accustomed to the rhythm. I haven't seen any differences from the beta yet, so I think—"

We'll be all right, I was about to finish, but Asuna cut me off with a sobering note.

"But Kirito, if any more of them get paralyzed…it'll make a temporary retreat much harder."

"…!"

I tensed and clenched the handle of my Anneal Blade. The weapon wouldn't fall unless I intentionally dropped it (or an external factor caused me to fumble it), but my subconscious was working in overdrive after witnessing the prior scene with the spearman.

The boss chambers in Aincrad, at least as far as I'd seen, did not lock the players inside once the battle had begun. If things got hairy, it was always possible to beat a hasty retreat. That didn't mean it was a simple matter, of course; there was a considerable distance between the battle zone and the door, so if everyone took off running at once, the boss would catch up to us in no time and cause delays, stunning, and ultimately, death.

So in a way, escaping from the boss chamber required a trickier coordinated effort than actually fighting the adversary. Could we even pull it off, burdened by a large number of paralyzed fighters?

For one thing, lifting an immobile player in your arms to carry them out required a significant strength value. I couldn't lift Asuna up with my skinny arms when she had passed out in the first-floor labyrinth, so I had had to drag her out using a sleeping bag—an emergency measure still fresh in my memory.

From what I could see, about four-fifths of Lind and Kibaou's forces were balanced or speed-first fighters, with only a few pure-strength tanks. As Asuna pointed out, if many more players got paralyzed, it would be much harder to disengage.

"We might need to refocus and prioritize dealing with the numbing," I said, stepping out of the way of a three-part hammer combo from Nato. Asuna nimbly matched my steps beside me.

"I agree. But if we start calling out orders for the main force, it's only going to confuse the chain of command. We need to get our ideas to Lind's ears."

Her hazel eyes darted over the HP of team H, and then Colonel Nato.

"We can handle him with just five. Go and talk to Lind, Kirito."

"Um…a-are you sure?"

"Yeah, no problem!" boomed Agil, who must have overheard. "The four of us can handle guarding for now! You've easily got two or three minutes to go talk with him!"

I turned back to look at the chocolate-skinned warrior and his friends, who seemed resolute, and I made up my mind. The key to defeating Baran was to keep his paralysis out of the equation. The battle was holding up for now thanks to our large number and high average level, but if this was the same party that tackled him in the beta, we'd be wiped out by now.

"All right, just for a bit! I'll be right back!"

Before I left, I unleashed a Vertical Arc into Nato's back as he stood frozen after missing with a big attack, and sped off for my target.

I shot across the coliseum-styled chamber, more than a hundred yards across, and headed for the main battle in the back. My pasty, skinny real body back home would be lucky to break fourteen seconds in the hundred-meter dash, but the agility-heavy Kirito crossed the space in ten flat. My bootheels screeched to a halt as I lined up next to a blue cape at the rear.

For a moment, it occurred to me that this was the first time I'd ever been face-to-face with Lind, leader of this raid and former confidant of Diavel the knight.

Ten days earlier, just after we defeated the previous boss, he'd screamed, *Why did you abandon Diavel to die? You knew the moves the boss was using! If you'd told us that information to start with, Diavel wouldn't have died!*

I hadn't apologized. I'd met him with a cold smile.

I'm a beater. Don't you ever insult my skill by calling me a former tester.

And having said my piece, I had put on the Coat of Midnight I was still wearing, and left the first-floor boss chamber. I hadn't interacted with Lind since that very moment.

So it shouldn't have been a surprise that when I sidled up next to him, Lind's first reaction was a grimace of disgust. His narrow eyes went wide, his blade-sharp chin trembled, and his thin lips went even thinner.

But that manifestation of his true emotions soon sank back beneath his skin. It bothered me that both he and Kibaou were attempting to mask their true feelings about me—though it also wasn't my business to care about it—but now was not the time to worry about feelings.

"I ordered you to handle the sub-boss. Why are you—" he growled before I interrupted with the line I'd prepared.

"Let's regroup. If any more members get paralyzed, it's going to make escape nearly impossible."

The raid leader looked back at the seven or eight players waiting to recover, then at the state of the fight itself. Following his lead, I checked the HP bar of General Baran. Out of his five bars, they'd lowered the third to the halfway point—we were already half-done with the boss.

"We're halfway there. Why would we need to retreat now?"

I had to admit, there was a part of me that thought it would be a waste to give up now. In the ten minutes since we had started the battle, several people had been paralyzed, but no one's HP had fallen into the red zone, and the pace of our damage against the boss was better than expected. There was more than a small chance that we could continue to press on, and make it through...

But as if seeing through my hesitation, a voice rang out from behind us.

"How's about we pull back if one more person gets paralyzed?"

I turned around to see Kibaou's familiar, light-brown spikes of hair. No doubt he was also filled with a powerful disgust at me for being a tried-and-true beta tester, but the look on his face was honest and forthright.

"Everyone's got the hang of the numbing range and timing. They're focused, an' morale is high. We been poundin' paralysis and healing potions, so if we stop now, we might not have the supplies ta give it another shot until tomorrow."

"..."

Again, I let my mind race for half a second before reaching a conclusion.

The most important thing here was not the number of tries or the sum of spent resources but human life. We had to succeed without losing anyone. That was the first rule of any boss battle in Aincrad.

But Lind and Kibaou already knew that. And if the leader and sub-leader of the raid decided that we could still win, the only thing that a single fighter from an outlying party would do by disagreeing was sabotage the chain of command—obviously, a bad decision. And on top of that, my own instincts were telling me that if we could just maintain our current progress, we *could* defeat Baran without any casualties.

"All right, one more. Just be careful when we get down to the last HP gauge," I said. Kibaou growled in acknowledgment and turned back to his station. Lind nodded silently and resumed his command.

"Team E, prepare to retreat! Team G, prepare to advance! Switch at the next stagger!" he ordered as I turned back and crossed the coliseum to rejoin team H.

Asuna wasted no time in asking, "What happened?!"

"We'll pull back if one more person gets paralyzed! But at our current pace, we can probably make it!"

"I see..." She briefly looked upset and glanced over at the main battle, but grudgingly agreed with the decision. "All right.

In that case, let's finish off this blue guy quick, so we can join the others."

"Yeah!"

Having reached a rapid consensus, we turned back to see that Colonel Nato had just unleashed a massive attack that was expertly blocked by Agil's group. There was just a bit over one full HP bar left. With perfect precision, we hit the beast with sword skills to either flank.

That attack brought Nato to his final HP bar, and the blue-skinned minotaur bellowed up at the ceiling. He stamped the ground with hooves as big as buckets, then hunched over to expose his horns and tensed like a coiled spring. It was a new pattern to this fight, but not one I'd never seen before.

"He's gonna charge! Watch the tail, not the head! He'll go along that diagonal!"

Nato turned to his left and charged right for Agil. But the axe-warrior, poised and prepared, easily dodged out of the way and unloaded his double-handed combo, Whirlwind. He stepped back, and Asuna and I switched in to continue the onslaught. The damage was so great that spinning yellow rings appeared over the colonel's head, and he began to wobble. We'd inflicted our own stun status on him.

"Now's our chance! Everyone use two full-power attacks!!"

"Raaah!!"

All six of us surrounded the taurus and pummeled him with flashes of light in red, blue, and green. His HP bar lost refreshingly large chunks in quick succession and soon plunged into the yellow zone that signified less than half remained.

Our full attack a success, we held distance once more, and the taurus's skin turned purple as he raged even louder. This berserk state before he died was, again, the same as in the beta. His attack speed was half again as fast as before, but with a calm head, this was not an issue.

On the other side of the chamber, the players let out a roar. I nearly lost my balance for a moment before I realized it was a cry of high spirits. General Baran's final HP bar had gone yellow as well. Meanwhile, the number of paralyzed along the wall had not risen but had shrunk to five.

"It's a good thing there weren't any surprises since the beta," Asuna opined to me while we waited for our skills to cool down behind Agil's protective wall. I looked back to the battle at hand and nodded.

"Yeah. But if we'd been paying attention against the kobold lord, we'd have noticed that the weapon on his back was a katana, not a talwar. And General Baran hasn't changed an inch from the beta. So…"

I suddenly realized that a shadow had passed across Asuna's face. "What's wrong?"

"Um…nothing. I'm just overthinking things…I was just noticing that it's weird the first-floor boss was a lord, but the second one is only a…"

Ga-gong!

A sudden crash interrupted our conversation. We all turned as one to the source of the sound—the center of the coliseum chamber.

But there was nothing there. Only a series of concentric floor rings made of blackish stone…

No. It was moving. The three circles of paving stones were sliding, rotating counterclockwise and slowly picking up speed. The stones were rising from the floor before my eyes, elevating into a three-step stage at the center of the room.

Suddenly, the view of the far wall over the center platform began to waver.

"Uh-oh…" I grunted. That was the visual effect that signaled a very large object being generated into the map. As I feared, the wavering in the air rapidly spread and began to generate a thick, menacing shadow at the center.

The shadow soon coalesced into a humanoid form and grew two legs thick as tree trunks that thudded heavily onto the stage. Sturdy, dark chainmail covered the figure's waist, but its torso was, as usual, bare. This one had a long, twisted beard that hung down to its stomach. The head was that of a bull, but it had six horns instead of two, and atop the center of its head was a round accessory of silvery platinum—a crown.

The mammoth figure, so black it might as well have been painted with ink, reared back, and the third and largest of the tauruses let out a roar. Flashes of lightning spread around the minotaur, filling the chamber with blinding light.

Finally, a six-part HP bar appeared so high in my field of view that it seemed to be stuck to the ceiling. I gazed dully at the letters that appeared.

Asterios the Taurus King.

Keep your mind moving! Think! I told myself so hard that if I wasn't gritting my teeth, I'd have spoken the words aloud.

It was clear what had just happened. General Baran, whom every player present, including me, had assumed was the second-floor boss, was just as much an opening act as Colonel Nato.

Baran's final HP bar turning yellow must have been the trigger to generate the true boss—the pitch-black King Asterios. But speculation about the origin of the creature was pointless. What mattered was what we did next.

There was no need to think. We had to retreat out of the chamber. We didn't even know how this monster would attack...and the risks of fighting this taurus king were clearly far greater than that of the general.

The problem was that Asterios had spawned in the center of the chamber, and the raid party was fighting in the back of the room. The group would need to charge through his attack range in order to reach the exit. Team H, fighting Colonel Nato, was the closest to the exit, and we could probably make it out safely now, if we broke for it...but if we did that, and teams A through G were wiped out by the king, our chances of beating this game of death disappeared along with them.

How to evacuate a forty-seven-man raid party? The first step was eliminating our present foes as quickly as possible.

Time seemed to spring back into motion once our path became clear, and I promptly raised my sword high and shouted, "All units, all-out attack!!"

I tore my eyes away from Asterios atop his three-step stage, and fixed a gaze on the berserk Colonel Nato. I leapt as hard as I could, following the path of his hammer as he raised it behind him.

As a speed-focused swordsman with no heavy metal armor, I could jump about six feet from a standing position. Nato was closer to seven or eight feet, but with the added reach of my sword, I could easily get to his head.

My Slant skill hit the shining black horns directly. Nato's attack motion stopped partway, and he reared back and roared. The tauruses of the second-floor labyrinth, excepting only a few (say, the Taurus Ironguard, which wore a heavy metal helm), were weak to blows to the horns. I hadn't tried to strike their foreheads at any point until now because jumping attacks were inherently risky, and even a clean hit from a sword skill was no guarantee that the opponent would suffer a movement delay. But this situation called for desperate measures.

At the exact moment I landed, Asuna and Agil's team followed up with attacks of their own, knocking Nato's HP into the red zone. His delay wore off, and the minotaur roared and began his motion for a numbing skill. In any other case, now was the time to pull back, but I pushed forward.

"Raaah!"

With a roar of my own, I unleashed my very best Horizontal. Even if I hit the beast's weak point, I couldn't stagger the creature on consecutive attacks, but it wasn't the forehead I was aiming for—it was Nato's giant hammer. The timing window was extremely short, but if I hit his sword skill with one of my own just before he fired it off, it was possible to cancel the attacks out.

There was a piercing clang that seemed to strike directly into the center of my brain, and my sword shot backward. Meanwhile, the hammer was pushed back overhead. Without missing their chance, my five companions proceeded to launch another wave of attacks. Only a few pixels of HP remained.

Under normal circumstances, chaining sword skills together was impossible. But I knew from our hunting of the Windwasps the other day that you could get past that limitation if you used weapons of different categories. I curled up in midair and kicked out with my left foot. The resulting Crescent Moon, a vertical kick attack as I spun backward, caught Nato right on the forehead.

The taurus hurtled backward and let out a high-pitched screech before freezing stiff, then exploding into a massive cloud of polygons. It must have been treated as a proper sub-boss, not just a typical mob, because I promptly saw a Last Attack bonus readout. I didn't have time for that, however; I spun around as I hit the ground.

The first thing I saw across the room was a towering ebony back. King Asterios was on the move. Fortunately, he hadn't targeted any of the five paralyzed along the east wall, but his destination was the thirty-six remaining fighters of the main party—who were still busy with General Baran.

My worst fear was that the main force would fall into total panicked chaos and retreat if faced by a boss on either side. Fortunately, that was not happening. But very soon, his lumbering steps would take him within attack range of the raid. We had to defeat the general before then.

"Let's go, Kirito!" said Asuna, her voice tense. But I wasn't sure if I should agree. It wasn't that I was afraid for my own life—for some reason that I couldn't explain, I was gripped with a sudden feeling that once I set foot into the battle ahead, I could not guarantee that she'd survive.

I knew damn well just how good Asuna was. I wasn't even sure if I could beat her in a one-on-one duel. But there was no denying my urge to force her to escape right there and then.

After I had abandoned my first and only friend at the start of this game, and was nearly killed by a fellow beta tester just hours later, I had sworn to live as a solo player, relying on no one but myself. The week that we had just spent as a partnership-of-sorts was only a means to uncovering and stopping Nezha's fraud. Nothing more.

So why was I being ruled by this emotion...this sentimentality?

Why was I so desperate to keep Asuna from dying?

"Asuna, you need..."

To run, I wanted to say—but I saw the powerful light in her hazel eyes. They told me that she knew full well what I was thinking. Her eyes were full of an emotion that was neither anger nor sadness but something even purer. Again, she said, "Let's go."

There was enough strength in that voice that it bottled up the fear that had overtaken me.

"...All right," I said, and looked back at Agil's party. The axe-warrior nodded at me, not frightened in the least.

"We'll swing around the right flank and defeat Baran first. If the king attacks before then, we've got to pull him away as best we can to help buy them time."

"Got it!" the others shouted. Bolstered by their courage, I leapt forward. By the time I reached full speed, my hesitation was gone.

The monster's reaction zone, also called its "aggro range," was invisible to the naked eye. But the more experience one built, the more it felt like a tangible thing. I followed my instinct and circled around the right side of the plodding King Asterios toward the main party.

Baran's HP bar was already down into the red zone. But as with Nato when he was nearly dead, Baran had gone into a berserk state and was using his Numbing Detonation at every possible chance, slowing the group's attack progress.

We had thirty seconds until the king started to attack, I gauged. I darted right between the wide-eyed Lind and Kibaou, directly in front of General Baran, and leapt high into the air, aiming for his blazing orange horns. But the general was nearly twice the size of the colonel. Even my highest jump combined with my longest reach couldn't make it all the way.

"Rrraah!"

At the apex of my jump, I took pains to hold my stance and just barely managed to throw off a sword skill. My Anneal Blade glowed green, and my body sped back into motion as though pushed by invisible hands: Sonic Leap, a one-handed sword charge skill.

This desperate attack hit him right in the weak point, and the general's body arched backward. This staggering was our final chance.

Asuna and the other four didn't need my order to know what to do. They raced in to land blows, then pulled back. The rest of the raid followed their lead, and General Baran was enveloped in flashing effects of every color.

But once again, it wasn't quite enough. There was still a pixel or two left on his HP bar.

"Not again!" I cursed, clenching my left fist. Coming out of a major sword skill off-balance, my only option was a simple attack. I roared and swung forward with a Flash Blow, hitting him square in the chest. It was just enough damage to do the job, and that tiny little jab sent the massive body expanding...and exploding.

I landed hard, ignoring the LA bonus readout entirely, and took a deep breath to command everyone to retreat back against the wall. There was no time to worry about whether I was over-stepping my bounds or not.

But my breath caught in my throat before I could speak.

The onyx taurus king, who should have still been ten seconds away, was leaning backward, his massive chest bulging like a bar-rel. That looked like...

A breath attack. Long range.

And right in his path, back to him, her eyes fixed straight at me, was Asuna.

If she didn't move now, there would be no escape. I couldn't waste time racing over to her. But that kind of logical reasoning went out the window.

"Asuna, jump to your right!" I shouted as I dashed toward her. There were other players in the breath range, of course, but my tunnel vision was fixed on no one but the hooded fencer. She must have sensed the danger approaching from behind in my voice and expression. She leapt as I commanded, not bothering to turn around.

As soon as her boots left the black paving stone, I reached her and slipped my left arm around her slender body, leaping in the same direction to add to our momentum. Even at full strength, the jump speed was unbearably slow. The arabesque pattern in the floor flowed past, glacial in pace...

The right side of my vision went pure white.

The dry shockwave that hit me was exactly like a clap of thunder. Asterios the Taurus King's breath attack was not poison or fire but lightning. And by the time we realized it, the both of us, and over twenty other players in the raid, were enveloped in its white blaze.

There was no such thing as attack, healing, or support magic in *Sword Art Online*. But that didn't mean that all traces of magic were absent from the game world. There was an infinite variety of magical items to be found that raised stats or provided buff effects, and the blessing of an NPC priest at a church in one of the bigger towns granted a player's weapon a temporary holy effect.

But those supernatural effects did not exist solely for our benefit. In fact, the majority were a detriment. For example, the many special attack skills employed by monsters: poison, fire, ice, and lightning breath.

The most powerful breath attack in terms of damage was fire, but lightning was no joke. For one, it was instantaneous—it traveled the full length of its range in the instant it was unleashed. Worse, it had a very high chance of stunning its victims, with the worst-case scenario involving an even more dangerous debuff.

Asuna and I took Asterios's lightning breath to our legs, and we both lost close to 20 percent of our health in one go. A green border began to blink around the gauge, and a debuff icon of the same color appeared as well.

Instantly, I felt my physical senses growing distant. I couldn't move my legs to land upright, even if I tried. Asuna and I slammed into the ground on our backs. This was no mere tumble effect—after all of my warnings, we were now paralyzed.

"Asu...na," I rasped. She was laid across my chest like an immobile plank. "Heal with...potion."

I tried desperately to move my stiff hand. There were two red HP potions and one green paralysis antidote in the belt pouch on my right side. Somehow, I felt around and grabbed the green one, popped the cork and held it up to my lips, even as the rumbling footsteps grew closer.

Once I finished the minty liquid, I hesitantly looked up to see that the massive taurus king was barely ten yards away. His attack had hit several other players with paralysis, and over a dozen of them littered the ground between us and him.

The other thirty players who escaped the lightning breath were making their way around the slowly moving boss, but they weren't sure how to react. The reason why was clear: The raid's leader and sub-leader, Lind and Kibaou, were both paralyzed, and the closest to the boss's position. They were desperately trying to give orders, but a whisper was the best anyone suffering from paralysis could produce. None of the players outside Asterios's attack range could hear them.

But very close to my ears came the sound of a fragile, beautiful voice.

"Why...did you come?"

I looked back to see two very large hazel eyes right in front of my face. Asuna was collapsed directly on top of me, empty potion bottle clutched in her hand. She repeated herself.

"Why...?"

She was asking me why I'd run toward her when I realized the

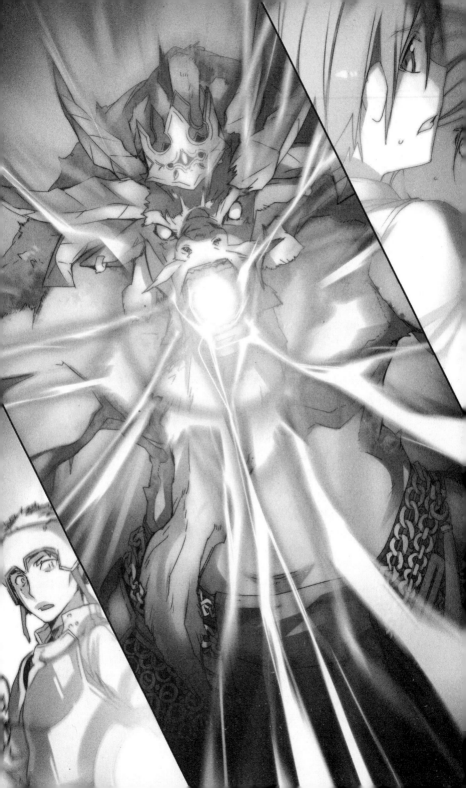

taurus's breath attack was coming, rather than darting directly out of harm's way. I wondered what the answer was myself, but it did not become apparent. All I could say was "I don't know."

And for reasons that were once again a mystery to me, she smiled gently, closed her eyes, and set her hooded head against my shoulder.

I looked over Asuna's back to see Asterios raising his massive hammer high overhead. The crushing implement, twice as large as even Baran's, was aimed right at Lind and Kibaou.

So this is it, I told myself.

If our two leaders died, the rest of the raid party would flee out of the boss chamber, leaving behind the ten or so paralyzed, including me and Asuna, to die... But at some later point in time, they would be able to use the information gleaned from Asterios's appearance and attacks to launch a second attempt.

The worst regret of all this was that I wasn't able to save Asuna and her limitless potential. As I'd told her after the first-floor boss, she could have one day led an enormous guild and been a leader to the player population. Like a shooting star, endlessly lighting up the sky of this dark, hopeless game of death.

I hallucinated a strange light, passing across the ceiling of the dim chamber.

But even after opening my eyes wider, the shining arc did not disappear. It reached an apex and began to fall, heading right for the crown on Asterios's brow as he was preparing to swing his hammer...

It wasn't until a high-pitched squeal of metal rang through the coliseum and Asterios lurched in pain that I realized the light wasn't a trick of the eye.

That was a long-range attack that shouldn't have been possible at this point in *SAO*, a sword skill under the Throwing Knife category. But the thrown weapon didn't simply fall to the ground after hitting the boss's weak point; it spun around and flew back across the room, as though pulled by an invisible string.

Asterios recovered from his delay and roared in anger, making a slow turn back to his attacker. That was the first actual hit on the boss, so it automatically drew the enemy's attention.

Suddenly, a powerful set of arms pulled me and Asuna off the floor. The mighty warrior, holding two people aloft without any help, spoke in a deep baritone.

"Sorry about that! I actually got a little spooked!"

Agil the axe-warrior carried us over to the eastern wall. His three companions were also busy moving paralyzed party members to a safer position. As if brought to their senses, the remainders of the blue and green teams raced over to the other immobilized fighters.

I tried to crane my neck up so I could see as he ferried us under his arms like suitcases. As we moved, the southern side of the coliseum came into view behind the boss's massive bulk.

About thirty feet from the entrance, a small figure clutching a bizarre weapon was staring up at the looming giant with a resolute look on his face.

"Isn't that—?!" Agil cried in surprise as he dropped us on the floor against the wall. And it wasn't just him—virtually everyone in the chamber was staring with shock at this new, forty-eighth player.

Not because he had suddenly appeared just before the boss routed us, or because he used a strange and unfamiliar weapon. It was because we had all seen this man hammering away at an anvil in the eastern plaza of Taran just a few days ago. It was Nezha the blacksmith.

He was dressed much differently now, of course. The brown leather apron was replaced by a bronze breastplate, gauntlets of the same material, and an open-faced helmet. But the image of a beardless dwarf that his short, stocky build and round, dour face created hadn't been neutralized by this new look; if anything, his outfit accentuated it.

The entire raid was shocked that a blacksmith would be here, participating in the boss raid, with only two exceptions: Asuna and me, the ones who'd convinced him to change careers in the first place. I was surprised as well, of course, but only because I hadn't expected him to be able to charge straight through the labyrinth alone, after just three days of training.

But there were others here who would be shocked in a much different way from the rest of us. As soon as the thought occurred to me, a group rushed forward from the raid party in the center of the room. They came to a stop once they reached an angle that gave them a clear view of Nezha's face around the side of the boss. It was team G...the Legend Braves.

"Nez..."

Orlando started to call the name of his missing partner, but he held back at the last instant. It seemed the Braves were still trying to hide the fact that Nezha was part of their guild.

For an instant, Nezha looked back at his silent former companions with a pained look, but he composed himself and yelled, "I'll draw the boss away! Get everyone back on their feet now, while you can!"

Asterios's walking speed—for the first of his many HP bars, at least—was quite slow. If Nezha used the hundred-yard hall effectively, he could probably continue to occupy the enemy's attention all by himself. If he held out until all of the paralyzed had recovered, we might be able to evacuate the entire raid group safely...

But no. It wouldn't work. The boss moved slowly, yes, but he had that instantaneous lightning breath to make up for it. There was no way to dodge that onslaught on your very first encounter with it. And based on the moment of Nezha's appearance, he probably hadn't seen Asterios's first attack.

"Agil, warn him about..."

The breath attack, I wanted to say, but I was already too late. Asterios stopped still and pulled his head back again, sucking in breath. His chest puffed up into a round ball, and little sparks crackled out of his nostrils. Nezha was standing still, looking up at the boss's head.

"Move..." I rasped.

"Get out of the way!!" someone in the raid shouted. But Nezha nimbly leapt aside before the words were even out of his mouth. The next instant, a brilliant cone of white lightning shot from the boss's gaping mouth. The breath attack reached nearly to the exit of the room, but Nezha was clear of its path by a good six feet.

The way he moved...Did he know exactly when to dodge?

My eyes went wide, and I suddenly heard a very familiar voice... but not one I would have expected to hear here, of all places.

"The boss's eyes glow just before the breath attack."

I looked up from the floor, stunned, to see the tile pattern on the wall warp out of place. An even smaller figure than Nezha appeared out of thin air. My mouth fell open (as did Asuna's and Agil's, if I had to guess) as I stared at that familiar whiskered face—Argo the Rat, the information dealer.

It was only afterward that I learned that she'd undertaken a series of quests beginning in the jungle outside the labyrinth that eventually earned her information on Asterios the Taurus King, the true boss of this floor. She learned not just his attack patterns, but the best way to counteract him—such as staggering him with a thrown weapon to the crown atop his head.

When Argo discovered that quest, she zipped around turning in objectives, and only finished just after the raid party entered the labyrinth. Messages couldn't reach anyone in a dungeon, and it was a question whether Argo and her agility-heavy build could make it through the labyrinth alone.

As she wavered with indecision outside the tower, she happened across Nezha, who was also preparing to brave the dangers of the labyrinth alone. They worked together—using Argo's Hiding skill and Nezha's throwing weapons to avoid or lure mobs out of their way—and reached the boss chamber just before Asterios appeared and threw the battle into chaos.

"Why are you still lying around? You're not paralyzed anymore," Argo said. I finally noticed that the paralysis icon beneath my HP bar was gone. I sprang to my feet and sprinted over to the Anneal Blade where it lay after I was hit by the breath attack. Asuna's Wind Fleuret was also nearby, so I brought them both back to the wall. I considered whether or not to address what Asuna said while we were on the ground, then decided it wasn't the right moment.

A quick look around told me that nearly everyone else had recovered from their paralysis. Lind and Kibaou were on their feet, but I saw Argo marching over toward them. For an instant, I even forgot that Nezha was single-handedly keeping the boss occupied.

Argo the Rat was, along with me, one of the most prominent publicly known beta testers in the game, and Lind and Kibaou were leaders of the anti-tester movement. As I expected, Lind didn't even pretend to hide his disgust, while Kibaou's expression was more uneasy and uncertain.

"Hey, spiky. Long time no see," Argo greeted Kibaou, ignoring Lind entirely. That's when it hit me.

Kibaou was the very man who'd attempted to buy my Anneal Blade through Argo. It was the kind of shady dealing that no leader would want associated with him, and Argo could sell the details to anyone who paid the price.

He didn't respond to her greeting, so she continued, "If you're gonna pull out, better do it now. But if you want info, I can sell it to you. For the low, low price of... nothing."

The moment Asterios's lightning breath hit Lind and Kibaou, they were at the greatest risk of dying of anyone in the raid. So it was a bit of a surprise to me that after just a few seconds of deliberation, they chose to continue the fight. Of course, we wouldn't know if that was the right choice or not until the end of the fight. But the tables had turned significantly since the moment just after the boss appeared. Nezha had successfully pulled Asterios's aggro for over two minutes, giving the rest of the raid enough time to recover from paralysis and refill their HP. On top of that, now we had the details on the boss's patterns.

"All right, let's begin the attack! Teams A and D, forward!" Lind ordered. The heavily armored tanks rushed in at King Asterios. Their body-blow charge hit him in the legs, finally drawing his attention away from Nezha.

Instantly, he started to sway, as though all of the tension keeping him upright had snapped. Asuna and I raced over.

"Nezha!"

The former blacksmith looked up, his expression as weak as usual...but with a new core of strength behind his smile. He held up the throwing weapon in his right hand.

It was the weapon I'd given him—a thick, bladed, circular throwing tool about eight inches across. The only way to get it at this point was as a rare drop from the Taurus Ringhurler enemies in this labyrinth. It fell under the Chakram subcategory of throwing knives, but unlike the actual chakrams from ancient India, this one had a leather grip along part of the circle. The grip made it useful for both throwing like a disc, or augmenting a punch like a set of brass knuckles.

Because of that versatility, chakrams in *SAO* couldn't be used with the Throwing Knives skill alone. They also required the mastery of Martial Arts, the extra skill that could only be learned from the bearded master hidden deep in the mountains.

As he said himself three days ago, he could hit monsters with a thrown weapon without having to worry too much about his perspective issues. But orthodox throwing knives were a quantifiable weapon that ran out over time and weren't suited for a main weapon. But the chakram was like a boomerang: It returned to the thrower's hand automatically. Thanks to that, he didn't need to worry about ammunition.

Nezha steadied his weary legs and held up his chakram. The blade was glowing yellow. Even though I was the one who'd given him the weapon, I didn't know the name of this sword skill.

"*Yaah!*"

With a powerful cry, his hand flashed, and the sparkling ring flew high in the air. It raced across the ceiling, a brilliant burst of light, and hit Asterios on the crown with perfect accuracy as he raised his giant hammer. There was another high-pitched *clang*, and the boss's muscled torso writhed. One of the attackers in Kibaou's team shouted, "Nice!" from the taurus king's feet.

The chakram hurtled back with alarming speed and smacked right back into Nezha's hand, thanks to the assistance of the game engine. He turned to me and Asuna and smiled again as though he were about to burst into tears.

"It's like a dream come true. Here I am...in the boss battle, playing a role..."

His voice quavered and died out there. Nezha swallowed and tried again.

"I'll be fine! Go ahead and join the battle!"

"All right. Do your best to read his lightning breath ahead of time and stagger him before he uses it. You're the key to our victory!"

I turned around and saw not just Asuna but Agil and his band of hearty toughs, ready for action.

Wasn't Agil supposed to be the leader of this team? I'll have to apologize to him later for taking over.

I shouted an order to the group. "Let's go!"

They echoed my call, and we headed for the unceasing series of sword flashes centered around our foe.

The true boss of the second floor of Aincrad, Asterios the Taurus King, was a third bigger than even Baran the General Taurus. His paralyzing lightning breath had terrified us momentarily, but with Argo's knowledge of his patterns, the group had devised a safe and steady strategy that was chipping away at his health.

The greatest role in the battle was undoubtedly Nezha and his throwing weapon, but it soon became clear that the single strongest group was team G—not Lind or Kibaou's forces, but the Legend Braves.

Like General Baran, Asterios used the area-effect skill Numbing Detonation, but Orlando and his team were able to take the numbing effects at very close range without ever being stunned.

When the king lifted his mighty hammer, the other groups had to evacuate to safety, but team G stayed right on him, continuing their assault without fear of his detrimental attacks. Even Lind had no idea when to give the order for them to retreat.

All of the Braves had high debuff resistance, thanks to their heavily upgraded gear. The unfortunate truth was that they'd "earned" the money for that herculean task through Nezha's upgrading scam, but now that Nezha was no longer a blacksmith, there was no longer any chance that they'd take the heat for it.

"...It's a complicated feeling, isn't it?" Asuna mumbled when we retreated temporarily to drink healing potions.

"Yeah. But at least they shouldn't be able to do it anymore," I replied, referring to the weapon-switching fraud. "If they're able to help us advance through the game like this, we'll just have to accept it. I still feel bad for those who lost their weapons, though."

"Yeah..."

She still looked conflicted, so I took her mind off things by leaning in close and sharing an idea.

"Y'know, I don't really feel like letting them win the battle MVP, so how about we fight back a little bit? If the timing permits it, of course."

"Fight back...?"

I lifted the edge of her hood and whispered into her ear. Asuna's eyes looked skeptical and exasperated, but she nodded in agreement. When she pulled the hood back up over her head, I thought I detected a hint of a smile on her lips, but I couldn't peer in close for a second look.

"Hey, Kirito," Agil rumbled from behind, with an odd tone in his voice and an empty bottle in his hand, "You said you weren't a pair, right?"

Asuna straightened up and pivoted on her heel. Her voice was frosty.

"We are not."

Fortunately, I didn't need to weigh in on the topic, because a cheer broke out from the direction of the battle. Asterios's last

HP bar had gone red. Our team's HP had just hit maximum again, which was perfect timing.

"Team E, pull back! Team H, up forward!" Lind commanded. I held up my free hand and clenched my Anneal Blade +6. Even if it was our turn in the rotation, it spoke to Lind's fairness as a leader that he didn't try to hold me back.

"Okay, hang on," I said, waiting for the right timing. "Go!"

We darted in to take the place of green team E along the boss's left flank. First, Asuna and I traded off with single skills against those tree-trunk legs. The monster roared in rage and swiped at us, which Agil and his friends blocked as they switched in.

Asterios's size was certainly frightening, but on the other hand, the larger a monster was, the more people could attack it at once. One full party was all that could fight Colonel Nato at a time, while two could tackle General Baran, and King Asterios was large enough for three at once.

Team H took the left side, blue team B handled him front and center, and Orlando's team G was still tearing away at his right flank. The king's black skin was burning through like coal, a sign of his berserk state, but we were on pace to finish him off with this set.

"*Vrrruaaraagh!!*"

With a terrible, primal roar, Asterios began to suck in air again. I didn't need to see the sparks around his mouth to know he was preparing his breath attack. But just as quickly as he started, the chakram flew in and struck him on the crown. Lightning exploded harmlessly from the king's nostrils.

If this was a normal MMO, that 100-percent-guaranteed stagger from the chakram would get nerfed to oblivion, I thought to myself, referring to the practice of reducing its power to restore proper game balance.

Floor bosses in *SAO* were a one-time affair—once defeated, they would never return. If Akihiko Kayaba was indeed watching over the battle from afar, would he be gnashing his teeth at the sight of his guardian, unable to stay poised long enough to unleash its best attack? Or would he be applauding the ingenuity (and luck) of the players who hit upon this unlikely strategy?

We're going to beat your second floor in just ten days, Kayaba! I thought triumphantly. A glance at the king's HP bar showed just a tiny sliver of red about to disappear. He raged even harder, stomping three times in succession before raising his hammer. Team B pulled back, recognizing the Numbing Detonation motion, while team G readied their best sword skills.

If the Legend Braves seized the Last Attack bonus here, they'd go from the backup force during the Bullbous Bow fight to the best fighters in the game. But I wasn't charitable enough to sit back and let them reap those rewards. I had a beater reputation to uphold.

"Now, Asuna!"

I leapt as high as I could. The fencer kept right up with me—in fact, her jumping speed was faster than mine. The force ripped the hood off of her head, and long chestnut-brown hair flowed through the air.

"*Vraaaah!!*"

Asterios brought down the hammer. A circular shockwave spread from the impact point, followed by bursts of sparks. Two of the Braves couldn't fully resist, succumbing to the stun effect of this final attack. Numbing Impact was weaker, but Detonation couldn't be avoided just by jumping, so Asuna and I would suffer the same effects once we touched the ground.

But...

"*Sey-yaaaa!*"

Asuna unleashed a fierce cry and shot off the rapier charge attack Shooting Star in midair.

"*Rrrraaaah!*"

I followed her with the one-handed sword charge attack Sonic Leap. We both shot up vertically, followed by trails of blue and green light. We were headed straight for the forehead of King Asterios, which was protected by his metal crown.

Out of the corner of my eye, I saw the flashing of the three mobile members of the Legend Braves firing off their own sword skills.

The next instant, our Anneal Blade and Wind Fleuret pierced the crown entirely and sank deep into the enemy's head. The crown splintered and cracked into pieces.

The massive body of King Asterios burst in an explosion that filled the entire coliseum chamber.

13

"CONGRATULATIONS," CAME A FAMILIAR VOICE, MAKing a familiar statement in English with a familiar native accent.

Asuna and I turned, exhausted after the long battle, to see Agil's smiling face. His meaty hand was curved into a thumbs-up, which I returned. Asuna didn't bother with that, but there was a rare smile on her beautiful face.

Agil lowered his hand and let his eyes gaze into the distance. "Your skill and teamwork are as brilliant as ever. But this victory doesn't belong to you...it's his."

"Yeah. If it wasn't for him, we'd have lost at least ten people in this fight," I replied. Asuna nodded in agreement.

Standing alone on the far side of the celebrating mass of players was the small figure of Nezha the former blacksmith. He stared up at the ceiling, watching the vanishing fragments of the boss, golden ring clutched in his hand.

I was distracted by a sudden cheer that rose from the group. At the center, Lind and Kibaou were locked in a bracing handshake. The blue and green squads were applauding wildly, and I joined in by clapping.

"Sheesh. They're best friends after all..."

"At least until we reach the third floor," Asuna noted sardonically. I got to my feet, whispered thanks to my Anneal Blade for its duty, and returned it to the sheath. After pulling Asuna up to a standing position and sharing a brief fist bump, I finally felt the satisfaction of the victory...of winning safe and sound.

We'd finished the second floor of Aincrad. It had taken us ten days, and there were zero fatalities in the boss battle.

After taking an entire month on the first floor, and losing our promising leader Diavel in the fight, this was better than I could have hoped for. But I reminded myself that we were a hairsbreadth from being wiped out entirely. The sudden and surprising appearance of King Asterios nearly killed Lind and Kibaou, not to mention Asuna and me.

We learned two lessons from this battle.

One, fulfill every quest around the last town and the labyrinth, because they might impart info on the boss.

And two, we had to assume that every boss from this point on had been changed in some way from the beta test. Of course, we'd only made it to the ninth floor in the beta, so once we reached the tenth, it was all new to us regardless.

Not only did gathering info through quests become important, but so would scouting out the boss first. The latter would not be easy, however. Most boss monsters didn't appear until you reached the back of the chamber and destroyed some key object, so there was no guarantee that a reconnaissance party would escape safely. There were a fair number of speedy scout types among us, but very few that could use throwing tools.

From this point on, the role of Nezha the chakram-thrower, as well as Argo, would become even more crucial.

I took a quick look around the room and didn't see the Rat, even with my Search skill—she must be hiding again. I nudged Asuna and we made our way over to Nezha.

When the ex-blacksmith saw us, he smiled radiantly, as though a great weight had been lifted from his shoulders. Nezha bowed and said, "Great work, Kirito and Asuna. That last midair sword skill was incredible."

"Well, actually..."

I scratched my head uncomfortably. I didn't want to tell him that it was just me trying to make sure I beat Orlando's group to the prize. Instead, Asuna answered for me.

"Incredible? That was your appearance. How did you manage to use a brand-new weapon with such skill? You must have practiced quite a lot."

"No, it didn't seem hard to me. I mean, I finally got to be what I'd always wanted. Really…thank you so much. Now I have…"

He trailed off and bowed deeply one more time, then turned back to face the center of the room. I followed his gaze and saw a group of five about twenty yards from the crowd. They were lined up and exchanging handshakes—Orlando with Lind, Beowulf with Kibaou, and the three others with other leading players. They wore the proud smiles of true heroes.

If you looked at the results screen for the battle against Asterios, the score based on damage defended and caused by the Legend Braves would easily outclass any other team. They'd found their place front and center among the best players in the game. I didn't know if they'd end up joining Lind's Dragon Knights or Kibaou's Liberation Squad, or if they'd start their own guild. But…

"Nezha, shouldn't you be there with them?" I asked. But the single most important person in the fight simply shook his head.

"No, it's fine. There's something else I still need to do."

"Huh? What's that?" I asked. Nezha looked at me and then at Asuna, whose brows were furrowed in apparent understanding. He bowed once more, then lovingly traced the surface of his chakram's blade with a finger, and began to walk away.

That's when I noticed that three players from the raid were coming this way. At first, I assumed they were coming to thank and congratulate Nezha, but their faces were hard. After examining the tall man in front with the broadsword, I finally realized why. This man, now wearing a breastplate over the blue doublet of Lind's group, was none other than Shivata, the man who'd asked Nezha to upgrade his sword five days ago. Next to him was another man in blue, and the third wore the green of Kibaou's team. They were all scowling.

Shivata pulled up in front of the Nezha and growled, "You're the blacksmith who was working in Urbus and Taran just a few days ago, aren't you?"

"...Yes," Nezha replied.

"Why did you switch to a fighter? And how'd you get that rare weapon? It's a drop-only item, isn't it? Did you make that much money from smithing?"

Oh, no.

Shivata's tone of voice said that he already suspected Nezha of shady dealing. Even if he didn't have a clue about the weapon-switching trick, he was clearly guessing that some kind of foul play had occurred.

In truth, Nezha's chakram was a rare weapon, but not particularly valuable. After all, it required both the Throwing Knives supplementary skill and the Martial Arts extra skill to use. But explaining all of that wouldn't remove the suspicion from Shivata's mind.

Eventually, all of the celebrating players fell silent, including Lind, Kibaou, and the Legend Braves, watching this new turn of events. Most had looks of grave concern, but even at a distance, the panic and tension on the faces of the Legend Braves was written plain as day.

In the moment, neither I nor Asuna knew what to do.

It would be easy to speak up and say that I gave him that chakram. But was deflecting the brunt of Shivata's anger and forcing him to back down really the right choice? It was undeniable truth that Nezha had seized Shivata's precious, treasured Stout Blade and broken a spent weapon in exchange.

Shivata used all of his willpower to control himself at that moment. He left without insulting or blaming Nezha. The broadsword he wore now was two ranks below his old Stout Blade. Shivata had done his best to power it up in the five days between then and now, and had managed to survive through this terrible battle. Did we really have the right to trick him again, to lead him away from the truth?

Nezha sidestepped my indecision entirely. He laid his chakram on the ground and got down on his knees, then pressed his hands to the ground and lowered his head.

"I deceived you, Shivata, and the two others with you. I switched out your swords before attempting to upgrade them, replacing them with spent weapons that I broke instead."

The coliseum was full of a silence even heavier than the one before the battle, ear-piercing and thick.

Sword Art Online had an astonishing system of re-creating players' emotions on their virtual avatars, but if there was one glaring weakness, it was a tendency to exaggerate for effect. I hadn't seen it for myself, but from what others said, it took very little time for sadness to manifest as tears. A happy feeling translated to a wide smile, and anger was represented by a reddened face and a bulging vein on the forehead.

So the fact that Shivata's only response was a furrowed brow was a true testament to his self-control. By contrast, the two men at his sides looked as though they were ready to explode, but they held it in as well.

I looked over at Asuna and saw that she was trying to suppress her feelings as well, but her face was visibly paler than usual. I must have looked the same way.

Shivata's hoarse voice finally broke the painful silence.

"Do you still have the weapons you stole?"

Nezha shook his head, hands still firmly on the floor.

"No...I already sold them for money," he rasped.

Shivata clenched his eyes shut at the answer, but he knew it was coming. He only grunted, then asked, "Can you pay me back the value?"

This time, Nezha had no immediate answer. Asuna and I held our breath. Far behind Shivata, standing at the left edge of the raid, Orlando's group was visibly uncomfortable.

In terms of simple feasibility, the sum of money that he'd taken from them was far from impossible to raise again.

Only ten days had passed since Nezha and the Legend Braves had started their fraud. The market prices for those items couldn't have changed that much, so if they sold off the assets they'd bought with the money they received, it should turn back into roughly the same amount.

But that was where the problem lay.

It wasn't just Nezha who had spent the money they'd unfairly earned, but the entire Legend Braves. The brightly gleaming armor covering their bodies was that very sum of money in physical form. In order to pay back their victims in col, Orlando and his group would have to sell off their equipment. After they'd just played a major role in this boss battle, would they really just give up the source of their power? And more fundamentally, how did Nezha plan to get out of this situation?

As I watched, holding my breath, the short ex-blacksmith answered, forehead still scraped against the floor tiles.

"No...I cannot repay you now. I used all of the money on all-you-can-eat meals at expensive restaurants, and high-priced inns."

Asuna sucked in a sharp breath.

Nezha wasn't trying to weasel his way out of anything. He was going to take responsibility for all of the crimes, and force Shivata and the others to focus their anger and hatred solely on him. He was covering for his companions, the ones who treated him like a nuisance and egged him into committing those acts.

The large member of Lind's team to Shivata's right finally snapped.

"You...why, you filthy—!!" He raised a clenched fist and stomped his right boot on the ground multiple times. "Do you have any idea what it's like to see your favorite, beloved sword smashed to pieces?! And you sold it off...to have yourself a feast?! To stay in deluxe hotels?! Then you use the rest to buy yourself a valuable weapon, barge into the boss battle, and fancy yourself a hero?!"

Kibaou's companion on the left shrieked, "When I lost my sword, I thought I'd never fight on the front line again! But my friends donated some funds to me and helped me gather materials... You didn't just betray us, you stabbed everyone fighting to complete this game in the back!"

And like a lit fuse, those shouts caused all the other players who'd been silently watching this scene to explode.

"Traitor!"

"Do you have any idea what you've done?!"

"You caused our pace to slow down!"

"Apologizing isn't going to fix anything!"

Dozens of voices overlapped into one mass of angry noise. Nezha's lonely back shrank, as though succumbing to the pressure of all that rage.

When the crowd's anger at beta testers threatened to explode during the planning for the first-floor boss battle, Agil had been the voice of reason. But there was nothing he could do here. He and his companions stood off at a distance, watching pensively.

Orlando's group was equally quiet. The five of them were whispering to each other, but it was inaudible over all the angry bellowing.

I couldn't do anything but watch, either. There was no magic word to solve the situation at this point. Now that the truth of Shivata's weapon was open knowledge, the only thing that could mend the wrongdoing was an equal sum of col, or something similarly heavy...

Suddenly, I remembered something Nezha had said just minutes before.

I finally got to be what I'd always wanted. Really... thank you so much. Now I have...

...nothing left to regret.

Those were the final words he'd said, the ones I couldn't hear.

"Nezha...you can't mean..." I mumbled.

One of the two people who had the power to bring this scene to a close strode forward, his hand held high. Blue hair and blue cape. A shining silver scimitar at his waist. Lind, the leader of the raid.

Shivata's trio stepped back to give him the stage, and the furious shouts that filled the chamber gradually died down. When it was at least quiet enough to have a conversation, he spoke.

"Will you tell us your name?"

At that point, I realized that Nezha was never a part of the raid party as classified by the system. It was one thing for Argo, who passed on her info and split, but Nezha took on a crucial role in hitting the boss's weak point. He deserved to be part of the raid, and we'd been one short of the limit, anyway. The only team with five members was G...the Legend Braves.

Something rubbed me wrong about the fact that Orlando hadn't extended a party offer to Nezha, a friend since before the days of *SAO*. But more important than that was how Lind decided to rule on this situation.

"...It's Nezha," the ex-blacksmith said, still prostrate on the ground. Lind nodded a few times. His features were sharp by nature, but he looked more nervous now than he did in the midst of the battle. He cleared his throat.

"I see. Your cursor is still green, Nezha...but that speaks to the severity of your crime. If you'd committed a properly recognized crime and turned orange, it would be possible to return it to green through good karma quests. But no quest will wipe your sins clean now. If you cannot repay what you owe to others in the game...we will have to find a different means of punishment."

He can't, I thought to myself, teeth gritted. Lind's thin lips grimaced, then opened again.

"It was not just swords that you stole from Shivata and others. It was a great amount of time that they poured into those blades. Therefore..."

Some of the weight lifted off my shoulders. Lind was about to demand that Nezha pay back his crimes by contributing to the game's advancement, and most likely regular payments over a long-term period. It was the same punishment that Diavel would have meted out if this had happened ten days earlier.

However…

Before Lind could finish, a high-pitched voice drowned him out.

"No…it wasn't just time that he stole!"

A green-clad member of Kibaou's team ran forward. His skinny body shook left and right as he screeched—

"I…I know the truth! There are plenty more players he stole weapons from! One of them had to use a cheap store-bought weapon, and ended up getting killed by mobs he'd handled just fine before!!"

The vast, masterless chamber fell silent once more.

After a few seconds, the blue-clad man next to Shivata spoke again, his voice hoarse.

"If…if someone's died because of this…then he's not just a swindler anymore. He's a puh…puh…"

The scrawny green man jabbed a finger forward and said what the other one couldn't.

"That's right! He's a murderer! A PKer!!"

It was the first time I'd heard the term PK in the open since we'd been trapped in the flying castle.

It was one of the most well-known terms among all the many MMOs out there. It wasn't short for "penalty kick," or "psychokinesis," or anything like that. It stood for "player kill," or "player killer"—the act of killing another player, rather than a monster.

Unlike most MMORPGs made these days, PK-ing was possible in *SAO*. There was absolute safety within any town, thanks to a stringent anti-crime code, but that protection disappeared outside of town limits. The only things that protected players then were their own equipment, skills, and trusted companions.

In the month-long beta test, a thousand players cooperated and competed in a race upward, sometimes erupting into combat where players crossed swords with one another. But PK did not apply to honest duels between two willing combatants. A player killer was someone who set upon unsuspecting adventurers in the wilderness or dungeons, a pejorative term slapped on those who killed for fun and profit.

Several times during the beta, I'd been attacked by PKers, but not once since the full game launched. On the very first night, I was nearly killed by another former tester who formed a party with me, via MPK: a monster player kill, using monsters to do his dirty work. But that was a passive means of killing and done in an attempt to win a quest item to further his own survival.

Now that the chaos of that initial starting dash had died down, it was impossible to imagine someone committing a true PK for the purpose of sick pleasure.

With the linking of our virtual and physical fates, PK-ing was out-and-out murder. In a normal MMO, engaging in such behavior was a form of roleplay, but that excuse didn't fly anymore. After all, killing players—in particular, players who showed enough willpower to venture into the wilderness and fight for themselves—only prolonged the possibility of our eventual freedom.

The day I met Asuna again in Urbus and we went Windwasp-hunting together, I said that wearing a burlap sack for a mask would make me look like a PKer. The only reason I made a joke like that was my belief that no one in Aincrad would actually stoop to such a thing. But here we were, and that ugly term was out in the open.

The skinny dagger user from Kibaou's team kept shrieking, his finger still pointed at Nezha's head.

"A few bows and scrapes can't make up for a PK! No amount of apologizing or money is going to bring back the dead! What's your plan? How are you gonna make this right? Well?!"

There was a painful edge to his voice, a screech like the point of a knife scraping against metal. Within a cold, sobered corner of my mind, I wondered where I'd heard it before. The memory came within an instant.

This dagger-wielding man had leveled a similar charge against me, right after we beat the first-floor boss. "I know the truth! He's a beta tester!" rang the voice in my ears. I'd shut him up by haughtily demanding that he not lump me in with the other testers, but that trick wouldn't work here.

Nezha's tiny back absorbed all of the accusations hurled at it. He clenched his fists atop the stones and spoke, his voice trembling.

"I will accept…whatever judgment you decide upon."

Another silence.

I felt like every person present understood the meaning behind the word "judgment." The air in the coliseum grew even colder and pricklier than before. That invisible energy reached a critical point, everyone waiting for the one person who would break the tension.

Eventually, I succumbed, ready to tell everyone to just wait a moment, even though I didn't have any ideas of how to follow it up.

But I was half a second too late. One of the dozens of raid members who'd been inching up on Nezha finally uttered a short burst.

"Then pay the price."

It was just four words, a statement that didn't hold any specific meaning of its own. But it was like a pin that burst an overinflated balloon.

Suddenly the chamber was full with a roar of noise. Dozens of players were shouting all at once: "Yeah, pay the price!" "Go apologize to the ones who died!" "Live by the PK, die by the PK!"

Their cries grew more and more overt until spilling into direct threats.

"Pay with your life, fraudster!"

"Settle your account by dying, you PK-ing bastard!"

"Kill him! Kill the filthy scheming scum!"

I couldn't help but feel like the rage on their faces wasn't entirely anger at his crime. There was fury and hatred for the game of

Sword Art Online that had trapped them here, as well. It was the thirty-eighth day since we'd been locked in this flying fortress. Ninety-eight floors remained to conquer. The overwhelming, desperate pressure of those astronomical odds had finally found an outlet, a target ripe for punishment: a swindler and murderer among our ranks.

Neither Lind nor Kibaou had the means to resolve this situation now. Even I'd just been sitting on my heels the entire time, watching the scene unfold, since Nezha had admitted to his crimes. My eyes wandered until they happened across the five Legend Braves standing at the side of the raid. They weren't shouting like the others but staring down at the ground, avoiding looking at Nezha.

You should have known this could happen someday, Orlando...Didn't you ever see it coming? I asked silently, but there was no answer. In fact, if I was making accusations, the same went for the man in the black poncho who'd taught them the trick. If he was generous enough to show them a fancy trick for free, why didn't he explain the potential dangers to them?

Unless...

What if this situation—the group turning on Nezha, demanding his execution—was exactly what the black poncho was hoping for in return?

In that case, what he wanted was not the help of the Braves, but the opposite. He wanted Nezha to be killed at the express desire of all the top players in the game for his direct role in the scam. That would create a precedent for direct player-on-player killing and lower the mental hurdle to reaching the act of murder across Aincrad.

If my fears were correct, that man in the black poncho was the real PKer here. But rather than soil his own hands with the act, he set up other players to do the dirty work for him, dragging them down to his level.

This was bad. We couldn't allow his devious plan to work. We couldn't have Nezha publicly executed. After all, I was the one who recommended that Nezha switch to a combat role and make up for his crimes by helping advance the game. In effect, I brought him here to this situation. I had a responsibility to prevent his death.

Amidst the hail of jeers, someone finally moved into action. Not Lind, not Kibaou, not even Nezha—but the Legend Braves.

They slowly crossed the vast room, metal armor clanking, toward the prostrate Nezha. Orlando's bascinet visor was half-down, so I couldn't see his face. The other four marched in step with him, their faces downcast.

The semicircle of Lind, the dagger user, and Shivata sensed that something was happening, and they stepped back to make room for the newcomers.

The group came to a halt with heavy footsteps. Nezha must have sensed the approach of his former comrades, but he did not look up. His fists were still balled on the floor, his forehead pressed to the tile. Orlando stopped directly across from Nezha, the chakram placed on the floor in between. His right hand moved to his left side. Asuna gasped.

His gauntleted hand gripped the hilt of his sword and pulled.

Orlando's weapon was, like mine, an Anneal Blade. It appeared to be powered up to a similar level. If he was going to strike Nezha's unprotected back, it would only take three or four hits to finish the job.

"Orlando…"

I called out the name of the paladin who had just helped defeat the boss monster minutes ago.

You spent far more time with Nezha than I ever did. But I can't stand here and watch you kill him—no matter what that does to my reputation.

I put all of my weight into my right foot, preparing to dart forward the instant he raised his blade. At the same time, I sensed Asuna shifting position as well.

"Don't do anything, Asuna."

"No," she said flatly.

"Don't you get it? If you interfere with this, you won't be allowed among this group anymore. You might even be labeled a criminal."

"I still won't stop. Don't you remember what I said the first time we met? I left the Town of Beginnings so that I could be myself."

"..."

I didn't have any time or arguments with which to convince her. Instead, I merely sighed in resignation and nodded.

Somehow, the angry shouting that filled the coliseum had turned to silence again. Everyone watched wide-eyed, waiting with bated breath for the fateful moment.

And perhaps because I was concentrating so hard...I picked out the quiet voice from Orlando's helmet, even though I was nowhere near close enough to hear it.

"I'm sorry...I'm so sorry, Nezuo."

The paladin laid down his sword next to the chakram on the ground. He took a few steps and got down on his knees next to Nezha, facing the same direction, removed his helmet, and put his hands flat on the tile.

Beowulf, Cuchulainn, Gilgamesh, and Enkidu followed his lead, setting down their weapons and helmets and getting into a line with Nezha at the center.

Amid dead silence, the five—no, six Legend Braves bowed in apology to the rest of the raid.

Eventually, Orlando spoke up, his trembling voice the only sound in the coliseum.

"Nezuo...Nezha is our partner. We're the ones who forced him to commit that fraud."

14

"SO WHY DO WE HAVE TO BE THE ERRAND-RUNNERS here?" Asuna grumbled as she trudged along.

I shrugged and answered, "What can you do? It's just the way it is."

"No, not that! We were a party of two during the first boss fight, but this time we had a full six!"

"Only because Agil was considerate enough to let us join him. We'll need to thank him when this all blows over."

Asuna raised an eyebrow at me.

"Wh-what?"

"Nothing. I'm just wondering if your skill at getting along is earning a few proficiency points."

"That's..." *my line*, I wanted to say, but I held it in. "That should be clear, since I have a gift for him, too."

"Oh? What's that, the Mighty Straps you found in the labyrinth?"

"...Ooh, good idea. I'll have to give those to him, too." I patted my fist into my palm.

Asuna looked at me doubtfully, then her eyes went wide with understanding.

"Oh, I know! You're going to foist that thing you've been keeping in the inn chest off on Agil!"

"Indeed."

She was referring to the large Vendor's Carpet that Nezha left with me when he abandoned his blacksmithing and went off to learn the Martial Arts skill. It was an expensive and useful item, but offered little benefit to a combat-focused character. Plus, it couldn't be placed in one's inventory, so it had to be rolled up and hoisted around by hand.

"Agil might be a warrior, but he seems likely to know some promising future blacksmiths, wouldn't you suspect? I'm sure Nezha would be happy knowing that it went to good use."

"But what if Agil himself wakes up to the lures of running his own business?"

"...Then I'll be his first customer," I answered glibly.

Asuna sighed and glanced ahead. We were walking up the spiral staircase between the second and third floors. But for some unknown design purpose, the stairs spiraled around the entire eight-hundred-foot-wide tower, meaning that we actually had to walk a distance of over 2,500 feet...plus height.

But because there were no monsters on the staircase, it was still a much easier exit from the tower than going from the boss chamber all the way down to the front entrance.

As the roving strikers (or, if you prefer, leftovers) of the raid, Asuna and I had been given our orders by Lind: to leave the labyrinth, which was shut off from all instant messages, and deliver the news of our victory to all the players who were eagerly awaiting an update.

Normally this would be the job—no, privilege—of Lind or Kibaou. But the main raid force could not leave the boss chamber for another hour or so. Not because they were locked inside but because they were too busy talking. The debate raged on about how to deal with Nezha and the Legend Braves.

But I no longer had any concerns about the outcome of that discussion. The instant that Orlando and his partners had laid down their weapons and admitted their sins, the conclusion was foretold. No matter how heated up the group was, they weren't so bloodthirsty that they would execute a group of six players, and the addition of the Braves to the guilty side changed the equation: Now Shivata and the others could realistically be repaid for their lost weapons.

Orlando explained every last detail of the deception and removed all of his equipment, not just the sword and helm. The other four followed his lead, and produced a small mountain of high-level gear that would fetch a price beyond my estimation.

He told the group that if they turned all of these items into cash, it would surpass the value of the lost weapons—they'd sunk their own honestly earned money into the armor as well—and serve as a repayment for all the victims of their scheme. If there was col left over, it could be used as a potion fund for the next boss battle.

Now that the damages were able to be repaid, the remaining problem was the player who died because his weapon was stolen.

Under the current configuration of *SAO*, no amount of money could make up for a lost life. The Legend Braves offered to go find the fellow's companions and apologize in person, if that would help in any way. When they asked the dagger user who'd brought this story up, he backed down on his assertion, saying that it was just a rumor and he didn't know the name.

In the end, the group decided to ask the information agent to discover the truth of the matter. The first controversy over player-swindling in Aincrad was about to reach a close without bloodshed, but there was one problem remaining: how to convert the dozens of pieces of high-powered equipment into cash.

There was always the option of selling them to NPC merchants in town. But the NPC's prices were always kept below the market rate by the "invisible hand" of the system in order to combat inflation. If we were going to get the maximum value, the transactions had to be with other players.

The people with the most col and the largest need for good equipment were the front-line players. So Lind and Kibaou considered the possibility of selling that equipment to the few dozen players present in the boss chamber and donating the money to

Shivata's group of three. Of course, there were more victims of the scheme than just the people present here, so proper payment would need to be made once everyone went back to town.

So the delay in leaving the boss chamber was due to a spontaneous auction. Sadly, none of the items was suitable for agile leather-wearers like me and Asuna—and even if there were some, I wouldn't have been in the mood to buy and equip them. As we stood around feeling relieved that a peaceful solution was found, Lind came over and said, "If you don't have anything better to do, could you leave the dungeon and tell the newspapers that our conquest was successful?"

I couldn't find a good reason to decline his request, so I prodded the reluctant Asuna, and we went out the door in the back of the chamber to the next floor. Agil and his friends waved goodbye, but we didn't have an opportunity to say anything to Nezha the former blacksmith.

As soon as Orlando and his friends lined up around him, his little back trembled and shook with constant sobs.

"Well, it seems like the case of fraud is going to wrap up safely…What do you suppose Nezha and the Braves are going to do next?" Asuna wondered as she climbed the gently sloping staircase.

I mulled it over. "Depends on them. They can't prevent the tale of the Braves' shady behavior from spreading around the front line. Either they'll have to avoid everyone here and go back down to the Town of Beginnings, or start over from scratch and try to reach our level again. Before we left, Lind told me that if they wanted to, he'd allow them to keep a minimum of col necessary for the equipment they'll need to hang around. But no matter what they choose, they won't treat Nezha like a third wheel."

"Hmm…To be honest, I'm still not sure how I feel about Orlando…But if they do make it back to the front line, I'll do my best to work with them. I mean, even you did all right with Lind and Kibaou, didn't you?"

I nearly missed a step.

"I-I haven't changed my attitude a bit! If anything, they're the ones who are acting weird. Kibaou's totally anti-tester, and Lind's trying to raise an elite fighting force, so solos like me are only an obstacle to his goals. And yet, both of them were being oddly normal..."

Asuna momentarily looked frosty when I uttered the word *solo*. She sighed and said, "As usual, you're completely clueless."

"Huh? How so?"

"If all of the frontier players were under the lead of either Lind or Kibaou alone, they would have been much more open about excluding you. But the blue Dragon Knights and the green Aincrad Liberation Squad are jockeying for power even as they work together, right?"

"Um, yeah..."

"In the current situation, they're both on edge. They think that if they antagonize you too much, you'll end up aligning with the other team."

"Me? With either blue or green?" I came to a standstill and chuckled. "Ha-ha, no way. They'd shut the door in my face, even if I actually wanted to join. I'm the evil beater, right? I mean, even today..."

I shut my mouth and started hopping up the steps. Asuna hurried to catch up, looking skeptical, then raised a finger in sudden understanding.

"Hey, by the way, what happened to the boss's last attack bonus? On Asterios the Taurus King, I mean. I didn't get the prompt."

"Uhh, ahh, umm..."

"And now that I think about it, didn't you win the LA on Colonel Nato *and* General Baran? You didn't get the king too, did you...?"

"Um, well, that's, uh—hey, is that the exit?"

"Oh, no, you don't! You *did* win it, didn't you? What did he drop? Tell me!"

Suddenly we were both jogging up the stairs. At the end of the gently curving staircase was a thick door decorated with a relief. The scene was of two swordsmen facing off among gnarled old trees. The left was dark-skinned, and the right was pale, but both were slender and fragile, with pointed ears.

The picture was meant to represent the theme of the floor ahead, I thought to myself.

Nezha—no, Nataku. You were the real MVP of the second floor. Come on back to us. The front line's a scary, dangerous place… but it's where you'll find what you really wanted. And the front line needs you, too. After all…

"In a way, the third floor is where *SAO* really starts," I said aloud. Asuna caught up to me, looking puzzled rather than harassing me more about the LA.

"It is? Why is that?"

I started off with my now-familiar, unhelpful refrain: "Um, well…"

And savoring each and every step, I crossed the final thirty feet of the second floor of Aincrad.

AFTERWORD

Hello, this is Reki Kawahara, author of *Sword Art Online Progressive 1*.

The word *progressive* might make you think of video formats, but in this case it is meant in the "incremental increase" sense. I chose this title to represent the task of conquering Aincrad bit by bit, from the very first floor. From this point on, I'll be using the abbreviation *SAOP*.

So first of all, I should explain why I decided to start writing this series.

If you'll permit me to repeat what I said in the afterword of the first volume of *SAO*, I wrote the story as a submission for the Dengeki Novel Award, so I had to finish the story with the game being beaten, right in the very first installment. Later on, I wrote a number of shorter prequel stories that filled in gaps (see Volumes 2 and 8), but they're more like little episodes, and don't focus on the meat and potatoes of the players advancing through the game.

So I've always harbored a secret desire to write about how Kirito and the others cleared each floor and defeated each boss in the game, it just didn't really happen until now. Because I'm now trying to write it all over again from the first floor, it creates a number of issues.

Biggest of all is how to deal with Asuna, the heroine. In the previously published series, Kirito doesn't get to know Asuna until much, much later. If I depicted Kirito as working with Asuna on the first and second floor of Aincrad, it would contradict what I've already published.

For a long time, I wavered between two options: avoiding that contradiction by starting off *Progressive* with a different heroine, or embracing the contradiction and going with Asuna right from the start. Ultimately, I admitted to myself that it didn't feel right having anyone but Asuna at Kirito's side, and I suspect that most of my readers feel the same way. So I decided to have Kirito meet Asuna right away.

Of course, I'm certain that some readers will not be able to accept the contradictions with what I've written before, and that's okay. But I will do my utmost to make sure that the choices I make line up with the established events as best I can. My hope is that you'll be able to overcome my inconsistency and enjoy this new series for what it is.

Now that I've gotten my customary apologies out of the way, let's go over each of these stories.

"Aria of a Starless Night," the story of the first floor of Aincrad, picks up right after the story of "The First Day," which is found in Volume 8 of the main series. We see characters that had only appeared in name before, such as Kibaou, future leader of the Army, and the information dealer, Argo the Rat. Then, of course, there are old favorites like Agil before he became a businessman, and Asuna when she was just a beginner to MMORPGs. It was a very strange mix of the new and familiar as I was writing. Of course, Kirito is still Kirito.

Part of the point of *Progressive* is to explain the systems of *SAO* in greater detail, so "Aria" spends a lot of time covering the concept of a "boss raid." I hope you really got the feel for a great big group of eight parties of six members each. If it didn't make sense to you, watch the second episode of the *SAO* anime series, please! Ha-ha.

The story of the second floor, "Rondo of a Fragile Blade," features a whole host of new faces. It took me quite a while to decide if the character of Nezha should be a man or a woman. Eventually, I got the feeling that having him be a girl would pose a whole new set of problems, so I took the easy route in making him a man.

I meant to have this tale feature the weapon upgrading system, but I let it slip away from me a bit, and the result was more of a mystery story surrounding the concept of upgrade fraud. Since there wasn't much fighting in the early part of the story, I wanted to feature a nice, meaty boss battle, and ended up bringing out quite a nasty boss for just the second floor of the game. If that happened in a real MMO, I would totally throw in the towel!

Those two stories made up the first volume of *SAOP*. I've already got the title of the third-floor story picked out: "Concerto of Black and White." In game system terms, I'm going to focus on the theme of campaign quests.

Well, now that I've gone and done a sneak peek for the next volume, I should probably come clean and admit that I don't think I can write more than one volume of *Progressive* a year. So if I cover two floors a year, when will I actually get to the seventy-fifth floor...? I'm too scared to consider the possibilities! Hope to see you in Volume 2!

And of course, I'll be continuing with the main *SAO* series. Part Three of the Alicization arc, Volume 11, should be coming out in December. Kirito and Eugeo will be tackling the mysteries of the Underworld. Please check it out.

Also, the continuation of *SAO* means that I'll need to skip *Accel World* this time around. Deep apologies! But since Volumes 9 and 10 of that came out in quick succession, it should be back to its normal schedule now. I'm not sure how long I will be able to keep up writing a book every other month (in fact, it's already looking hairy)…but I'll do my best!

Thanks once again to my illustrator abec for eagerly tackling two series at once, to my editor Mr. Miki for eagerly (I think) tackling this five hundred–page monster of a book, and to my vice editor Mr. Tsuchiya for dealing with the ulcers (I assume) of waiting for my very late replies to every message. And to those of you who read to the end of this very thick book, the greatest LA bonus of my gratitude!

Reki Kawahara—August 2012

HAVE YOU BEEN TURNED ON TO LIGHT NOVELS YET?

SWORD ART ONLINE, VOL. 1–3

The chart-topping light novel series that spawned the explosively popular anime and manga adaptations!

MANGA ADAPTATION AVAILABLE NOW!

SWORD ART ONLINE © Reki Kawahara ILLUSTRATION: abec
KADOKAWA CORPORATION ASCII MEDIA WORKS

ACCEL WORLD, VOL. 1–2

Prepare to accelerate with an action-packed cyber-thriller from the bestselling author of *Sword Art Online*.

MANGA ADAPTATION AVAILABLE NOW!

ACCEL WORLD © Reki Kawahara ILLUSTRATION: HIMA
KADOKAWA CORPORATION ASCII MEDIA WORKS

SPICE AND WOLF, VOL. 1–13

A disgruntled goddess joins a traveling merchant in this light novel series that inspired the *New York Times* bestselling manga.

MANGA ADAPTATION AVAILABLE NOW!

SPICE AND WOLF © Isuna Hasekura ILLUSTRATION: Jyuu Ayakura
KADOKAWA CORPORATION ASCII MEDIA WORKS